CODE 13

Paul Gilmour

Code 13

Copyright © 2020 Paul Gilmour

This is a work of fiction. The characters, incidents and dialogue are drawn from the author's imagination and are not to be construed as real. Any resemblance to actual events or persons, living or dead, is entirely coincidental.

ISBN: 978-0-6488497-0-4 (Paperback)
eISBN: 978-0-6488497-1-1 (ebook)

A sequel to "Jeremiah's Codes"

Prologue

Guiana Highlands, Venezuela

A dark silhouette moved swiftly and silently along a candle lit corridor leaving behind a trail of death. Bodies scattered with their throats slashed, bled freely across the ancient stone floor of the thousand year old temple. Driven by his feverish desire to find her, the assassin pushed deeper into the dungeon, gun in one hand and razor knife in the other. Educated from a young age to inflict death upon those the United States Government chose as the enemy, killing had become a large part of his everyday life.

Tonight's mission was different though, it was personal. Three long intense months of searching since the heart wrenching phone call in the dead of night. In the end, it led him to the Monk's sacred asylum high up in the secluded mountains of Venezuela.

He reached a row of weathered wooden doors all bolted shut, except for one. In the dim flicker of one near exhausted candle, a door waited half ajar at the furthest end. He edged his way forward, stopping abruptly at the distinct sound of something up ahead. There it was again, a chinking sound like chains rattling.

Focusing on the sound, he took two slow silent steps closer, when suddenly something massive leapt from the shadows. A wild beast or herculean man he couldn't quite tell, charged at him knocking him backwards off his feet and slamming him mercilessly against the wall. His weapons clattered to the floor as the man growling like a wild dog, pounced at him swinging punch after punch. Fists the size of dinner plates pulverised the assassin's face draining the life from him and like a rag doll, he was tossed to the floor.

Twisting and turning under the man's weight, the assassin fought back, kicking his legs up around the man's head and shoulders. Imitating a boa constrictor snake strangling a goat, he

1

latched his legs around the man's throat and used all his strength to squeeze the life from his assailant. Weighing over three hundred pounds, the man lifted himself off the floor and dropped all his bone crushing weight back down against the assassin's chest.

It knocked him hard, cracking ribs and driving the air from his lungs. The onslaught of blows to his face had ceased and instead, the hands had latched around his throat severing his fight to refill his lungs. Above him, the man lent in close tightening his grip. His breath stank of stale wine and long beads of drool dangled from his mouth as he clenched his rotting teeth.

The assassin tossed and turned, arching his back while desperately wrestling the man's fingers open, but he was too strong.

As his life faded, four words flashed through his head.

'Jon please help me.'

The phone call and his plight to rescue his lost love had invaded his last conscious thought. Adrenaline surged through his body to every muscle as he pushed the man up a few inches. The tiny freedom to move gave him space to angle his hips off the floor and drive upwards with his arms. The grip on his throat loosened and at last, he gulped air like a fish out of water fighting for its life.

'Jon please help me.'

The constant thought empowered his strength, he had come too far not to succeed. He extended his arms to the side and wrestled himself free a few inches until his hand touched metal.

But as quick as he gained the leverage, the big man retaliated using his enormous weight to thrust his knee into the assassin's belly and throw himself back on top. The fury of punches recommenced smashing his face, fracturing his jaw and splitting his skin like an overripe melon.

'Jon please help me.'

Under the flicker of light, the assassin looked into the man's eyes and mumbled "Fuck you!"

With lightning speed, his hand snapped closed around the knife handle and he thrust it up into the man's eye socket, not relenting until his hand hit flesh. The blade penetrated his brain, inflicting immediate death.

He staggered to his feet, heaving for breath and cringing from the pain in his ribs while his face felt on fire. Blood blurred his vision as he took unsteady steps towards the partly open door. The fight had depleted his strength but the thought of her energised his every step until he reached the doorway and paused. The anticipation of finding her had suddenly overwhelmed him. What if she wasn't in there, he agonised.

Repressed by the solid weight and the rusted hinges, the door creaked as he pushed it further open. Dim flickering light spilled out into the corridor and the assassin caught his first glimpse of the room.

At first his heart sank, there was no prisoner in there, just an old wooden bed with thick chains bundled on top of a dirty blood stained mattress. The cell was a ten feet square cubicle reeking of human excrement and the musty smell of age. A single candle burning in the corner presented a dull yellow ambiance to the room reflecting off the stone walls that gave him a clearer view of the bed as he entered.

His heart skipped a beat and tears welled in his eyes. Among the chains, a long slender body lay twisted and motionless. Her clothes were in tatters, her long earthy brown hair matted with blood and her dirty skin was streaked with trails of sweat. The stench of excrement suffocated his nostrils and he gasped.

Suddenly her eyes flicked open and sensing his presence, she shrunk to the head of the bed like a constantly beaten child desperately trying to distance herself from harm.

"Please don't hurt me!" she cried as the assassin lifted his gun and fired two rounds.

The padlock disintegrated on impact from the two bullets and he rushed to the bed pulling the chains free from around her ankles and wrists.

"It's okay, it's okay, it's me... it's Jon," he said softly reaching out to touch her hand.

Haunted by the memories of losing her, a tear tumbled across his bloodied cheek as his love for her erupted like a volcano. Her exquisite beauty filtered through the dirt and blood, revealing high cheek bones and her tantalising crystal green eyes. She lay degradingly half naked with only a shirt that had been shredded to expose her breasts and finely moulded abdominals. Bruises and lacerations covered her long athletic legs, some fresh with thin trails of wet blood dripping to the bed.

Their eyes met and at first, she cowered further into the bed until his warm touch brought her back to him. Next to the bed, used syringes were scattered across the floor and her arms showed a line of well tracked needle marks.

"Jon! Is that really you?" she slurred, and her eyes wavered from the concoction of sedatives flowing through her veins.

"I'm here, you're safe now," he whispered pulling her in close to the loving warmth of his body.

They had endured a secret battle to save the planet against *The Trust's* evil plans and in that short space of time, had kindled a love unbreakable by death. Nicholette Sponarava had been, like him, a lethal fighting machine moulded by the needs of governments and in her case, the Russian KGB.

They embraced tightly as their lips met, pressing passionately before he reluctantly broke away, "We have to get going, get out of here before it's day light."

Subdued by weakness she fell back into his arms, caressing her head against his chest and inhaled his aura.

"I love you so much, I knew you'd come," she sobbed.

As tears tracked down through his blood caked shirt, Bennett besieged with happiness, cradled her and kissed her forehead, "You are my princess and I am your knight. My world was broken without you."

A tidal wave of tears pursued, and she shook uncontrollably with emotion.

"I must kill the Monk," she muttered into his chest, displaying a snippet of her former self.

4

The Monk had once been their ally against *The Trust* but ended up their enemy when his men stole her dead body. Then, through wizardry from another world, they injected life back into her and imprisoned her.

"You will get your chance but not now, he has too many guards upstairs. Time to be patient."

"Fat fuck guard will be making his rounds soon," she slurred.

"You mean dead fat fuck guard," he replied helping her to her feet.

She sneered with satisfaction, she loved that his sense of humour was a mirror of hers and she'd missed that. The Monk had kept her bound by chains the whole time and at night, the guard would inject her with barbiturates before violating her womanhood. Every time she was too weak and restricted by the chains to engage her own retribution.

"The Monk says you destroyed *The Trust*," she stuttered.

He nodded, "Yes, they are no longer a threat."

"He says it's not over, a bigger enemy is out there, waiting for the right time to strike. Jon we're all going to die, every one of us," she wept, leaning against him as they staggered from the cell.

He had heard the Monk's apocalyptic prophecies many times before, but unlike the rhetoric verses by doomsday cults, it wasn't about the end of the world. His visions were different, he declared the fate of humanity would be decided by the arrival.

"He's an insane old religious fool, there's no truth to his sermons. The sun will be up soon, we must hurry."

They left the desolation of the temple's prison and commenced the long journey home, neither of them knowing the truth, or the real enemy.

1.

<u>Eckhard</u>

Lake Ouachita, Arkansas
August 15, 1955

The water surface once tranquil and soothing, had become a boiling pot of froth and emotions. The birds had scattered high with a crescendo of squawking and a mass flutter of wings breaking the late afternoon stillness. Beneath it, one lone eighteen-year-old boy wrestled something in the waist deep water of the lake's edge.

Eckhard pushed with all his weight and strength against his victim's fight for life. He clenched his teeth and his arms screamed with exhaustion as he kept pushing, just a few more seconds, he begged of his courage.

"Eke… please… I can't breathe," Simon screamed as he broke loose of Eckhard's clutches and his head breached the surface for the first time.

Simon gasped for what would be his last breath as Eckhard threw himself onto him, like a crocodile he death rolled his victim back under the water with everything he had left.

On the bank, a young woman stood watching nervously whilst checking their surroundings.

"Hurry Eke, I think someone's coming," she shouted.

Eckhard had all but run out of strength as the body in his hands fell limp under the water and the struggle ended.

"Judith help me get him to the bank," he called.

She rushed into the water grabbed the lifeless body and together they dragged it to the dry sand as a man appeared from the tree line.

"Hey are you okay?" he called.

"Mister can you get help, my young brother has drowned," Eckhard screamed back at him.

The man hesitated.

"Go get the doctor, tell him it's Arthur Banks's kid, Simon," Judith commanded.

"Please hurry," Eckhard added.

The man turned on his heel at the mention of Arthur Banks and vanished into the trees running as fast as he could.

The others fell back laughing, their plan was well underway, and it would take over half an hour for the stranger to reach the closest doctor. Simon Banks would not be revived.

"I love you," she exclaimed pulling his hand to her breast.

He responded, pushing her back onto the sand and stripped her of her wet clothes. Both were aroused by the moment, but she was more excited by the control she constantly had over him.

Eckhard and Judith were deeply in love and had been for some time much to the disapproval of their parents, particularly his. Arthur Banks was a well-respected businessman and a prominent member of congress, so he constantly faced public scrutiny for the doings of his family. The shame of his eighteen-year-old son dating a woman in her late twenties was difficult to digest and the press didn't let up on it.

Eckhard rolled onto his back satisfied by the sex and a growing excitement about their plan.

"It will be all yours now Eke," Judith announced putting her clothes back on.

He made no reply, busy in thought about the next part of their plan.

"What's wrong, are you chickening out because if you are then you just murdered your brother for nothing. Think about the big picture," she added running her hands through his long dark hair and kissing his neck.

They had planned this day for months, waiting until they were alone at the lake.

"I don't know if I can do the next part," he blurted out.

His father's wealth was in the billions and with Simon gone it would be all his, but it meant killing his parents.

"You can my darling, but we must be patient and wait for the right moment," she said.

He was an intelligent kid, scoring the highest grades at school and as many of his teachers commented, was destined for greatness.

Today that journey had begun.

2.
The Soldier

St Ives, UK
June 1, 2004

The freezing ocean grappled at his tiring body, pulling and pushing him each way with the surge of the currents. The young British soldier scanned every direction to the desolate sight of dark water and a landless horizon. Above him storm clouds intensified and lightning streaked the evening sky while beneath him his worst nightmare was unravelling.

A down burst of icy air dropped from the circling clouds and the water responded with a surging swell battering the Lieutenant's body. Swimming had never been his favourite past time and now he was regretting missing those childhood lessons. As he clawed and kicked to stay afloat, the undercurrent wrestled tirelessly to drag him under.

Sea spray strangled his every breath until a rogue wave crashed across his head and drove him downwards. After what seemed like minutes, he thrashed his way to the surface as something heavy nudged his side.

Around him the wind had mysteriously eased, and the ocean was losing its ferocity under the sudden hammering of heavy rain. The storm had opened its bowels and the deluge had commenced. Jagged bolts of lightning, purple, crimson and blue illuminated the sky for brief moments followed instantaneously by the sonic boom of thunder drowning out the roar of rain.

He was frantic, thrashing to stay afloat and fearing what had touched him. With every flash of lightning he caught a glimpse of something moving, a silhouetted triangular shape slicing through the water.

He watched in terror as another huge shark fin appeared and then two smaller ones, all circling at a distance showcased by the storm's light display. Then one by one the sharks sank below the surface leaving just the clatter of rain bouncing off the ocean.

The numbing sting of the north Atlantic Ocean was debilitating, hypothermia smothered his breath and his legs struggled to keep him buoyant. His greatest fear growing up was to die at the teeth of a shark, to be ripped apart in a feeding frenzy by a pack of blood enraged predators and somewhere in the blackness they waited their attack.

Behind him in the distance a small boat approached from the north. A bright search light swayed back and forth across its path and he could just make out the darkened shapes of men on the front deck. Then as the light brushed his position, he flapped his arms in a frantic bid for rescue. The boat spun hard and the engine roared louder.

Overhead the storm wasn't letting up, the rain more blinding, and an incoming gale was whipping up a whitewash of surface chop. The spotlight remained fixed on his position as the boat steamed at speed towards him and the men waved and pointed.

Somewhere over his shoulder movement caught his eye and he realised in horror it wasn't him they pointed at. At that moment the sea erupted and swallowed him. Water surged past while he wrestled to recover the surface and draw breath, but he was pulled deeper.

He couldn't kick, his legs were paralysed, or so he thought.

A few more drowning seconds and he gained traction clawing his way upwards, towards a bright light flickering through the surging white water. Like a bubble from the depths, his head burst through the surface to the sight of the boat and the men onboard standing watching him. They just stood motionless, peering down almost visionless and strangely, not making any attempt to save him.

The water around him had turned bright red and he realised in terror, it was his blood and his life polluting the sea. The shark had severed his leg mid-thigh leaving the flesh and bone flapping in the wind swept current.

In a flurry of panic-stricken slaps against the water he tried to swim towards the boat, screaming for help.

"Help me please."

He was tiring quickly and his blood boiled around him in the surging water now smothering his face. A feeding frenzy was about to unleash as the scent of his blood spread deeper and sharks raced towards him from the ocean depths.

"Please help me...PLEASE!" he pleaded one more time as his head sank under the surface and he swallowed sea water.

A voice broke above the idling engine, "Where is it, tell us where it is, and we will save you. More sharks are coming, tell us and we will save you."

He could not think, his subconscious was in a complete grip of fear and he knew that within seconds his body would be ripped apart.

"I don't know, get me out," he screamed.

A large fin appeared cutting the water at speed towards him. "This one will finish you, tell us and you will live."

At twenty feet and closing, the shark submerged for the kill.

"Under the floorboards next to the fireplace ... FUCKING GET ME OUT ... NOW"

He had no idea what was happening, his subconscious and conscious minds were locked in a fierce battle. He was in the water fighting for his survival, yet his most recent memory confused him. How did he end up in the water in the first place, he thought?

He was clutched from the water, one leg missing and blood gushing from the ruptured artery. It was disorientating and as quickly as it started, it stopped, and he discovered himself still strapped inside his St Ives home.

"What the fuck just happened?" he gasped finding his breath and looking down at his two legs, no blood in sight and no sharks.

Around him the same men from the boat laughed.

The lieutenant had enlisted with the British Army when he was just fresh out of school and shipped straight to the Gulf War of `91. By the time he was deployed during the invasion of Iraq, he was well accustomed to the pros and cons of war.

He just hadn't thought stealing something so small from the treasures of Saddam Hussein would become his greatest abomination. The underground vault on the outskirts of Hillah had developed into a feeding banquet for the greedy, all pocketing what they could. Taking one small artefact was nothing in his eyes to the truck loads stolen by others.

The straps around his ankles and wrists were excruciatingly tight preventing his escape. On either side two heavily battle-scarred men clutching Beretta handguns presided over him while another stood in front with a small black device in his hand. All wore dark military style outfits and automatic rifles slung across their shoulders.

"Thankyou Lieutenant?" the man holding the device said, divulging a slight hint of an American accent.

Another armed man walked into the room carrying a dark Hessian bag and handed it to the lead man. Nothing was said.

He watched as the man opened the bag and removed a dull grey marble sphere with hundreds of small alien like hieroglyphs etched into the surface. The man smiled and rolled it around in his hands like he would a basketball, for it was that approximate size.

"What the fuck did you do to me?" the Lieutenant asked again.

"Technology, it's amazing don't you think? How we can trick the human mind into thinking whatever we want it to think" the lead man answered still inspecting his newly acquired trophy.

The Lieutenant could feel a metal spike in the back of his neck and he grimaced in pain with every slight movement of his head.

"You have a six-inch spike into the spinal cord of your neck so I suggest no sudden movements," the man replied breaking from the hypnotic effect the Sphere had on him.

"This here device controls your thoughts and just how terrifying I wish them to be. You see if I turn up this dial, your worst fear comes to life, and to you it's real. I believe in your case it came in the form of a shark attack," he added laughing to the accompaniment of the others smirking.

He and the other men had charged into the Lieutenant's home an hour earlier searching for the stolen artefact and attempted an interrogation in the traditional sense. They had punched him and threatened greater harm, but he had remained strong minded refusing to hand over the artefact.

Since discovering it in Iraq he had always experienced some unusual connection to it. At times it would resonate a soft harmonious purr like that of a content house cat and occasionally the symbols turned a shade of vibrant blue. Though each occurrence lasted only a few minutes he was convinced the sphere was home to some form of organism, perhaps extraterrestrial.

"Why do you want that?" he asked looking at the Sphere.

"Lieutenant, the Sphere was not yours to take and likewise, it was not Saddam Hussein's either," he replied.

"What's it worth?" the Lieutenant asked.

"Your life," he quickly replied raising his silenced Beretta and squeezing the trigger twice in quick succession.

The Lieutenant's body slumped lifeless as blood and brain oozed from the two exit wounds in the back of his head.

The men vacated the house hoping not to raise suspicions from neighbours and drove slowly away.

3.
Heist

500 nautical miles west of
San Antonio, Chile
June 10, 2004

Andre stepped from the ship's control room into the escalating fury of an approaching storm. He battled the handrail, clutching hand over hand as the stealth warship lunged forward and pitched high against the barrage of a mountainous eight metre swell. A gale force wind lashed his face and in the freezing rain, it stung like a hundred razor blades shredding his weather-beaten skin. It would be an hour before the early morning sun penetrated the thundercloud overhead and offered the warmth they desperately needed.

He and his squad of commandos had been steaming all night at twenty-five knots towards a small cluster of remote islands five hundred miles west of San Antonio. The closer they approached, the storm dealt more, unleashing greater fury as if warning them away. The lightning had become more frequent and the cracking thunder grew louder by the minute. It wasn't about to relent anytime soon.

He raised his night vision binoculars and scanned the horizon, mostly vast wild ocean shielded by the early morning darkness. He checked his watch, they were making good time, he thought, two minutes past four meant they would be at their target by close on four thirty.

At that moment, a rogue thirty-footer slammed without mercy into the bow and he lost his footing, slipping backwards but staying upright gripping desperately at the deck rail.

"Damn this fucking ocean!" he muttered.

Andre Matheson wasn't a companion of the open sea, he preferred the dry hard ground where he had the control and confidence without the slithering and tilting of a wild ocean. Like the others in his team, he was a trained mercenary, a hired hand to do the dirty work that most didn't want to do. Matheson had hand selected each member, mostly for their abilities in the art of war, but more for their commitment and devotion to him. Each had at some point in their previous military service been under his command and so he knew them all well.

He righted himself, tightening his grip on the rail and raised his binoculars again.

To the west he could just make out the silhouette of the island's jagged coastline and the massive heart rising abruptly from the sea into the low clouds. It was a semi barren fragment of rock, the tip of an enormous mountain resting sedately on the seabed. To the untrained eye, it appeared somewhat docile yet at the same time, mysteriously eerie with its near vertical cliff faces and the ocean forever grinding at its base with wave after wave.

It certainly didn't look inviting Matheson thought, as he focussed his binoculars towards the northern shoreline, a five-mile-long platform of volcanic rock that rose fifty feet above the water. It resembled a gargantuan rectangular pillar laid on its side as a wall to guard the island. But he knew what lay beneath it and he signalled to the ship's captain to steer towards it.

From orbit, the island had a more militarised appearance. Cut between two towering mountain peaks a three-thousand-yard asphalt runway stretched from north to south. Along the northern side three massive hangars concealed the elevators giving access to an eight-level underground facility.

"Boss, is that the island?"

Matheson lowered his binoculars and turned towards the voice yelling above the roaring wind. Carl Balfour had been his right-hand man since the attack on Area 47 and never far from his side. Three years earlier he and the same men had carried out the militarised assault on the US Government's sister site to Area 51 where they stole Lucifer's Funnel, a small but deadly fragment from the 1947 Roswell crash. Up until that day, he and his men had never accepted the well disputed conspiracies of the crashed alien craft. The raid on Area 47 quickly changed those beliefs.

Matheson nodded, handing him the binoculars. Balfour took them and started his own reconnaissance of the dark mass looming up ahead.

"I hope your intel is good. If not, we could be sailing into a slaughter. Could be any number of guns mounted on them cliffs," Balfour pointed out in his rough south African accent.

"My intel is always good, you know that," he replied as his satellite phone chimed and he stepped into the ship's helm to answer it.

Balfour watched him, waiting.

"It's a go, neurotoxin has been released," Matheson said as he disconnected the call.

"Can't believe they found their way through that storm," Balfour said shaking his head in amazement and added walking off, "I will get the men ready."

"Good, we disembark in twenty minutes," Matheson called to him.

He stood for a minute longer wondering the same thing. An hour earlier, four elite paratroopers had haloed from thirty thousand feet onto the island and dispersed a deadly neurotoxin into the ventilation system. It acted within a minute spreading throughout the entire facility and eradicated the occupants like rats. Some died instantly but most suffered a harrowing death lasting minutes with their internal organs first to dissolve, followed by their skin liquefying.

The ship pushed forward at full speed as the surrounding water hissed and hurled across the bow. Up ahead at three hundred yards, a narrow opening in the cliff face appeared. At first it was just a dark blemish on the rock face but as they approached closer, it emerged as a crevice barely wide enough for their ship to pass through. The skipper steered it slowly at ten knots wrestling the ocean's surge and cursing as the hull scraped and buffered the rocks either side. The whole passage lasted fifteen minutes until they reached a small tranquil lagoon surrounded by steep cliffs and sheltered from the storm's ferocity.

Matheson and his men leapt into an inflatable boat and charged across the still water to the facility's dock where the four paratroopers waited.

"Sir, neurotoxin will be non-lethal in eight minutes," the lead paratrooper declared as he shook Matheson's hand.

"Good work soldier. How was the ride in?"

"Scary as all fuck, rode the lightning all the way!" he laughed.

They all donned breathing apparatus and descended three levels past dozens of mangled and bloodied bodies until they reached their destination.

"Holy shit!" Balfour exclaimed stripping away his mask and stepping into a brightly lit room roughly twenty meters square.

He turned to Matheson, "Looks like your intel was good."

They stood at the entrance for a moment while the other men removed their masks and shuffled for a better view. On the floor scattered around the room, half a dozen men in white lab coats lay bleeding out onto the white tiles.

"Have you ever seen anything like that before?" Matheson asked nodding towards the large reflective silver object in the centre of the room.

"No, I can't say I have and it's not what I expected," Balfour replied taking a few cautious steps closer and caressing its polished surface.

"I am not sure an ancient artefact is the correct description either," Matheson chuckled.

He reached for his satellite phone and placed a call.

It rang once and to his surprise, a woman's voice answered.

"Do you have it?"

"Yes, it will be loaded and shipped within the hour to the coordinates you requested."

"Good now finish your mission," she commanded.

"Yes ma'am!" he replied but she'd cut him off.

He turned to Balfour, "That's one icy bitch! You have half an hour to get this thing out of here and onto the ship."

While his second in command went about his business, Matheson took a small backpack from one of the other men and hurried to the lowest level.

He found a location deep inside one of the many rooms and opened the bag to expose a digital keypad and series of orange, green and red buttons. He set the timer for two hours and keyed in a series of nine digits before he rested back on his knees for a moment thinking and chuckling to himself.

He pressed the red button and stood.

The timer display illuminated, and the countdown commenced, signalling the nuclear device was armed.

4.
<u>Apocalypse of Night</u>

Location unknown

The sun was moments from setting behind a backdrop of darkening clouds. Something was not right; the air was too cold and a strange blustery wind clawed almost suction like at his clothes.

Bennett stood motionless watching the mountainous horizon to the west ignoring his instinct to flee. Under his boots the loose stone quivered while around him, people carried on with their everyday lives not perturbed by the man standing nervously in the middle of their street. He kept deliberating that something was not right, none of it was meant to happen now, the sphere and codebook had all been destroyed.

His feet refused to move, fixed to the ground as the second pulse of vibrant blue light split the clouds to the north. The roadway under his feet started to heave upwards and yet he stood paralysed, frozen in time. Lightning sprayed across the darkening sky to the accompaniment of a deep thunderous rumble.

One by one the local villagers stopped and stood watching him oblivious to what was coming.

The northern horizon of a once lush palm forest was now a hundred-foot wave of rock and earth tumbling towards them at an increasing velocity. Infernos erupted as gas lines burst and the deafening roar announced its arrival.

People around him began screaming and running while the land tsunami gained momentum, tossing and crushing all in its path. Nothing could stop it and somewhere further west another pulse of blue light struck the earth with annihilating force.

Bennett wrestled against the rolling ground trying desperately to force his boots free of the stranglehold it had on him. Down the street a man was running towards him, yelling, but as he drew closer, Bennett had a sudden realisation.

The earth below them erupted and the man stumbled to the ground clawing his way towards Bennett. He looked up and through the agony of the fire engulfing his body he muttered a few painful words.

"It is too late Jon, you failed... we are all dead!"

Bennett was staring into the bleeding eyes of himself. His aged and weathered face reflected crimson in the reflection of fire and the scars signalled a violent life. Behind him and rising higher, the land tsunami continued its path of extinction upturning the earth and decimating every structure in seconds.

Molten earth engulfed the man's body and Bennett felt his own skin melt and peel as the intense heat hit him. The roar of death was deafening as the wall of rock crushed his body to pulp.

5.
Relief

Luanda, Angola
May 4, 2005

Bennett jolted upright, drenched in sweat and swamped in relief. His apocalyptic torment had been another of his reoccurring nightmares plaguing him every night for the past week. All that remained was a dull headache and a racing heart rate as he looked around the darkness of his hotel room. Suddenly it all came rushing back and he remembered where he was, a dingy hotel in the south of Luanda.

Four years had passed since he single-handedly took down the six men at the helm of *The Trust* and averted the execution of their devastating plan. A new world order had been their goal but first it needed the annihilation of the world's population, a restart of the planet so to speak.

He glanced at the bedside clock massaging the sleep from his eyes. Illuminated in red, it was a few minutes past two in the morning.

Next to him the bed was empty, just the shallow impression of where a body once slept with the bed sheets scrunched to the side. Silence surrounded him until somewhere off in the distance a car backfired.

"Nik?" he called softly scanning the room for movement.

No reply.

He reached under the bed and grabbed his Beretta 9mm, his handgun of choice, and quietly racked a round into the chamber. The room was dingy with one well used double bed consuming most of the floor space. Off to one side an open doorway exposed a tiny bathroom and he gave it a quick look. Nicholette was nowhere to be seen.

Bennett raised his gun and pulled open the door. He snapped a quick peek in both directions along an empty hallway. *Why hadn't she woken him?*

He moved quickly along the dimly lit hallway and down a stairwell to the street below. There he paused watching the deserted street, mostly in darkness except for the occasional flicker of light emanating from a row of shops across the road. Above him, the half-moon was attempting to break free of the scattered clouds and offer him some light.

Somewhere in the distance, a short burst of gunfire broke the silence and then two quick rounds rang out. He raised his gun to eye level and sprinted in the direction it had sounded, a side alley just forty yards to his left.

As he approached the alley, a dark shadow emerged walking quickly towards him.

"Okay that's far enough, show me your hands," he called from over the top of his gun sights.

As more moonlight broke through, the shadow materialised to reveal a woman dressed in jeans and a tight t-shirt exposing a nice breast line and slender muscular arms.

"Whoa don't shoot! It's me Jon."

Bennett lowered his weapon to stare into the seductive green eyes of his fiancée.

"What the hell are you doing out here and who was shooting?" he asked looking past her into the dark alley.

"Two dead Russian agents back there," she answered with a flick of her head towards the alley.

Bennett nodded, he wasn't surprised.

Nicholette Sponarava was still the most wanted fugitive in Russia, worth one million US dollars captured alive. They had no interest in the 'Butcher of Volgograd' dead, she held too many secrets but most of all, they wanted to witness her suffer a brutal punishment for the many murders she had committed. Once a highly respected member of the Russian Special Forces and then the Russian Foreign Military Intelligence Unit she quickly elevated to become their most ruthless assassin, superior and effective in every way. It wasn't until she dissented and started executing their own murderous politicians that her life transcended into a daily contest of survival, constantly looking over her shoulder and on the run.

They raced to their hotel room and from there they watched the street and the main hotel entrance down below. The gun fire had woken a few of the locals as lights came on and silhouetted figures appeared at the windows across the street.

"We can't stay here, they know our location," Nicholette whispered, thinking the room could be bugged.

He agreed with a nod and pulled her in close to his chest, kissing her forehead.

They had become quite a team, combining their lethal prowess and engaging private contracts for six figure fees. Most involved assassinations however, by their justification, they were deserving punishments for the crimes the targets had committed, mostly genocide and other war like crimes. Occasionally a wealthy father sought revenge for the murder of his child and he willingly paid an extra hundred thousand dollars to stare into the perpetrator's eyes as they exhaled their last breath.

They shared a covert and fast paced lifestyle, travelling to all ends of the Earth under the pseudonym, 'Hansel and Gretel', a trademark name Nicholette had insisted on. The fairy tale had been one of only a few good memories from her childhood, growing up in Moscow under the dictatorship of her abusive father. Bennett didn't care about the name, it made her happy and that's all that counted in his opinion. He loved her and would do anything for her while she felt the same for him. He'd been her saviour.

Four years earlier she had died in Orto-Tokoy and without explanation, her body had vanished leaving Bennett distraught. But then that phone call in the dead of night reinvigorated his zest for life, she was alive. For the next three months, he spent every day and night searching for her, pulling on old acquaintances who owed him a favour however, no one could help him. It was his aunt Rose who delivered in the end.

Rose Bennett had been like a mother to Jon after his mother died at a time when he was too young to remember and his father, Viktor Bennett, was too busy travelling the globe from one CIA assignment to the next.

When Rose came to him, he was overwhelmed with relief that Nicholette was alive. The last time he'd seen her, she had died in his arms from a gunshot wound at the hands of Logan Bannister the same man, who murdered his father. Then her body had vanished without a trace leaving just the blood on the ground as evidence. It was unexplainable until Rose showed up with answers.

She had always been deep inside the government's covert departments and had developed a plethora of contacts. Bennett never knew just how close Rose was to the truth.

They both sat at the window watching the street while Bennett contemplated their next step. They had a mission to complete and for their efforts, half a million dollars.

Sponarava spoke again, "Jon are you listening? What now, they know we're here!"

"Nic you can't do that shit."

"What are you talking about?"

"Going off in the middle of the night, not waking me, you know that macho shit of yours. *The Nicholette Sponarava I'm so tough routine, I can do anything shit.*"

In the last few minutes, he had become pissed off at her stupidity.

Since the first couple of attempts on her life last year he had become overprotective of her. The Russians wanted her and he knew what that meant. They would stop at nothing to find and capture her. The only problem in his opinion was Nicholette herself. She would fight till the death, there would be no possible option of capture and Bennett knew it would end in her death. That angered him.

"I can handle myself babe, you know that so please stop worrying," she replied and changed the topic quickly, "Anyway isn't it usually you people want to kill, or have you slipped down on the most hated list. Poor baby not pissing enough people off these days and he's becoming jealous of me!" She laughed.

Bennett joined in the laughter. She had made a good point, he had slipped and yes, she could handle herself, probably better than him he conceded.

"What happened tonight?" he asked.

"The fools were smoking. Clearly they don't teach that in covert surveillance anymore back in the motherland," she laughed.

"I spotted the glow of their cigarettes from our window. After an hour, I'd had enough, it was time to find out who they were. They spotted me walking out the front door and both took off down the alleyway. Hey, they shot first and well, you know the rest, two dead Russians."

"You sure, they were Russians?" he asked.

"I'm lucky they want me alive, best thing for me, gives me a fighting chance I reckon. They were Foreign Intelligence Service for sure, both had the right markings."

Bennett nodded, he had started thinking of how she came back into his life and wasn't keen to lose her again.

"Okay, next time you decide to go it alone in the wee hours then tell me. Promise me that."

"Yes babe, absolutely!" she sheepishly responded leaning forward into his arms.

He wrapped her up in his warmth and their lips pressed together. Like the first time it still had the same euphoric kick, a scintillating tingle running rampant across his whole body starting in his loins. They held each other enjoying the moment until movement outside in the street caught her eye.

Bennett reluctantly pulled away, disappointed he couldn't take her right there.

Across the street in the shadows of the shop awnings three men appeared moving slowly at first but hastening their pace towards the hotel entrance. Each carried an automatic rifle pointed in the direction they moved.

6.
Russians

Luanda, Angola
May 4, 2005

"Okay I guess that's our cue!" Sponarava announced.

"I have a plan, grab all the weapons you can carry," Bennett responded.

She stopped, staring at him.

"You care to share your plan then?" she asked.

"No time, come on. I figure we have two minutes before they come barging through that door."

Like everywhere they went, Bennett had a quick escape pack all set to go. Inside a duffle bag next to the door, a small selection of their favourite handguns and assault rifles were neatly packed plus plenty of ammunition. It was a safeguard he'd come to rely on when needing to make that urgent escape like what was happening now.

Nicholette grabbed the bag and tossed it over her shoulder like it weighed nothing yet it was close on twenty kilograms. She loved her gym workouts, lifting heavy weights and challenging Bennett whenever she could to an arm wrestle. Sometimes she would win but not without a little cheating, her penetrating green eyes often swaying Bennett's concentration followed quickly by a left jab to his ribs. Win by any means she would declare as he'd throw her to the gym floor and take his playful revenge.

They left their hotel room and sprinted down the hallway towards the fire escape. He stopped, wedged the escape open.

"What are you doing?" Sponarava yelled.

"It's part of my plan."

"Again, knowing your plan would be nice," she returned with an overabundance of sarcasm.

"Soon, we have to keep moving."

"Okay boss but you're the one stopping to make it easier for them," she said as the first of the men appeared at the opposite end of the hallway.

A shot nicked the doorframe above their heads and they leapt down the narrow metal stairs, three treads at a time.

"We keep these goons on our tail all the way to the target," Bennett said in between breaths as they ran.

"The target, what do you mean? Are we advancing the schedule?"

"We get to the car, let them see us and then head across town."

"Oh ingenious!" she exclaimed.

Sponarava was on Bennett's wavelength.

Their assigned target, an ex-Angolan Army General lived on the northern side of Luanda on the way to Panguila. He had under his charge, an army of over three thousand men and women, all ready to overthrow the Angolan government at any moment on his orders. Nelson Buhari lived two miles south of Panguila on a heavily forested section of land and guarded by a small number of troops. His three-story cement and brick home stood out amongst the trees presiding over the locals like an Angolan king. But he was no king to the people, most feared him, and many had died at the hands of his rebel troops. Like so many of their previous contracts, he was another genocidal warlord maniac wanting control and power.

Bennett and Sponarava's mission was to 'cut the head off the snake' so to speak, before the rebel army could expand any further and take control. Their brief on Buhari showed him as merciless, a man raging with his own greed to control Angola no matter who he had to murder along the way. Latest intelligence suggested dissention building among some of his more senior leaders and with Buhari dead, could mean the dissolution of the army. It was a contract 'Hansel and Gretel' accepted without a second thought.

Bennett started their car, an old Mercedes diesel worth far less than what he had paid, but he didn't care. Once the mission was over, they would be leaving it on the side of the road or someplace where a lesser fortunate could use it. He checked the mirror as the first volley of rounds shattered the rear window.

"Cutting it a little close, aren't we?" Sponarava heckled and lifted her Kalashnikov AK102 assault rifle.

Soviet made guns were still the best in her opinion and Bennett would never sway her for the German and American alternatives. She returned a short-controlled burst of a few rounds through the gaping hole in the back window towards the shooters. They scattered for cover giving Bennett enough time to fishtail the car around the next corner leaving a small dust storm in their wake.

At that early hour, cars were scarce on the roads and as expected distant car lights appeared in the rear-view mirror, two sets of lights driving at speed in their direction.

"Okay, the plan has not changed for Buhari, we stick to what we discussed. Agreed?" he asked.

"Agreed. We may not have enough time though, they are gaining fast," Sponarava replied sitting beside him and half turned to watch the two cars approaching.

Bennett pushed down harder on the pedal and the Mercedes lurched forward giving him another ten miles per hour, but that was about it for their old machine. The steering wheel had a violent shudder made worse by the cracks and potholes in the asphalt. They still had a few hours of darkness before sunrise and only a mile out from the target's residence.

"The front gate is about two hundred yards up ahead. You take out the guards but remember, keep it quiet," he said easing up on the accelerator and added, "We don't need to be waking up Buhari's army."

"What are you going to do?" she asked.

"Buy us some time I hope," he laughed giving her a wink as she checked her weapons.

"Meet you at the gate in fifteen minutes after you've silenced the guards," he added pressing hard on the brake pedal and yanking the handbrake. At the same time, he extinguished the head lights and released the brake pedal. Back behind him the pursuers failed to notice the manoeuvre.

"Go! Remember, silence is the key," Bennett said as she opened her door and leapt to the roadside into a nicely executed roll before rebounding to her feet.

Bennett slammed down hard on the pedal and accelerated towards the north with the others in pursuit a few hundred yards behind him.

Less than ten minutes later, the three guards were dead each with a single gunshot to their head. Like most of the soldiers in Buhari's army they were not well trained and never stood a chance against Sponarava's stealth approach or the accuracy of her silenced handgun. While she did her part, Bennett fought hard to shake off their followers, giving his best to keep the car on the weather-beaten road at over a hundred miles per hour. Every corner was death defying as the car fishtailed and slid, clinging loosely to the road while back behind him the other car quickly narrowed the distance.

The old Mercedes lacked the horsepower to break free from the pursuit, so he released the accelerator and spun the wheel while yanking hard on the handbrake. The car shook violently against the rough road surface and the back end slid outwards as the rear wheels locked up. At that moment he released the handbrake and gave the engine a fresh spurt of life with his foot. The car initially struggled to regain traction and he had to wrestle the wheel to stop the overspin until the tyres bit down hard into the dirt.

Feeling like a Formula One champion he drove at speed towards the oncoming headlights, while risking a head on collision he waited until the very last second to turn his lights back on at high beam. The driver of the first car followed his natural reaction and pulled hard right away from the sudden bright headlights blinding him. The car spun out of control into a ditch while the driver of the second car with a little more time to react narrowly missed rear ending the lead car. It spun uncontrollably across the road slamming side on into a small tree. Bennett kept his foot firm against the accelerator speeding away.

A few minutes later he was back at the entrance to Buhari's estate where he left the car and ran the twenty yards to the sentry point. By the time he'd found Sponarava waiting in the darkness, they could hear a car approaching at high speed.

"Thought you were going to take care of them," she said with a flick of her head towards the sound of the roaring car engine.

Bennett brushed away the sarcasm with a slick chuckle. It was always a competition between them and he knew on this occasion she had clearly beaten him. The three dead bodies with single gunshots to their head meant he didn't need to ask how she fared.

"Let's move, Buhari's house is eighty yards up this road," he said pushing past her.

A few minutes later, they had silenced two more guards and were inside Buhari's house. They moved fast clearing each room advancing towards Buhari's bedroom on the second floor, the furthest room off to the right overlooking the compound behind the house. Inside the compound, a squad of fifty men slept unaware of what was happening.

Like all their assignments, they had spent the previous few days preparing, scouring satellite images of the compound and thermals of the residence. Despite the constant battle to outdo each other, they had become a formidable team, constantly anticipating each other's moves and rarely making mistakes.

"Wait!" Bennett whispered as he snapped a quick peek into the room, pushing the door open a few inches.

He nodded towards the room, raised his gun and they barged in at speed.

7.
<u>Nelson Buhari</u>

Luanda, Angola
May 4, 2005

A startled Buhari jumped to his feet, staring back at them, eyes wide glaring into the muzzles of two handguns pointed at his head from a few metres away. He resembled a large black gorilla about to beat his chest in anger.

"How dare you barge into my house. Do you know who I am?" he bellowed.

A size eight boot in his chest was the response as he fell backwards onto the bed next to a young naked girl, no more than eleven. She was just one of the many selected from the local village to satisfy his sexual appetite. Though their mothers resisted, there was little they could do except grieve, their daughters would never return.

Sponarava had lost control at the sight of the girl and pounced, unleashing a fury of repeated fists into his face, breaking the man's jaw in two places. Bennett grabbed the girl and covered her mouth, beckoning with his other for her not to scream.

He knew Sponarava's years of sexual abuse at the hands of her father still plagued her day and night.

"You are a filthy piece of shit," she said lifting her handgun.
PEW

A single tap of a silenced gunshot and Buhari grabbed his bloodied crutch while she glared at him from two feet away.

Bennett released his hand from the girl's mouth and she made no sound, just looked back at Sponarava's tears trickling down her face.

"I am sorry this animal has tormented you," she said as Buhari screamed to waken his soldiers.

Without taking her eyes from the small girl, she fired two quick rounds, each dead centre in his forehead. His head exploded as his brains splattered across the wall behind the bed.

Bennett turned to Sponarava with a quizzical look.

"What? We were going to kill him anyway!" she replied with a small shrug of her shoulders.

"Yeah but did you need to shoot his dick off first," Bennett said with a hint of sarcasm.

She shrugged again and smiled back at him, taking the young girl in her arms and motioning for her to go home. They knew about his fetish for young girls and it was the real reason in her eyes to kill him and not the acts of genocide he was responsible for.

"Now for the fun part," Bennett said.

He walked to the window and looked out over the compound in darkness and seemingly unresponsive to Buhari's brief scream for help. He suspected somewhere down there, the Russians from the car were lurking, searching for Nicholette. It was time to make things interesting, he thought.

He unstrapped the Heckler and Koch HK33 assault rifle from across his shoulders and through the open window, he sprayed a wide arc of ten rounds into the air. The compound exploded to life, men yelling and running in all directions. Some fired wildly into the air not knowing who was shooting or where it was coming from.

The Russians had been sneaking through the compound heading towards the house when Bennett appeared at the window. Only one of them had spotted him as the gunfire started.

"Let's go, stick to the plan," Bennett called.

Suddenly a half-dressed man stood in the doorway, gun up and about to squeeze the trigger as Sponarava charged him, lifting him clear off the floor and ramming him backwards, driving his head into the opposite wall. In the same movement, she raised her Tokarev pistol and shot up through his chin into his head. He collapsed lifeless to the floor.

Outside in the compound the Russians were fighting for their lives dropping their share of soldiers but soon their time would be up. As the first of the four Russians died, Bennett and Sponarava were back at the car.

"Do you still have Buhari's photograph?" he called to her after spotting the Russian's car parked outside the entrance.

"Yes," she replied digging into the duffle bag and pulling out a six by four picture of their target.

She handed it to him and he dropped it onto the front floor of the Russian's car.

"This way when the Angolan police arrive, they will discover a photograph of the victim in the Russian's car and they become the obvious suspects," he said smiling.

"Those Russians know me, know us, what if they talk to the police," she added.

Bennett chuckled listening to the gun battle coming from behind the trees. "Do you really think they will survive that?" he replied nodding his head towards the compound.

She conceded with a brief smile as he started the car and slowly drove away.

Back inside the compound, the Russians had all been killed except one, he'd been shot twice in the stomach and once through his left lung. He dialled his cell phone and in his last few breaths he spoke into the phone.

"We lost Bennett...still in Angola with the woman."

The phone fell from his hand as he took his last breath.

The person on the other end was furious, they needed Bennett but more importantly, they needed the Thirteenth Code he carried upon his chest.

8.
<u>Blue Crystal</u>

Namori, Ghana
May 5, 2005

Threatening to suspend their afternoon training session, a bank of black storm clouds rose swiftly in the south. The entire village had turned out to chant the victory song and pay homage to their champion football team, each silently praying for a successful passage into the national finals. For Duku and his teammates, it was an honour to spend their last workout under the watchful eyes of the townsfolk and they eagerly absorbed the moment.

As the whistle blew signalling the start of training, something in the sky caught Duku's attention. Slowly the others joined to stand with him watching the northern skyline as a small silver cylindrical object floated towards them, high above the ground. At first, it appeared to drift and slip sideways dropping closer until it veered hard right towards the football field.

"Hey what's that?" one of the boys behind him said.

The spectators driven by curiosity did the same, stopped to stare skyward as the object accelerated overhead at five hundred feet and vanished to the south. There had been no sound until the screaming started.

None of them had noticed their football team drop to the ground.

Duku was one of the first to fall, collapsing helplessly to his knees, twisting face down into the hard earth. Blood spewed freely from his mouth and eyes while he howled in agony as his life drained into the dirt. His heart rate accelerated and exploded inside his chest like a grenade, ripping away the last few seconds of his young existence.

It all happened quickly, sixty brutal excruciating deaths in less than twenty seconds.

Ten thousand miles away, a small group of men and women sat watching the event unfold on a satellite feed. A few clapped while others shook hands. Their first live test had been successful, aerial dispersal of the blue crystal dust at altitude was effective. That they all knew meant millions would die.

One man in particular was more pleased than the others. It meant his plan was coming together.

9.
<u>Soldier of the New World</u>

Manhattan, New York City
May 5, 2005

A single high calibre gunshot resembling the intense crack of a whip split the rumbling drone of the late afternoon traffic. Down on the sidewalk people screamed and scurried for their lives. The street without warning had transformed from the impatient hustle of the 'end of day' workers to a bloody mayhem as they scrambled for the sanctuary of nearby buildings.

Behind them sprawled on the pavement, an elderly silver haired gentleman dressed in an immaculate Caraceni suit bled out from a two-inch gaping hole in his chest. The round had desecrated his heart on impact extinguishing his life instantly and ending his twenty-five-year reign at the helm of America's largest bank.

Somewhere further across Greenwich Street, his assassin concealed behind the walls of a high vantage point, dismantled his sniper rifle for the journey home. He was not a contracted assassin but a lone wolf terrorist with his own brutal agenda, selecting high ranking officials of both the corporate world and the political arena.

His marksmanship was impeccable, never missing his target which he owed to the teachings of his father. Today's execution had elevated his total into triple figures and like the other murders, this one had a specific purpose. He researched meticulously to select the best candidates for his crosshairs, men and women with the political clout to push society further into chaos by their very greed for greater power and wealth. Like the banker dead on the sidewalk, they had high ranking involvement in the ownership of sinister business enterprises that kept the world in a perpetual state of conflict. He carried a distinct hatred of those who profiteered from death and suffering, but he failed to see any positive impact conventional protesting was having around the world.

He considered himself a new age visionary, a man on a crusade to save the planet by an unorthodox tactic. He was all about halting the financial atrocities and the corporate corruption through acts of terror. His assassinations were always quick and without warning, never following the same routine. Within twenty-four hours of the execution, a typed letter would arrive at the target's office. It always read the same and never did it provide the authorities with any physical evidence.

By the hand of God, you were executed for the atrocities you support. The world we share is dying and it is men and women like you who care not for its survival but how to make more profit.

Greed is our criminal sin and you were found guilty. Let it be a warning to others like you that if you continue to prosper from war, mineral wealth or population expansion then more will die at my hand. You must desist from further progress and convince all those around you. You are not immune from my gunsight, make change or die at my hand.

At the end it was always signed, *The Soldier of the New World*.

It was a name that quickly became the topic of frustration among senior law enforcers worldwide. It wasn't until he turned his killing spree towards key government officials of the British and American administrations did the investigation receive the full grunt of the CIA and MI6. At that point *The Soldier* crossed over from serial murderer to political assassin and the man hunt unfolded.

A month earlier he had executed a prominent British Government minister while he sailed aboard his luxury yacht on the Thames. An easy target *The Soldier* considered, as he pulled the trigger eight hundred yards away hidden among the cover of the riverbank shrubbery. The next day when his message arrived at 10 Downing Street, it caused political panic and the war on terrorism gained greater momentum while the assassin basked in the glory of one more triumph.

The FBI and Interpol had nothing, no evidential leads and no clue who he was or whether the assassin was a man or woman. The assassin's never-failing accuracy hinted military expertise but of what nationality was one of the endless intelligence gaps confronting the world's best investigators.

While the police swarmed the New York crime scene, *The Soldier of the New World* boarded Lufthansa flight 907 bound for Berlin in preparation for his next target.

10.
Impact

Washington DC
May 9, 2005

The bedside telephone blurted to life in the dead of night.

"Yes," a half-asleep President responded.

"Mr President, its George, we have a situation in northern China. Less than an hour ago a large-scale ground impact was detected in northern Shenyang, possibly nuclear."

"Assemble the Joint Chiefs," the President demanded and hung up as his Secret Service agents stood waiting for him to shower and dress.

Less than ten minutes later, Bill Armstrong walked confidently into the Situation Room to a wall of video monitors ablaze with satellite images and media broadcasts. He was a tall man, towering over most in the room and easy to spot in a crowd. He never cared much for the formal attire a President should adhere to and so he entered the room wearing jeans and a light-coloured polo, partly concealed under a dark casual jacket. He was there to do a job not become a fashion topic for Vogue, he always said. He had been the President for a little over nine months and he was still finding his feet among the rigid politics of the White House and how best to play the bureaucratic game they all liked so much.

George Whitman on the other hand was no stranger to politics having grown up in a three-generation family of Senators. His father, grandfather and great grandfather had each served impressive terms as United States Senators in Massachusetts. George chose to break that trend. He instead enlisted in the Army at a young age until during the Gulf War of 1991 where he was badly wounded and forced to leave the military. His father convinced him to enter politics and his lineage soon showed.

Fourteen years later Bill Armstrong selected him as his Secretary of Defense. It had been expected considering they had been friends for a long time and he was an American patriot through and through.

He met the President at the door with notes in hand and a full briefing at the ready.

"What do we have George?" he asked with a slight exchange of pleasantries.

"Substantial damage, half the city destroyed, a million or more dead. Satellite imaging confirms ground impact of colossal size," Whitman answered.

"Any idea what caused it, are we talking nuclear strike?" the President asked fixated on the aerial images of a blazing holocaust.

"A team is analysing the images but yes, it is looking nuclear. A ground impact by the size of the crater and the destruction surrounding it. A five-mile radius has been flattened as if the ground swallowed the city."

"What about a meteor strike? Could that be a possibility?" the President asked.

"The team is divided, some believe it's more likely an extraterrestrial impact, a small to medium size asteroid like the Tunguska event in Siberia during 1908. The remainder of the team aren't so convinced, they believe the destruction pattern is typical of a large nuclear ground impact. What we do know is that something hit the ground seconds before the explosion. Eyewitness reports from over a hundred miles away describe a bright flash of blue light in the sky moments before the explosion."

"Blue light? What are the experts saying about that?"

"They can't explain it though they suspect it's probably light refracting off either the missile or the meteor trail."

"Okay any word on how the Chinese are responding?"

"It's early, the Chinese Government are yet to make a statement. We do know that the Shenyang military base was ground zero."

The President caught the Secretary's eye and he could see the concern, or perhaps fear, he thought.

The Chief of Staff approached, "Mr President, the video link up is ready, the joint chiefs are assembled."

The next few hours unravelled heated discussions and arguments as the overall nervousness in the room escalated at the preliminary thought of a nuclear war. The Chinese President had responded, claiming an act of aggression against his nation using an unknown weapon of mass destruction and immediately his military were mobilising on the defensive.

The Joint Chiefs expressed mixed concerns; some suspected a nuclear strike by North Korea while others continued along the meteor principle. The President wasn't so convinced, he had his own suspicions and apprehensively ordered the country's state of alert to DEFCON 4.

One man in the room had a more informed view, congratulating himself on a job well done. Soon the world would be at war, making his mission that much easier.

11.
Warning

Nias Island
May 10, 2005

Seductive and tantalising, Nicholette's hands crept slowly down Bennett's chest, kissing his neck as she did.

"Morning babe," she whispered into his ear.

She loved his robust physique, tall and strong with only a slight hint of aging, mostly the speckling of grey through his dark hair. At forty-five, he was in peak physical condition and like her, maintained a daily regimented appetite for exercise. Each morning at sunrise they'd run the ten miles to the closest village, indulge in the locally brewed coffee before racing each other home, driven by their insatiable competitive spirits. At last count, he had the slight edge in the victory tally and though she didn't show it, he knew it annoyed her.

He turned towards her, staring into her penetrating green eyes as their lips pressed. At first, they kissed slowly with the gentle passion of two people deeply in love but then as their sexual hunger took over, they tore the clothes from each other. The next hour rolled by as they wrestled in and out of ecstasy, both reaching their own sexual heights until fatigue became too great.

It had taken a few days from executing Buhari to arriving back to the swaying palm trees of Nias Island. Home as they called it, was set on the southern end of the island, a secluded section of tropical grandeur facing a wide span of the Indian Ocean. Bennett had chosen the spot for not only its 'off the grid' feel but, also the nearby surfing points. He loved his surfing and at every opportunity, he waxed the board and paddled out into the line-up. Lefts were plentiful rolling in from three thousand miles of unobstructed ocean and he would surf until his shoulders ached from exhaustion.

Nicholette on the other hand was not so keen. Instead she preferred the groupie thing, dressing down to a skimpy bikini and sunning herself on the beach watching her lover find a barrel or two. She was her own spectacle with her sleek but curvy body, ample breasts and sharp Russian features. Long muscular legs rising to finely tuned buttocks under a brightly coloured G-string gave the local boys something to fantasize over. At thirty-nine years of age she still had the physique of a twenty-year-old and Bennett loved it.

Their house was set high on a cliff overlooking two surfing points yet far enough back among the trees to conceal it from view. He had built most of it with the help of the locals though some parts he'd kept hidden from their eyes. Encircling the entire upper floor, a wide timber deck provided a spectacular view of both the tropical jungle behind and the wind-swept ocean in front. Hammocks and soft lounges lined each side of the deck and depending on the wind direction, they could always relax in coolness. It was every surfer's dream house.

Bennett liked his privacy and seclusion, it had kept him alive through the years as a wanted spy, but more because of what he carried upon his chest. Four years earlier, he had learnt of Jeremiah's Codes and the secrets contained within the ancient spheres. But more importantly, he had discovered he was the carrier of the Thirteenth Code. It had appeared one day out of nowhere, a series of thirteen alien like symbols tattooed in vibrant blue across his chest forming a neat arc from shoulder to shoulder.

His tattoo was one of thirteen unique sets shared among thirteen different carriers around the world, some known and some still unidentified. The sets of symbols had become known as Jeremiah's Codes after a young boy named Jeremiah was found mysteriously adrift in the waters off Bermuda during 1941. His only communication was to ramble undecipherable nonsense and scribe strange symbols and text onto the linen of his hospital bed. Bennett's father had been sent by the CIA to investigate and it was him who recorded everything the boy wrote into his notebook. It was that book that became priceless once the connection between the symbols and the ancient sphere became known.

The boy had a set tattooed across his chest and it was that sequence of thirteen symbols that activated the sphere to display the original technology to build the world's first atomic bomb. It was later identified as the third code in the book. Bennett's tattoo was the thirteenth and the last code illustrated in the book. It was also the most dangerous of all the thirteen different codes.

"Hey! How's the surf?" Nicholette asked as she walked onto the deck handing him his coffee, a long unsweetened black.

"Not much today, too blown out," he replied taking her in his arms and holding her close while he stared out to sea, mesmerised by the constant pounding of white water across the reef.

The sun was well into the morning sky and enshrouded them in warmth, the rays already biting into their naked skin.

"Money is in the account," she said.

Hansel and Gretel's fees were always paid on time, half on acceptance and then the remainder when the job was completed. Everything was done electronically and concealed behind the security of false bank accounts and heavy encryption. Law enforcement didn't have the resources or investigative abilities to track them and Bennett made sure of that by paying expert hackers to ensure their anonymity.

"Why do you worry about me so much?" she asked feeling the love of his embrace.

"Huh?"

"That night in Luanda, you seemed so worried about me going off by myself. Don't you think I'm capable of looking after myself?"

"Capability doesn't come into it, most of the time you're more capable than me. No, it's just that everyone has an expiration. I just don't see why you need to increase the odds of finding yours. Besides, I never want to lose you again," he replied looking deep into her eyes and giving her another long kiss.

After those three protracted months of searching, he'd found her imprisoned by the Monk in a temple deep inside the Guiana Highlands of Venezuela. He was stunned and confused to learn that the Monk's men had taken her dead body and somehow revived her. It was something he had not expected from the self-appointed religious leader of the world. The Monk commanded the World Supreme Council made up of all the highest leaders of every religious faith on the planet. Their mission was about ensuring one common goal, pushing aside their petty disagreements and protecting the earth. It had nothing to do with religion they all knew, it was about protecting humanity and preventing the bleak future the Monk had witnessed in his visions. A deep dark secret of what was to come that no one suspected.

The Monk had a legion of devoted worshippers known as the 'Guardians of Gaia' and it was them who had taken her body. Returning someone's life was something they had learnt from the Monk; a simple injection was all it took. She had been a loyal Guardian for many years since leaving the Soviet secret police and the Monk wasn't about to lose her valuable skills. She protested his decision wanting desperately to return to Bennett but that resulted in her imprisonment.

Bennett had landed in Venezuela within twenty-four hours of Rose's information and rescued her. Fifteen Guardians died silently that night, but the Monk escaped without harm.

"You won't lose me, babe," she replied and walked back into the house where a breaking news story was unfolding on the television.

Everyday Bennett loved to soak up the day's events on Fox News, CNN or whatever news show was playing at the time, he had no favourite. He despised most news reporters for the sensationalism and lies they told just to sell a story. It was his ritual each morning to update himself on world events while downing two cups of rich coffee and filtering out the bullshit in each story.

Nicholette couldn't give a damn what was happening elsewhere, she had seen enough in her time and knew the world was collapsing. She had heard it time and time again from the Monk in his sermons about humanity needing to save itself. Greed and the urgency for domination were taking over and subsequently, people were dying. The earth's population continued to expand at an exponential rate and already most of the third world countries were starving to death with no reprieve in sight. It pissed her off to say the least.

"Don't know why you watch that shit Jon," she announced from the kitchen.

She enjoyed cooking, expanding her culinary skills whenever she could and trying to be a good 'soon to be' wife. It bugged her that she wasn't good with home duties and that all she could do was fight and kill. Tonight they would feast Russian style after more pleasure in the bedroom, she expected.

"Oh my, check this out. Meteor strike in northern Shenyang, over a million dead and half the city has been flattened," Bennett announced in a somewhat saddened and shocked voice.

She stood beside him in disbelief at what she was watching.

"Those poor people," she remarked behind a welling tear in her eye.

The news reader came over the air saying, "Okay we have in the studio with us, Professor Jim Reynolds, a renowned leader in the field of meteoritics. So, Professor what can you tell us about this meteor impact in Shenyang?"

"Simply that isn't a meteor strike, I am not seeing any evidence that indicates to me that an extraterrestrial body impacted the earth at that location."

Sponarava sat down next to Bennett and joined him, fixated on what the professor was saying.

The news commentator continued, "So if you're saying it's not a meteor then what caused the devastation?"

"For it to be a meteor impact, then I would expect more of a deep crater in the centre and the rimming of earth around the outside. There would be complete destruction in the middle, everything I would expect to be flattened from the impact. There is some minor evidence I see but the earth appears to have been folded upwards over itself."

He pointed at a large satellite image the commentator handed him.

"You see there the ground formations are concentric radiating out from the epicentre. I am not convinced it's the result of a meteor, but I would need more data from the scene."

The commentator pushed him for answers, "In my limited knowledge, the only other event that could cause something like this could be a nuclear blast. Am I correct in saying this Professor?".

"Nuclear detonations are not my area of expertise but yes, a nuclear ground impact would be similar in its destructive pattern to a meteor strike, but you would need to ask an expert in that field."

"Do you think this was a nuclear strike Professor?" the commentator baited.

"I could not possibly answer that question without further data from the scene, but I would think there'd be devastating radiation within miles of that site if it was a nuclear detonation. Meteors don't have anywhere the same levels."

The commentator cut him off as the channel went to an advertisement.

Bennett quickly changed to another news broadcast but this one was covering a different disaster, a nine-point-seven magnitude earthquake in Kashmir, thousands believed dead and half the city now appearing as if turned upside down.

"Kind a looks the same as the meteor impact, don't you think?" she suggested.

"Yes, it does. Can you believe this? Look at the headlines, a tsunami reported in the Pacific off Japan has claimed a thousand lives and they're saying close to three thousand people are still unaccounted for," he replied.

"Too much disaster for one morning Jon, I'm going for a swim, want to join me?" she beckoned accompanied by a naughty little smile.

He didn't budge from the couch, engulfed in the devastation occurring worldwide and starting to feel uneasy about it.

"What the fuck is going on? Meteors, earthquakes, tsunamis and then there's this," he said pointing at a documentary on Discovery. He had changed channels to a recent story on a new epidemic sweeping across Central Africa.

Nicholette walked back disappointed her offer had been overshadowed by world events. On the screen, an onsite doctor from the World Health Organisation in a small village in Ghana was talking to the camera, "People are dying all around me and there is nothing we can do to stop it. I have never seen anything like it in all my years. It makes Ebola seem like the common cold in comparison. But I think the worst part is the victim's appearance at death, their skin turns blue and the body dissolves within days like massively accelerated decomposition. There are so many dead here that we're continually running out of body bags as you can see behind me."

For someone so tough and resilient, she had to look away when the camera panned across the rows of dead decomposing bodies laid out on the bare ground.

"Do you think it has something to do with ...".

Bennett interrupted her, finishing her sentence, "*The Trust*... maybe? That description does sound like the blue death."

"But *The Trust* was destroyed four years ago, could it have rebuilt?" she asked.

"Possibly! I removed the six directors, but the Monk always claimed there were two older men at the helm of it but, no one knew who they were, and I never identified them. So yes, maybe they have rebuilt the organisation."

He drifted into deep thought at the mention of *The Trust* and the quick agonising death caused by exposure to the blue crystal radiation. Only a chosen few survived an exposure and those who did were left with a set of symbols like his tattooed across their chest. How it happened, he never understood but he was one of the survivors.

He sat staring at the screen now showing a rerun of the news headlines, *Over a million dead... meteor strike in Shenyang City... Chinese military on alert...*

All had gone quiet except for the morning birds outside chirping up a song. Inside, Bennett turned off the television and tried to relax sinking back into the lounge. The upper floor of their house was one open aired room with kitchen and master bedroom separated by low privacy walls. In the centre, a sixty-inch plasma screen mounted on the wall looked down on the lounge room. All around, large windows gave an even greater open feel and permitted the cooling sea breeze to sweep through. Downstairs more bedrooms ran the length of the house.

He had found tranquillity in the past four years with Nicholette but the events leading to the death of the six directors still played on his mind. The deceit and lies had taken its toll and since the nightmares started, he had become troubled. Though he tried to hide it, she sensed his growing vulnerability.

"You've gone quiet, what's wrong?" she asked.

"I had another nightmare in Angola, the night you went out after those Russians."

"What? You didn't tell me. Was it the same as the others?"

The nightmares had started two months earlier, all ending the same; with his failure. An apocalyptic event caused by the energy pulse weapon in orbit built from what he carried on his chest. The thirteen symbols across his chest held the key to schematic plans for a weapon far beyond the technical capabilities of humans and possessing a greater destructive force than the world's nuclear arsenal combined. But like the other twelve codes, it had to be physically entered into the sphere to release the plans.

Two ancient spheres existed somewhere on the planet though their exact location remained a mystery to Bennett. Likewise, their origins weren't known, though quite distinctly extraterrestrial in design and constructed of a grey marble material not found anywhere on earth. Covering the entirety of the outer skin were three hundred alien-like symbols, each capable of being depressed to activate the symbol.

There had once been three in existence until Bennett destroyed one in Germany by activating its self-destruct protocol. The result of that had been a thermonuclear explosion destroying one of *The Trust's* key research facilities. That sphere had been dubbed the 'Sphere of Anubis' after it had been uncovered among treasure located in the ancient Egyptian tomb of Anubis, the God of Death. The second was discovered in a Mayan temple and the third had never been uncovered though *The Trust* spent years searching Iraq believing it was somewhere among Saddam Hussein's treasures.

Bennett started thinking. There must be a connection between the nightmares and the sudden increase in disasters.

"Yes, the same, always ending with me looking at myself crawling from the fires saying something about I failed and then the ground rises up and engulfs me," he answered.

"What do you think it means?" she asked.

"Not sure! But I'm concerned. Could these latest events be the result of pulse strikes?"

"How could it be? Aren't you the only carrier of the Thirteenth Code?" she replied.

He nodded, "Yes I believe so."

"Then how could it be possible?" she asked.

"I don't know but if my nightmares are not a coincidence then are they warning me? If so, then these were pulse strikes and we need to start worrying."

She stood watching him for a moment from the kitchen, concerned that his usual ruggedness was wavering, slowly being consumed by the sudden onset of the nightmares. They knew each other well, but him trying to conceal it only frustrated her and escalated her concern.

He turned the television back on to CNN and more news stories, this time coming out of Massachusetts.

"Can you imagine having the wealth of this guy?"

"Who?" she responded from the kitchen.

An elderly man dressed in a dark Italian suit stood before a captive audience of news reporters and photographers. Either side of him, bodyguards shielded him like he was the United States President and he was enjoying the moment.

Bennett answered, "Eckhard Banks, CEO for the Orionis Andromeda Corporation. He has just announced the takeover of Ramadon Missiles, the world's largest manufacturer of missile systems. It is speculated upwards of a five hundred-billion-dollar deal. Unbelievable!"

"Isn't that the guy who struck a deal with the Chinese to sell them intercontinental ballistic missiles together with the nuclear warheads? I remember reading about how the United Nations tried to block the trade but some loophole in the nuclear treaty meant it was fully legal," she added.

"Yes, that's him, his guided launch systems are state of the art, I think we have his systems installed at our missile sites and now with Ramadon, he will control ninety percent of the world's high-tech ballistic weaponry including the manufacture of nuclear warheads. Humanity will never learn, here we are allowing this maniac to advocate nuclear war to make his billions! How much is enough? Seriously unbelievable! Now he is one guy I would love to see on our contract list," Bennett said in disgust and turned the television off.

The laptop chimed in the background as an encrypted message arrived.

"We have another contract," Nicholette said opening the email.

"Fuck!" she exclaimed.

"What is it?" Bennett asked.

"Two million dollars."

"Who's the target worth that much?"

The most they'd ever been paid had been half a million to take out a Mexican drug lord and his three Lieutenants operating in Guatemala. Their client had remained the same for the past year, an untraceable email account that Bennett suspected was the CIA, yet they still accepted the payment.

"Some lunatic calling himself the "Soldier of the New World", she replied.

12.
Secret Plans

Washington DC
May 10, 2005

The cause of the impact at Shenyang was yet to be determined, a rock from space or an act of war, no one knew. One thing was certain, the military base had taken the full force of the strike leaving nothing except flattened lifeless ground.

Tensions were escalating as the Chinese tirelessly pursued the blame and the North Koreans crept closer to a full nuclear alert while six thousand miles away, the United States President had just terminated an overheated discussion with the Joint Chiefs.

"Mr President, I strongly urge you to reconsider your stand on this. You've seen the satellite imagery, the Chinese are mobilising their nuclear arsenal and we've lost tracking of three of their subs in the Pacific," the Secretary of Defense appealed as the President took his seat back in his office.

"George I'm not about to act like it was us that caused this. If we go into a ready state of war, then what message does that send? We need more information out of Shenyang before I'm going to make any decision that could place this nation at risk of nuclear attack," the President responded.

He and George had been good friends since their early political days in New York and he was the only one he trusted to be his right-hand man.

"Bill, the impact screams nuclear and you know it. The only ones capable of a stealth strike like that is us or the Russians. If they launch, we have thirty-eight minutes to respond before we lose the cities on the west coast. Those subs in the Pacific carry enough nuclear firepower to take out the rest of the country. Please Bill, we need to be at DEFCON 2."

"George, I have just spent the past two hours arguing with the Chiefs, I have made my decision for now, we remain at DEFCON 4 and that's final."

Whitman edged forward on his chair to push his point further, he was an ex hard core commando and disapproved the diplomacy approach the government took towards acts of terrorism or war. This, he believed was an act of terrorism to start a world war and a strike on United States soil would be next.

"George, is there something you're not telling me?" a curious President demanded after witnessing the Secretary's reluctance to leave the office.

"No Mr President," he replied and stood as the President's phone chimed.

"Wait George, turn on NBN," the President instructed, placing the phone back down.

The massive wall screen across the room lit up to a scene of chaos and devastation. News reporters anxious to inform the world, spoke fast and deliberate.

"Looks like another earthquake, this time in Kashmir," Whitman said as he walked closer and read the update across the lower screen. He paused and added, "Oh my! Nine point seven! This could be the largest ever recorded."

"Yes I think you're right, a nine point five was recorded near Valdivia in Chile in 1960," the President replied as he stepped from behind his over-sized red cedar desk. It had been a gift from the Canadian Prime Minister and was carved from thousand-year-old timber, something that annoyed him. He was a conservationist at heart and strongly opposed to the rape of earth's ancient forests or the extinction of wildlife.

He added, "There's been an unprecedented increase lately of large earthquakes. Should we be concerned George?"

"Climate change, global warming, the earth moving on its axis, who knows, anything could be causing them. Sir you need to look at it in perspective, most occur in third world countries where the buildings are old and poorly constructed. I would expect the damage to be high even with the lower scale tremors," Whitman answered.

The President nodded, he wasn't convinced by the Secretary's response and ushered him to leave.

In the privacy of his office, he removed his encrypted cell phone from his pocket and made a phone call. The call would be untraceable, something the Secret Service reluctantly set up for him at his request.

A male voice answered, and the President spoke quickly, no names were to be used.

"Do you have the target?" he asked.

"Yes."

"Very good, proceed with the plan," the President said and hung up.

13.
Murder

Southern Venezuela
May 10, 2005

The knife penetrated deep, driven hard by years of resentment. His death had not been foreseen or prophesied and yet it signalled the beginnings of a new era in religious turmoil. The Monk had reigned supreme for five decades delivering stability to the world's religious realm and negotiating peace among the conflicting theologies.

Shrouded in tall jungle and hanging vines, the Monk's temple set deep inside the Guiana Highlands of Venezuela had become his sanctum. Like his temple destroyed in Nepal, this one offered the same seclusion and inaccessibility.

He had always felt protected within the walls, never once feeling vulnerability behind the stronghold of his band of loyal guardians. But to be murdered by someone close was absurd, he thought.

As he slumped to the cold stone floor and the last few breaths brushed his lips, he watched his killer walk boldly from the room stopping momentarily to turn and smile goodbye.

Outside the Monk's chamber no one noticed the stealth intruder exit the temple and vanish into the darkness of the jungle. Held tightly in their hands, a spherical shaped object reflected what little light there was that night and once again, the Mayan Sphere had become a threat to humanity.

14.
Contract

London
May 13, 2005

Bennett and Sponarava had been caught in traffic for the past hour, at a standstill. Further east along the M4, a crash had occurred. One car had side swiped another at high speed, setting off a chain reaction of tyres screeching, passengers screaming and a milk tanker eventually rolling and blocking both city inbound lanes.

They had landed at Heathrow shortly before nine that morning into a dreary overcast day and temperatures not expected to rise much above ten degrees Celsius. Nicholette had elected to drive the fifteen miles to Barnsbury but now she was cursing her eagerness, she had no patience for traffic congestion and after a short while, it was starting to show. What she thought would be a thirty-minute drive was more likely to be three hours.

"I hate fucking traffic jams!" she screamed at the steering wheel.

Bennett beside her was deep into the brief about their target.

"Be patient, there's nothing we can do about it and besides there's no hurry," he said flicking through a twenty-page dossier that didn't really give him help with understanding their next target.

The day before they had been enjoying the balmy temperatures of Nias Island, dripping in sweat from sunup to sundown and now, a complete reversal rugged up in jackets, jeans and boots.

"I love you in jeans and boots, very sexy!" he announced out of the blue.

She turned to him, flicked her long dark hair to the side and said, "Thanks babe, but I still hate traffic jams!"

He laughed and she joined in. For the next twenty minutes, they talked and laughed, reminiscing past good times while not realising it, the traffic had started to move freely again. Bennett and Nicholette had chosen to marry in six months at a place high up in the alps of Nepal, a temple with breathtaking views, clinging to the edge of a four hundred foot cliff face. It was her dream to marry her loved one in a place of sanctity, somewhere innocent and clean of societal influence. She wasn't like most women, longing for that fancy church service with the glamorous white gown trailing ten feet behind, while the bride maids preferred to think it was all about them. She just wanted their privacy and to share the moment with the man she loved.

In the two years together, she and Bennett had become a phenomenal team, built on trust, both knew how to play the other and most of all, they had each other's back.

"Who calls themselves the Soldier of the New World, seriously?" Bennett said.

"What's more absurd is that someone is paying us two million dollars to kill him, so who the fuck is he?" she asked.

Bennett reopened the dossier to refresh himself on what he had already read during the flight over. It had arrived the day after they accepted the contract and the fifty percent deposit cleared the bank. That afternoon they were on a flight out of Pandang via Singapore to London.

"No one really knows. I see here that both the CIA and MI6 have narrowed him down to possibly somewhere in the Barnsbury area but no name, well not listed in this brief anyway. We know how secretive our friends at those agencies are!" he said thinking back to his days in the CIA.

"As expected, the FBI have nothing," he chuckled flicking over the page.

"This guy is one messed up nut job, listen to what he leaves in a note on the victims. By the hand of God, you were executed for the atrocities you commit. The world we share is dying and it is men and women like you who care not for its survival but how to make more profit. Greed is our enemy and you were found guilty of this sin. Let it be a warning to others like you that if you continue to prosper from war, mineral wealth or population expansion then more will die at my hand. You must desist from further progress and convince all those around you. You are not immune from my gun sight, make change or die at my hand. Signed the Soldier of the New World."

"How does he think that will make any difference? He's just another terrorist fighting his own cause, just in an unorthodox way. And who made him judge, jury and executioner? Don't even get me started on the hand of God part," she said.

"How is that any different to what we do?" Bennett asked.

Sponarava looked at him briefly and returned her eyes to the road ahead, "I would hope to think that what we do has some good in it, some benefit to the world. We assassinate only those deserving it. Right?"

"Yes, but do we offer them fair trial?"

"Ahh no we don't but there is no such thing as fair trial when it comes to most of the people we execute. For example, Buhari in Angola, do you think a trial was the best option for him? The man had ordered the genocide of thousands of Angolan Muslims so he would have received the death penalty anyway, so we just sped the process up at a massive discount. It would have cost the United Nations and the Angolan government tenfold what we were paid."

Bennett knew she had a point, but he enjoyed tossing a bait her way every now and then.

"According to this, he has killed eight men and two women, all with a single gunshot to the head at long range."

"What distances are we talking?" she asked.

"Most in excess of a thousand yards except the latest one in New York. That one he set up across the street in a fourth story apartment. The distance was sixty-five yards."

"Hmmm… thousand yards means our Soldier has undergone military training somewhere, no one can shoot accurately over that distance without some form of high-level training."

"His targets so far have been bankers and politicians, that last one in New York was the CEO of Citigroup."

He flicked through the pages of homicide reports scanning for the victim details for each assassination.

"The other victims included the CEO's of UBS in Zurich, Mizuho in Tokyo, Crédit Agricole and BNP Paribas in Paris, and ING in Amsterdam. Looks like most are bankers, only one political official I see, a member of the British Government."

"Why banks I wonder?" she thought out loud.

"If it's banks he likes to target then what about Eckhard Banks," he laughed and she joined him.

Outside the traffic had slowed once again as they entered the congested Marylebone Road heading east. Bennett had eased up on his reading, there wasn't enough in the brief to give them an exact starting point except somewhere in Barnsbury. How MI6 pinpointed him to that area had him intrigued.

As if reading his mind, she asked, "How do they know he's in the Barnsbury area?"

"MI6 tracked the paper he printed on. All the notes left on the victims came from the same printer. Did you know this? I mean did you know every piece of paper ever printed on can be traced?" Bennett asked.

"No but I did hear the NSA were working on something like that."

"Yes, well it appears they have perfected it. Every printer manufactured after 2001 must have a unique microscopic signature code. Before that it was only a few printer manufacturers who were doing this but now every manufacturer must. Each page printed is stamped in the centre with this tag and gives the printer serial number, IP address and the date time stamp. Each note had a different IP address according to this. Oh clever?" Bennett added.

"What?" she asked.

"He may be nowhere near London, he's bounced the IP through servers in the Ukraine, Poland, Australia, Russia, Slovakia and here in London. He's using hacking software to disguise the IP on the final printout.

"So, he is bouncing his printed message off multiple printers around the world using the printer's local network," she confirmed.

"Appears that way according to this report. The furthest back they could trace it was from a server in Barnsbury. The problem is they checked that one and its physical address doesn't exist."

"Okay I can see why you're saying he may be nowhere near London."

Bennett went silent staring out the window as they passed Kings Cross Station a few minutes out from their hotel. Nicholette darted and weaved among the traffic manoeuvring around the endless convoy of red double-deckers, a sight London was famous for. Something on the side of one the buses caught his eye. He flicked open the brief again, across to the pages of victim details.

He opened their laptop and quickly typed in the letters, 'HSBC Bank'. The internet result led to more searching, this time, Stephen Greenwich the CEO of HSBC.

"Surely it can't be this simple," he declared out loud.

"What is simple?"

"See the sign on that double-decker there," pointing at the bus beside them.

"Yeah, Charity Golf event at Royal Wimbledon this weekend," she said.

"Its sponsor is the HSBC Bank."

"Yeah so!" she replied still looking at the billboard moving ahead of them in the traffic.

"The victims are bankers representing big banks, right? Well it just so happens that the six banks are coincidentally in the top seven banks in the world."

"Top seven? Don't tell me. The seventh is the HSBC Bank, right?" she added.

"No, it's actually the fourth largest but all the others make up the remainder of the top seven, he missed this one by the looks. But wait, the clincher is this. The CEO of HSBC, Stephen Greenwich is a mad keen golfer, plays off a handicap of one and lives here in London. I'm betting he will be playing in this charity event and our Soldier boy may be there too."

"A golf course is a wide-open space, perfect for a sniper," she added.

Bennett nodded already pulling up satellite imagery of the course and the surrounding buildings.

Nicholette gave off a small moaning sound.

"You okay?"

"Yeah, don't think airline food agrees with me, I've been feeling a little off all morning," she replied rubbing her belly.

"You are looking pale, rest when we get to the room. I'm heading out to do some reconnaissance of Royal Wimbledon."

They had a day to prepare before the event started.

Further back in the traffic a black Range Rover moved at the same speed, concealing itself behind buses. The occupants, two armed men in their early thirties, never removed their eyes from Bennett's car.

15.
__Royal Wimbledon__

Royal Wimbledon Golf Course
May 14, 2005

Next morning, they strolled casually onto the golf course blending into the hundreds of spectators all eager to catch a glimpse of their favourite celebrity. It was to be a big day with special guests from all over the world attending, musicians to movie stars. Professional golfers teamed up with celebrities in teams of four and together they played to win with the lowest aggregate score. The winning team of the weekend won a million pounds for a charity of their choice. The next three teams each won two hundred thousand pounds for their charity. The losing three teams had to donate one hundred thousand pounds each to a charity nominated by the organisers. It was an event for the wealthy only, yet, each year it continued to gain greater public momentum and more celebrities participated. The real winners were the local children's hospitals, cancer research institutes, disadvantaged kids, the world's starving and the Salvation Army to name a few.

The day had started with clear skies, but forecasters predicted rain later in the morning much to the disappointment of the event organisers. Golf wasn't a game that coexisted well with rain, not many of the players enjoyed carrying umbrellas and the drenching each time they took their shot. The thing in their favour was the higher than fifty per cent odds, the forecasters were likely to be wrong.

"I'm not sure about this Jon," Nicholette said spotting Dennis Quaid and Hugh Grant fighting it out on the fourth.

"Yeah, I'm not sure they will be happy having Sinéad O'Connor on their team, she's still back in the sticks looking for her ball. A bit like my golf," he laughed.

"No idiot, I'm talking about the Soldier assassinating Greenwich here, there are no high points and too many trees lining the fairways. He'd have to get in too close and run the risk of being seen."

"I'm relying on him using the tree line if he's here, I don't see any other way," Bennett replied.

They kept walking watching, searching for anyone looking out of place. People lined the fairways and the players kept coming, team after team.

"There he is," Bennett announced easing up on the pace as Nicholette spun around reaching for her handgun hidden under her shirt.

"No, I mean Greenwich," he quickly corrected himself before she created an incident on the green.

At the next tee-off on the fifth, two men and two women stood laughing amongst themselves while they prepared to hit off down the one hundred and sixty-six yard par three. Stephen Greenwich was the tallest of the four and had broken from the group readying himself with his seven iron for the short fairway to the green. For one of the wealthiest men in the world and the weekend's sponsor, his dress style didn't show it. He was casual, wearing dark baggy trousers like a teenager and a bright pink shirt as if inviting a bullet.

The others, none of whom they recognised, watched on as he whacked the ball. They clapped as the ball landed a few feet from the hole and the next team member moved to the tee.

"He should have just painted a bullseye on himself with that shirt!" Bennett chuckled.

Bennett's cell phone blipped.

"Right on time," he said as he opened the incoming message.

An image opened on his phone and attached to it were a dozen thermal images of the tree line around the golf course.

"I actually didn't think this would work, satellite thermal taken five minutes ago," Bennett declared zooming into a heavily treed area south of the eighth green.

"Well well well, look at that!" he said passing the phone to Nicholette.

Set back five yards into the southern forest a human shape was visible, a body configuration lying flat resembling a gunman in the prone position, one leg pulled up for comfort.

"Good positioning, that's where I'd be too, quick escape through Barham Road," she added.

"Or motorbike it through Wimbledon Common, opens plenty of escape options that way," he suggested.

"Greenwich is halfway to the green, come on, but we can't spook him", Bennett said.

They moved quickly keeping their attention on the golfers so not to stand out and making sure to stop occasionally and study the event program. Ten minutes it took them to edge their way around the fourth, third and ninth to arrive on the northern side of the eighth.

The first of the teams had just teed off and were making their way along the fairway while groups of spectators followed along beside them on the edges. It was perfect timing, they had beaten the crowds to the green and to the gunman they would appear as eager spectators.

"Okay the imagery places him just behind the advertising banners, it's an ideal position, spectators can't block his line of sight and they are high enough above the ground to shoot under them," Bennett said looking down at his program.

"This guy has done his homework, there is a clear shot straight down the fairway to the tee from under those banners, an easy four hundred yard shot," she added speaking into her program.

"So what's the plan now?" she asked.

"Wait for the crowds and move with them around to the other side of the green to get a closer view of his position. He will be camouflaged under the leaves I'd imagine. Kind a like looking for the snake about to pounce on the mouse don't you reckon?"

A helicopter buzzed overhead, flying low and almost appeared as if it was going to land but then diverted north.

"Bloody media, always in the way," Bennett snarled.

The players and the crowds arrived and swept them across to the green. Bennett separated from Nicholette and walked further behind the spectators into the edge of the trees. He just didn't know he was being watched by both the sniper and two spectators near Nicholette.

Bennett took a few steps back into the wooded area towards where he thought the sniper was positioned. The ground was littered deep in gold and brown leaves from the dense canopy of oak trees above him. The sniper could have been anywhere he thought, as he scanned the forest in the best non-conspicuous way he could.

Back behind him, someone was calling for help.

16.
Emergency

Royal Wimbledon Golf Course
May 14, 2005

Bennett turned in time to see Nicholette collapse to the ground next to the green with spectators crowding around her in a panic. At the same moment, the forest floor behind him came alive and the leaves transformed into a human shape. Bennett caught glimpse of the monster rising behind him and he drew his handgun. He could hear people calling for an ambulance and the quietness expected at golf tournaments had been shattered.

His gun was at eye level, finger firmly on the trigger and staring into the eyes of a leaf covered giant. Standing three yards over among the shadow of the dense tree canopy, the Soldier of the New World zeroed his rifle on Bennett's head. Both didn't flinch though Bennett's concentration faltered, concerned for what had happened so suddenly to Nicholette.

The man stood a good three inches above Bennett and at least forty pounds heavier in comparison. His clothing was military camouflage for the autumn forest floor blended with a leaf net covering his entire body like a shawl. His face gave nothing of his identity, concealed under a blackened mask. His weapon was state of the art military grade for long range killing, Bennett could see by the size and length, it was a Barrett M82, the weapon of choice in modern war. They were in a Mexican stand-off, both staring at each other, though either could have shot at any time.

The sniper spoke, "Jon, your girlfriend is in trouble."

"Who are you? How do you know me?" Bennett asked, taken by surprise that their target knew him.

A sudden burst of violent screaming sounded from behind him after a spectator wandered too far away from the green.

"GUN... HE'S GOT A GUN!"

Mayhem broke and people scampered off the fairway. So too did the sniper, firing three shots into the air to aid his escape. He vanished deeper into the forest behind a long row of trees while Bennett raced back to Nicholette lying unconscious on the ground. He dropped to her side; she was alive but panting like a dog in the middle of a heat wave. Her pulse was shallow and her skin clammy. Bennett had no idea what had happened in that brief time they were separated but she was alive, and to him, that was all that mattered.

A young nervous looking man dressed neatly in the event uniform rushed over to him keeping his head low like he was running to board a helicopter.

"Sir, an ambulance is on its way," he called.

Bennett nodded as he partially lifted her onto his lap. The green and fairway was now mostly clear of people including the players, they'd been first to run at the sound of gunshots. Soon it would be swarming with police and that meant too many questions.

"Did you see the guy with the gun," Bennett asked him.

"No I didn't, but someone said there were two guys with guns in the forest."

He'd been seen, that wasn't good, Bennett thought.

Thirty minutes later, still unconscious, Nicholette was wheeled on a stretcher into the emergency ward at St George's Hospital a short distance away in Tooting. Bennett had been relegated to the waiting room where he was forced to sit for two anxious hours before a doctor finally appeared.

"Mr Johnson I am Doctor Winston, has your wife suffered any seizures lately?"

They rarely travelled under their real identities; it was too dangerous knowing they were wanted in a dozen countries across the globe. This trip they chose Steve and Veronica Johnson, a newly wedded couple from Tennessee on holiday in the United Kingdom for three weeks.

Bennett shook his head, "No... Is she okay? Can I see her?"

"She has regained consciousness, but she is still weak and not too well. Has she been feeling ill at all lately?" the doctor asked, a woman in her late forties.

Bennett paused and thought quickly, "Yes yesterday morning she complained of stomach illness, you know feeling queasy, she just blamed it on the airline food."

The doctor made some notes on Nicholette's chart and carried on with her questioning, "We ran some blood tests, she has some abnormally high white blood levels."

"What's that mean?" Bennett asked impatiently.

"It means she is fighting an infection in her body, maybe a virus. We will need to run some more tests to narrow it down. But now she needs her rest," she informed him and then turned to leave before adding, "Mr Johnson, I am concerned about the baby, the heartrate is too low."

"What... back up doc? What do you mean, Baby?"

"Oh! I'm sorry haven't you and your wife spoken, she is six weeks pregnant."

Bennett stood there in shock, no they had not spoken, did Nicholette even know he pondered.

"Anyway, I want her to stay overnight so we can run the tests and monitor the baby's vital signs," she commanded and walked off. She had a long list of patients to see and had no time for chit chat, she had delivered her diagnosis.

Ten long minutes later, Bennett entered Nicholette's room to her half sitting, saline drip in her arm and looking like she was ready to escape. Their eyes met the moment he walked through the doorway and she stood, a little shaky at first, and then she steadied herself. He grabbed her and they kissed.

"Hey babe, how are you feeling?" he asked pushing her back a little to gaze into her eyes.

"I'm sorry, I let you down," she replied.

"What are you talking about? No, you didn't."

"The target? We missed the target! It's not good for our reputation."

She was rambling, tears welling in her eyes and becoming more agitated by the second. Nurses came and went but mostly they were left alone.

"Nic listen to me. I don't give one fuck about the target, the client can have their million back, all that matters to me is you. You got that... YOU and our baby!" he said pulling her close and kissing her head.

She burst into tears and fell limp in his arms.

"So you know," she sobbed.

"Yes now I do. It is such wonderful news, I am so happy."

"I was going to tell you, but I have been worried Jon."

"Worried...why?"

"There is something going on inside me. Something doesn't feel right."

"Of course there is, you are having a baby. You have a life growing inside you," he said comforting her.

"No you don't understand. I think my nanobots are attacking the baby," she cried into his chest.

Like the Thirteenth Code releasing the plans to build the orbital weapon, the Eighth Code released alien technology to manufacture self-replicating human cell nanobots. These microscopic organisms gave new life to their host, extending lifespans by hundreds of years and enhancing strength beyond comprehension. Composed entirely of a synthetic cytoplasm and a gel CPU, they'd develop their own neural networks throughout the body and transmit new commands to the body's existing cells. They destroyed disease, quickly healed injuries and greatly improved the efficient functioning of the body's natural life support system.

Both Bennett and Sponarava had these flowing actively through their bodies. Bennett had been impregnated at a young age while Sponarava had received hers at the hands of *The Trust* after she suffered exposure to the blue death. It had saved her life.

Bennett had only ever thought of the nanobots as good things until now. They gave life not took it, he thought. Microscopic robots charging through their blood working overtime to repair damaged cells. Had a host ever been pregnant, he wondered. To his recollection, there had only been a small handful of people injected with active nanobots and a few of them he had killed a few years earlier. His thoughts were scaring him, perhaps they'd never been tested against an unborn child.

"Sounds absurd, why do you think that?" he whispered hoping no one heard her.

"It's just a feeling, I can't explain it, but it feels real."

The doctor returned within the hour and this time she appeared more concerned. A nurse followed close behind pushing a machine on small wheels.

"The first series of tests have come back, we need to do an immediate ultrasound of the baby," she announced pushing her way in front of Bennett and slipping her hands into some rather tight rubber gloves.

The nurse started up the machine and the doctor smeared cold gel across Nicholette's belly.

"You have nice abdominals young lady," she commented looking down at Nicholette's muscular physique and inwardly jealous she didn't have the same. Instead she was plump from the permanent shift work and lazy eating ritual it caused.

She applied the probe through the gel in slow steady movements and studied the monitor.

"There it is," she said looking closer at the screen and taking snapshots as she did.

"As expected at six weeks it is very small and there's the heartbeat," she added.

"Is our baby okay doctor?" Nicholette asked anxiously.

"Yes my dear, all looks normal," the doctor lied.

She handed the probe to the nurse and turned to Bennett, "Can we speak privately please."

Bennett gave Nicholette an encouraging wink and followed the doctor out into the hallway. He could feel Nicholette's eyes on him every step of the way. He wasn't used to her frightened, she had always been strong, emotionless at times and most of all, resilient but now he too, was worried.

"Mr Bennett, I will be blunt, I think your wife will miscarry soon, maybe in the next day or so. To be honest I haven't seen anything quite like this, the amniotic sac and embryo are encased in what I would describe as some unusual thick skin cocoon. If I wasn't mistaken, I would say the white blood cells are attacking the embryo. Apart from that, the embryo looks normal."

She hesitated, "I would like to bring a specialist in to have a look, it is quite unusual."

Bennett was trying to absorb what had been said and how he was going to tell his fiancée.

"Her blood workup is quite unusual too, its best she stays overnight and then tomorrow the specialist can have a look at her."

"Specialist? Why?" Bennett asked.

"I have a good friend over at the University research hospital, he specialises in blood disorders. I'd like him to look at the anomalies I picked up in her blood."

Bennett nodded and broke from the conversation hurrying back to Nicholette.

"We have a problem, the doc has seen the nanobots in your blood. Some blood disorder expert is coming to have a look," he said quickly.

Nicholette had already ripped the cannula from her hand and was on her feet heading for the door. Bennett could only laugh at her haste and raced after her. Back behind them no one noticed they had left; the hospital staff were too busy in their hectic routines.

They rushed to their car and headed straight for their hotel through the free-flowing mid-afternoon traffic. Back behind them the same black late model Range Rover from the previous day scooted around cars to catch up. The same two men dressed in dark suits onboard the Rover watched Bennett's every move. One picked up his cell phone and made a call.

"Sir we have Bennett in our sights, they are about to enter their hotel. What are your orders?"

He listened and gave a quick nod to the driver.

17.
Distracted

London
May 15, 2005

They hadn't spoken much on their drive to the hotel, she had been deep in thought about their baby while Bennett had been much the same. Though she appeared strong and unbreakable on the outside, he was concerned how losing the baby would affect her mental state.

"When were you going to tell me?" he blurted.

"Huh? Sorry, I wasn't listening!"

"The baby, when were you going to tell me?"

"Soon, but it doesn't matter now," she replied and burst into tears.

They had just entered the hotel's underground carpark and slipped into the first spot he found. Five cars over, the black Range Rover entered a carpark. Inside, the two men watched as Bennett reached over and pulled Nicholette into his arms.

"Babe it's going to be okay, we will find a way around this, I promise. Come on let's go up to the room," he said knowing he'd probably just lied to her. On the short walk to the lift he told her what the doctor had said, carefully leaving out the miscarriage part.

Two men dressed in dark business suits and pulling small overnighter bags pushed in front of them at the lifts. They all entered together and exchanged short pleasantries about the weather and the hotel. Nicholette didn't say much but she could feel the two men's eyes undressing her and it both excited and angered her at the same time. She had always been conscious of her beauty and at times, she used it as her weapon, seducing the enemy in a vulnerable position before killing them. Bennett stood beside her obstructing their view and continued to chat freely with them.

The taller of the two men kept the general conversation rolling as the lift ascended.

"You men here on business?" Bennett asked.

"Yes, just today and tomorrow, then back home."

"Home? Where's home?" Bennett asked detecting an American accent.

"Boston Massachusetts," he quickly replied moving forward slightly. The other man had already taken one step back.

Had Bennett and Sponarava not been distracted by her health, they would have noticed the man at the rear with his hands constantly in his pockets, though it was warm inside the lift.

"Nic… GUN!" Bennett yelled as his world went black and he collapsed to the floor.

The lift was a tight space for at the most, six people, yet Sponarava spun on her heel kicking her other leg out and around into the gunman's face. He'd been taken by surprise at her retaliatory speed. She leapt at him like a wild jungle cat drawing her Tokarev from under her belt and firing two shots as her world faded black to join Bennett on the floor.

The lift doors opened.

18.
The President

London
May 15, 2005

Bennett woke, dazed and uncertain where he was at first. His vision was blurry, and he vaguely recalled the penetrating sting of the tranquilising dart in his neck. It had been fired at close range and within seconds, the neurotoxin had strangled his consciousness. He was sprawled on a large bed with his hands restrained while opposite him, a man in his late thirties sat relaxed, watching him. A Glock handgun rested steadily on his leg.

Bennett sprang to his feet though lost his balance, a lingering effect of the drug and slipped back onto the bed.

"Steady Jon, the toxin wears off quick, you'll be okay in a minute or so," the man now standing said, not taking any changes with his fingers edging closer towards his handgun. His orders had been simple but did not include himself being killed.

Bennett recognised the man as the taller of the two they had encountered in the lift. His suit jacket was partly open to expose an empty shoulder holster and Bennett suspected he was a Government employee.

"Where is Nicholette?" Bennett demanded looking around the small room.

"I assure you Jon she is safe in the next room, no harm has come to her," the man replied holding his handgun by his side, trying not to intimidate Bennett.

"Who are you and what do you want?"

"I'm not your enemy, my name is Ryan Adams and I'm here on behalf of the President of the United States. It is important he talks with you," the man said slowly placing his gun on the table beside him as a gesture of trust and stepping closer towards Bennett.

Bennett sensed the seriousness and lifted himself up to sit on the edge of the bed.

"Secret Service?" Bennett asked.

"Yes I am, Special Agent Ryan Adams. I am sorry we had to take these extremes to speak with you, but we didn't want to take any risks. It is well known you are not the easiest person to track down and engage contact."

Bennett laughed because it was true.

"Where am I?" he asked holding his bound hands up.

Adams was already at his side cutting him loose of the zip ties.

"A hotel not far from the hospital," Adams replied and turned his back on Bennett.

It was a test Bennett knew, an opportunity for him to overpower Adams and take his gun. He resisted the urge more because he was curious why the President had gone to this length to contact him.

He watched Adams pick up a black briefcase and place it gently on the only table in the room. Next to it he unfolded a small antennae dish.

"I want to see Sponarava," he said.

"Yes of course," he replied and he made a quick phone call.

"How did you find me?" Bennett asked.

"We've been tracking you for a month now. You and Nicholette arriving in London today was unexpected, saved us falling onto one of your mantraps around your house on Nias Island," Adams replied continuing to set up the laptop and satellite connection.

The door behind him opened and two agents walked in with Nicholette in front. Her hands were still bound and she raced to embrace Bennett as Adams ordered the restraints be removed.

"What's going on Jon, what do they want with us?" she asked.

"Hello Jon, I apologise for this intrusion," a new voice in the room stopped Bennett from replying to her.

He turned to face the laptop screen and President Armstrong sat looking back at him in high definition resolution.

"Mr President, I am intrigued why you needed to drug and abduct us."

"My Agents assured me you would not be harmed and that this was a necessary measure considering your lethal abilities."

Nicholette watched on not saying anything.

Bennett just nodded in agreement while the President continued.

"Jon no one knows about this meeting except us and it must remain that way, do you understand?"

"Yes sir but I'm a little confused. What's this all about?"

"You won't be confused after I explain myself. I am aware of your involvement in taking down a group of men a few years back who had sinister ideas for our future. Though I feel rather under informed of the events that took place, my source tells me you are one very important individual. Since taking up office nine months ago I have learnt many secrets, some I understand are best kept classified but it wasn't until recently that I became overwhelmingly suspicious of something closer to you."

Bennett lent forward to pay attention, he had an inclination where the briefing was heading.

The President continued, "Jon, you might have noticed the increase in earthquakes around the globe during the past year, but you may not be aware of the changing dynamics of the destruction patterns."

Bennett interrupted, "How have they changed? I'm not following."

The President ignored his question and proceeded.

"Twenty-four hours ago an event of colossal magnitude occurred in Northern China. At first, we thought it was a meteor impact but initial damage reports indicate something entirely different. Half the city of Shenyang has been flattened and at least five hundred thousand are dead or missing. To make matters worse, ground zero was China's main northern military base."

Bennett shook his head in disbelief, he knew the political ramifications if the Chinese suspected it was a deliberate hostile attack.

"Was it nuclear?" Bennett asked.

"No reported radiation and the ground damage was somewhat different to that of a nuclear strike," the President answered.

"What are the Chinese saying?"

"That's the problem, they are convinced it's a nuclear attack by either us or the North Koreans and are mobilising their military machine into a ready state for war."

"But don't they realise there is no radiation so there has been no nuclear detonation," Bennett responded.

"Yes this has been pointed out to the Chinese President but he refuses to listen or negotiate."

"Okay you mentioned something about the damage patterns being different, what do you mean?" he asked.

The President answered, "The destruction in Shenyang was not similar to that of either a nuclear strike or an earthquake and there was no distinctive crater like you'd expect from a meteor impact. The ground appeared to have rolled over the building structures leaving nothing but barren terrain in its wake. It was like nothing I have ever seen before until I looked at a few recent earthquakes in China and Pakistan. They all had similar destruction patterns but to a much lesser degree than Shenyang. They all looked like a freshly ploughed field but to a much greater scale."

The President paused waiting for Adams to pass Bennett a series of photographs each showing large areas of mutilated earth once towns and cities. Bennett immediately noticed the distinct pattern. He passed them to Nicholette.

"Mr President I would describe it as a land tsunami radiating out from the epicentre," Bennett said.

The President hadn't thought of it in that way and was deliberating the notion while Bennett continued to talk.

"Sir I don't know what you are wanting from me and I certainly don't understand why you are holding secret meetings with me or why you are conducting your own research?"

"Jon I suspect the pulse weapon is semi operational but needs something to provide its full destructive power," the President announced knowing that would reward him with Bennett's full attention.

Bennett felt a burning sensation ignite inside his chest and he knew under his shirt the symbols would be glowing. It was not possible, he had destroyed Meredith four years earlier, the only platform in orbit capable of unleashing the full destructive force of the blue crystal. Without the thirteenth code, Bennett had been confident it would never threaten the existence of life on Earth.

The nightmares were now making sense to him.

"Jon, I need your help to verify my suspicions, but we must keep it strictly off the radar."

"Mr President, if what you are saying is correct then the weapon is nowhere near full strength meaning whoever has it will need the thirteenth code. The Shenyang images show it at about ten per cent or less."

The President's jaw dropped, his source had not informed him of the full destructive potential.

"Things as you'd expect are heating up, my military advisers are pushing for full war readiness which of course implies a potential nuclear response. I can't allow it to go that far, I can only hold them off in negotiations for so long, but it is the North Koreans I am concerned about, they have started mobilising troops towards the Chinese border and our latest intelligence indicates they have access to at least fifty mobile nuclear warheads."

The President had paused momentarily to collect his thoughts.

"Jon I need you to verify the pulse weapon was used on Shenyang and it needs to be done quickly. Whatever it takes, but I need condemning evidence to expose whoever is responsible. We need to find it and neutralise it."

"What if I refuse to help," Bennett responded.

"Your payment will be quite substantial but more importantly, your name will be officially cleared with the Senate. You were not responsible for the Kuwaiti slaughter; I know it was the preliminary testing of the orbital weapon and you were set up."

Bennett had suffered years of humiliation at the hands of Senator Brown, the one who so boldly spearheaded *The Trust* until his rightful assassination. To hear the United States President say he was innocent and would be exonerated was overwhelming, an offer he could not refuse.

"Okay but where do I start? I destroyed the killer satellite four years ago and I know that the Thirteenth Code hasn't been activated yet so how is it we have an active pulse weapon?" Bennett asked.

"My source told me *The Trust* uncovered a completely intact weapon on board an alien craft deep in Antarctica a few years back. Where it is now, we do not know but I suspect that is what was used over Shenyang."

"What do you mean, alien craft?" Sponarava spoke for the first time.

"I have little information however, I believe it was too advanced in technology to have been built on Earth," the President replied still attempting to maintain some level of secrecy.

Bennett knew they had limited time and didn't push the subject, he suspected it was another craft like the one so many believed crashed near Roswell.

They spoke for another ten minutes while Bennett extracted what he could from the President. At the conclusion he asked one final question.

"Mr President you have a well-informed source, who is it?"

"Under normal circumstances I would never disclose my source however, since his death it is no longer a risk," he said before pausing and adding, "the Monk."

"Dead, how?" Bennett asked in shock.

Nicholette mirrored his surprise, astounded as well.

"Murdered a few days ago in Venezuela, no suspects at this stage though it had to have been someone close to him inside his temple," the President answered. He added, "Ryan will provide you everything you need and you are only to report to him or myself but please, time is critical, good luck."

Bennett sat staring at the screen as the President terminated the connection. He did not feel sorrow or pity, it was more about the aftermath that would soon follow. The Monk dead wasn't something he had expected.

19.
Rose Bennett

Lisbon, Portugal
May 16, 2005

British Airways Flight 502 was on time arriving at Lisbon International which pleased Bennett. He checked his watch and as promised, they were disembarking at exactly 5.45pm into a comfortably cool night. They cleared customs as Mr Bryon Wilson and his fiancée Rebecca Gleeson from Colorado Springs visiting Portugal on their first vacation together. They proceeded straight to the rental cars and in no time, they were travelling west on the A5 heading to Cascais, a forty minute drive with Bennett behind the wheel. He wasn't a fan of Nicholette's driving, she was always too erratic and careless. Road trips with her behind the wheel weren't for the light-hearted. He could never work out whether she was just impatient or just loved to piss him off at times, getting satisfaction from watching him clutch the door handle and turn pale.

The sun had just set, sinking below the watery horizon of the north Atlantic Ocean as they reached their destination. They sat for a few minutes absorbing the scenery and though it was darkening quickly, they could still make out the expanse of ocean running parallel to the road. On the right, a large mansion sat presiding over a lush lawn and gardens. A massive concrete wall ran the length of the frontage giving it an impenetrable feel, while behind it a series of high spotlights shone down like as if it were a prison.

It was no prison.

Rose Bennett lived in a multimillion dollar mansion set on five acres of immaculate gardens with breathtaking views westward over the Atlantic Ocean. At the front, a massive iron gate blocked their entry until an armed guard appeared from behind the wall.

"Mr Bennett, Rose has been expecting you," he said and the gate opened.

"Whoa! What's with all the guns," Nicholette commented as they drove slowly up the fifty metre long driveway towards a three story glass palace.

"Yeah and they have some heavy duty weaponry," Bennett remarked looking from left to right across the massive lawns and gardens surrounding the house. Spotlights amongst the gardens gave it a real luxury resort feel.

In total, they counted ten men across the yard, all dressed in dark military style outfits and each carrying a Belgium made F2000 Bullpup assault rifle, a sophisticated and deadly weapon. Two more men appeared as they pulled up out front and opened their doors once the car stopped. Bennett couldn't help thinking it was like arriving at a plush hotel with the concierge greeting them and the bag boys fussing for their luggage.

An average height older woman appeared from inside and half ran down the three short steps to embrace Bennett. Rose Bennett was approaching eighty years, but her appearance had her looking closer to fifty, she too had the artificial cellular nanobots active in her body and clearly, they were doing their job. Each year for the past three, she had been getting younger and more agile, and her mental capacity was that of a young woman. The eighth code technology was worth billions if not trillions for its rejuvenation abilities, but it brought to the table many issues. If there was no aging population then six billion people would quickly become twelve billion, twenty billion and so on until the planet could no longer support life. It was partly for that reason *The Trust* never exposed the existence of the technology to the science community.

Rose embraced her nephew for a few minutes and looked him up and down. She had always been critical of his life, always looking out for him and wanting the best for him. She liked Sponarava, she witnessed a change in Jon, a new happy Bennett, a man with love in his step. She particularly enjoyed the way

Sponarava carried herself, all tall and confident in her stride and most of all, lovingly devoted towards her nephew.

She and Nicholette exchanged a tight hug like the one she gave Bennett and exchanged a long conversation about each other's health like good friends do. Since helping Bennett find her in Venezuela, they had unintentionally drifted apart but only because of their covert lifestyle and no other reason. Rose had known Sponarava when she worked for the Monk and grew to admire her skills and feisty determination.

"Why the small army?" Bennett asked breaking up their little chit chat.

"A precaution since the Monk was murdered. I assume you have heard the news about the Monk's death," she said.

"Yes, we heard he was killed by an intruder slitting his throat," Nicholette replied. She had been close to the Monk when she worked for him but quickly changed her opinion after he locked her away in his dungeons. Now she felt no sorrow at all.

"Correct, there are no suspects, but I am sure that is not why you are here!"

"I would have killed him myself and it would have been painful, a cut throat was too merciful," she said in anger as Bennett grabbed her arm and squeezed it. She knew to stop because Rose had been and still was a fan of the Monk, she believed in his prophecies and bizarre beliefs about the true ancestors of humanity.

Rose led them into the house. It was enormous, massive high ceilings and an ancient Egyptian feel to the décor with bronze statues and paintings symbolising ancient royalty lining various walls.

"WOW!" Nicholette was in awe, she had never seen anything like it.

"Impressive," Bennett responded.

"Come, let's talk," Rose commanded adopting a more authoritarian persona than friendly aunt.

They were led down a long wide tiled hallway to a smaller room with no windows. It resembled a small conference room with a huge wall screen at the far end and a round table in the middle accommodating ten high back chairs. They each took a seat and Rose's guard closed the door behind him as he left.

"This room is completely soundproof, no one can hear what is said in here," she started.

The others nodded in acknowledgement and did their own inspection of the room.

Nicholette wondered why she needed a room for secrecy, who really was Rose Bennett, she thought.

"We need your help," Bennett blurted.

Rose returned a quizzical expression and beckoned Bennett to go on.

"We believe *The Trust* is active again and somehow have built their version of the orbital weapon."

"Really, why do you think this?" she asked.

Bennett and Sponarava took turns to explain their reasoning focusing on the devastating world events. Neither of them mentioned the meeting with the President.

"Interesting! It may not be their version," Rose remarked.

"How's that, what are you saying?" Sponarava asked.

"The Monk had always claimed an undamaged alien craft existed somewhere in Antarctica, one that had a fully functional energy pulse weapon onboard. The craft that crashed at Roswell resulted in the weapon breaking apart on impact, only the lens was recovered from the weapon," she answered.

Sponarava glanced sideways at Bennett, she still struggled to accept the conspiracies of the Roswell crash were factual. "Lens?" she asked.

"Lucifer's Funnel, the red diamond used to magnify the force of the pulse beam," Bennett answered, adding "But without the rest of the weapon, it was useless."

He continued.

"I think there is a prototype out there or maybe the real thing. Either way we must find it and eliminate it. I don't need to remind you of its capabilities and ramifications for the planet," Bennett said in a serious tone.

They all nodded remembering the Monk's warnings. Fire it too many times at the earth and the consequences would be a chain reaction splitting the earth's crust open.

The energy pulse weapon was designed to annihilate sections of ground many times that of the largest cities. It directed an energy pulse deep into the earth's crust that then radiated outwards and upwards creating a massive rippling effect across the earth's surface crushing everything in its path. Ripples or best described as land tsunamis would reach heights of two hundred feet rolling unstoppable across the earth. The aftermath resembled a freshly ploughed field except on an unthinkable scale. The weapon used Lucifer's Funnel to intensify the power of the blue crystal into a laser beam with the destructive force beyond anything scientists ever imagined.

"How do we find it Rose?" Bennett asked.

"Your old friend, Dom Whittaker documented much of *The Trust's* experiments and facilities around the world. I had heard *The Trust* were searching for the craft in Antarctica but then Dom died and that ended my source of information," Rose said.

"Hmmm yes unfortunate," Bennett commented sarcastically.

He hadn't heard Whittaker's name in the past three years and wasn't too excited to hear it now. Dom Whittaker had once been National Director of Intelligence and his best friend, until Iran. There he had materialised as his enemy after Bennett discovered the truth and the betrayal shadowing most of his life.

"My dear, are you feeling okay?" Rose asked Nicholette.

"Yes just a little tired," she replied looking down away from Rose's stare.

"How long have you been pregnant?" Rose asked examining her all over with her eyes.

Both looked at Rose, shocked that she knew.

"How did you know?" Bennett asked.

"Jon I can feel the changes in the energy around her, the Monk taught me many things about human behaviour."

"So maybe a Christmas baby!" Rose announced in her often abrupt way.

She had been a massive influence in Bennett's life, stepping in after his mother died and teaching him how to survive in the constant absence of his father. She was his father's only sister and like his father, she had been well connected within the US government's clandestine organisations. Much of that changed when Jon lost his mother and she returned to Australia to care for the then four-year-old Bennett. Rose had been in her ninth year with the US Defence Intelligence Agency and before that, ten years in the National Security Agency. Giving it all away to care for her brother's kid had been a difficult decision at the time though she loved her brother and would do anything for him.

The decision so difficult to make, became the best one she had ever made. She never imagined how raising a young child could be so rewarding and particularly, when she never experienced any maternal instincts to want her own child. Rose and Jon bonded as mother and son.

"Maybe? What do you mean, maybe? Do you know something?" Nicholette asked sounding concerned.

Rose paused looking at Jon with a worried look not knowing what to say.

Bennett took Nicholette's hand and nodded at Rose.

"My child, I am sorry. All three of us have the eighth code running through our bodies and though, it is a good thing, now it is working against you Nicholette. I can sense it is attacking the embryo and your body's natural immune system is in battle with it. You have a re-engineered version of the eighth code as you know. It was altered with one purpose and that was to fight the effects of the blue death."

Four years earlier, Nicholette had been with Bennett in Namibia where they were exposed to the lethal blue crystal, a highly radioactive material planted on earth by a meteor thousands of years ago. Bennett survived but she would have died if it hadn't been for the injection of the eighth code.

"Is there anything that can be done?" Bennett asked Rose.

"You have to remove that version of the eighth code from her body, that is the only way," Rose replied standing and taking Nicholette in her arms.

Sponarava broke down in tears.

"Please I don't want to lose our baby!" she pleaded.

"There is only one way to remove it," Rose said and continued to speak.

"The First Code deactivates the nanobots and over time they flush from the body. You must be present when the code is entered into the sphere. It was a safeguard against wrongful activations of the eighth code. Just remember it means anyone else near the activated sphere with the eighth code will be rendered inactive as well."

"Well that raises a dilemma, doesn't it?" Bennett said.

"Yes it does. As far as I am aware the first code has never been revealed," Rose replied.

"What about the sphere, do you have any idea where the other two are?" he asked.

"The Mayan Sphere was stolen when the Monk was murdered and as for the Sumerian Sphere, it has never been seen. I am not even sure it exists."

Bennett sat staring at nothing while beside him, Nicholette had composed herself.

"We need to find it," she said staring at him.

Bennett nodded without a clue where to start searching.

"Jeremiah! You need to find Jeremiah. He is the only one who knows all thirteen codes," Rose declared.

It was Jeremiah as a young boy who gave Bennett's father the codes in the early 1940's. He had been found adrift at sea off Bermuda after a mysterious sinking of a US freighter. At the time, it was suspected to be the result of a new advanced torpedo by the Germans and Viktor Bennett was sent to investigate. He gained nothing about an advanced torpedo or involvement by the Germans. Instead he encountered a young ten year old boy rambling, making no sense and drawing combinations of thirteen symbols on anything he could write on.

"Any ideas where we can find him?" Sponarava asked.

"Jeremiah has always been elusive, the Monk tried to find him but failed."

"Okay then what about the sphere, where do we start looking for the Mayan Sphere?" Bennett asked.

Rose thought for a moment, "Find the weapon and you will find the sphere, that's my guess. I will reconnect with a few old sources and see what I can dig up," she answered as a small knock sounded from the door.

A large man dressed in a black and white chef's outfit appeared.

"Madam Rose, dinner is served," he announced.

Rose Bennett was happily wealthy after a lifetime of investments in commercial property projects around the world predominantly in third world countries. Her share portfolio alone was worth close on two hundred million dollars and growing every day. It all contributed to her lush lifestyle on the shores of the Atlantic.

They moved to the dining room and for the remainder of the night, they wined and dined enjoying stories from Bennett's younger days in Australia and Rose's recent holiday adventures. Nicholette sat listening, laughing and occasionally contributing to the conversation but most of the time she was not there, her mind in deep thought about her baby's fate.

A hundred metres down the road seated on a hard timber bench overlooking the moonlit ocean, a tall red-haired man glanced at the house every few minutes. His face was severely scarred down one side from an unfortunate accident ten years earlier and he had become a hideous sight. The man looked like a vagrant by the way he was dressed and had been there for hours waiting for his moment to attack.

20.
Chase

Cascais, Portugal
May 17, 2005

The next morning, Bennett and Nicholette hit the road early to make their ten o'clock flight back to Sumatra via Rome and Mumbai. They preferred to vary their stop overs and not be predictable in their travel patterns. Each wore some form of disguise, Nicholette with a long black wig and heavy makeup while Bennett showcased a greying beard. Both had become experts at concealing themselves from those intelligence agencies scouring the closed-circuit camera feeds at international airports.

Arriving early was his thing, he loved the pre-flight time just relaxing, drinking coffee and watching the hustle and bustle of travellers. Nicholette on the other hand preferred to just go, no purpose in sitting around waiting for a flight, in her eyes it was a ridiculous waste of time. But today he had his way and they left Rose's house early, cruising onto the A5 at just after seven.

The day was picture perfect, no clouds and the warmth of the sun low to the east was soothing on their skin. Bennett drove keeping to the advertised speed limit and overtaking slower motorists only when he had to. Traffic was light making their travel time to the airport an expected forty minutes.

"We have a friend, four cars back, silver sedan, one occupant," he announced.

Nicholette adjusted her side mirror and spotted the car maintaining their speed and partially concealed behind a large white van.

"Male driver, large build, looks like a late model Mercedes," she confirmed.

"Time for some fun," Bennett said and changed lanes while accelerating just enough to overtake the truck ahead of them. He repeated it with the next vehicle in front of them.

"Yes he is following us, copying our moves. Who the fuck is he?" Nicholette thought out loud.

"I think we're about to find out," Bennett called pushing his foot hard down on the pedal followed by him yelling, "GUN."

Sponarava reacted with lightning speed to snatch her handgun as a short barrage of automatic gunfire shredded the rear window and she ducked for cover. Bennett swerved across the two lanes and their car lurched forward with more speed. A stray bullet hit a car in front of them and it spun wildly out of control off the motorway into the side ditch. Other motorists braked and scampered from the roadway while the gunman gave chase closing the distance quickly. Bennett had reached eighty miles an hour and their rental had more to offer. He floored the pedal.

Sponarava opened fire leaning out the passenger window but their assailant kept gaining on them. His Mercedes was much faster than their standard Ford Focus and he was making quick work of catching them. Another burst of automatic gunfire, this time missing, but it forced Bennett to pull hard right onto the gravel road edge where their car fishtailed in a frenzy.

The gunman had the advantage and raced alongside them, firing his handgun. The bullets hit the driver's door narrowly missing Bennett, fragmenting the windshield into a spider web of a thousand cracks.

He swung the car hard left smashing into the side of the Mercedes however, the gunman anticipated the move and accelerated full power into them. The weight of his car pushed the Ford sideways at high speed and it flipped upwards at first then end on end off the motorway onto the gravel. There it rolled a few more times and careered through the guard rail down a steep thirty meter embankment into the rear yard of a large warehouse.

The gunman raced at high speed off the next exit as people started to gather on the roadway, some making their way hastily down the embankment towards the upturned wreck. Others just stood watching in disbelief.

The few running down the hill reached the wreck in time for it to explode in a vibrant myriad of orange and red, followed by a funnel of black smoke rising high into the clear sky. The blast shockwave threw them backwards while the flames ravaged the wreck.

21.
<u>Revenge</u>

Lisbon, Portugal
May 17, 2005

Sirens were drawing nearer as the wreck blazed out of control. Bennett and Sponarava had jumped during the final roll, before it slammed through a wire fence behind the warehouse. Dazed but quick on their feet they sprinted for the cover of an alleyway between two old derelict buildings. They kept running another fifty yards until they reached a wide open desolate street and stopped in the shadows of the building.

"What now?" she asked catching her breath.

Both had suffered minor scratches in the crash, nothing serious to slow them down.

"I think it's a safe bet we need a new car," he said sarcastically pointing towards the black smoke billowing over the top of the roof behind them.

"Come on, nothing here and this place will be swarming with cops soon," she replied and they crossed the street towards another alleyway.

Bennett carried his two Beretta 9mm handguns, one under his belt and the other in his hand. Sponarava had her single Tokarev out scanning both directions. The sound of a car engine at high speed caught their attention and it appeared to the north racing towards them. The silver Mercedes from the highway was now bearing down on them from three hundred yards away.

Bennett grabbed Nicholette's arm and they sprinted for the alleyway, an extension of the one they had just emerged from. Either side the buildings stood four stories high and like the other ones, distinctly aged and ready for demolition.

The Mercedes skidded wildly into the alleyway with just enough space either side to straighten and accelerate towards them. Bennett glanced quickly over his shoulder and stopped mid stride. Sponarava copied him.

They both raised their guns and fired half a magazine at the approaching car, some striking the windshield and others smashing through the radiator and ricocheting off the engine block. A couple sliced through the front right tyre and the car veered uncontrollably into the wall before the driver regathered control and pulled it back straight. He wasn't stopping.

He returned rapid fire holding his gun out the window with one hand and driving with the other.

Bennett ducked for the cover of the surrounding building out of the way of the Mercedes swerving to hit him. Sponarava had leapt to the other side of the alley and rolled across the concreted roadway to lift herself back up into a shooting stance. She fired, emptied her magazine and shredded both back tyres as the car flipped on its side. It continued under the momentum throwing up sparks as it scraped across the concrete before slamming into the wall.

By the time she dropped her empty magazine and reloaded, the driver was out and firing at her. Some of the rounds hissed by while others hit the wall next to her as she sprinted the four strides to Bennett's outstretched hand.

"COME ON!" Bennett screamed, returning a burst of random shots in the gunman's general direction. He'd found an open doorway.

He grabbed and pulled her into the cover of the building where they ran, ducking and weaving. They were inside an old disused factory with a forty foot ceiling and long chains hanging down from pulleys attached to a rail from one side to the other. Across the floor a disused conveyor belt split the factory in two with timber crates lining one side and a row of rusted steel vats on the other. The building stank of rotting meat and the sign above them told them why. *Nelo Pet Foods, the finest in all of Portugal.*

A once thriving business was now scheduled for the wrecking ball like the others around it. The whole five blocks of warehouses and factories had been sold to make way for

Portugal's first Disneyland style theme park at a cost of over a hundred million Euros. The owners had accepted an irresistible offer while others just closed their doors leaving everything behind to the mercy of the rats.

They moved quickly among the rows of empty shipping crates stacked ten feet high until they'd reached the protection of the steel vats. Above them a second floor extended twenty feet from the southern wall with a straight stairway leading to it from behind the vats and out of sight to most of the floor.

"We need height, take this asshole out," Sponarava suggested.

Somewhere overhead, the low thump of helicopter rotor blades could be heard hovering above the building but then vanished as quick. *Was it the police?* They both thought.

"We can't stay here," Bennett said.

She heard him but was halfway up the ladder before he realised she was gone. She edged her way across the landing keeping low and with her gun leading the way. Bennett watched as she positioned herself and he made his way back towards where they had entered the building. He crept low and slow around the crates, glancing up at her for signals every few seconds and scanning from behind his gun sights.

The building had gone dead quiet. He looked up and Sponarava had one finger up pointing towards the door. She flattened her body hard against the landing floor, extended her gun forward and waited.

Suddenly a loud deep voice broke the silence.

"Bennett your time is up, you cannot run!"

Bennett looked up at Sponarava, she was shaking her head, she couldn't see their assailant.

"Show yourself Bennett, you are a coward hiding."

The gunman's voice seemed to echo and bounce off the high ceiling.

"Who are you and what do you want?" Bennett responded, crawling low towards the door.

Above him, four shots rang out. Sponarava had caught a glimpse of the gunman not far from Bennett's position but it was her mistake.

She missed her mark by an inch and the subsequent retaliatory gunfire obliterated the suspended flooring she stood on. Timber shattered as twenty rounds sliced through the floorboards and pursued the fleeing Russian. A few feet over she reached the stairs at the same moment a timber crate beside her exploded from the spray of bullets. Shards of jagged timber ripped through the air and sliced through her gun hand. The Tokarev slipped from her grasp and tumbled to the floor below with a clatter of metal against hard polished concrete. Sponarava fell, hitting the stair railing with excruciating pain.

Bennett witnessing her fall, launched to face his enemy, rapidly squeezing the trigger to blast four rounds at where he thought the gunfire had originated. They all missed, the assailant had traversed across the crates and landed on the other side. For a big man, he moved like a world class gymnast leaping the crates in no time to quickly reappear behind Bennett.

The first Bennett knew of the move was when he heard the soft thud of boots behind him and he spun with his gun up.

"On your knees and toss your gun over to me," the gunman called from five yards.

Standing before him was a tall red-haired man dressed in a dark battle jacket and black pants. A massive scar ran the length of his face down the left-hand side and he spoke with a deep American accent. Cradled across his arms and pointed at Bennett was a Chinese made T86 assault rifle.

Bennett did as he was commanded and tossed his Beretta before lowering slowly to his knees.

"Hands behind your head," the gunman commanded.

"Who are you?" Bennett called thinking he knew the face but couldn't place him.

"What you don't recognise me? That just insults me Jon. You murder my father and you don't have the decency to acknowledge who I am," he replied scowling at Bennett.

"Then why don't you tell me hero?" Bennett called, remaining bold and fearless while slowly edging his arms down.

Sponarava in mid-air flight above him caught the gunman's eye seconds before her boot connected with his face. Bennett reacted yanking the spare gun from under his belt as the gunman squeezed the trigger of his assault rifle. The high calibre bullet hit Bennett tossing him backwards, stumbling and smashing against a crate.

Sponarava landed like a cat and swung another roundhouse kick into the gunman's chest striking him hard with her size nine boot. The impact pushed him off balance and his rifle dropped to the floor with a weighted clank. She glanced at Bennett sprawled on the floor and pounced at the gunman swinging left and right punches into his head. The first two connected but the next he blocked, and he retaliated with his own strikes. A quick combination of three strikes to her head knocked her backwards as he pulled his handgun out. She lunged and grabbed it, wrestling and pushing it towards the ceiling as the chambered round fired. Blood streamed from a gash in her hand and sprayed the floor creating a slippery mess.

Both locked eyes, her crystal green and his steely grey while they wrestled with the gun. He was much stronger than her but Sponarava was a veteran at fighting for her life and swiftly with all her strength, drove her knee into his groin while at the same time, snapping downwards on the gun. It all worked perfectly, and Sponarava had the gun pointing at him until her own blood became her hindrance and she slipped.

Sponarava tried to regather her balance but her opponent proved too fast, he snatched the gun back and kicked her full frontal in the head. She fell backwards and rolled to her knees glaring up at him, sweaty hair dangling across her face and her eyes snarling like a cornered lion. Blood poured from her nose and she swallowed the bitter metallic taste as it trickled into her mouth, and she spat it out.

"It's a shame you have to die, this was just about your boyfriend," the gunman announced.

She said nothing, just stared at the scarred man and the muzzle of the Glock 9mm. She had never seen him before.

He raised his gun and three gunshots echoed across the room.

22.
<u>Joshua</u>

Lisbon, Portugal
May 17, 2005

The three bullets hit the gunman dead centre in the chest and he dropped to the floor. Bennett had fired from three yards over the top of Sponarava and from his prone position. Ten seconds earlier he had regained consciousness from the bullet striking his head. He'd been lucky, it had hit him on the side and deflected off his skull leaving just a bloodied gash.

He raced to Nicholette covered in blood and he thought the worst.

"Where you hit?" he asked grabbing her and pulling her up into his arms unaware of the others who had just entered the building.

"JON!" she screamed and he spun raising his gun at the same time.

Standing before him, the gunman was poised with two handguns, one directed at his head and the other at Nicholette on the floor. He could see the bullet proof vest protruding from under the man's jacket and took a higher aim, it would have to be a head shot he calculated.

"Bennett drop your gun…or she dies."

The gunman's face at closer range revealed a mosaic of smaller crimson red and purple scars intermeshed to distort half his face. The man was ugly Bennett thought, but something about him he found strangely familiar. He stepped forward closing the distance between them.

"One more step and she's dead," he declared.

"Who are you?" Bennett asked. He knew it was an easy shot at three yards to take the man's head off but he couldn't risk a reflex shot hitting Nicholette.

"I've been waiting for this moment a long time Jon, to watch you die like you did my father."

A Mexican standoff was unfolding, both with guns aimed at each other and both wanting answers.

"Shoot him Jon," Nicholette commanded from the floor.

Somewhere off to his right a familiar voice called from the shadows of the building.

"JOSH … DON'T SHOOT HIM."

The gunman half turned his head towards the voice and Bennett launched. He charged him front on driving his full body weight into the gunman while disarming his right hand. The left was still pointed at Nicholette and with incredible speed, he snatched that gun and turned it around pointing back at the gunman's face. It all happened in a couple of seconds and Bennett was in control. Nicholette had retrieved her Tokarev and moved to take aim beside him.

The voice again, this time closer.

"Jon please don't shoot him, it's Joshua."

Bennett turned to face a woman in her sixties pacing towards him, stately dressed in black business attire, long skirt and a loose blouse top.

"Silvia? What the fuck are you doing here?"

At that moment, they heard a muffled shot and the gunman collapsed to the floor with a small yellow dart in his neck. Nicholette stepped forward quickly with her gun up aimed at the woman approaching and the two men at her side. Both wore dark military battledress and carried tranquiliser rifles more commonly used in the wilderness of Africa to sedate and capture the biggest of beasts.

Silvia Whittaker stepped forward of the men and approached Bennett. It had been a few years since he'd seen her. The last time was just before she vanished underground after Dom's death and not wanting to face the truth of her dead husband's shameful life.

Bennett returned his attention to the gunman, studying what remained of his natural face. He could see some resemblance to the younger Joshua Whittaker he once knew.

He glanced back at her, she had not aged in the few years and appeared confident in her posture as they embraced. They had always been close friends but the betrayal by Dominique Whittaker had left a foul stench on his mind and right now, he was suspicious of her sudden appearance.

"He won't be out for long," she announced nodding her head towards the gunman sprawled on the floor.

"The tranquilizer is just a safeguard," she added.

"I don't understand any of this, what is going on, why are you here?" Bennett asked.

"Who is this woman?" Nicholette asked refusing to lower her weapon.

"It's okay Nik, lower your gun. This is Silvia Whittaker, Dom's wife."

"What about him?" She responded pointing her gun towards the unconscious gunman.

"A ghost!" he slowly replied.

"Jon, it is true, this is Joshua," Silvia interjected.

"Josh died a long time ago. I was there when Dom ordered the life support be terminated," he replied looking at Silvia.

"Yes, that is what Dom wanted us all to believe, it was another of his deceptions," she replied.

"What? Why?" Bennett asked utterly confused.

"He staged his death, Jon. Like so many things we discovered in Dom's life, it was all a set up. He paid off the hospital staff to make it look like Joshua was on life support."

"Why would he do that?" Bennett rebutted.

"After Dom died, I found a bunch of his old diaries hidden in the basement and for weeks afterwards I trawled through them, learning things that to this day, I still find despicable. Dom Whittaker was a stranger to me, he was my husband, yet I knew nothing of his other life."

She paused trying not to smear her makeup and wipe away a small tear.

"Jon, I am so sorry. I had no idea about what he had done to you, the deceit and betrayal must have almost killed you."

Bennett nodded and added, "It's a time I've come to forget and move on from."

She paused a moment looking closer at Bennett, regathering her thoughts.

She continued, "When I was disposing of his belongings, I found a small leather bound journal packed inside an old pair of dungarees. That journal is why I am here."

Bennett and Nicholette stood listening.

"The journal revealed information that Joshua hadn't died from a drug overdose as you and I believe. Dom staged it all, had it look like an overdose, paid the hospital to fake the life support and eventually his death. He then smuggled him out of the country. Joshua was a hunted man, he had murdered a prominent street gang member in Washington, a suspected drug deal gone bad and he ended up with a bounty on his head. Dom did what he had to do, fake his death and get him out. It was perfect, not even I knew."

"Okay so Scarface over there is Joshua Whittaker, why is he hunting Jon?" Sponarava asked.

"I have tried to convince him otherwise, but he believes Jon murdered Dom. He wants revenge."

"Silvia you know I didn't, but I had every reason to. How did you find him and what happened to his face?" Bennett asked.

"After the journal, I knew I had to find him so for two years I searched relentlessly. The journal was an anthology of one murderous act after the other. He had become Dom's private killing contractor, committing the murders the Agency would not sanction because of the political ramifications if ever revealed. But I don't need to be telling you about that Jon, do I? Like you know that life and so did Dom."

Bennett nodded partly in disgrace at his former life working for the Agency.

"And the scars?" he asked.

"Result of him building his own incendiary devices while living in Somalia in about 1998. He almost died for real that time," she chuckled and added, "The hideous scars are his reminder of stupidity." Silvia had always had a good sense of humour, she had to, living with Dom Whittaker.

Silvia continued to speak.

"Three months ago, I had a lucky break. One of my contacts sent me a photograph of him passing through JFK International. Red hair and that massive scar was a dead giveaway. Some groundwork and I tracked him down to a hotel in Manhattan."

Bennett gave her a quizzical look.

"Oh come on Jon, I was married to a spy for twenty years, did you not think I would learn a few tricks of your trade," she laughed.

"I went to Manhattan, knocked on his hotel door. At first, he didn't want to know me, very distant and cold. Dom had drummed into him to stay dead, never contact me or anybody who could reveal the truth of his existence. It took some work, but I found his heart again. Then a few days ago I received a strange message from him. He was talking about finally getting his revenge. I knew he meant you, he'd said it too many times about one day killing you."

On the floor next to them, Joshua was starting to stir, his eyes flickering. Bennett and Nicholette reacted quickly raising their guns. So too did Silvia's guards but their aim was on them not Joshua.

"I'm not taking any chances Jon, one wrong move and he's dead," Nicholette declared closing her grip and aligning herself for the quickest reaction.

"Wait! There is another reason I am here Jon," Silvia said.

Bennett gestured with his hand for Nicholette to back off and she took two steps back but not relenting her aim.

"What is it?" Bennett asked.

"It's something I was sworn to secrecy a very long time ago."

The scarred gunman edged up into a sitting position staring at the green eyed Russian and her Tokarev zeroed on his head. He made no attempt to stand, instead transferred his focus to Bennett.

"Mother what are you doing here?" he asked keeping his eyes on Bennett.

"To stop you from making a mistake," she replied.

He wasn't listening and cut her off midsentence, "Hello Jon, mother here has probably told you about me rising from the dead."

"Yes she did, she was deceived by your father just like I was," Bennett responded before quickly adding, "But I didn't kill him."

"He did what he had to do and I do not believe you," Whittaker responded.

"I was with your father when he was killed. Sepehr Airport in Tehran, four years ago and yes, I wanted to kill him after what he'd done to me, but I didn't. That is the truth."

Whittaker spat at Bennett and for his efforts, Nicholette's boot landed square in his face hurling him over onto his belly.

The others reacted, Bennett with his gun on Whittaker and the guards holding Nicholette back.

"ENOUGH," Silvia yelled and they all stopped mostly shocked at her sudden outburst.

Bennett for one, had never heard her raise her voice or sound angered in all his years he'd known her.

"Now both of you listen to me. I am sorry but Joshua you are not my biological son."

"What are you talking about?" Whittaker asked confused, as was Bennett standing next to him still with his gun aimed at him.

"Your father wanted a child and I could not give him one."

She continued in her usual softer voice, "I did not know until many years later at which time it was too late to change anything. He told me your parents both died in a car accident and you were the only survivor. He arranged the legal guardianship or so he led me to believe."

"Why are you telling me this now?" Joshua asked.

"Because of what else I discovered. Your father kept so much from you and me, his deceit has damaged many lives but not as much as it did for Jon."

She paused watching them both, Bennett with his gun targeting Whittaker sitting on the floor with blood trickling from a split lip, remnants of Nicholette's boot.

"But there is more you both do not know!"

23.
<u>Deception</u>

Lisbon, Portugal
May 17, 2005

Bennett looked at her, he was confused at where the conversation was heading and Joshua was growing more agitated the longer he sat under Bennett's gun.

"I know who your real parents were Joshua. Your mother's name was Grace Montgomery and your father was...," she said now turning her attention to Bennett.

He lowered his gun in disbelief, more shock than anything and finished her sentence, "Viktor Bennett!"

"Yes, your mother and father Jon," she confirmed.

"What the fuck! Are you saying Bennett is my brother?" Whittaker yelled as it started to sink in what his mother was saying.

"Yes he is your older blood brother," she replied.

"That is not possible, it is another one of Dom's lies. My mother died when I was four," Bennett said. He was busy doing his math in his head.

"Your mother had cancer and the doctors did not expect her to live. Viktor didn't accept it and took her to a CIA funded medical research facility in Romania. The treatment was a success but not without serious side effects. Her mental state deteriorated badly over the next couple of months, but your father never gave up on her. He kept her well looked after in a villa somewhere in Greece overlooking the Mediterranean. It was there where she gave birth to Joshua. After that I do not know what happened to her or whether she is still alive."

"How did Joshua end up with you and Dom?" Bennett asked.

"Dom knew I desperately wanted a child but couldn't bear one, so I think Viktor presented a viable solution. Your mother wasn't in any mental state to care for a child and he made up the story about Josh's parents dying in a car crash. I had no idea of the truth."

Bennett had become well accustomed to the deceit by his old friend Dom Whittaker but this one was difficult to digest. Next to him Nicholette was looking pale and sat down. He broke from his gun sights covering Whittaker and moved quickly to her side while she continually argued she was okay. Bennett knew different but for now, she was fine.

"Josh I am sorry I didn't tell you sooner, but I thought it would just complicate things," Silvia pleaded.

He ignored his mother and called out, "Bennett, how did my father die then?"

"I was held prisoner in a hangar at Sepehr Airport by your father and an Iranian operative by the name of Soheil Mahdavi. Things went to shit and Mahdavi shot Dom, though he managed to escape. I found him outside the hangar bleeding badly where we came under fire from a team of mercenaries led by Logan Bannister. One of them launched a rocket at us and Dom was killed."

He paused and added, "I will be honest, after what I discovered about your father, I wanted to kill him but couldn't bring myself to do it and that's pretty much it."

Josh nodded while he processed the information before asking, "I don't understand why you were his prisoner and why the mercenaries were shooting at you and him."

"It's a long story," Bennett replied and for the next hour he and Nicholette explained Jeremiah's Codes, *The Trust* and Dom's involvement.

By the end, Josh visualised his father in a slightly different light and he could feel Bennett's torment. Parts of the briefing made sense, his father had loosely mentioned *The Trust* and the ancient codes.

"What now then?" Josh asked.

"We need to find the weapon and destroy it," Bennett replied looking towards Nicholette who had deteriorated. He added, "And we need to find the third Sphere."

"My father did speak about *The Trust* and their vision for a New World Order though I just thought it was him talking absolute lunacy and really didn't pay much attention. He spoke of genocide on a grand scale to restore the population balance to the planet. I used to laugh; I was the one declared a sadistic killer but here was my father talking about murdering five billion people. What you have told me Bennett does fit with my father's ramblings. After all this time, he was serious. Wow! I can't believe it."

Silvia interjected, "This weapon, how do we find it?"

"I do not know. *The Trust* need the Thirteenth Code to fully activate it which they do not have. They must have built another killer satellite like Meredith, that's the only possible way," Bennett said.

"There is one other possibility," Josh almost whispered thinking of what his father had rambled about.

The immediate silence and curious looks gave Josh the floor.

"My father spoke about some alien craft hidden in the mountains of eastern Antarctica and once they unearthed it, the ultimate power to conquer the world would be in their hands. He had raved on about some anomaly they had detected a thousand feet inside the ice that displayed distinct disc like similarities to the Roswell craft. Back then I just thought he had lost his mind and didn't buy into his stories."

"Okay I think it's probably safe to assume *The Trust* have uncovered the craft however, the magnitude of the ground destruction in China indicates the onboard weapon is not functioning to its full capacity," Bennett said.

"So they need the Thirteenth Code to give it full power?" Silvia asked.

"Yes in a way. The code is needed to release the schematics from the Sphere," Bennett answered.

"Then they need you, right?" she added.

Bennett nodded.

"Where to from here?" Nicholette asked. She had quickly regained her colour and energy though it was causing her immense grief, the feeling of impending doom for her baby was excruciating.

"*The Trust* had a third facility in the South Pacific off Chile. It was in one of the memos on Dom's PDA, a reference to the headquarters for the America's Division like Kehlstein was the head of Europe. It was somewhere on the Juan Fernandez Islands I think from the pictures," Bennett remembered.

"Hang on, you mentioned pictures? My father sent me a photograph in the mail once of an island with jagged mountainous coastlines, volcanic like dropping sharply to a savage almost black ocean that no seaman would sail. It looked pure evil like some lost world."

"You just described the photos I had of the island. Why did he send you the photo?" Bennett asked.

"It came in the mail a few months before he was killed. No accompanying letter except written in his handwriting on the back was *Josh never lose this, it is your bargaining chip*. I had no idea what it meant, just some picture of an eerie looking island."

Bennett snapped to his feet, "We need Dom's PDA, he liked to embed encrypted documents into picture files. I'm betting there will be some clue in that file."

"Where's the PDA now?" Josh asked.

"Back on Nias Island, well hidden."

"I have a jet at Lisbon International, we can use that," Silvia suggested.

"You have a jet?" Bennett asked puzzled at her sudden wealth.

"Cessna Citation, it's an old one but reliable and I know what you are thinking. Yes Dom did leave me a substantial sum and no I don't want to think about where it came from," she replied pushing aside Bennett's curious appraisal of her.

Within another hour they had boarded her business jet and were airborne heading towards Binaka Airport on Nias Island. They just didn't know their flight was being tracked.

24.

__Ashes__

Nias Island
May 18, 2005

The single thin funnel of lingering grey smoke reaching for the clouds was a disturbing sight as Bennett banked their aircraft towards the small grassy airstrip. Half an hour earlier they had touched down at Binaka Airport and transferred to Bennett's twin engine Beechcraft leaving Silvia's men to guard her jet.

The rain had eased to a light drizzle while the sky was opening to the early afternoon sun reflecting a golden brilliance across the ocean. Bennett flew a wide cautious circle around the smouldering pile of timber and tin roofing they once called home. Their island shack had been desecrated to rubble by presumably a missile of sorts and now embers flickered the last remaining life.

He and Nicholette looked at each other, he'd seen the look on her face before, it was one of revenge and hatred though saddened at the same time. She had come to love their secluded home at the ocean's edge and the privacy it had provided. Now she was realising her life had reverted to the days of her dark murderous past. Like Bennett she hated that life and for the past four years they had grown to love each other under a normal lifestyle of domestic bliss.

Bennett lowered the wheels and they descended onto the airstrip, a patch of open ground he'd spent a month bulldozing and stripping the palm jungle. The gusting sea breeze made the aircraft bounce as the wheels touched down on the moist grass and skidded as he pushed hard on the brakes. He had always talked about one day extending the airstrip to make take-offs and landings less risky, but he enjoyed the challenge. When Nicholette ranted about the dangers of flying fuelled by her phobia he just laughed it off.

The strong wind pushing onshore from the ocean had evacuated most of the smoke leaving just a thin plume leaning towards the north. They walked the two hundred yards from the airstrip to the blackened ruins through a dense palm infiltrated forest following one of the many tracks Bennett had carved out over the years.

They stood staring at the charred remnants, the timber building framework completely incinerated, and the tin roof collapsed over it. The house had sat elevated on sturdy timber poles to give a clear view of the surf break fifty metres away and best protection against the increasing number of tsunamis encountered in the region.

"Definite missile strike," Bennett remarked.

"Yeah that's for sure, the debris is too spread for just a fire," Josh commented while Nicholette walked among the ashes searching for anything worth salvaging, there was nothing.

"Okay come on, let's get the PDA and clear out. I reckon whoever did this will be back," Bennett commanded turning back towards the airstrip.

They walked to the edge of the strip where Bennett knelt down and started digging in the dirt. "Josh give me a hand."

After a few busy minutes they had unearthed a rusted metal hatch the size of a small doorway. Bennett grabbed the handle ring and lifted with all his strength to expose a dark pit.

"Come on, we need weapons," he said descending a narrow steel ladder into the darkness.

Nicholette and Josh followed taking cautious steps down the dozen steel rungs into the pitch black confinement. Suddenly the bunker exploded in bright green neon light and Whittaker gasped with both shock and excitement.

"Fuck Bennett, you planning on starting a war?"

Bennett had found the light sticks and cracked two open to give them visibility and exposure to his arsenal. Stacked to the ceiling on either side were fifty different types of assault rifles, handguns and explosives. At the far end was his heavy artillery mostly rocket launchers, anti-aircraft weapons and two electric Miniguns chambered with three hundred rounds ready to go.

Bennett laughed briefly, making no comment at Whittaker's remark but instead kicked up a couple of floorboards under his feet. He knelt and fumbled underneath the floor cavity with his hand until his arm had vanished up to his shoulder.

"Okay got it," he said and pushed himself back onto his feet.

The room gave plenty of head height as he straightened and directed the light stick over the PDA device in his hand. Nicholette had already shouldered her choice weapons and was climbing back out of the bunker leaving Whittaker still staring in amazement at Bennett's collection of sniper rifles.

"Take whatever," Bennett suggested pushing past him filling a duffel bag with assorted high powered automatic weapons and ammunition.

Whittaker grabbed a Remington M24 with the biggest scope he'd ever seen, more resembling a telescope, he thought.

"What do you plan on taking out astronauts on the moon!" he chuckled raising it to feel the line of sight.

Bennett laughed, "Well that's assuming astronauts have actually been on the moon!"

"Just like the old man, conspiracy theorist disbelieving everything. He never stopped talking about government lies and the cover ups. Always the cynical one, my father," Whittaker replied.

"Yeah Josh, you forget one thing my friend. We were both CIA!" Bennett laughed with a hint of sarcasm taking his first few steps up the ladder while wrestling the weighted bag of weapons and the PDA in his spare hand.

The PDA had been Dom Whittaker's insurance policy against *The Trust's* leadership containing the only known evidence of their identity and the imposed criminal liability of their master plan.

Josh hurried himself along to catch up to Bennett and load the aircraft. The others were already strapped in and within ten minutes, the Beechcraft was skimming the treetops at over two hundred knots heading back to Binaka.

Not much was said, Nicholette still saddened by the devastation of her home and Bennett focused on his flying. Josh and Silvia sat in the back staring at the passing jungle fifty feet below them occasionally glancing towards each other.

None of them had noticed the tiny silver blip in the sky to the north.

25.
__PDA__

Binaka Airport, Nias Island
May 18, 2005

Bennett took his seat near the rear of the jet with Nicholette close at his side. Across from them, Silvia and Josh were absorbed in deep conversation about Dom's involvement with *The Trust.* Bennett had only just started to notice the mother son bond between them and in the aircraft's lighting, the man's facial scarring was more hideous than he first thought. One side of his face was worse than the other but collectively, the melted mosaic of red and purple skin gave it the heinousness that parents shielded their children from seeing.

The jet rolled out onto the runway into a gentle south easterly breeze, gaining momentum and lifting towards the broken clouds. Further to the north the silver object gained altitude and accelerated past Mach six into a sub-orbital flight path heading towards the border separating China and Russia. The two pilots shared a guilty conscience for what they had been ordered to complete and they knew the consequences would be far greater than the destruction of Shenyang.

Bennett booted up the PDA and scrolled through hundreds of files until he reached the memos about the South Pacific facility. Not much was detailed in the correspondence mostly just inventories and construction costings interspersed with maintenance schedules. It was listed as the headquarters for the America's Division and like Kelhstein and Kyrgyzstan, it was completely underground except one difference. It had been excavated into the side of a mountain.

"Any of these pictures look familiar," Bennett asked Josh passing the device across.

"Yes that one, that's it," he replied pointing to one image in the middle of three.

"As I thought, that picture file is ten times bigger than the other two," Bennett commented and immediately extracted the encrypted contents hidden inside the file.

"Two hidden files, one text and the other is a video," Bennett said.

"Sneaky bastard!" Josh remarked pushing forward for a front row view.

Bennett opened the text file displaying a set of latitude and longitude coordinates.

$$33°44'48.24"S \quad 80°49'32.46"W$$

Nicholette punched them into an Internet search and it returned a point on the north western shoreline of San Fernandez Island in the Pacific Ocean off Chile.

"Okay, we can assume that is the facility," Bennett said as he double clicked the video file.

At first the screen remained black, lifeless for a few seconds. Then a voice broke through the PDA's speaker.

"That's Dom," Silvia blurted.

"Josh if you are watching this then I am surely dead. The following video provides proof of those behind *The Trust* and confirms their master plan discussed at a meeting held on seventeenth November 1994 at Kehlstein in Germany. Those present are Hiedler, Walter Heathermann, Denzil Brown, Richard Koehler, Herman Schwartz, Stirling Kaumheimer, Dierk Klotzer, Vinson Weber and myself. It is imperative you terminate these men before the execution of the plan's final phase. Once the systematic firing of the pulse weapon commences there can be no return and our planet will be destroyed."

The footage changed from pitch black to a brightly lit room displaying a group of men sitting around a long rectangular table. The low black and white resolution was typical of the small covert cameras of the time and though it was grainy, it clearly showed the faces of the men at the table. The way the footage panned the room in jerky motions meant the small camera was attached somewhere on the front of Whittaker's shirt and he was walking around the room.

The sound recording wasn't the best quality however, it gave them a hefty insight into the sinister ways and expectations of the Fourth Reich. It declared their plans for the most sadistic massacre of human life in the history of the planet. Phase one with the widespread dispersal of blue crystal dust would exterminate close to one billion people whereas phase two obliterated another four billion using the pulse weapon.

Bennett and the others sat silent, in disbelief at what they were witnessing.

"Is that who I think it is?" Nicholette questioned.

"I recognise most of these men, they were known as the Six," Bennett said without any feeling of guilt or shame. He had assassinated them four years prior to halt their atrocities.

"I'll be damned, that is Adolf Hitler, older but somehow younger. I don't understand, how is this possible?" Josh asked.

"The eighth code nanobots I would assume, they allow the host to live longer and rejuvenate the body in the process," Bennett explained before adding, "It certainly explains the direction of their master plan, the genocide and the overzealous desire for supremacy." He paused and added, "Hiedler!"

"Who?" Nicholette asked.

"Dom says Hiedler is one of the ones who was present. He is referring to Hitler! Conspiracy theorists around the world have always claimed that Hitler never died at the end of the war but instead was smuggled out to South America onboard a German U-boat. Many claimed he took on his original family name Hiedler," Bennett answered.

"The other fella must be Walter Heathermann," Nicholette said as Bennett's cell phone chimed and he stood to answer it.

"Hello Jon," the caller said.

Bennett looked back over his shoulder towards Nicholette who was watching him suspecting the caller was Rose. She was correct.

"I have some information Jon," she continued.

Bennett changed the subject, "Rose did you know I have a brother?"

The line went silent for a moment.

"Rose you there?" Bennett asked.

"Yes, but I am shocked that you know this. I can only assume Silvia has found you."

"Yes, she says Joshua Whittaker is my brother. How much do you know about this?" Bennett asked.

"Do you believe it Jon? Think, where did Silvia disappear to for all those years, not even you could find her."

"Rose are you saying it's not true and I shouldn't trust Silvia," Bennett asked lowering his voice out of hearing.

"I am saying that you should tread carefully, I am not convinced it is true," she answered.

For the next few minutes Rose briefed him on her research into the Antarctica craft and *The Trust* until the line went dead. Each time he called back, he was greeted with static silence.

"Forget San Fernandez Island, it's been destroyed, and the weapon has been stolen," he announced walking back to the group and interrupting Silvia mid-sentence.

He could see their puzzled expressions and for the next few minutes he briefed them on the phone call, omitting Rose's suspicions about Silvia.

Nicholette was first to comment, "Silvia has confirmed the other older man as Walter Heathermann, he was a British spy during World War II and became a double agent near the end of the war. Attempts were made by the British to arrest him, but he managed to elude them every time."

"What happened to him?" Bennett asked.

"Don't know, last I heard he too was somewhere in South America but that was many years ago," Silvia answered.

"I know exactly where he is," Bennett said.

They all turned watching him scan through the PDA.

"I remember seeing the name Walter and a list of countries in one of the directories," he said scrolling through the directory and arriving at the heading of Bolivia. A list of fifteen first names became visible.

"There it is, the name Walter and just what I was hoping for, another set of latitude and longitude coordinates," he announced.

21°55'50.89"S   64°47'18.82"W

"Those coordinates come back to Bolivia, five miles southwest of a small town called Padcaya in the south of the country. Massive house set amongst the trees," Nicholette said turning the laptop's monitor for the others to view.

"Why there I wonder?" Josh said not realising he had spoken out loud.

"Bolivia became a well-known sanctuary for Nazi war criminals after the war, perhaps *The Trust* based their coordination from that part of the world. Anyway, I think we need to find Heathermann if he's still alive, and extract some answers," Bennett replied.

They all nodded in agreement.

26.
Zavitinsk

Zavitinsk, Russia
May 18, 2005

Milena despised the freezing cold and the winters in Zavitinsk were the worst, she longed for the balmy climates of southern Europe. A few more weeks was all she had to endure she hoped, while her husband finished his deployment. As the Lieutenant General of a small military air base a few miles north of the town he enjoyed his work, though he impatiently waited the news of his promotion to the Ministry of Defence in Moscow. It had been long overdue and a reward for his five long years commanding Russia's most eastern land-based secret.

His wife appreciated the importance of his job, but she was ignorant of the underground arsenal of two hundred nuclear intercontinental ballistic missiles. Each had the capability of reaching the most southern cities of the United States and any target in Europe. The Russian Administration had deliberately failed to declare the weapons as part of the world disarmament agreement and now each missile stood poised in a launch ready state.

The suspicious explosion flattening Shenyang six hundred miles to the south had become his nightmare. His superiors handed him disturbing instructions for an immediate launch standby; he just didn't know all the targets.

At first, he had been ordered to target the North Korean city of Chongjin. The fifty-megaton warhead would decimate the city in a few seconds and the radiation fall out would kill thousands if not millions.

But when the targets changed to three cities in the United States, he rang to order his wife into their bomb shelter. She knew the drill having spent the best part of twenty years following him around Russia to military installations in the north and the south. She didn't question his decision, instead she placed the phone down and took a long look out her window to the north towards the base. She didn't know how long it would be until she would see the sky again. A bright flash in the distance caught her attention.

The sky was cloudless but to see a single flash of blue lightning was bizarre, she thought. It was an unusual sight, lightning as straight as an arrow hitting the ground like a laser shot from the sky. She grabbed the phone and dialled her husband's direct number. The line was dead and she started to worry.

Under her feet the floorboards started to shake like a small earth tremor. She looked north again but this time something appeared out of place and she ran to the street. The earthly horizon was rising, gaining height by the second.

Other people had emerged from their homes, all facing north, mesmerised by what was coming. She heard someone scream and saw them point as the roadway started to tremble and break apart.

"Milena… RUN!"

Her neighbour screamed at her as the leading edge of the earth tsunami hit the northern edge of the town.

She turned and ran slowly at first until she found traction on the icy asphalt. Others around her did the same, stampeding from their own deaths.

The Earth's surface rolled forward crushing and tossing everything it touched, houses, roads, nothing was exempt. The roaring rumble of the ground rolling like a hundred-foot wave was deafening and as she glimpsed behind, her ankles knocked and she stumbled.

With her hands outstretched to soften her impact she fell with a flesh scraping thud to the roadway where she tumbled onto her back.

Behind her the mountain of rocks and debris had slowed, replaced by bursting gas lines and raging infernos devouring everything. She lay there, shivering with fear yet her thoughts were with her husband. She knew he was dead, that dreaded day he'd spoken so much about had come. The Americans had struck with a nuclear missile and as the ground below her tore apart, her death came quickly and without pain.

Ten miles above her, a silver craft abruptly changed course at Mach seven towards Nevada.

27.
Bolivia

South of Tarija, Bolivia
May 20, 2005

Shielded behind a solid ten-foot rock wall and a sizable grassy moat, Walter Heathermann's massive retreat resembled a more modern era castle, an ideal fortress for a war criminal escaping prosecution.

The cottage largely built on timber and stone sat nestled amongst a deep forested area within the lower mountainous region of southern Bolivia. A tight gravel roadway split the tree line opening onto an immaculate manicured lawn, enshrouded in lush gardens leading to the front entry. Back beyond on the southern side, the lawn fell sharply away to a small lake edged by densely packed mahoganies and tall conifers.

Bennett and the others had flown in through Tarija during the morning and drove the thirty miles south in a rental van to Heathermann's estate. The trip had been slow, impeded by the old neglected winding road navigating through steep ravines until they reached their destination, an area of thick forest half a mile west from the house. From there they trekked to within sight of the estate where Josh merged himself with the underbrush and readied his weapon.

"No sign of life," he remarked from behind the sights of his Remington M24 sniper rifle.

"Yeah maybe early siesta," Bennett chuckled accompanied by an affirmative grin from Nicholette crouching to his right.

She stood and Bennett did the same checking his ammunition and drawing his Beretta. He signalled to Silvia to keep low out of sight behind a thick Balsa tree before turning to Josh, "Cover us."

Nicholette took the lead sprinting the thirty metres across the lawn with Bennett on her heels keeping his eyes fixed on the upstairs windows. Distinctly out of place in the Bolivian countryside the building advertised a European design with its steep pitched roof and shutter covered windows ideal for a gunman perched high waiting their arrival.

Something was wrong they realised approaching the house, the rear door ajar enough to display the blood splatter across the walls. Just inside a lone male was visible sprawled in his own sea of blood, as Bennett pushed cautiously through the doorway.

Five more lifeless bodies with bullet wounds lined the floor.

"All shot in the back of the head. Looks like an execution," Nicholette whispered.

Bennett nodded rolling each body over to inspect their faces while Nicholette maintained watch for the perpetrator.

"Heathermann's not among this lot, all too young," Bennett commented.

He returned to her side and together they finished the sweep of the house as Whittaker appeared.

"All okay in here?" he asked looking down at the dead.

"Yeah, Heathermann isn't here though," Nicholette responded.

"Might be his blood trail outside on the lawn. Looks badly injured too going by the amount that leads south into the forest," Whittaker said pointing towards the same door he entered through.

They hurried outside into the open to the sight of Silvia waving her hands frantically and pointing at the sky back over the house.

"GET DOWN," Bennett yelled.

The whistling hum of two missiles rushing in low from somewhere to the east gave meaning to her distress as the house detonated, brick and timber exploding in all directions.

28.
The Old Englishman

South of Tarija, Bolivia
May 20, 2005

The two Hellfire missiles tore the house apart on impact as it were made of tissue paper. Timber and stone erupted skyward blanketing the site in flaming debris as fire and black smoke ravaged the shredded remains.

Sprawled across the lawn, Bennett struggled to find his feet while his ears felt as though they'd been ripped from his head. Beside him Nicholette was up and helping Silvia to her feet. Josh on the other hand had been hit harder by the blast wave tossing him against the base of an old mahogany. He was unconscious and bleeding from a deep gash to his head.

"We can't stay here, give me a hand to move him," Bennett called reaching for Whittaker.

Behind them the deep snarling thump of helicopter rotors cutting the air drew their attention.

Bennett spun, yanked his rifle off his shoulder, raised it towards the Sikorsky Black Hawk materialising through the swirling smoke and unleashed half a magazine directly at the cockpit. It pushed skyward to expose a heavy armament of missiles hanging from the underside.

Bennett continued to fire as another missile launched, low over their heads to the west and ignited the forest. He watched the helicopter bank away to the north, scanning it for markings though the black metallic skin gave away nothing of their enemy's identity.

Further over, three men brandishing Heckler & Koch machine guns appeared from behind the burning house. Unaware they were running at him, Bennett expended his last few rounds at the retreating helicopter, determined to bring it down.

"Jon!" Nicholette screamed.

He turned in time to watch her drop to one knee and cut the three men down in one wide sweep of her rifle.

"Motorbikes!" he beckoned towards the driveway.

He had spotted two Kawasaki dirt bikes overturned on the roadway and their riders sprawled covered in blood next to them. Victims of the same three gunmen she has just killed, he suspected.

"You and Silvia take the bikes, meet you at the van," Bennett shouted over the new sounds of high revolution gunfire from above. The helicopter had returned and one gunman hung from the side clutching the electric Minigun firing what seemed a thousand rounds but unexpectedly, none came close. It was then he realised they weren't trying to kill him.

Nicholette doubled Silvia on the fastest of the two bikes, a Kawasaki 450 and revved it hard into a fishtailing frenzy out the gravel driveway towards the road. She was no stranger to high speed motorcycle riding having spent half her life evading the Russian Militsiya during her days as a rebel freedom fighter. Silvia on the other hand had only ever been on a motorbike once and clung nervously, her arms strangling Nicholette's waist.

Abandoning the containment gunfire on Bennett, the pilot spun the Black Hawk around, angled the nose down and fed the hungry turbines more fuel. Less than a few seconds and his rotors were snapping at the motorbike's rear wheel at sixty miles per hour.

Sponarava didn't need to look, she could taste its presence as the thundering swoosh of the rotors carved downwards through the air sparing Silvia's life by inches.

"Hold on," she yelled and yanked violently at the throttle.

Using her left boot like a professional motocross rider to skate the loose gravel, she dragged the handlebars tight left and accelerated towards an opening in the tree line.

The pilot watched, smirking as he depressed the missile's trigger. The helicopter's last Hellfire shot out from under its left stub wing and struck the earth a few feet behind the fleeing motorbike.

Seventy yards to the south, Bennett battled a new deluge of gunfire. An advancing group of four soldiers had emerged from the trees near the lake and started shooting, pushing him sprinting for the protection of the closest trees. But as he threw himself to the forest floor, a sudden sharp jolt of pain shot through his body. Under him, the hard steel barrel of Whittaker's M24 had flicked up hitting him in the sternum and briefly, he lay there in agony cursing to himself.

The sudden roar of the Hellfire exploding hurled him to his feet and he grabbed the sniper rifle.

The gunfire had stopped but the four soldiers were still moving quickly towards him using the tree line to disguise their approach. Using a low hanging branch to rest the weight of the sniper rifle, he steadied his aim and waited impatiently as the dust cleared from the explosion.

The Black Hawk hung low above the ground, edging slowly forward towards two dark figures scrambling across the open ground. From behind his dark mirrored helmet, the pilot watched Silvia stumble to the ground and Sponarava turn to grab her arm, yelling something at her. He glanced to the man sitting next to him.

"Kill them," the man ordered into his radio.

The soldier hanging from the rear door swung the Minigun around, took aim towards the women and fired.

"Noooo! You fucker!" Bennett screamed, squeezing the M24 trigger.

With the gunman centred behind the crosshairs he fired the weapon twice, the first ripped through the man's left arm while the second, a more unforgiving shot tore half his head off.

The pilot spun the Black Hawk in time to witness the muzzle flash of Bennett's rifle. The round pierced the windshield, passing within a few inches of killing the pilot and shot through the cockpit, past the man sitting next to him. Andre Matheson breathed a sigh of relief and grabbed the pilot's arm.

"WE NEED HIM ALIVE."

The pilot eased his finger off the Gatling gun trigger and instead, pulled the Black Hawk skyward away from the incoming rounds. Bennett kept up the barrage while the women clambered back onto the motorbike and escaped past the tree line.

As the thump of helicopter rotors dissipated, the sounds of the four approaching soldiers grew louder. He covered Whittaker's unconscious body with fallen leaves and fled deeper into the forest. Overhead the Black Hawk banked high in the sky and rolled back towards his position, buzzing low across the tree canopy while he clambered quickly under and around tree vines and small forest bushes. The distance between him and the soldiers grew greater and it wasn't long before he had disappeared into the darkness of the thick underbrush.

Somewhere to his left, a stifled moaning caught his attention. Crouching low and concealed, he edged forward, scrutinising the jungle from behind the sights of his handgun. Slowly pushing the low hanging branches aside with his free hand, he found the source of the sound, an old man partly hidden among the exposed roots of a ten-foot-wide mahogany. Walter Heathermann was near death, his shirt covered in blood oozing from a two inch hole in his chest. He peered up from his half-closed eyes and a smirk crossed his mouth.

"Arhh Mr Bennett we finally meet after all this time," he gasped as a trickle of blood spilled from the corner of his mouth.

"You're Walter Heathermann?"

"Yes, and not for much longer," acknowledging his impending death.

"What happened here?" Bennett asked.

"Your government wiping out any remaining trace of *The Trust*," he sniggered and added with a hint of sarcasm, "Cleaning up what you missed Jon."

Bennett ignored the comment. "Where is the weapon?"

Heathermann fought the onset of a violent coughing fit to answer as more blood burst from his mouth. "The weapon and the craft were stolen from us a year ago, where it is now, I do not know."

"Who stole it?"

"Your government."

"Why, I don't understand. Who in the government?"

"There is much you don't know. *The Trust* were never the real enemy Jon. We were about saving mankind."

"Real enemy, who's the real enemy?"

Heathermann paused sucking in a deep breath and allowing a sudden burst of pain to pass.

"Are you a Holy man, I mean, do you believe in God?" he asked.

Bennett half shook his head and Heathermann continued, "The Holy Bible speaks of two distinct immortals, God and Satan, the good and the bad as it's told. I was never a believer myself until I met the Fuhrer and he taught me a new understanding of the biblical scriptures. Before the war he had come into possession of an ancient scroll he believed originated from the Sumerian civilisation of five thousand years BC."

"Come on old man get to the point," Bennett demanded keeping watch around them for movement.

"Yes...yes... Those scriptures provided a new somewhat radical insight into the events leading up to the times of the Bible. When you consider the published conspiracy theory that the Sumerian people had not originated from Earth then the scroll had colossal meaning. In the first few months of World War II, the Fuhrer received a visit from an old Monk claiming he could offer him the complete domination of the world without the bloody ground war. Adolf laughed it off at first until the Monk shared his vision, a cataclysmic future of an unprecedented kind. It wasn't a world he planned on conquering. He witnessed in these visions, the true enemy."

Though the sun was still high in the afternoon sky, the darkness cast by the overhead tree canopy shielded their position to the approaching gunman thirty feet to the west.

"Who's the real enemy?" Bennett whispered after a flock of birds scattered from the trees just to their left.

"The Fuhrer was hysterical and enraged at what he'd seen. He ordered an immediate meeting with his most senior military advisers and they devised their extermination program, the death of the Jews."

"So, you're saying the Jews are the real enemy?" Bennett half snickered.

"He thought they were at the time, however the Monk's vision had not been clear," he declared as somewhere close by a branch snapped.

Bennett hurled himself from sight as a single gunshot rang out, echoing throughout the forest. In the darkness of the neighbouring dense shrubs, he watched as the shooter moved quickly to within a foot and fired another round into Heathermann's lifeless body for good measures.

Poor rambling fool, Bennett thought as he watched the gunman lift his radio mic to his mouth. "Sir, Red Wolf reporting, Heathermann is dead, it's a confirmed kill."

Bennett pounced, gun outstretched. "Drop your weapon, NOW."

The gunman, a tall blonde-haired man dressed in green unmarked fatigues ignored Bennett and swung towards him.

Two shots sounded but each from separate guns.

The gunman dropped to his knees, screaming in agony at the bullet hole in his chest, an inch from his heart. Bennett had been quicker in pulling the trigger while the blonde man's shot went high.

"Who are you?" Bennett demanded stepping in closer to remove his weapons.

"Fuck off Bennett, you're next on the list after Heathermann," he growled.

The radio crackled to life, "Red Wolf, do you have a fix on Bennett?"

"I guess you do." Bennett ripped the radio mic from the man's jacket lapel.

"Red Wolf is unable to take this call right now, perhaps call back later. Oh, and yes he has Bennett's position," Bennett answered in his usual sarcastic way.

"Still a smart ass I hear, well your time is up, surrender yourself now and Sponarava lives, do I make myself clear?" the radio spat back.

"Who is this?" Bennett challenged while he maintained his gun sight on his prisoner who was grinning a little too much for his liking.

"Who I am does not matter, it's what I want that does."

"And what's that?"

"What everyone wants Jon, the code. So, cut this bullshit chatting and show yourself back at the house or your girl dies."

Matheson wasn't one for negotiation, he had worked countless secret missions for the US Government and *The Trust* and knew how to play the game. Right now, he had a gun to Sponarava's head and enough weaponry around him to feel in control. He pushed the radio to her and said, "Convince your boyfriend."

"Jon, there's five of them here, KILL THEM ALL."

Blood sprayed across the lawn as her lip split open from the butt of Matheson's handgun.

"You harm her and your death will be more excruciating than you could ever imagine," Bennett calmly said into the radio and pulled the trigger killing his prisoner instantly.

29.

<u>Matheson</u>

South of Tarija, Bolivia
May 20, 2005

Bennett crawled on his belly under low growing shrubs towards the demolished house still suppressed by a raging inferno. Not far to his right, the Sikorsky sat resting on a section of open lawn, its rotors stationary and no sign of life. Further over to his left he caught a glimpse of Nicholette on her knees and by the blood across her face she had been beaten.

"Big mistake fucker," he uttered to no one.

Spread out in a circle around her were four men heavily armed with Heckler & Koch assault rifles and another who stood guard a few feet behind them. They each wore the distinctive green camouflage battle dress of the military and maintained a scanning vigilance over the tree line with their guns at the ready.

Bennett recognised the one behind her, an ex-Green Beret who led strike teams for the CIA during his own time in the Agency. Andre Matheson had a ruthless reputation and a prestigious combat record that complimented his rugged serious stance. Though a few years younger than Bennett, he appeared well aged with greying dark hair and a weathered face. At two hundred and fifty pounds, he was physically threatening, exuding intimidation with his every move.

For Bennett, looking at him now returned the discomfort of his past. The horrific memory had been instantaneous. Clinching the rifle he had stolen from the dead gunman; he resisted the invading urge to pull back the trigger and obliterate Matheson with bullets.

They had worked together on CIA missions in Afghanistan and Somalia assassinating key members of various terrorist outfits, but it was the Kuwait fiasco that ended his career. Six years earlier, a Senate Inquiry had declared him responsible for the deaths of forty innocent Kuwait citizens during a militarised assault on a suspect terrorist cell in Kuwait City. There had been no terrorist cell in the target apartment building, just innocent men, women and children.

Matheson testified at the Inquiry placing Bennett at the crime and leading the charge. He lied. Bennett was never present. Instead of appealing innocence, he chose to protect the lives of his Agents in Moscow where he was at the time of the murders. Disturbingly, the Agency hung him out to dry never revealing his true location. But when it came time to determine his fate, all fell silent and he walked free, just burdened by the humiliation of the dismissal from the Agency.

He had not laid eyes on Matheson since the Inquiry until now.

"Bennett show yourself or she dies," Matheson called.

Bennett cringed at the sound of the man's deep southern accent and waited a moment before unveiling his position.

He raised himself up and stepped out into the open to the sound of men shouting to drop his gun. He and Nicholette locked eyes while he let his rifle topple to the ground.

"On your knees Bennett," Matheson called grabbing her long ponytail and pressing his handgun into the back of her head.

It wasn't the first time she had been forced into a hostage situation and Bennett knew it. They made eye contact again and her confidence exuded in her smile.

"Matheson, let her go, you have me now," he shouted as the sudden surge of bitter pain across the back of his legs made him collapse uncontrollably. One gunman bound his hands behind his back while a second stood guard with his rifle inches from his head.

Matheson kicked Sponarava in the back pushing her forward to kiss the ground while he ordered one of his men to tie her up. Bennett watched from his kneeling position as Matheson approached him to within a few feet and stopped.

"Rip his shirt open," he ordered the man to his left.

Buttons popped and scattered loosely across the grass as the soldier wrenched the shirt back over Bennett's shoulders.

"What the fuck, where's the code Bennett?" Matheson demanded bending down to take a closer inspection.

"You let her go and I will show you," Bennett replied calmly. He had mastered the ability to cloak the tattoo though how, he couldn't explain. He had woken one day to find it vanished but faintly reappeared when he thought about it. The more he focused on it, the brighter it presented.

"Don't Jon, you know you can't," Nicholette yelled inviting the soldier closest to her to slam his rifle butt into her head. A new gash opened and fresh blood trickled down the side of her face.

"You're dead." Bennett glared at Nicholette's attacker.

Matheson reached into his pocket and pulled out a small digital camera.

"Blue Fox, kill her," Matheson ordered while maintaining eye contact with Bennett.

"WAIT!" Bennett screamed, "Okay you win, I'll show you."

Matheson side glanced over at the soldier he called Blue Fox and raised his hand. Sponarava scowled and swore as the soldier lowered his gun from her head.

Bennett waited a few seconds and closed his eyes emptying his mind of all thoughts. At first the symbols appeared faint, a blotchy discolouration on the skin until the passing of a few more seconds. Then the manifestation was complete.

Matheson stood watching, mesmerised and in awe at the one sight so many had sought. Thirteen unusually shaped symbols had illuminated in iridescent blue across Bennett's chest in an arc from shoulder to shoulder. Under the sunlight they appeared to glisten and pulsate in tune with his heartbeat.

Matheson raised the camera and snapped a few shots.

"Thank you Jon, finally we have your code recorded and I guess that means there is no longer a need for you," he laughed.

"Why are you doing this? Who do you work for now Matheson?" Bennett challenged.

"That really doesn't concern you Bennett, let's just say that the people you work for are no different to those who employ me."

Bennett ignored him continuing to maintain his stare, "So Matheson why'd you lie at the Senate Inquiry?"

"Jesus Christ Bennett that was eons ago, I was just following orders, nothing personal."

"Who's orders?" Bennett returned immediately.

"Senator Brown but I think you already knew that," he replied.

Bennett did however, he was just trying to buy some time.

"So many missions together you had my back Andre, so why turn against me?"

"Money my friend and lots of it," he replied pocketing the camera and turning towards the helicopter.

"Kill them both," he ordered as he walked off.

30.
Metal Storm

South of Tarija, Bolivia
May 20, 2005

An urgent succession of shots rushed in low from some distant position south of them along the tree line. The first obliterated the chest of the soldier to Bennett's right while the second took out the other. He jumped to his feet and dashed towards Nicholette. Her guard had been third to fall from a direct head shot, his brains spraying across her face.

Matheson sprinted towards the helicopter, firing randomly at the tree line and screaming orders into his radio.

Behind him, Bennett and Nicholette hastily removed their hand restraints and armed themselves with the dead men's weapons.

At thirty feet from the chopper, the tormenting crack of a high-speed projectile passing his head flung Matheson off balance and into the path of the sniper's next round. It spiralled cleanly through his upper leg and he stumbled dropping to one knee. The third shot nicked his shoulder as he crawled behind a section of building untouched by the earlier missile strikes.

The pilot cursed, the massive fourteen metre rotors were taking too long to reach take off speed. More gunfire, this time not far behind the helicopter, chinked off the tail assembly.

"Matheson... COME ON!" he screamed across the radio, turning his head in time to spot his leader bleeding and stumbling amid the barrage of Sponarava's gunfire. She had spotted him escaping and opened fire closing quickly on his position until his retaliatory shots drove her to the ground.

Fifty metres to the pilot's right and cloaked under a blanket of dead leaves, Whittaker shifted his sniper rifle. He compressed the trigger with infinite finesse and the pilot slumped forward, blood gushing from the gaping bullet hole in the side of his neck.

Bennett charged through the swirling rotor wash and yanked the dead pilot from his seat. Automatic rifle fire clattered in the background where Nicholette had Matheson pinned on the far side of the burning house. For the moment, he was out of her sight and bleeding badly.

He reached inside his jacket pocket.

"Hey Sponarava, I can save your baby, I have the sphere and the first code," he yelled across the crackle of fire and the roar of the chopper.

She had heard him and paused her advance reflecting on the thoughts of her unborn child.

"What do you want?" she called back.

"The helicopter and I will take you to it," he replied standing with his gun pointing loosely to the sky in an act of surrender.

She raised herself enough for him to calculate the distance.

Whittaker had made it halfway across the clearing when the flash of the explosion blinded him temporarily and it spun him face down into the dirt. Bennett had been scanning the instrument panel when the shock wave rocked the Sikorsky off its wheels and the machine lurched sideways.

The miniature concussion grenade detonated a few feet above the ground and like Thor's Hammer hurtling through the air slammed into Nicholette's chest. Matheson had waited for just the right moment before tossing it towards her before he dropped away from the impact.

Whittaker clawed forward clutching his weapon in one hand and pushing himself upright staggering each step towards Sponarava sprawled motionless on the ground. Behind him the helicopter's turbines were winding down and Bennett was in full sprint towards her.

"Nicholette!" he screamed, not caring who was left to shoot at him.

Somewhere further over behind the burning building a motorbike engine roared to life and accelerated away. Whittaker had seen it and charged past Sponarava firing his handgun at the vanishing taillight. At over thirty yards, each shot missed and Matheson was gone.

Bennett slid across the ground as Nicholette's eyes flickered open and she clutched at the pounding ache in her chest.

"Damn that hurt," she murmured through laboured breath pushing herself upright and accepting Bennett's comforting arms. The impact had been mostly deflected by the surrounding house wreckage and passed over her.

"He photographed the code, we need to get that camera," she said clutching at his arm to raise herself up, mostly unphased by the impact.

"He won't get far, come on we'll take the chopper," he replied and turned to Whittaker, "Good shooting, thanks, I owe you one."

"Where's my mother?"

"I told her to meet at the drop off point, the motorbike ran out of fuel and the chopper was back on us. I left her to divert it away," Sponarava answered.

He glared at her, disappointed and angry. "What the fuck, you left her."

"Whittaker!" Bennett yelled to get his attention.

"Go find her, we'll be back once we retrieve that camera," Bennett ordered, staring him down. He knew Whittaker's fate if he took Sponarava on.

They climbed on-board the chopper and within a few minutes were airborne over the densely forested hills north of the house site. Bennett maintained a low flight path scouring the only road, a narrow strip of dirt and gravel flowing through the base of a deep ravine heading towards Chaguaya. The heavy thump of the rotors echoed an intimidating presence across the valley and Matheson knew they were about to snap at his heels.

Within seconds the mini gun spun to life and a stream of lead ensued spraying the roadway behind him. One round clipped the rear guard before deflecting into the drive shaft and the bike catapulted with a savage jerk sideways in the loose gravel. As if riding an outraged rodeo beast for the first time,

Matheson was tossed violently through the air onto the sun hardened ground. There he rolled to his back to catch sight of the Sikorsky hovering thirty feet above the road and Bennett, helmetless, glaring down at him.

Twenty miles to the north another aircraft approached at speed.

31.
Captive

South of Tarija, Bolivia
May 20, 2005

Matheson raised his handgun and fired a rapid succession of shots mostly striking the underbelly until one pierced the windshield. Bennett pulled the Black Hawk skyward away from the incoming threat while down below their target was on his feet running, half stumbling on his bloodied leg into the concealment of the trees.

The pulsating rumble of rotors snatching and biting the air echoed through the valley as Bennett yanked back hard left on the control, kicked at both foot pedals and fed the turbines full throttle. Instantaneously the Sikorsky with a thunderous clap rolled back over into a downward dive towards the now empty roadway.

"Can you see him?" he yelled above the deafening roar of the rotors.

Continuing to scour the terrain, she returned a shake of her head.

"The forest is too dense, looks like we're on foot," he called while circling back to land near the road clearing.

All they could see to the south was an almost impenetrable blanket of mountain forest set between jagged ridge lines and steep sandstone cliff faces. To the west, a wall of rocky skyscrapers intermingled with the dark swirling clouds of an impending afternoon storm while to the east gentle sloping farmlands saturated the horizon.

"He can't be far," Bennett beckoned grabbing what weapons he could find in the chopper's rear cabin.

Armed with M4 assault rifles, they moved quickly into the shadows of the tree line. Bennett chose to shoulder the rifle and lead with his Beretta handgun. Nicholette preferred the M4.

"He's injured and bleeding," she whispered pointing towards blood spots across the ground, "Leg wound I reckon and by the shoe prints, he's limping on his left leg."

"Okay, stay alert. He won't be trying to outrun us," Bennett chuckled.

The sun was breaking in and out from behind the expanding storm clouds devouring the light by the minute under the interwoven tree canopy. The temperature was dropping quick and by nightfall would edge close to freezing, possibly colder if the storm hit.

Bennett grabbed Nicholette's arm and raised his hand signalling her to stop. She reacted out of habit, dropped low amongst the shrubs and lifted her gun. Bennett had done the same and was pointing towards a tall rock outcrop twenty feet further over. Something had caught his eye, a brief reflection of light bouncing off Matheson's wristwatch.

Nicholette peered through the foliage as Matheson stepped from behind the rock.

"GUN!" Bennett yelled pushing her sideways and they both fell flat to the forest floor.

The whistle and ping of rounds shredding leaves around them was all they heard for the next few seconds until it was replaced by the distinctive click of Matheson's gun reaching empty. Bennett leapt forward, rifle up firing fully automatic in Matheson's direction however the man had fled.

"It's going to be dark soon, it'll be quicker finding him if we separate," Nicholette whispered.

Bennett moved quickly to outflank him while she continued tracking his blood trail through the forest.

After a few minutes of edging slowly through the thick undergrowth, Bennett froze at the sudden sound of a single gunshot followed by silence.

Thirty yards to his east, Sponarava was scrambling desperately for her weapon. Next to her, Matheson was doing the same. Just moments before, he had waited like a starving lion stalking a young wildebeest until she stepped into view.

Her peripheral senses had alerted her just in time to deflect the tree branch from pulverising her face. Matheson lunged and she spun, raised her gun and squeezed the trigger. The single round shot high as her boot clipped an exposed tree root and he charged his full weight into her. The impact threw her sideways and the rifle toppled from her grip, slipping from sight down a shallow embankment.

The ground under their feet broke loose and they fell, him punching her while she clawed for her handgun. Then as she yanked it from under her belt and turned it on him, he threw one massive punch into her face, nearly knocking her head from her shoulders and snatched the gun cleanly from her. She stumbled to her knees.

"Okay bitch, time for you to die," he growled.

She regained her balance and climbed slowly to her feet watching him as he tracked her movements with his gunsights.

"That's far enough."

She held her ground like a wild cat protecting her territory and secured her best footing. They locked eyes in a cold stare, her seductive green emeralds now expressionless killers as she transformed from expecting mother to the notorious Soviet assassin.

"I admire you Sponarava, you are one lethal bitch and for that I will make your death painless," he laughed.

"Nicholette, don't kill him, we need some answers."

He half turned towards Bennett stepping from the shadows of the forest with his hands raised above his head and smiling at her.

"Always the comedian hey Bennett! But this time, the laugh is on you," Matheson called and turned the gun towards him and pulled the trigger.

On cue, the glint of silver shot through the air while Sponarava returned her smile towards Bennett. He'd seen the small silver blade concealed in her hand and gave her the distraction she needed. At that exact moment Matheson turned his attention to Bennett, it gave her the opening and she struck like a viper. The four inch blade tore its way through his gun hand, slicing three fingers clean from his hand.

Bennett rushed across and grabbed the bloodied gun.

"Okay Andre you know the drill, you answer my questions and you get to limp out of here. If not, then I guess it's bad luck for you!"

Matheson sneered attempting to camouflage the searing agony while he cradled his damaged hand into his shirt. The torrent of blood from his leg gunshot had subsided to a trickle but his severed fingers were flooding his shirt.

"Where's the camera?" Bennett asked stepping in to search Matheson's clothing and pushing the Beretta's muzzle into the man's head.

"Don't know, must have dropped it," Matheson replied as Bennett moved back empty handed.

"Not the answer I was looking for," Bennett said looking over at Nicholette who had retrieved her rifle and stood poised with the barrel pointed at his head.

It was a side of her that Bennett knew all too well, the aggressive killer who still had a most wanted mugshot on the wall of most Russian Federal Security Service buildings. Her murderous past was nothing to be proud of and like Bennett, she had her share of skeletons in the closet, though life had now changed. The past couple of years had been her best, discovering real love for the first time with a man her equal and soon to be father of their child. It had softened her somewhat until now.

"You know Andre, you're lucky I showed up when I did. Nicholette here would have killed you without as much as a blink of an eye."

She returned her own smug grin towards Matheson while Bennett moved in close to him.

"Take your boots off," he said.

"Come on, as if I'm going to run?" Matheson replied.

Bennett plunged his gun muzzle into the man's shoulder, "I don't think it's worth you losing use of your shoulder now is it? Take off your boots."

Matheson complied and removed his boots followed quickly by Bennett stripping the laces and tossing the boots. With the help of Nicholette they dragged him backwards a few feet to the trunk of a small tree where they sat him upright against it. They pulled his hands back behind the tree and Bennett bound his hands with the laces.

"This just saves me shooting you in the back if you did run," Bennett laughed walking back around to face their prisoner.

"Now let's start this again. Where is the camera?"

"Like I said, I must have dropped it somewhere back there in the jungle," he replied motioning with his head behind them.

Bennett looked down at Matheson's smug expression and with a backhand, he flung the butt of his handgun across the man's face. A single line of blood trickled down from a small rupture in his cheek and dripped to his shirt.

He looked up shrugging off the attack and uttered, "I'm disappointed, I thought your first question would be the location of the pulse weapon. That is why the President sent you, isn't it Jon?"

Bennett hesitated as Nicholette interrupted, "What makes you think the President sent us?"

"Oh come on, the people I work for know more about you than you do yourself. London ring any bells? You of all people should know that, the US Administration is more corrupt than ever before and no one is exempt from greed. Four years ago, you decapitated *The Trust* but did you really think that it all ended there. If you did then you are ignorant fools."

"Okay Matheson cut the bullshit, then you tell us where the weapon is?" Bennett demanded.

Matheson grimaced from the fresh throbbing of his wound and snickered, "Do you really think I'm going to tell you anything, clearly you are mistaken Jon."

The forest around them had gone strangely quiet, the cicadas had ceased all song and the breeze slapping at the treetops had died to breathless. The only noise was the distant rumble of thunder way off to the west until Bennett moved in on their captive.

A tortuous howl fractured the stillness scattering birds to the heavens while down below Bennett pushed his hand in deeper. Matheson kicked and wrestled to escape but as Bennett's fingers penetrated his leg wound, he battled to maintain consciousness.

"FUCK YOU BENNETT," Matheson screamed and spat, fighting the agony of a man's fingers crawling inches inside his leg.

His face contorted around clenched teeth and sweat drowned his shirt as he resisted the defeat of torture.

"The location of the pulse weapon please Andre?"

Matheson pushed his head back staring to the treetops and feeling the boot laces slashing deeper into his wrists while he tugged desperately to break free.

"You know Jon, all will be revealed in time, our world will have no choice but to accept the changes coming. For too long we have suffered at the hands of corrupt political systems and the everyday lies. You follow your President, but he is really your enemy and for too long he and his predecessors have kept a great secret from the world," Matheson answered with increasing laboured breath.

"Where is the weapon? I won't ask again," Bennett repeated ignoring Matheson's attempt to deflect the conversation.

"I don't know," he replied snorting a retaliatory laugh looking over at Nicholette and instantly his pained expression faded. "Your baby will die, you know that don't you?" he said pausing a moment and adding, "But it doesn't have to."

She stepped past Bennett and grabbed him by his shirt collar raising his head to her level. "Where is the sphere?" she barked at him pulling him up higher exposing her ripped muscular arms and a distinct exhibition of her strength.

He just returned a silent smile and she hollered in his face this time with the bonus of raging spittle. The mention of her baby dying had struck the right nerve and triggered the resurgence of her old self. Maternal emotions had taken control. They locked eyes as Bennett placed his hand on her shoulder to calm her down.

"Don't worry, he will talk," Bennett reassured as she released her hold and he slipped back down against the tree.

Without warning, she raised her rifle and fired a single shot.

32.
Interrogation

South of Tarija, Bolivia
May 20, 2005

With his face a mosaic of contortion and howling in a dialect perhaps only the most insane could comprehend, Matheson glared back at Sponarava standing over him. His eyes fluttered under the strain of the intense burn of the bullet hole in his abdomen and he sensed the onset of shock as his legs trembled.

"WHERE IS THE SPHERE?" she screamed at him.

Bennett blinded by surprise had reacted too slow to stop her shooting Matheson. Her swiftness had always been unchallenged, something he had accepted though now he was cursing as he took the gun from her.

Matheson closed his eyes and clinched tight his jaws to fight the invading agony as fresh blood drenched the ground upon which he sat.

"Jon I am surprised you don't know more than you do," Matheson muttered.

"Then enlighten me," Bennett answered.

"Lying at the Inquiry wasn't my proudest moment I must admit but you need to understand there was more at stake if I didn't. Back then *The Trust* controlled everyone and everything political. I followed my orders and I stayed alive."

The bullet had missed vital organs, a deliberate action by Sponarava but still the pain it caused was intense.

"Yeah yeah, bullshit! The sphere and weapon, where are they?" Bennett demanded.

"Stand aside Jon, I will make him talk," she announced edging back into Matheson's face and advertising the razor sharp blade in her hand.

He sneered as Bennett seized the knife and pushed her away.

"Tell me what we need to know Andre," Bennett asked calmly staring closely at the silver blade in his hand.

Matheson looked up at the treetops and the scattered glimpses of the darkening sky, "Hear that? No matter what I tell you, none of you are getting out of here alive."

At that moment, the trees shuddered and birds took flight. A high pitched roar intensified somewhere above them as a military helicopter screamed past and banked north.

"Reinforcements Jon!" Matheson said half laughing but cut short by the intensifying pain gripping his belly.

Bennett stood scouring the sky through the gaps in the trees and then turned towards Matheson, "Well that's too bad for you."

He dropped to his knee and thrust the knife deep into Matheson's abdomen, an inch from the bullet hole and made one half twist. Matheson screamed and arched backwards, clenching his jaws as the fierce burning agony terrorised his body.

"Where is the sphere?" Bennett urged tilting the knife deeper.

"You know how this goes and you know how long I can keep this up." Bennett extracted the blade slowly and pressed it down into the bullet hole, starting to twist it as he did.

"Okay okay, you win," Matheson yelled as his mental breaking point was breached.

"The sphere is always in one man's physical possession, never out of his sight."

A single gunshot whistled through the trees ending with a fleshy thud followed by another slamming against the tree, inches above Matheson's head.

"SHOOTER!" Bennett yelled grabbing Matheson and pulling his body closer to the ground in the protection of the tree. Nicholette had already calculated the shooter's rough location near the summit of a nearby ridge and was saturating it with suppressive fire.

"He's been hit," Bennett called watching the fountain of blood pulsate from their prisoner's neck wound. The sniper's bullet had partly severed the man's artery and blood was squirting freely with every beat of his heart.

"Matheson stay with us, who has the sphere?"

Blood oozed profusely from under his hand as he pushed down with his clenched fist to slow the bleed.

"Andre, who has the sphere?"

"Eckhard Banks," he murmured.

"The CEO of the Orionis Andromeda Corporation?" Bennett quizzed.

Matheson nodded, "Yes."

"How do we find the weapon?" Nicholette asked urgently. Bennett had slowed the bleeding, but they were witnessing the swift arrival of his death, his skin becoming bloodless pale.

His head slumped forward, semi-conscious.

"Matheson, wake up, where is the weapon?" Bennett yelled, shaking the dying man's shoulders.

"Weapon needed... Provenance! Need to stop Provenance."

His speech had fatigued in the preceding seconds and his breathing was like the panting of an old dog on a scorching day.

"Provenance, what is Provenance?" Bennett demanded, pulling his head close to amplify his question.

"President's secret," Matheson replied as he expelled his last breath.

Bennett held the man's lifeless body for a few seconds before he let it slip back to the ground.

"What do you think that's all about?" Sponarava asked.

Bennett returned a bewildered shake of his head, "Come on, back to the chopper. We need answers."

They ran low ducking and weaving their way through tree branches in what Bennett hoped was the right direction towards the helicopter. He led the way with Nicholette cracking the same pace behind him and close enough he could hear her pounding breath. Around them the dense forest was opening to sporadic patches of bare exposed ground among scant trees.

"Jon ... GUN!" she screamed.

At full stride he caught glimpse of the M16 swing towards him and engage from ten metres away. Rounds cracked the trees either side and one clipped his arm shearing a shallow track of flesh while hurling him sideways. As he stumbled into the cover of nearby thick undergrowth, he raised his handgun and fired at the shooter. It did little to subdue his attacker as a new barrage of gunfire shredded the surrounding trees, forcing him to his belly among the vines and tall weeds. Then all went quiet, the rounds stopped and Bennett launched to his feet, gun out ready.

"Jon, you okay?" Nicholette called from a short distance away.

At her feet laid the attacker, dead. She had drilled two rounds into him, one in the head and the other in the chest while on the run. Her marksmanship had become her renown trademark having matured inside the training fields of the Soviet Special Forces. Single-handedly killing seventeen KGB officers in thirty minutes had earned her the notoriety as the 'Butcher of Volgograd' and the most feared assassin of the 90's. But executing her tyrant father in cold blood after years of violent sexual abuse had dictated her course in life.

Bennett acknowledged her shooting with an affirmative nod as he rummaged through the dead man's pockets. They found nothing of his identity or who he worked for and his black unmarked military like clothing offered no clues.

"Definitely US military by those tats," Bennett remarked pulling the dead man's sleeves up.

"We got company," Nicholette whispered pointing her gun across the clearing.

Fifty yards to the north, five men dressed in the same black battledress advanced from the tree-line.

"Come on, have to find another way to the chopper," Bennett called returning low into the cover of the dense forest.

They sprinted back the way they'd come through thick undergrowth until the sudden movement of another gunman blocking the path forced Bennett to fire.

"FUCK... Bennett don't shoot!" the gunman screamed with his hands and sniper rifle raised above his head.

Nicholette raced forward with her rifle raised and the crosshairs firmly on the man's head.

"Josh, what are you doing here? Where's Silvia?" she responded glancing across at Bennett who was peering over the top of his handgun sights.

"Where's Matheson, is he dead?" Whittaker asked lowering his hands.

"Not so fast Josh, answer the question, where's Silvia?" Bennett responded maintaining his sights on him. He was sensing Nicholette was thinking the same as him by the way her rifle barrel was still in Whittaker's face.

"Safe back at the van, another chopper arrived shortly after you left, flew in low and took off in your direction. I figured you could do with my help. Now can you get the guns out of my face," Whittaker appealed looking from Bennett to Nicholette.

"How did you get here?" Bennett asked half lowering his gun.

"Motorbike... the other one at the house."

"Yeah Matheson is dead," Nicholette added stepping back before asking "Are you injured?"

He looked down at his blood stained sleeve and laughed, "Nothing serious, near miss with a tree, motorbike wanted to go straight, I didn't!"

She laughed as Bennett made a hand gesture to start moving and briefed Whittaker, "We got five heavily armed soldiers between us and the chopper... need to find a way around them."

"Did Matheson say anything?" Whittaker asked.

Bennett didn't answer, he had raised his hand to signal silence and within seconds the reason became clear. A burst of gunfire cracked through the trees as two gunmen dressed in black emerged followed by another two. Sponarava was the first to return fire hitting one of them in the chest at thirty yards, though it did nothing to lessen the incoming barrage of lead.

"Come on, we can't stay here," Bennett screamed above the rattle of their automatic weapons and yanked at Nicholette to commence their retreat.

Whittaker held back firing into the trees at anything moving and called, "You go, I'll hold them off."

"What about you?" Nicholette returned from her crouching position beneath the bushes.

"Pick me up on that ridge," he answered pointing towards the east at a prominent sandstone cliff face rising high above the jungle top.

Bennett nodded his confirmation leaving Whittaker to continue the suppressive fire from the cover of a large tree.

They scurried low through the thick underbrush to the lessening sound of gun clatter until Bennett skidded to a halt and dropped to his knee. Ahead of him through a loose patch of shrubs and vines their Sikorsky sat motionless in the same road clearing where they'd left it.

"I don't like it, could be a trap," Nicholette interjected.

"Agree, but we have no choice, that chopper is our best escape plan," he replied and stepped into the open, "Cover me."

All remained quiet until Bennett ignited the turbines and the rotors commenced their windup. A loud whirring howl rebounded across the jungle growing with intensity as Bennett fed the machine more throttle and the Black Hawk lifted inches from the ground.

To his left, Nicholette was sprinting at full stride with a gun in both hands and screaming something at him. Within seconds bullets started piercing the cockpit.

"Hang on," he muttered and spun his bird around and depressed the trigger to the nose mounted Gatling.

The mini gun whirred to life with a high reverberating metallic hum as it spat lead at an unforgiving rate scattering the attackers back into the trees. Nicholette had reached the chopper and climbed onboard taking up a position behind the side mounted gun.

"Come on, let's get the fuck out of here," she screamed but the chopper shuddered violently sideways throwing her off balance against the gun and her footing slipped.

Up front, Bennett was facing a new dilemma.

33.
<u>Apache</u>

South of Tarija, Bolivia
May 20, 2005

"We got a big problem," Bennett called back to Nicholette who was dangling from the side gun and wrestling the machine's sway to climb back on board.

She scrambled forward into the cockpit to the sight of a demonic beast filling the windshield. Under each stub wing dangled an array of Stinger and Hellfire missiles while the underbelly M230 Chain Gun countered their every move. Like a spider ready to pounce on an entangled moth, the sleek Apache attack helicopter quivered in the air twenty feet from their position waiting to strike.

Bennett had a firm grasp on the controls but with each attempt to escape, the faster more agile Apache blocked their path.

The radio crackled to life, "Bennett, ground your bird... or I'll be forced to fire."

Bennett gradually edged their helicopter upwards clearing the treetops while the Apache mirrored the same move. He knew their opponent was far superior in fighting prowess, yet he continued to ignore the pilot's orders.

"Bennett this is your last warning, ground your helicopter NOW."

"Don't think so," Bennett mumbled, pushing the helicopter's nose forward and depressed the trigger.

His nose mounted Minigun spun to life inundating the Apache in a fury of over two hundred rounds, mostly missing their target.

Next to him Nicholette screamed, "Missile!"

In less than a second the Hellfire missile struck the tail assembly blasting it clean off and the Black Hawk spun like a child's spin top. Inside the cockpit the centrifugal forces smothered Bennett's attempt to pull back the power, while Sponarava's knuckles grew white from gripping the seat and her face drained the same shade. Flying had never been her friend and right now, crashing wasn't about to help her phobia.

"Hold on, it's going to be a rough one," he declared watching the ground invade the windshield as the nose slipped forward.

She grabbed what she could to hold herself up, staring outside at the revolving landscape as the helicopter spun and shuddered under Bennett's fight to keep them alive. To her it was like an 'out of control' sideshow ride and soon the connecting metal rods and hydraulics would snap tossing them to their death.

Then with an abrupt whiplash, they slammed nose down into the earth bouncing violently onto their sides jarring what felt like every bone in her body. The rotors severed in all directions ricocheting across the surrounding trees while up above the Apache pilot watched with a slight smile.

Bennett had braced himself unlike Nicholette who was flung without mercy against the instrument panel and belted unconscious. Then as the rotational momentum eased and the wounded helicopter ploughed to a grinding halt across the open ground, another hazard rushed forward.

Gale force winds from the Apache's rotors swept the crash site as a small group of armed men stormed the cockpit dragging Bennett resisting into the clearing. Behind him another two had the easier task of removing Nicholette's motionless body until she stirred.

The one to her left wore the full brunt of her retaliation with a hooking right arm across his jaw and cheek. She twisted and rolled to her feet as the second one slammed his handgun into the rear of her head and she collapsed to the ground.

Bennett had witnessed her break loose, but he was powerless to assist, his body was rapidly falling victim to a powerful neurotoxin injected into his neck. The men had been briefed well on their prisoners and weren't about to take any unnecessary risks.

As Nicholette suffered the same fate, another larger helicopter thumped overhead and shortly afterwards, landed next to the crashed Black Hawk. They were loaded onboard and within a few minutes it departed under the escort of the hovering Apache.

Four thousand miles away, Ryan Adams watched the satellite feed as the helicopters flew northwest towards El Alto.

He dialled an encrypted number, "Mr President, as expected Bennett and Sponarava have been captured in Bolivia."

"Excellent, keep me updated of their progress," he replied and added, "Ryan, I don't need to remind you of the urgency to get this done."

"Understand Sir. What about Whittaker and his mother?" Adams asked.

"We don't need them," he replied and hung up.

34.
Pods

Nevada, USA
May 21, 2005

At thirty thousand feet above the barrenness of the Nevada desert two cylindrical man-sized pods hurtled towards the earth, each spiralling and tumbling end on end against the planet's gravitational forces. Just moments before, an unmarked C-5 Galaxy flying north had jettisoned them while down below a small military unit waited impatiently on the ground.

Inside the metallic capsules, the cargo remained in their drug induced state of paralysis. Bennett and Sponarava had endured the ten hour flight from El Alto never once able to move or communicate. Around them their captors offered nothing of their identity, just men and women dressed in dark military attire. It wasn't until they started moving him to the pod that he caught sight of Nicholette imprisoned in the same manner. Fighting was futile, the chemicals in his veins had extinguished his movement and suppressed his senses.

He watched from a small round porthole as clouds rushed past and the barren mountainous horizon spun uncontrollably in all directions. Then abruptly the pod shuddered and jerked as a silver parachute plucked him from his spiralling death.

Less than fifty feet further over the same was happening to Sponarava's pod as she witnessed her own tumbling nightmare. She watched as the ground closed in just moments before her pod smacked hard against the rock and sand of Papoose Lake, an aged lakebed ravaged by decades of extreme heat and dryness.

The sun was slipping towards the west while a violent windstorm swept the terrain, heaving dust a mile high. In the thick of it and driving at speed a single large truck bearing similarity to an army troop carrier made a direct line for the downed pods. On board a heavily armed greeting party of six soldiers waited anxiously ready to retrieve their prisoners and retreat to the seclusion of their base.

As the truck skidded to a halt, they rushed forward battling the sand blasting their faces and hoisted the pods into the concealment of the rear canopy. The raging dust blanket overhead disguised their presence as the truck vanished into an elaborately camouflaged passageway tunnelled into the mountainside overlooking the lake.

The massive steel door shrieked and groaned as the hydraulics lowered it slowly to the floor and the locks slid into place. The truck's engine roared and it rolled forward into a long expertly machined tunnel ending at the doorway to a giant elevator. It ascended six levels at a low struggling speed until the doors opened onto a brightly lit hangar of exceptional magnitude, three football fields across.

Under the watchful eye of three people standing on the observation deck suspended forty feet above the floor, the truck drove slowly to the furthest end of the hangar where the soldiers alighted. The pods were quickly unloaded onto pushcarts while up above the three moved quickly from the deck.

Bennett watched from the small porthole as his pod shuddered along another well illuminated hallway, ceiling lights passing every few feet and all the while his thoughts rested with Nicholette and her fate.

The pushcart stopped and he witnessed for the first time the face of one of his captors. A man in his early thirties, curly red hair and narrow set blue eyes peered down at him. The paralytic drug ravaged his nervous system, deadening every muscle and terminating all movement. His eighth code nanobots had grossly failed him, the toxic incursion proving too powerful, resulting in a complete neuromuscular seizure.

The red headed man receded from view as a bright light swamped his vision accompanied by the metallic squeal as the pod opened. He was disorientated momentarily unable to see, except the ceiling above and the rushing of soldiers in his peripheral vision. Two dressed in desert fatigues moved to his side and dragged his powerless body from the pod.

The room was like one he'd encountered a few years earlier, an unusual design and only one true purpose he recalled. While the guards held his limp body loosely upright, he scoured the confines of the ten metre wide circular chamber. Above him an enormous stark white ceiling towered high over the very item he sought, a marble like solid sphere of archaeological influence sitting atop a three foot steel pedestal. Similar to the size of a basketball it displayed uniqueness, dull machined chrome with three hundred engraved hieroglyph symbols covering its extremity.

Bennett felt the tingling rush of anxiety tear through his body and yet he was powerless to move. The sphere was Nicholette's only chance of survival and here it was a few feet from his grasp. Like the Sphere of Anubis destroyed at Kehlstein four years earlier, this one originated from the same makers and appeared identical. Each symbol lightly carved into the surface depressed like a key on a keypad and with the correct sequence of thirteen symbols, the sphere activated in a brilliance of light.

Now it was lifeless, however, as Bennett was dragged closer and his boots scraped the hard tiled floor, a soft harmonious drone emanated from deep inside. The dull surface grew translucent and the symbols materialised brighter in a shade of azure blue. The two soldiers hesitated almost dropping Bennett while fixated on the transformation unfolding before them. Behind them the three from the observation deck entered the room.

"Remove his shirt," commanded the tallest of the three.

The soldiers yanked his shirt back over his shoulders exposing his bare chest. Bennett resisted but only in his mind, his body disobeyed.

The sphere appeared to hover, rising an inch above the pedestal and gyrate steadily exposing itself. The man passed by without making eye contact with Bennett and stood scrutinising the sphere like a child would a puppy in a pet store. Dressed in a dark business suit, the man displayed all the same characteristics as those of the Six, the insatiable hunger for domination. He turned to face their prisoner.

Bennett was staring into the cold dark eyes of Eckhard Banks.

Banks nodded and Bennett sensed someone to his right, as his peripherals detected a fluid filled syringe. Within seconds the sharp twinge in his neck confirmed the hypodermic needle piercing his skin and almost instantly, it took effect. A few more seconds and the symbols materialised across his chest, no longer concealed by the involuntary power of his mind.

His vision was blurred as he swayed loosely in a state of drugged delirium with no control or defence against those holding him upright. Banks commenced entering codes into the sphere pausing only to double check Bennett's chest before pressing the corresponding symbol. As each engaged, it illuminated brighter and the resonating sound intensified.

After the twelfth symbol he stopped, looked past Bennett and waited.

"I'll do it," echoed a voice from the rear of the room.

He stepped back watching his commander take centre stage and approach the sphere.

Bennett's eyes roared disbelief, his confusion muddled with the lack of clarity.

"Thankyou Jon," she said passing by him and pressing down the final symbol.

Vibrant white light erupted simultaneously from the three hundred symbols momentarily blinding the room. Bennett closed his eyes shielding the brilliance just as the drug reached maximum and his head slumped forward into the dawning of a new nightmare.

35.
<u>Lost</u>

3 miles south of Papoose Lake,
Nevada desert
May 22, 2005

A lone figure stumbled aimlessly across the naked terrain, his boots snagging rocks while his mind wavered under a drug induced narcosis. All around the land was flat, barren, littered with spindle grass and wind swept gullies. The surrounding horizon offered very little other than an alien world with mountainous ridge lines blurred by the eerie red haze of the sun setting behind a rising dust cloud.

Bennett had been wandering for hours without direction or purpose and with every step he fought impatiently to recall recent events. His mind was muddled, he had no recollection of who he was and a thumping ache behind his eyes tormented his every attempt to remember.

In the distance a narrow stretch of poorly maintained asphalt granted him purpose and his pace quickened as the rattling of an old diesel lorry drowned out the soft whistling breeze. He watched as the truck slowed to a squealing halt under the asphyxiating veil of black exhaust.

"Hey mister, you okay?" the driver, a man in his early twenties asked staring Bennett up and down.

"What ya doing way out here?" he continued without breath.

"That I don't know," Bennett replied hesitantly, alerting the young drivers' suspicions.

"What's ya name? I'm Kaden Bishop," the driver asked pushing the passenger door open and beckoning with his hand to get in.

"That I don't know either," Bennett replied hoisting himself up into the truck's cabin.

"So what do ya remember?" Bishop enquired.

Bennett shifted uncomfortably on the hard aged seat focusing his attention outside the cabin into the quick fading afternoon light.

"Nothing... I don't remember anything or who I am."

Bishop nudged the heavy lorry forward grinding up through the gears leaving behind a trail of engine smoke ruffling in the breeze.

"Where you heading?" Bennett asked still fixated on the horizon as if expecting his memory to instantly materialise.

"Indian Springs, it's about forty miles south of here. I have a friend there who might be able to help."

"Help? What kind of help do you think I need?" Bennett responded.

"Help you remember your past."

Bennett transferred his focus from the absence of outside to the driver of the rickety old lorry, "You say it like you've done this before."

"Some strange things happen out here in these places, you're not the first I've come across like this. There have been others without their memories."

"Others? Strange things? What are you talking about?" Bennett responded with an inquisitive expression.

"Some weird shit, people just wandering around and like you, no memory of how they ended up here. Most of my friends reckon its some alien abduction shit going on and the government is part of it."

"Huh! Alien abduction, do you really believe all that?"

"Don't know but it's the best explanation I've heard so far and well, kinda fits the area."

Bennett interjected, "What do you mean, fits the area?"

"To the north is Area 51 and just back there behind us is Papoose Lake."

Bennett returned a puzzled expression.

"You know, Area 51, the secret government underground facility. They got heaps of secret shit there. The big one though is Papoose Lake," he continued.

"Papoose Lake! What's there?" Bennett asked.

"Sector Four. Bunch of people reckon there's a secret alien base there somewhere, you know weird spaceship shit. They call it Sector Four. I find it all spooky and probably complete bullshit."

Bennett watched and listened to the young driver chatter for the next fifteen minutes about one conspiracy theory after the next while the truck chugged south towards Indian Springs. None of what he had said made any sense, his mind was still void of memories.

Headlights in their mirrors blinded them like a flash grenade and sudden gunfire drowned the gurgling drone of the truck engine.

"Fuck! Hang on, some fucker is shooting at us," Bishop yelled pulling hard at the wheel and slipping on the loose roadside gravel.

Another burst of gunfire, this time shredding the front left tyre and slicing through the cabin shattering the windscreen. Bishop slammed hard on the brakes in panic losing control as the old heavy lorry jack-knifed.

Sliding on its side, the truck howled and groaned in metallic agony as the steel frame scraped the asphalt, sparks flew and the noise echoed out across the valley floor.

Inside the cabin, Bennett and the driver held tight against the dominating force of momentum clawing at their bodies.

Ten yards back, two gunmen advanced slowly towards the settling truck wreck.

"Wait here," Bennett said, not fully comprehending why or what he was doing and climbed through the open windscreen.

The gunmen dressed in dark jackets and jeans rose their weapons at Bennett as he walked boldly towards them.

"That's far enough Bennett," the taller of the two instructed and fired one round into the road at his feet.

Bennett stopped mid stride.

"You know me? Who am I?" Bennett asked confused by their instant recognition of him but more because he didn't feel the slightest intimidation of two handguns in his face.

"On your knees," the gunman demanded pressing his gun closer towards him.

Bennett lowered himself slowly to the sounds of Bishop exiting the truck cabin behind him.

"Kill the driver," the gunman said with a small glance towards his colleague.

The second gunman was a few inches shorter but more muscular than his leader and pushed quickly past Bennett.

From the black abyss of his memory suppressed mind something snapped and Bennett rose up from his haunches, striking the second gunman in the throat.

The gunman fell clutching at his neck while Bennett snatched his loaded Glock, spun while firing two quick rounds into the first gunman. Both struck him in the face just above his eyes and he dropped lifeless to the road.

The second gunman recovered swiftly to his feet and tackled Bennett to the ground like a national league footballer blocking the game winning touchdown. Bennett crumpled under the driving force, falling backwards against the hardness of the road surface as the attacker kicked the gun from his hands.

Though smaller, the attacker was swift and powerful striking three times before Bennett could retaliate. Blood burst from his mouth, two punches had found their mark while the third deflected from the defensive swing of his arm just before he unleashed a karate style side kick to the attacker's chest. His size eleven boot winded the man and it gave Bennett an opening.

He pounced unleashing a volley of punches and head high kicks dropping the attacker dazed and desperately inhaling breath. It had taken him less than ten seconds to kill one and render the second defenceless as he snatched the man's handgun.

"Who are you and what's your purpose here?" Bennett demanded pointing the gun at the man's head.

"And how do you know me?" he added.

His prisoner spat blood but said nothing in reply, only glared at Bennett and pushed himself up onto his knees.

"I won't ask again," Bennett urged prepping the trigger and catching a glimpse of Bishop standing next to the truck's cabin watching, confused and dumbstruck at what he had witnessed.

In that split second he shifted his gaze, the man launched at Bennett, striding four short paces until the first of three bullets tore him down. Bennett had seen the movement in his peripherals and fired. Each round tore the man's chest apart and he collapsed dead onto the roadway to join his colleague.

But then as he turned, Bishop gasped. Blood poured from between Bennett's fingers as he clutched a small silver dagger lodged in his belly. He looked down at it realising the gunman had flung it at him the moment he'd pulled the trigger.

Bishop rushed and grabbed him to soften his fall as he buckled under the searing agony of the three inches of steel inside his abdomen.

"Take their car," Bennett murmured pointing back at the dead men's black SUV parked a short distance over.

"Okay hang in there," Bishop called dragging him to his feet towards the idle vehicle. Bennett was just on the heavy side of two hundred pounds and Bishop was half that, so lifting his near unconscious weight proved exhausting.

"Search them, I need to know who they are," Bennett muttered as he passed out.

Thirty minutes later Bishop drove at reckless speed fishtailing and raising dust along a narrow winding road into the isolated rugged mountains fifteen miles southwest of Indian Springs. On the back-seat Bennett drifted in and out of consciousness while his body trembled and shook as if battling an internal war against some supernatural demon.

Up ahead a massive silver disk spanning one hundred feet rose high above the road and a bright retina searing light beam sent them careering sideways.

36.
Charles Edmund

Southwest of Indian Springs
May 23, 2005

Bennett's eyes flickered and his body stirred to the muffled sounds of two men whispering. One he recognised as Bishop but the other, an older more educated voice he did not know. He vaguely remembered the hectic car trip and Bishop losing control under the invasive white light of a massive spotlight.

"You have to take him back, he can't stay here, too much trouble will come of it," the older man demanded in what Bennett sensed was an agitated tone.

"Professor, he is like the others, no memory and wandering alone near the lake." Bishop defended his actions.

"Yes, but this man is different to the others," he uttered glancing back over his shoulder at Bennett pulling himself up from the sofa.

Professor Charles Edmund had once been a well-respected astrophysicist at NASA and the Pentagon until a few years earlier when he suffered a psychological tragedy. His colleagues had seen it coming, his outlandish theories had transformed from theoretical to conspiracy in a matter of months and it wasn't long before he earned his nickname, 'Crazy Charlie'.

For two decades, Charles Edmund had led the way, delivering ground-breaking advances in the understanding of space evolution and the origins of the universe. But then one day it all changed, his professional career tumbled and spiralled into the oblivion of scepticism. His theories turned outrageous without an inkling of scientific proof or a solid premise to maintain his credibility among his colleagues. His theories about aliens visiting Earth through portals awarded him a place with the insane and conspiracy theorists worldwide. It was all part of the mental destruction of his career.

"That's not a good idea, you should rest," Edmund said stepping towards Bennett and beckoning for him to lay back down.

"Where am I?" Bennett defied Edmund and pushed himself to his feet but lost his balance. Bishop rushed to ease him back to the sofa.

"You have lost a lot of blood, but the wound has closed up now. You were lucky, it doesn't appear to have damaged anything vital, but you need rest," Edmund said.

"Are you a doctor?" Bennett asked, watching the man closely.

Dressed casually in jeans and an old t-shirt, Edmund was perhaps approaching his late sixties Bennett thought, though his dishevelled appearance possibly added a few years. His long scraggy unkept grey hair gave him the crazy professor look, yet he spoke with the distinct baritone of someone who possessed vast knowledge.

"No I am not, but I have been around plenty claiming themselves doctors to know a thing or two about the human anatomy. This surgery wasn't difficult, the knife entry was clean and it only needed a few sutures. What I do find phenomenal is your healing rate, already the wound looks a week old."

Bennett lifted his shirt and inspected Edmund's handiwork, a one-inch cut with six neat sutures evenly spaced.

"Nice work!" Bennett commented adding, "Who are you?"

"I am sorry, my name is Charles Edmund, you and my friend Bishop were attacked on the road out near Papoose Lake, some forty miles north of here. You were stabbed and he drove you here. Do you remember this?"

Bennett nodded glancing over at Bishop standing close by.

"Yes I remember, two men tried to kill us," Bennett responded.

"Yeah and both are dead now! Professor, you should have seen this guy take them down, pure magic, I have never seen anyone so quick," Bishop interjected.

"Well not quick enough I would say, he was still stabbed," Edmund sniggered leaning towards Bishop and whispering, "Go

165

check the perimeter, this guy being here only means trouble for us."

"Where are we?" Bennett asked as Bishop vanished from the room.

"My house, fifteen miles southwest of Indian Springs. It's my research station."

"Research?" Bennett queried.

"I am an astrophysicist, spent most of my career at NASA but now I work for myself. The satellite dish and telescope sitting over this house is the biggest in all of Nevada and responsible for some of the greatest galactic discoveries of the past decade. Bishop tells me he found you wandering lost and disorientated out on the old Papoose Lake road. He says you don't remember anything about yourself or your past!"

"Yes true, I have no idea who I am except one of the men I killed called me Bennett."

"Your name is Jon Bennett, you were once an employee of the CIA until about six years ago. After that I don't know anything about you. Your sacking was something that raised my suspicions, it just didn't add up. The Senate Inquiry stank of a cover up and you were hung out to dry. That's my guess!"

Bennett shook his head, "I have no idea what you are talking about, I don't remember anything."

"Well it certainly explains your combat skills, you had the reputation as the CIA's best field operative but also one with many enemies."

The sudden crack of gunfire engulfed the small room as Bishop raced back in yelling something indistinguishable and fell spraying blood from two rounds in his back. A group of four heavily armed men stampeded past and slammed Bennett to the floor. Edmund received the same treatment with a rifle butt rammed into his back dropping him to his knees next to Bennett.

"Don't move," one gunman yelled while the other three zeroed their aim on Bennett, not taking their eyes from him for a second.

On the floor at his boots, blood pooled as Bishop bled out, his body twitching with the last moments of life. Beside him, Edmund groaned and attempted a verbal retaliation.

"Who are you? How dare you barge into my home!" he growled with the distinct quiver of fear resonating in his voice.

"Shut up old man," one of the other men commanded stepping forward driving his rifle butt into Edmund's head and dropping him face down onto the floor.

Bennett catapulted forward from knees to feet in no time and snatched the gun. He spun the Heckler & Koch HK33 and depressed the trigger fully automatic across the three men, each ripped apart by the quick onslaught of high calibre bullets. The fourth gunman fired his weapon but missed when Bennett turned towards him with the rifle outstretched smashing him in the face. At the same time, he sliced down on the gunman's arm and his gun toppled to the floor. It all happened in three seconds to the disbelief of Edmund. He raised himself to his knees and looked around the room, he'd never experienced death so close. Bishop had been right in describing Bennett's speed, he thought, watching the ex-CIA agent standing over the fourth man on his knees.

"Who are you?" Bennett demanded, pointing the HK33 closer to the man's head.

He made no reply just glared at Bennett.

"Why are you here?" Bennett continued.

Again, the man said nothing.

Bennett pulled the trigger once and the man screamed in pain. A single round sliced through the man's leg, drilling a clean hole through the outer fleshy part of his thigh. Edmund watched in horror.

"Why are you here?"

The man stayed silent, instead he grimaced in agony and held his bleeding wound.

Edmund scampered to Bishop, lifting his dead body in his arms. "Poor Kaden, you didn't deserve this my boy," he murmured.

Behind him he heard Bennett say. "You will survive that last shot, the next you may not. Start talking."

Edmund turned to witness Bennett push the rifle barrel into the man's belly. He continued to watch as the man held his silence.

"Bennett, don't shoot him," Edmund shouted.

BANG

Bennett missed on purpose and the round penetrated deep into the timber floor at the man's knees.

In response, the man started laughing. "Soon you will remember nothing at all of your life. Now it's just your old memories but they too will vanish."

Edmund broke in. "You are from Sector Four, aren't you?"

He turned his gaze towards Edmund. "Arh… Crazy Charlie! Sector Four does not exist, you stupid old fool. You and your little conspiracy nut-jobs are wasting your time."

Bennett backhanded him with his rifle and blood burst from his ear.

"Why are you here?"

"I thought that was obvious Bennett. Kill you!"

"Why?" Bennett asked.

The man started laughing again except this time, it resonated a more sadistic tone.

"Because you are no longer needed, they have the code now."

Bennett was confused, he couldn't remember anything and strangely, his distant memories were slowly fading. Behind him, Edmund was as baffled.

"What code, what are you talking about?" Bennett asked.

"Who are they?" Edmund butted in.

"QUIET… listen," Bennett called above Edmund.

He kept his gun levelled at the man's head and looked towards the ceiling, listening to the increasing rumbling drone.

"Chopper inbound," he announced grabbing Edmund by the arm and dragging him backwards away from their prisoner.

"What about him?" Edmund shouted.

"He's dead," Bennett replied as the first missile struck the far side of the house and it erupted over the top of the man kneeling on the floor. His life evaporated in the fireball that ensued.

Another missile followed a few seconds later to claim the remaining house.

37.

Gunship

Southwest of Indian Springs
May 23, 2005

The pressure wave from the blast threw Bennett and Edmund against the only wall left standing, knocking the air from their lungs as they slid stunned to the floor. Above them the thunderous whining roar of an attack helicopter prepared to fire another missile at the remaining one third of the house.

"Edmund, wake up," Bennett yelled from two feet away.

The roof was caving in around them and the inferno grew more ravenous by the second. Either side of them, burning timber beams fell and ignited in a fury of flames while Bennett pushed himself to his feet, shielding himself from the intense heat. Edmund on the other hand was too dazed to respond.

Bennett grabbed his arm and hurled him over his shoulder then ran for the door as the darkness outside turned bright as the sun, accompanied by the deafening roar of turbine engines. Like a showman on centre stage, he and the dazed Edmund were in the helicopter's spotlight, standing in full view on the back patio with nowhere to escape. Behind them the entire house was ablaze and crumpling to the ground accompanied by the frightening screams only a burning house can make.

"Bunker, I have a bunker under the dish," Edmund murmured lifting his hand pointing towards the massive satellite dish array rising above them.

Standing at fifty feet above the ground and close to one hundred feet in diameter, the dish presented a colossal sight as they exited the burning house. Forty yards of open ground was all he had to run with Edmund on his shoulders. At twenty yards, the helicopter dropped in low under the dish.

Bennett slowed as he caught vision of their aggressor for the first time.

"What the fuck!"

Edmund twisted on Bennett's shoulders to gain his own view of what at first looked more similar to the futuristic flying machines from Terminator. It resembled an attack helicopter forged with a Lockheed F-117 Nighthawk stealth fighter jet and under the vibrant orange light of the flames exuded pure intimidation. Fifteen-foot wedge shaped wing appendages protruded out each side from a short but sleek fuselage, while at the rear a massive V tail gave the craft an impression of high speed. To give it the power for flight and immediate manoeuvrability, two jet turbines rotated on the tips of each wing providing the vehicle with upwards, downwards and horizontal flight.

It hovered just above the ground, watching them from far enough away for Bennett to see the single pilot staring at him through his raised helmet visor, sneering as if teasing Bennett to keep running. They locked eyes for a few seconds while he lowered Edmund to his feet.

"What is that thing?" Edmund shouted above the whirring turbines.

"Don't think we should hang around to find out," Bennett called back and pushed Edmund towards the building.

"GET DOWN!" Bennett screamed.

Edmund half turned not comprehending the urgency as he caught a glimpse of a blue flash of light. Bennett on the other hand had seen what was coming. Like an elongated blob of vivid blue light, a pulse shot out from under the gunship and struck the building underneath the dish. At first nothing happened, but then after a few seconds, the entire building blew outwards like fireworks in the sky. The ground under their feet shook as the satellite dish started to tilt. The blast threw them both ten yards backwards scraping and tumbling across the ground towards Edmund's burning house.

All the while, the gunship remained hovering at a safe distance as the pilot watched. He lowered his visor and his world turned a shade of green striated with bright white, where the fires burned. He slowly edged his machine forward a few feet off the ground until he caught sight of the two men crawling on hands and knees among the burning fragments of building and satellite dish.

"You have many lives Bennett," he stuttered to himself releasing the safety switch on the nose mounted canon.

He lined up his target and depressed the trigger.

At that exact same moment, Bennett stood full view and he felt the tatt tatt tatt of bullets piercing the cockpit and the gunship's fuselage. One round tore through his arm ripping his bicep in half and wedging in the firewall behind him. Blood sprayed across the instrument panel from the ruptured artery in his arm. He pulled his machine skyward away from the incoming rounds and banked high in the sky and back down towards Bennett standing with the HK33 in his hand. The pilot hovered his gunship and quickly configured his remaining pulse missiles to their full destructive capacity before firing all five towards where Bennett stood.

It had taken him just short of four seconds to complete the arming sequence while desperately and in an act of futility, he tried to halt the squirting fountain of blood from his arm.

The five pulses of energy shot out one after the other in rapid succession, each striking the ground at the same spot and vanishing into the earth. Like the building strike, the detonation took a few seconds. This time it was different.

"Oh shit! RUN!" Bennett screamed.

Edmund stumbled forward as the ground under his feet started shaking and quivering. He fell awkwardly to his knees.

"Come on, there's no time," Bennett yelled grabbing the old professor's arm and dragging him upright.

The area surrounding them was the size of a football field, on one side was the burning carcass of Edmund's house and on the other was the toppling mass of the satellite dish. In the middle where the energy pulses struck, the ground was erupting in waves of molten earth, like the ripple effect when a rock is dropped in a pond, the waves started rolling. The first uplifted everything in its path and like a giant plough churning across the ground, it tossed broken earth ten feet in the air.

"What is happening?" Edmund called in between his short-laboured breaths. He was out of condition and at sixty-five, he struggled to maintain pace with the younger and more athletic Bennett.

Bennett glanced back again at the rising ground and though it was dark, the fires presented an eerie orange halo and he could just make out the giant wall of rock and earth tumbling towards them destroying everything in its path. It gained speed as it advanced.

Twenty yards…. Fifteen yards…. Ten yards and then.

"OH FUCK! HANG ON!"

38.
Doomsday Prepper

Southwest of Indian Springs
May 23, 2005

Suddenly the orange ambiance was gone and they were in complete darkness. The deafening rumble of the approaching rock wall had lessened, becoming muffled, but seemed to reverberate around them as a violent downburst of air knocked them off their feet.

"Hold on!" Bennett screamed again as the earth under them dropped and lurched sideways.

The section of ground they stood on had become a long narrow splinter of earth with one end slipping twenty feet into a huge underground cavity. The abrupt fall of the ledge tossed them sliding and rolling, bouncing off rocks until they hit the cavity floor. Around them the muffled sounds of earth tumbling faded into the distance while above, the once star filled sky had vanished.

"You okay?" Bennett called, climbing to his feet and brushing loose dirt from himself.

Beside him, Edmund tried to lift himself yet slipped on each attempt as the ground under his feet continued to shift. Bennett grabbed his arm and hauled him upright.

"I'm okay, nothing broken. Just a few cuts and bruises."

"Yeah me too!" Bennett mumbled taking a few steps into the darkness, impatiently waiting for his eyes to adjust.

"What happened, why does it feel like we're in a concert hall?" Edmund asked listening to his voice echo around them.

"Your satellite dish collapsed on us," Bennett replied looking upwards.

In the pitch black it was faintly visible fifty feet above them. The dish had flipped over when it collapsed and rolled over the top of them as the energy pulse exploded thirty feet underground. The earth melted on impact and waves of molten rock rolled outwards until it hit the dish and the cavity below it. There the energy waves deflected either side and continued their destructive path for a short distance further.

"But how? What caused it?" Edmund asked.

"Some kind of energy pulse shot from that helicopter is my guess," he replied.

"Helicopter? Is that what you're calling it? I've never seen anything like that before," Edmund said, not so much a question but a statement.

"Energy pulse? Never seen anything like that before either," he added.

"We seemed to have fallen into an underground cavity," Bennett continued.

"It's my bunker," Edmund blurted.

"What are you talking about?"

"The underground cavity. The ground collapsed into my bunker," Edmund said moving quickly past Bennett until he was standing on a patch of hard concrete floor.

He raced further into the darkness moments before the low drone of a generator started somewhere off in the distance. A few seconds later, the lights started flickering on to expose a medium size room lined with rows of shelves like a storage warehouse. Each shelf was stocked to the ceiling with cans of food and plastic drums of water.

"It's my nuclear fallout shelter, you know for when the next big one starts," answering the bewildered look on Bennett's face.

"Doomsday prepper," Bennett sniggered.

"Call me what you wish but hey, it just saved our lives. Come I'll show you around."

Bennett had no response; the old scientist was right.

"Impressive!" Bennett followed him down long corridors and into three more rooms, much larger than the first one.

"Did you build this?" he asked.

"No most was already here. I think it's an old US Army facility from the Cold War days. Built pretty much for the same purpose I suspect," he replied pointing towards the old US military markings and the radiation symbols on the doors.

He continued, "I don't think it was ever used. All the furniture was still wrapped in plastic and the computers had never been booted."

"Computers?" Bennett asked.

"Yeah whole room of them back there, relics on today's standards," Edmund replied leading Bennett into a smaller room at the end of the corridor.

Lining one wall, Edmund had stacked the old unused computers in two piles while on the opposite side, he had arranged his own modern alternatives and several HF radios. He switched all three radios on and the sounds of static and distant voices filled the room.

"I haven't used these for years might take a while to zero in on local traffic."

"Sector Four? What is Sector Four?" Bennett asked.

"What?" Edmund responded but was busy tuning his radios to the squeals and chirps of far off radio transmissions.

"Upstairs, you asked that soldier if he was from Sector Four!"

"Yes, I did. Sector Four is the reason I am now called Crazy Charlie."

Bennett gave him a baffled look and a prompting gesture with his hands, inviting more information.

"The US government claims Sector Four does not exist but that is bullshit. My sources tell me there is an alien base in the hills near Papoose Lake. I bet you already know that, right?"

"What? I have no idea what you are talking about! Though I can see why the nickname! Seriously you think there are extraterrestrials living inside a mountain in Nevada. You can't be serious!"

"Yeah I didn't think you were going to confirm the truth, you were a company man after all," Edmund laughed not perturbed in the slightest by Bennett's dismissal of his beliefs and sanity.

"Truth? I'm not exactly the person to be confirming anything right now, I can only vaguely remember working for the CIA, let alone start confirming the existence of aliens," Bennett laughed.

"There have been others like you, I mean people found wandering alone in the desert near Papoose Lake. That's where Bishop found you, near where I'm talking about, near Sector Four."

"Others?" Bennett asked.

"Yes, I know of at least four other people in the past two years, all the same with no memory of their immediate past or who they were. The police and FBI showed no interest, claiming each was a case the person had simply become lost and was severely dehydrated. Doctors confirmed the memory loss was a result of prolonged sun exposure and the extreme lack of water. The unusual part of that story was the distinct lack of sunburn or any physical signs of sun exposure. I made my own inquiries with medical friends and if these people did suffer amnesia from extreme dehydration then it would have been very short term. Nothing like what actually happened."

"What happened?" Bennett asked.

"Within a few months every one of them developed advanced stage dementia and died."

"So, what are you saying? I'm going to die in the next few months," Bennett asked.

"You heard the soldier, he said soon you will remember nothing. I'm telling you it's all connected to Sector Four, it's too much of a coincidence."

"Okay let's say for argument sake, this Sector Four does exist. How did I get there? How did they erase my memory? And more importantly, why?" Bennett added.

"That we need to find out," Edmund concluded.

"How is it you believe this base exists anyway?"

"I worked for NASA for twenty years leading their deep space exploration team. We were discovering a new planetary system every few months in reaches of space no one even knew existed or fathomed could exist. It was exciting times until we stumbled across a strange singular dwarf planet by itself not orbiting any star and lightyears from any known system. We estimated its size to have been about five hundred miles in diameter, quite small on planetary scales. Actually we considered at first it was likely a rogue moon."

"Yeah what was so special about it?"

"Well apart from it being perfectly symmetrical and clearly not an asteroid," Edmund returned, hesitating a moment, "It was on a direct path towards Earth at an enormous speed, well past the speed of light."

"I don't understand! Can planets or moons do that?" Bennett asked.

"Normally no, but this wasn't a planet or moon! Our deep space scans showed it to be hollow," Edmund answered Bennett's dumbfounded look and he quickly added, "That was ten years ago, we never had the chance to fully investigate it."

"Why what happened?" Bennett asked.

"I made the mistake of reporting it up the chain in the early stages. We were excited and well, we wanted it known. Within a day I lost my job, my team all lost their jobs. There were no explanations given, we were simply told that budget cuts to the space exploration program meant we had to go."

"Why such a reaction?" Bennett challenged.

Edmund stayed silent for a moment and looked at Bennett.

"That discovery was the first of its kind and a game changer. That object was unusual, it had been made and I don't mean naturally."

"What are you saying that it was man made?" Bennett queried cynically.

"Yes, but not by man, no human could have made it. This object was over three thousand lightyears away."

Bennett slowly shook his head, "Are you suggesting advanced alien life?"

"I think so. But what we were looking at was three thousand years in our past, so before the existence of modern man. Before Christ if you're a religious man."

Edmund saw the confused expression on Bennett's face. "At one lightyear, the light emanated from a star or object in space takes one year to reach us, so if it is three thousand lightyears away then it takes three thousand years to reach us. Therefore, every star you see in the night sky is thousands of years in our past, actually millions of years. Do you understand?"

"Yes I do. So this object you discovered could be anywhere now, right?"

"Correct, might not even exist anymore because it would be three thousand years old on top of its age at the time."

"Where does Sector Four come into all this?"

"How far does your memory go back? Do you remember the Roswell crash?"

"Yes, allegedly an alien craft crashed but ended up being an experimental weather balloon."

"Good you remember. After I lost my job, I was approached by a man claiming he was once part of Majestic 12. He wouldn't tell me his name, so I nicknamed him MJ."

"Hang on, Majestic 12! I remember it. Wasn't it all bogus and just a bunch of whacko conspiracy theorists claiming UFO's and aliens were real? Didn't the FBI determine it was all just a scam?" Bennett interjected.

"Yes, that is what the government wanted everyone to believe. They were real… very real. They killed my NASA colleagues!" Edmund whispered as if he thought his bunker was bugged.

"What? Why do you say that?"

"After we lost our jobs, every one of my team except me, died within a few months. Some had sudden heart attacks, a couple died in car crashes and then there was poor old Jim Richards. He was savagely mauled by a grizzly bear whilst hiking near his home in Montana City. From reports there was nothing recognisable about him after the attack."

"How was Majestic 12 responsible?"

"I have no proof except what MJ said, my team was murdered to keep the secret secure."

"Secure?" Bennett raised his eyebrows, starting to see why the old scientist was aptly nicknamed, Crazy Charlie.

"Majestic 12's mission was to hide the existence of extraterrestrials and flying saucers; the world isn't ready for the truth, MJ said. What do you think would happen if our discovery was released to the mainstream population? How would they react knowing there is a death star looking object floating around in space?"

"Death star?" Bennett quizzed.

"You know, the Death Star from Star Wars. That is what we thought it looked like, a great big metallic ball floating through space."

"All sounding like some outlandish conspiracy theory to me," Bennett remarked.

"Yes, it does sound unbelievable, but my team are all dead and there are no records of what we discovered. That object, whatever it is, is out there somewhere and maybe nowhere near Earth but it proves the existence of perhaps advanced technology in space and therefore an advanced civilisation of extraterrestrial beings. This is the greatest discovery in the history of mankind and it's been silenced."

Bennett's memory was limited, he could only recall events in his younger life and nothing in the past ten years or so. He was listening to Edmund and trying to take it all in, but at the same time, he was struggling with his amnesia.

"Where does Sector Four fit into this?"

"MJ gave me the names of some people who could help me reveal the truth. Turns out the people were a bunch of ufologists based in Vegas, led by a strange Frenchman calling himself Xavier. They mostly watched the skies at night and listened to long range HF radio transmissions, often travelling to remote parts of America, spending days or even weeks camped in the wilderness alongside their cameras pointed skyward. But it was the area around Papoose Lake that had them most intrigued and curious."

"Sector Four?" Bennett offered.

"Yes, S4 as Xavier referred to it. Conspiracy theorists worldwide were making unverified claims of an alien base deep inside Papoose Mountain, a place where extraterrestrials lived and built their ships. Much of the speculation was based on the high volume of UFO sightings in the area and the strange happenings."

"You mean like me and the others found wandering without memory."

Edmund nodded and added, "Yes."

"In the beginning I wasn't a believer and tried to distance myself from Xavier. In the short few years I had been associating with him and his group, I lost all credibility in my field. It was like the government was making me appear crazy, continually discrediting me and ensuring my name appeared in documents linked to conspiracy theorists."

"Why ruin your career, I don't understand why you would become involved with such people."

"It wasn't until the radio transmission that I changed my views."

"What transmission?"

Edmund walked across the room to a row of shelves filled with hundreds of books, mostly academic science journals. He selected a small uninteresting looking textbook and opened it to about halfway. A piece of paper fell to the floor and he quickly scooped it up.

"Here read this," he said as he handed it to Bennett.

NASA Edmund has discovered the object, need to advise our friends at S4 and eliminate all knowledge. MJ-12

Bennett read it a few times.

"What is this?"

"It was a radio message intercepted the same day I reported the object to senior management at NASA," Edmund replied.

"How did you get this?"

"Xavier and his team spend every minute of every day scouring radio transmissions. This was one they discovered embedded among other transmissions. It wasn't until he met me and learnt of my discovery that he realised what it all meant. That message convinced me something was going on. MJ-12 is Majestic 12. Eliminating all knowledge had to mean killing my team and referencing our friends at S4 as well, that could imply alien friends! Don't you think?"

"Why are you still alive?" Bennett asked adding, "All your team are dead except you!"

"I don't know, maybe they consider me good as dead, I lost all credibility and so I'm not a threat to them any longer. As if anyone is going to believe crazy Charlie Edmund if he ever started talking about some massive alien mothership hurtling towards earth. Can you imagine the reaction? Crazy Charlie has watched one too many Sci-fi movies. You know Will Smith fighting aliens in Independence Day."

Bennett gave him a blank look.

"Oh, you don't remember, blockbuster movie a few years back. Will Smith saves the world from an alien invasion."

"No I don't recall it. I need to find this Sector Four you talk about and stop my memory loss. Not dying in a few months would be good too," he laughed.

"That might be a problem you see. No one has ever found it and those who have gone looking closer, never return. They just add to the missing person statistics."

"How many?" Bennett asked.

"Missing persons? At last count, I think twelve or thir..."

"Quiet, do you hear that?" Bennett broke in, silencing Edmund mid-sentence.

39.
Arsenal

Southwest of Indian Springs
May 23, 2005

Bennett jumped to his feet and sprinted up the platform to the ground surface. Above him slivers of light escaping from the bunker lit up the upside down satellite dish and for the first time, he witnessed the enormity of the chasm, they were under a dome. In the middle he could just make out the long feed horn protruding out from the centre and now touching the ground. The ground surface had an unusual ruffled appearance, all churned up like it had been freshly ploughed with a ten-foot blade.

He climbed over twenty yards of broken ground towards the edge of the dish where he stopped abruptly and dropped low, listening and watching.

A bright spotlight caressed the dome, breaking through the cracks in the metallic skin. It had split in places when it crashed to the ground from its housing and toppled over. The thunderous whine of turbine engines came next and more spotlights lit up the dome while three of the same advanced helicopter machines buzzed overhead. One lowered closer to the ground aiming its spotlight directly towards where he was standing. A wide crack big enough only for a small child to fit through allowed the light to swamp his position and like a deer in headlights, Bennett stood staring at the hovering helicopter.

"Okay not good!" he grumbled, turning and racing back towards the bunker to an overly anxious Edmund who was at the top of the platform, fixated on the light display shooting through the cracks.

"Come on!" Bennett yelled, grabbing him by the arm as he sprinted past.

"What's going on?" Edmund called.

There was no need to answer. The dome exploded and the first hole appeared. Shards of metal and fragments of dish blew inwards, narrowly missing Bennett as they disappeared down into the safety of the bunker. What was once a few cracks in the dome was now hundreds. Another explosion and this time, half the dome collapsed inwards sealing over the bunker entrance under forty tonnes of twisted metal. More missiles hit the dome and the remainder fell until the structure was completely flattened.

Inside the bunker, Bennett and Edmund moved quickly to avoid the incoming barrage of steel beams and aluminium sheets falling from the dish breaking apart. Within minutes, the entire opening had filled, blocking their exit while on the surface, foot soldiers started scouring the area under the watchful eyes of the gunships.

Bennett stood watching as the last piece of steel slipped and crashed to the bunker floor with an ear shattering screech of metal on metal, followed by the final thump as it hit the floor. Beside him, Edmund was laughing.

"What's so funny?" Bennett quizzed, not feeling the same humour of the moment.

"I always said my bunker would one day save my life and well, here we are alive," he cackled.

"Well I do hope there is another way out of here, otherwise the joke is on you professor?" Bennett retorted.

"Yes, there are two emergency exits but I think we may have a problem."

"Why?"

"Both exits are narrow tunnels to the surface, each about twenty feet long and wide enough for two persons side by side. The problem is whether they withstood those earth tremors, I saw the surface up there all ripped up."

"Where are they?"

Edmund led Bennett down a long corridor ending in a tee intersection with another corridor. To their left was a closed door while on the right, a small hatch.

"The hatch opens to the first tunnel," Edmund said.

Bennett moved in front of him and opened the hatch.

"Okay not good! Where's the other tunnel?" he said looking solemnly at a wall of earth. The tunnel had collapsed and filled with soil and rock.

"It is much further away on the other side, back past where the dish has collapsed in on the bunker."

They headed towards another long narrow corridor, leading them fifty yards to under his burning house. In places the concrete walls had cracked and tilted inwards under the load of the ground. They had to crouch low and uncomfortably to pass.

Another hatch door, similar to the first one, blocked their way.

"My house cellar is on the other side," Edmund said as he started to push the door lever.

"Wait!" Bennett stopped him.

He listened closely at the door while opening it slowly and pushing it an inch.

A rush of hot burning air smacked them both in the face and the cellar stank of hot wine. Smashed wine bottles littered the floor swimming in the leaked contents.

"Damn it, that was my finest collection," Edmund said looking around the mess covering his cellar. His anger had replaced his fear.

The cellar was small, ten feet across with a steep set of rusted steel stairs leading up into the house. At the top, an orange glow marked the entrance to the house. Bennett stepped up first, slowly edging his way and shielding his face from the intense heat, growing more unbearable on each step.

"Can you see anything?" Edmund called, waiting below.

Less than a minute later, Bennett rushed back down the stairs, face bright red and drenched in sweat.

"Fuck that was hot, your house is totally destroyed... sorry!" Bennett announced, searching the room to find water to cool himself down, but all he found was vintage wine.

"Normally I wouldn't say no to a fine red wine," he laughed.

"Can we get out up there?"

"Yeah but not going to be easy. There is a small opening under the roofing sheets, but it is still burning. Oh and the other problem is the soldiers and gunships. I heard at least three gunships buzzing around and a few men shouting. They are looking for us or at least looking for our bodies!"

He paused and added, "What time is sunrise around here?"

"Starts getting light about five, why?"

"It's now three thirty which means we have less than two hours to get out of here. In daylight we're sitting ducks which brings me to the next question. Do you have any weapons?"

Edmund looked at him, breaking a smile, "Come I think you might like this."

He led him back past the collapsed section to the closed door opposite the first hatch. He opened it.

"Well well well what do we have here? Were you planning on starting the next big war yourself?"

Edmund laughed.

Bennett entered the room, a fifteen by ten feet cubicle lined with gun racks holding all kinds of assault rifles, machine guns and sniper rifles. In the centre, a large table was jam packed with explosives, handguns and seemingly endless boxes of ammunition stacked almost to the ceiling. He walked around the room, selecting various weapons as he went behaving like a kid in a candy shop.

"There is more."

"What? Are you kidding?" Bennett quickly responded.

At the far end of the room another doorway opened into a smaller tighter space. Bennett stepped into it. His mouth dropped.

"You have been busy, where did you get all this?" he asked.

At his feet and stacked to head height were long cases in the distinctive army green colour. On the side of each box was stencilled 'FIM-92C Stinger'.

"Never know when you will need stinger missiles in an apocalyptic world, hey professor?" Bennett responded laughing.

Edmund nodded shrugging his shoulders, "Never can be too careful."

"I won't ask where it all came from."

He walked around the cases of stingers to another assortment of weapons, mostly grenade launchers and one massive heavy duty M2 machine gun leaning against the wall in the corner. He stopped, scanning the weapons, all were too big to lug through the tunnel.

"What's that?" he asked pointing towards a metal box with dials and wires attached, resembling some elongated space age amplifier.

"Oh that, yes. Experimental EMP generator," he shuffled to place a sheet over it.

"Why the fuck do you have an Electromagnetic Pulse device down here?" Bennett chuckled.

"My work at NASA wasn't always about space, there have been a few side jobs along the way. This was one."

"Does it work?"

"I don't know, I have never tested it. But it should."

"To what range?" Bennett asked.

"Maximum of five miles, I was contracted to develop portable tactical EMP devices to knock out military communication installations in the field."

"I have an idea." Bennett picked up the device.

"Wait, if your planning on setting it off, you need to know something. Its power source is generated from a very small fusion explosion."

"Whoa! Are you telling me this is a nuke?"

"No but similar in a much smaller version without the destruction. It's not important that you understand how it works, just that it doesn't emit radioactivity when detonated. The chain reaction is enough energy to set off the EMP. But you need to get it to the surface to affect the helicopters. That is your plan I am assuming?"

"Yeah it is, however, first we need to prepare."

For the next thirty minutes Edmund lugged as many weapons as he could to the cellar while Bennett suffered the intense heat clearing a wider passage through the roof debris up top. The gunships were still searching the site, buzzing low at times over the house site fanning the fire with turbine wash and each time Bennett froze, waiting for a missile to launch him into oblivion.

The EMP generator was heavy and at over three feet long, made it hard work moving it along the tunnel and up the stairs to its place among the roofing sheets.

"Okay what now?" Edmund asked as Bennett came back down the stairs.

"We set it off and then fight our way out. That way we only have to contend with the ground troops and not the airborne enemy."

Edmund went a shade of grey matching his hair. "Fight? I can't fight, I'm a scientist not a soldier!"

Bennett scoffed, "What? You don't want to be called a soldier, but you stockpile enough weapons for a small guerrilla outfit. Do you see how funny that is? Have you ever fired a weapon?"

"I used to live on a farm in Nebraska, so yes I've fired guns, just not the big military ones," he replied ignoring Bennett's sarcasm.

Suddenly the cellar shook and more wine toppled to the floor smashing as it fell. The cracks in the concrete ceiling grew larger and it started to warp in places. Bennett grabbed the closest assault rifle and raced up the stairs two treads at a time. At the top he crawled low ignoring the heat clawing at his back until he could see out under the twisted roof metal. At a hundred yards, a group of soldiers dug at the ground while one of the gunships hovered overhead, shining its spotlight over them. Then they all scattered and the gunship launched a blue pulse into the spot and another violent tremor tore through under his feet.

"We have no time, they are digging in through the other tunnel," Bennett called sliding back down the stairs.

They both took turns carrying guns to the surface and stacking them neatly under the roof sheeting. The fire was dying with nothing but metal and concrete left to devour while the heat was quickly losing its bite. They positioned themselves and

Bennett prepared two M16 rifles and slipped three fully loaded handguns under his belt.

"Professor, what happens when we set the device off?"

"A small explosion about the size of a grenade. Then the primary charge ignites. You have two minutes once it's activated."

"How do I do that?" he asked.

Edmund showed him the simple steps of flicking two switches.

"It will work won't it?" he asked looking directly at Edmund searching and hoping for a sign of confidence.

"It should, though like I said, it's never been tested."

"Well professor if it doesn't, we're dead so you better hope your PhD in whatever, pays off."

Edmund held silent.

Bennett lifted the device and edged his way under the last few sheets of iron. In the distance the soldiers were busy digging while one helicopter stayed overhead and the other two patrolled low on either side of the dome.

He crept from the concealment of the iron sheeting and positioned the EMP device in the open a few yards over from where he had waited. As instructed by Edmund he flicked the switches and a two-minute countdown illuminated on the panel, flashing in red, as the timer counted down.

01:57 01:56 01:55....

He rushed back into hiding and paused, looking back over his shoulder as one of the gunships changed course. At first it banked towards his position and then at the last second, stopped and hovered over a raised section of earth fifty yards over. There it swamped the ground in bright light searching from left to right.

He stayed low under the debris watching curiously for a few seconds. He had never witnessed anything like it. What he had first thought was a new advanced design of helicopter was not entirely accurate. The machine had no rotors on top like a modern-day helicopter. Recessed at the ends of the long winglets, hung four jet engines, two each side pointing at the ground that tilted forward to give it speed. Each burned orange hot and as it came closer, the whining turbine sound grew deafening.

01:34 01:33 01:32....

He continued to watch, fascinated by its futuristic design as it continued to scour the area at low altitude. Each time it turned, the flickering light from the ground fires reflected off its body making its black metal fuselage glisten like the skin of a wet snake.

It stopped, hovering over a clump of twisted metal, ten feet above the ground. At the front, the narrow cockpit big enough for one pilot was fully shielded in glass and resembled more the nose of a fighter jet. The pilot sat hidden behind a mirrored visor scanning the ground below him and was oblivious to Bennett watching him from thirty yards away.

Suddenly two long mechanical arms dropped from its underbelly and started clawing through the metal and tossing it aside as if it were paper. It took on the appearance of a giant praying mantis with its long slender raptorial forelegs foraging through the waste. He kept watching, forgetting the time.

00:59 00:58 00:57....

A voice close-by severed his fixation on the machine and he retreated a few feet back under the roofing iron. Two soldiers appeared close by, both with battle rifles in their hands at the ready.

Bennett checked his watch.

"Shit!" he muttered to himself.

"Hey what's that?" he heard one say.

Bennett leapt from under the iron and raised his M16 firing as he bounded four steps towards the device and the two soldiers leaning down to look at it. Neither had seen him coming and died on the spot with three bullets each obliterating their hearts.

The sound of rapid gunfire alerted the others and worse, the closest gunship was already swinging around towards him.

40.
Firebird

Southwest of Indian Springs
May 23, 2005

Gunfire swamped his position as he sprinted back for the cover of his hiding place. Something metallic snagged his leg and flipped him onto his back with brutal force. At first, he thought he'd been shot in the leg until he looked up. Above him, the praying mantis had him in its grip, one of the long forelegs with its metal claw had him pinned to the ground. He struggled to break free while the pilot laughed and the claw tightened around his hips.

Then as the machine lifted him, he wrestled desperately against the twisting action of the claw to reach for his handgun tucked under his belt. For a brief moment, he had a clear shot of the pilot until the claw tightened and the pain amplified. The handgun fell.

Under him a small group of soldiers traversed the churned-up ground making their way towards him. Further over, Edmund was crouched in the darkness, trembling in fear. He had crawled out at the sounds of the shooting, just in time to see Bennett running and the long claw of the gunship snatch him.

The soldiers arrived and the lead man beckoned at the pilot to drop their prisoner to the ground. None of them, including the pilot, had seen the device.

00:03   00:02   00:01....

The blast wave ripped all four men off their feet and drove them backwards twenty feet through the air. Two were killed instantly from the impact while the other two were paralysed with pain. Unlike a grenade, there had been no shrapnel to shred their bodies, instead it was an intense compacting force like a massive hammer expanding outwards at an incredible rate, crushing all their bones at once.

Bennett on the other hand, had been lucky. Most of the blast had washed under him as he hung from the claw rising higher above the ground. For what seemed like minutes was only a few seconds when a sudden violent shudder vibrated through the claw, almost snapping his back. The screaming whine of turbines had ceased and the machine slipped sideways. The EMP had detonated, destroying every piece of active circuitry for three miles or more. The other two gunships had been much closer to the ground and the pilots with less time to react, hit the surface in spectacular fireballs.

The pilot in Bennett's machine held it airborne for a short while longer, but powerless gliding wasn't a feature of its design and it plummeted, tilting over onto its side. As it impacted nose first into the ground, the two forelegs snapped and Bennett was hurled clear of the ensuing explosion. He rolled and tumbled end on end across the uneven ground before slamming into one of the dead soldiers.

"Bennett wake up, come on, wake up!" Edmund screamed at his side.

He had emerged from under the debris moments after the device detonated and watched as Bennett and the machine plummeted to the ground. He shielded his eyes from the blast and raced the ten paces to drag him back to the bunker though slipped, losing his footing and slumped onto Bennett. In the distance the other soldiers were running towards them, stopping only to shoot while around them, the three gunships burnt out of control.

"Get off me professor." Bennett pushed himself up and tossed the old man aside.

"Thought you'd be dead for sure!" Edmund replied and stood.

"Get down you fool," Bennett yelled.

Edmund collapsed to the ground screaming in pain as a bullet clipped his arm spinning him around while the next three rounds narrowly missed his head.

Bennett grabbed the closest dead soldier's rifle, a Kalashnikov AK-9 and started return fire from his kneeling position. He had never been a fan of the Russian AK rifles, but it wasn't a time to be fussy and he kept the pressure on the trigger, dispersing the onslaught of enemy soldiers.

"GO! Get back to the bunker… GO," he screamed at Edmund in between short bursts of gunfire.

The first spray of bullets dropped and killed the two closest soldiers. The next volley wasn't so accurate, shooting over the heads of the others. The sudden bombardment of firepower was enough however, for Edmund to scurry like a startled rabbit disappearing into the small crevice under the debris, not looking back. He had always been timid, not one to face danger or take a fight head on. Right now, it was no different as he sunk deeper into the protection of his cellar.

Outside, Bennett grabbed two rifles, slung one across his shoulders and readied the other. He sprinted, firing at the soldiers before dropping low behind a crumpled section of the satellite dish. The house fire had died, but the crashed gunships were still ablaze, offering some light to the battlefield though at the best, it was dim. In the flickering light, he counted five dark shapes edging slowly towards him, all keeping low to the ground. The soldiers had seen him too and were already spreading to flank him.

Bennett waited, keeping out of sight.

The first of the soldiers appeared, a dark human shape silhouetted against the backdrop of the fires. Then two more. They crouched low taking cautious steps towards him, three directly in front at fifteen yards and one each side.

RAT-A-TAT-TAT-TAT-TAT-TAT

The gunfire started, automatic rounds punished the dish wreckage and he dropped lower to the ground, hearing and feeling the shots pierce the thin metal. He was pinned with no escape. To his right, one of the flanking soldiers stood and started firing, forcing him onto his belly out of the soldier's line of sight.

A loud explosion close by shook the ground and he felt the searing hot blast wave scrape his back. He jumped to his feet, raised his rifle and fired fully automatic. A large fire burned to his right where the flanking soldier once stood. The other three advancing soldiers lay mangled, arms and legs torn from their bodies as if a giant wild beast had dropped from the sky and attacked. Bennett stopped shooting and looked around at the human carnage, not quite understanding what had happened, until a voice interrupted his thoughts.

"Bennett COME ON!"

He looked towards the sound and was shocked to see Edmund standing there still with the rocket grenade launcher on his shoulder.

"What the fuck, you can't shoot a gun, but you can fucking fire a rocket!" Bennett called to him shaking his head in disbelief.

Gunfire sounded, this time from behind them. The other flanking soldier was still alive and wildly firing from thirty yards away. The explosion had given the battlefield new light and Bennett dropped to his knee and took aim. Edmund had already fallen flat to his belly mostly from loss of balance with the weight of the launcher on his shoulder.

"Okay you fucker, cop this!" Bennett mumbled as he squeezed the trigger.

The single bullet sliced through the soldier's head splitting it open like a melon, blood and brains spewed to the ground at the same time his body dropped lifeless with a thud.

"Nice shooting," Edmund remarked.

Bennett didn't acknowledge him, instead he stood and scanned the area for movement. Nothing caught his eye.

"Is that it? Are they all dead?" Edmund asked lifting himself to his feet.

"Thanks for that professor," Bennett said nodding towards the rocket launcher on the ground and adding, "I think you may have just saved my life."

"I don't know what came over me, I heard the shooting and saw you pinned down. I just pointed and pulled the trigger"

"You did good, but we have to get out of here, reinforcements won't be too far away," Bennett replied feeling a little lightheaded.

"You okay?" Edmund asked watching him massage his forehead with an expression of pain on his face.

"Yeah just a thumping headache coming on, a weird feeling like suddenly I can remember more things, but it's all muddled and doesn't make any sense."

"I know somewhere safe, but it's in Vegas," Edmund responded.

"How far is that?"

"Forty miles."

"There's our wheels over there," Bennett pointed towards three dark coloured Humvees parked a short distance away, two looked driveable but one had been half swallowed by the ground.

He started jogging, quickening his stride.

"No good, the EMP would have fried their electronics," Edmund called and Bennett stopped.

The old professor continued to walk pushing past him, "Come on, I have something better."

They walked briskly a hundred yards down a steep dirt road to a small wooden shed hidden amongst the trees. Edmund lived on two hundred acres of barren ground atop a low-lying mountain range with a splattering of tall pines and conifers. The house site was situated on the highest peak with the satellite dish once towering high above the trees and an impressive sight for anyone approaching.

Edmund eased and looked back up the road towards the trails of black smoke. The first rays of sunlight had broken the eastern horizon and the night was becoming day, giving them both visibility over the carnage.

"Ever seen anything like this?" Bennett asked.

As far as they could see, the land resembled the surface of a wild mountainous ocean frozen in time, ten-foot rifts of earth stacked like crashing waves.

"Yes once, but a long time ago. NASA were working on developing mining technologies for the moon that used lasers to break the ground apart. I don't think they had much success with it though."

"Hmmm maybe they did!" Bennett remarked brushing aside the apocalyptic vision and turned towards the shed, opening the door.

"Oh yeah, now we're talking!" he shouted as Edmund pulled the dust covered tarp from his pride and joy.

"Thought you might like her, my 1979 Pontiac…"

Bennett interrupted, "Pontiac Firebird Trans AM, 345 horsepower of pure grunt. My father used to have one of these, the best damn car I've ever driven."

"You can remember some things!" Edmund said.

"Things in my distant past I can like my childhood, however nothing recent," he said as he moved closer to caress and admire the two door highway beast.

"450 horsepower and six on the floor," Edmund announced.

"What?"

"I made a few modifications to the engine and added a new gear box," the professor replied watching Bennett idolising his car.

"So quite a fair bit faster than your father's," he added proudly.

Bennett didn't consider himself an expert in cars, it was more about going fast that he cared for.

"Will it start?" he asked anxiously.

Edmund opened the door and turned the key.

The V8 engine roared to life, thumping with power and purring to the beat of a satanic tune.

"EMP resistant, not much in the way of electronics to fry," Edmund declared as Bennett pushed past him, taking the driver's seat without question.

"Okay you're driving then!" Edmund said sarcastically and hesitantly hurled himself into the passenger seat.

For the next ten minutes, Bennett drove at nail biting speeds while his passenger dug his nails into the leather seat refusing to relinquish his eyes from the dirt road ahead. Bennett watched and laughed but didn't ease off, he pushed harder and faster. To a distant onlooker, they were just a single dot racing across the flat barren stretch of desert ahead of a dust plume trailing skyward. The sun had broken above the eastern mountain range presenting another cloudless day and again, heading towards a scorcher. They kept driving east towards Las Vegas.

Further to the north, a group of Black Hawk helicopters lifted off, loaded with more soldiers and flew south at top speed.

41.
Blackout

Highway 95, Las Vegas
May 23, 2005

"That soldier said something about a code and no longer needing you. Do you know what he meant by that?" Edmund asked.

"What?" Bennett replied confused, taking a brief look at the professor.

They had reached Highway 95, rocketed through Indian Springs at over a hundred miles per hour until the early morning traffic slowed their arrival into the western suburbs of Las Vegas. Edmund played his own rendition of a Navman, giving Bennett directions most of the way, to the point it was annoying Bennett. To hear Edmund say something other than, turn left, turn right, stay on this for the next five miles, was pleasure to his ears.

"The soldiers back at the house, the ones who killed Kaden, the one in charge said something about a code?"

Bennett shook his head, "I don't know, but I'm starting to remember more things."

"What things?"

"More of my past, I know I worked at the CIA and I keep seeing a silver ball covered in symbols, like it's supposed to mean something to me," Bennett responded massaging his head because the pain was intensifying.

"But with the memories comes this excruciating migraine like I think my head is building to explode," he added.

"When did your memories start coming back?" Edmund asked.

"I had a massive flashback of memories all muddled together, well I think they were memories. Me as a child and then grown up flying fighter jets, getting shot down, being tortured and killing people," he replied pausing to think about what he had just said about killing people.

"Okay but when did these flashbacks start?" the professor asked impatiently before adding, "Did it happen before or after the EMP going off?"

"After," he replied.

"Just what I thought, I am thinking you have some sort of memory suppressing device in your head and the EMP has knocked it out. This would be why now your memories are returning."

"That same soldier said something about soon my memories would be all gone, maybe you are right, maybe I do have a device in my head. So, what now?" Bennett asked.

"My friend Xavier might know what to do," Edmund said as the car suddenly swerved right.

"BENNETT!" Edmund screamed clawing desperately at the wheel to straighten the car back into the correct lane.

Bennett had fallen against the wheel, unconscious while the car first swerved right and then hard left into the oncoming traffic. Edmund had reacted in time to pull the car back narrowly missing a family of five in a wagon doing sixty miles per hour.

"FUCK what happened?" Bennett reacted and like a professional car racer spun the wheel back around, flooring the engine to regain control in the loose gravel of the roadside.

"You blacked out for a few seconds."

He eased the car's speed back and pulled off to the side of the road as a new wave of agony suffocated him and again, all went dark.

42.
Xavier Roland

Las Vegas
May 23, 2005

Thirty minutes had passed and Bennett started to wake, rubbing his eyes at first and then fiercely at the back of his head. The pain had worsened, localised to the base of his skull and like someone was slowly hammering a large nail into his head, it was growing more painful by the minute. He looked around a medium sized dimly lit room and it became clear, he was in someone's loungeroom by the homely furnishings, television and the dull coloured shag pile carpet. Somewhere behind him men were talking softly, but it was quickly drowned out by a more threatening noise close by, a deep growling sound.

The source of the sound appeared, teeth baring and white froth dripping from jaws powerful enough to rip his arm clean off.

"Ziggy, it's okay buddy, leave our quest alone!"

The Bullmastiff was close on sixty kilograms and at a few inches from Bennett's face, he seemed more like a hundred.

"Where am I?" he asked ignoring the row of teeth and turning towards the voice.

Two men stood watching him from the far side of the room, one was Edmund but the other he'd never seen before. A tall dark haired man in his early fifties bearing resemblance to someone who had just escaped a Nazi concentration camp. His skin was sickly pale, almost death like and his face had drooped one side to give him a more eerie appearance.

"Jon, good you are awake," Edmund announced walking quickly towards him with the tall man close behind.

"I see you have met Ziggy Stardust, a good faithful dog this one," the tall man said as he pushed past Edmund to take a closer look at Bennett.

"This is Xavier Roland, my friend I told you about," Edmund said.

"Where am I? What happened?" Bennett asked shaking Xavier's hand. He had an unexpectedly strong grip for a man presenting so timid and weak.

"You are in my house, just north of Las Vegas and Charlie here, says you blacked out," Xavier replied in his heavy French accent.

Bennett couldn't remember much of it; his head was pounding too much. The last thing was the attack on Edmund's house.

"I have so much to ask you Jon. Charlie has told me many things but first, I suspect you have an alien device in your head," the Frenchman declared.

"What the fuck? Edmund, who is this nutjob?" Bennett pulled back, distancing himself from Roland.

"Hear him out, I think your life may depend on it," Edmund replied.

"Jon, I have spent most of my life investigating countless claims of alien abductions around the world, some I'll admit were hoaxes but many I believe actually happened."

Bennett interrupted impatiently, "Oh come on, are you saying I was abducted by aliens?"

"Yes, I think maybe you were. You were found wandering alone in the desert out near Papoose Lake?"

"Yes, but that doesn't mean I was abducted!"

"Maybe not, but did you know you are the fifth person to be found in this past year. All just like you, wandering disorientated without memories in the middle of nowhere. None could explain how they ended up there and strangely, all were a long way from home."

"What do you mean, long way from home?"

"From all over the world, Poland, Germany, Soviet Union, Australia. It had the local authorities baffled, completely unexplained mysteries and would you believe, no records of them ever entering the United States."

"What was the result of the investigation?" Bennett asked.

Roland laughed, "What investigation? Homeland Security took over every case and from there on, all went silent. The FBI weren't even involved which don't you think is a little unusual?"

"I told him," Edmund interjected.

"How do you know this?" Bennett directed at Roland.

"A good source inside the FBI. Their directive to stay away came from high up in the US administration."

"Tell him about Sector Four," Edmund showing impatience.

"Arh yes, Sector Four. This goes to add more weight to my theories. It is well speculated among my colleagues that buried deep inside Papoose Mountain is a facility originally built by the US Government but now used by a race of alien visitors. I believe this is why so many people claim to see UFO's in the area and not so much because Area 51 up the road."

Bennett studied the man sitting opposite him, watching his every move and how his eyes reacted to his speech. Was this Frenchman a whacko conspiracy theorist who had taken one too many acid trips in his younger days or was there truth to what he was saying? Bennett kept listening to him rattling on about alien encounters.

"Where are these other people? What have they said?" Bennett asked referring to the others found wandering the desert.

"All dead! All died within a few months, each never regaining their memories, suffering the rapid onset of dementia," the Frenchman replied.

"Yeah but I can remember things and I'm slowly starting to recall more," Bennett refuted.

"Yes, that is very interesting and it goes to prove my theory of alien abduction."

"How's so?"

"I always thought the memory loss was caused by an implant of some kind and then when Charlie told me about the EMP, it all made sense. It's the only logical explanation why now you are starting to remember more things. The EMP destroyed whatever it is you have in your head stopping your memories. My guess is the blackouts and headaches are a result."

Bennett took a minute to digest what he was saying yet he struggled to accept it. He had always needed solid evidence before believing most things. He was cynical and distrusting of everyone particularly after Dom Whittaker's betrayal. Without his recent memories, the thought of aliens and abductions sounded complete nonsense.

"There are some distinct differences between those found wandering near Papoose Lake and the hundreds of others claiming to have been abducted," Xavier said pausing to look closer at Bennett.

"What differences?" Bennett asked.

"This is where it becomes really interesting, Jon. There are many documented reports of abductees with markings on their skin, usually unexplained scars or small dots on the hands, arms and neck. The ones found near Papoose Lake had none of these, instead, they had a vibrant blue tattoo across their chests."

"What kind of tattoo?" Bennett asked.

"One exactly like that," Roland replied pointing curiously at Bennett's slightly exposed chest.

Bennett peered down at the small area of exposed chest and yanked his shirt over his head.

"Wow! What is that?" Edmund asked, moving in closer.

Bennett stood half naked, staring down at the sparse scattering of dark chest hair, but it was the vibrant blue tattoo reaching in a wide arc from one shoulder to the other that had his attention. He raced to the bathroom with the others close on his heels.

In his reflection, he was greeted with thirteen astronomical like symbols spread evenly across his chest and each appearing to pulsate a soft blue radiance. At the same moment, an avalanche of memories swamped his mind and he collapsed unconscious to the hard tile floor.

Thirty minutes later, he regained consciousness to the watchful eyes of Edmund and Roland sitting opposite him.

"Jon, you passed out again," Edmund announced.

"What? Where am I?" he asked looking around the confines of a small sterile white room.

"You are at Centennial Hills Hospital," Edmund replied as Roland barged into the room with an CT scan in his hand.

"I was right, damn it, I knew all along," he called from the doorway.

He lifted the CT to the light and it needed no explanation.

"What is that?" Bennett asked.

"That my friend is proof of alien abduction. It is a metallic device with tentacles intertwined into your spinal cord."

He took the CT and held it closer to the light. At the third cervical vertebra, a small cylindrical object a few millimetres in length was clearly visible. Reaching out from each end were an abundance of long thin wispy wires intertwined through the bone structure of his neck and meshed upwards into the base of his skull.

"How do we get it out?" Bennett asked reaching behind his neck to massage and search for it.

"I have no idea but my guess, it's not going to be easy."

"You are correct Mr Roland."

They all turned towards the new voice in the room.

43.
<u>Agent Watson</u>

Centennial Hills Hospital
Las Vegas
May 23, 2005

Two men moved swiftly across the room to surround Bennett while the third, the one talking engaged a more sedate entrance taking his time to approach Roland.

"Who are you?" Roland asked nervously. He'd seen men like this before and he knew what was coming.

"Department of Homeland Security, I am Agent Watson, these here are Agents Roberts and Johns. We have some questions for Mr Bennett."

Bennett looked them over, he had seen the handguns on their hips fitted neatly under their opened suit coats. One had made it more obvious as a likely sign of power or warning to him and pulled his jacket back. The one talking looked familiar, he thought, red hair and narrow set blue eyes but he brushed it away as the two beside him edged closer.

"Jon we just want to talk, no need for hostility," the redhaired man said calmly watching Bennett embrace a defensive position.

"What's this all about?" Roland demanded from a few feet further over and Edmund at his side.

The room had become crowded with the six of them and the massive CT scanner taking up most of the space.

"This is not your concern Mr Roland, we just need to take Jon for a few questions, that's all," the agent replied nodding his head towards Bennett and his colleagues.

"Well I'm flattered you know who I am, but you're not taking Jon anywhere, he needs to stay in hospital," Roland replied.

"How do I know you?" Bennett interjected.

"You don't," Agent Watson replied.

Bennett studied the man and glanced to his side, the other two had edged closer exposing their sidearms.

"What do you want with me? What questions?" he asked as the agent to his left took a quick step towards him.

Bennett spun with lightning speed, his hands outstretched snatching the man's sidearm with ease. In one fluid motion, he dropped a few feet backwards and fired two rounds in quick succession. It all happened in less than two seconds and caught them off-guard as the first round struck the second of the two men. The other shot killed the man closest to him. The one calling himself Watson was next as Bennett confirmed his grip and zeroed on the man's head.

"Toss your gun over," he demanded.

Watson spread his hands out, letting his handgun dangle loosely.

"Think about what you've done Bennett, you just killed two Federal agents. Not looking good for you so I suggest you cooperate and you might not face the electric chair."

"My suggestion to you is start talking or you will join them," Bennett responded.

Watson stood his ground and said nothing.

Roland and Edmund were stunned, both peering down at the dead men bleeding from small holes in their foreheads.

The gunfire as expected, had set the hospital on lock down and the pandemonium followed. Nurses ran to shut the wards, patients screamed in fright while the hospital's security detail raced towards the source of the gun shots. Two quick shots were all they had heard and then nothing more.

"What the fuck Bennett, you just killed two federal agents," Roland screamed.

"They're not federal agents. I know this one," Bennett said calmly staring at the one calling himself Agent Watson.

"How can you be so sure?" Roland asked.

"My memories, they are returning quickly. I was being held prisoner in a massive aircraft hangar and this guy here, he was there. I am assuming it was this place you call Sector Four," Bennett replied.

"And our government never issues Soviet made sidearms like the Makarovs these ones have," he added.

Bennett raised the handgun and waved it at Watson.

"Have you come from Sector Four? Is this true?" Roland asked.

Watson glared at them, "You are all dead, you have no idea what you are dealing with."

"Answer him, is it true? Why was I there?" Bennett barked.

Watson started laughing.

"Your memories fail you, but soon you will be dead so none of this will matter."

"Your threats mean nothing, now tell me why I was there," Bennett demanded tightening his grip of the Makarov.

"They all die, it's unavoidable," he said.

"What are you talking about?" Bennett asked.

"The implant in your head, that's why you are here isn't it? The scans show something attached to your spinal cord, am I right?"

Bennett looked to Roland and Edmund standing next to him. Both returned a concerned nod.

"Yes, you are, how do I remove it?"

Watson again started laughing, "You can't."

"Then there is no need for you," Bennett replied pointing his gun at the man's leg and firing.

"ARHH... FUCK YOU BENNETT!" he screamed collapsing to the floor.

"Tell me, how do I remove it," Bennett yelled at him.

"FUCK YOU," he returned defiantly.

Edmund grabbed Bennett's arm, "Enough, no more, we can't stay here, police are coming," Edmund interrupted at the distant sound of sirens.

Bennett grabbed the remaining handguns and headed to the door.

"What about him?" Roland asked.

"We take him with us," Bennett replied striking him in the head with the butt of his gun. He grabbed a bandage and tossed it to Roland, "Wrap the wound, we need to ask him more questions."

The round had exited cleanly through the edge of Watson's knee and the bleeding was controllable.

"Grab a trolley and here, throw these on," he called to the other two who had caught on quickly to what Bennett's plan was.

He had found two hospital uniform overcoats hanging behind the door as he checked the corridor outside the room. Roland knew the layout of the hospital well and had selected an area closed off for refurbishment but still equipped with medical machinery. Roland and Edmund hurled the unconscious Watson onto a trolley and covered him under a sheet.

"Okay all clear outside, let's get moving."

They hurried along the empty corridor, pushing the trolley like they belonged. Once they reached the populated section and the chaos, their exit became easy. No one noticed them descend to the underground carpark and across to the Pontiac parked on the far side where they dumped Watson's unconscious body into the trunk. Somewhere above them, the police sirens had intensified with the first two patrol cars arriving at the hospital's main entrance.

Roland was first to notice and pushed quickly past Edmund. Bennett had slumped to the car's trunk clutching his head like he was fighting to stop it exploding. His fingers white as they squeezed both sides of his skull.

"BENNETT! Stay with us, Charlie help me get him in the car."

They pushed and crammed his semi-conscious body into the rear seat accompanied by his agonising growls and attempts to speak. Neither understood what he was saying, they both thought it was a different language. Edmund took the driver's seat and they sped from the carpark unsure of their next move.

He reached forward and grabbed Edmund's arm, "Stop, need to know how to get rid of this thing."

His voice was quivering with pain from the increasing pressure mounting inside his head as the tentacled device penetrated deeper into his brain, exterminating cells as it advanced. The pain was surging in waves and whereas the episodes had been once every few hours were becoming more frequent. Unbeknown to him, his eighth code nanobots were fighting the intrusion but slowly were losing the battle.

"How? You heard him, you can't remove it!" Roland returned keeping his eyes on the congested traffic heading north towards Highway 95 and back towards Indian Springs.

"He was lying," Bennett said briefly.

"How are you going to make him talk?" Edmund asked but quickly added while shaking his head, "Don't answer that." He knew the answer.

Roland smirked. He was excited in the presence of Bennett; his past twenty years had been dedicated to hunting the truth and exposing government secrets. But like many of his colleagues, he was tainted as a lunatic, an extremist conspiracy theorist who the newspapers enjoyed ridiculing. That to him was another conspiracy, the government forcing the media to discredit him, he thought.

Behind him, Bennett was sitting up, colour returning to his face.

"How's the pain?" Edmund asked.

"Short bursts, mostly gone now."

"What can you remember? You said you were in a hangar?" Roland eagerly asked. The past few years for him had been about proving the existence of Sector Four at Papoose Lake.

"That's all I remember, a massive hangar, nothing else."

They slipped from the midday traffic and headed south along a narrow gravel road.

"Where are we going?" Bennett asked.

"Somewhere private so our friend will talk," Roland answered pointing towards a metal structure a few miles in front of them.

"It's an abandoned scrap metal yard, no one goes there. You know so plenty of privacy for you to make him talk!" Roland added.

"My recent memories are not good but there is something going on," Bennett announced leaning forward again.

"What?" Edmund asked.

"Something is urging me to return and I don't know what it is or why, just this feeling there is something there I need."

"Or someone!" Roland interjected.

"What do you mean?"

"The something you speak of could be a someone. It may not have been just you there," Roland replied.

Bennett sat back again in deep thought, trawling the memories he had, but nothing surfaced. It was all his distant past, childhood memories, his time in the Navy and the beginning of his CIA days. Like the pieces of a scrambled jigsaw, nothing would make sense until more constructed segments were revealed.

They drove to the back side of the metal yard where they were hidden from view of the highway. A few minutes was all it took Bennett, he had attached wires to the car's battery and dragged their semi-conscious prisoner from the trunk. The bleeding had stopped.

Roland helped tie the prisoner to the car bumper while Bennett tested the current, slapping the wires together. A bright cracking spark erupted fully alerting their prisoner, he knew what was coming.

"Okay by the look on your face, you know the rules so no need for me to explain them," Bennett said.

Watson said nothing.

"Xavier, can you remove our friend's clothes."

Edmund stood watching from a distance, he wasn't a supporter of what was about to happen.

"Jon, is this really necessary?" he called.

Bennett ignored him and prodded the prisoner's bare flesh with the wires.

An agonising scream rang out and Edmund turned away in disgust. Watson's body tightened, every muscle contracted against the electric charge.

"How do I remove it?"

"Fuck you Bennett!" he screamed.

"Wrong answer!" Bennett said and pushed the wires into his bare stomach.

Watson cringed, pulling forward on his hand restraints, muscles tense and veins almost exploding from under his skin. Sweat beaded across his face while he fought to hold his composure.

"Tell me how I remove it," Bennett demanded lowering the wires towards his manhood.

Watson remained silent, watching as the wires drew closer to his groin.

"WAIT... STOP!" he yelped as the wire nicked his testicles.

The pain was instantly crippling, ripping through his genitals like a burning hot poker fresh from the furnace.

"The device can only be removed using the same machine that implanted it."

"Where is this machine?" Bennett demanded.

"Same place you were two days ago, second level, room 21C."

"Where was he two days ago? It was Sector Four, wasn't it?" Roland interrupted.

Watson laughed staring at Roland saying nothing.

Roland unleashed a right hook square to the man's face, splitting his lip clean open. Blood spilled down the side of his chin and dripped to his bare chest.

"Tell me, where is it, where is Sector Four," he yelled grabbing Watson's head and pulling it close to his so that his angered spit showered the man.

Behind him Bennett watched, shocked at Roland's sudden outburst.

"I know who you are, you don't fool us," Watson whispered through his clenched teeth staring directly into Roland's dark eyes.

"What the fuck are you doing?" Bennett screamed pulling Roland back with the help of Edmund who was just as shocked at the sudden aggressive discharge.

"I'm sorry, I don't know what came over me!"

"You know Bennett, even if you do manage to remove the device, you won't stop her," Watson said.

"What? Who won't I stop?" Bennett asked. At the same time, a sudden rush of movement threw him off balance and he fell backwards to the hard desert floor.

Watson had broken free and attacked Bennett in three quick strides and a volley of strikes to his head. They wrestled for a few seconds before Bennett punched and kicked his way free to the sudden sound of a gun shot at close range.

Their prisoner collapsed to the ground holding the bloodied hole in his chest.

"You idiot, we needed him," Bennett screamed at Roland still aiming his handgun at the dying man on the ground.

"Who is she?" Bennett demanded, peering down into the man's dark eyes fading from life.

His expression went lifeless and he took his last breath.

Bennett slumped back onto his knees and glared at Roland, "At least tell me, you know where this Sector Four is?"

"No but I have an idea. I think I know where a back entrance is. There is only one problem."

"Yeah what's that?"

"It's a one-way ticket, no one has ever returned when they've gone searching."

Bennett stood for a moment studying his French companion, wondering what it was he found familiar about him. A fractured memory perhaps, he thought, but the last few minutes showcased Roland in a different light.

They disposed of Watson's body and left the scrapyard heading back towards Las Vegas.

Overhead at ten thousand feet, a prototype surveillance drone was relaying ground images back to a control room in Washington DC.

44.
Papoose Lake

Papoose Lake
May 24, 2005

Twelve hours later under the secrecy of the early morning darkness they advanced their way slowly along a small narrow ravine carved from years of wind and rain. Bennett moved the quickest with Roland close behind, but Edmund struggled to keep pace on the uneven rocky ground. His aging body to blame. The desert around them was peacefully quiet except for the occasional rush of wind channelling like a rolling surge of water along the ravine. Either side, the walls were tall, well above their heads making it ideal for a covert approach towards their target.

For the past hour they had been edging closer, keeping out of sight they hoped, towards an area two miles east of Papoose Lake. An expanse of rocky terrain pitted with old abandoned mine shafts condemned by local authorities. Signage every fifty yards had unnerved Edmund and he was becoming more hesitant on every step.

RESTRICTED AREA
US GOVERNMENT PROPERTY
NO TRESPASSING

"Don't all these signs worry you?" he called from a few yards back.

"Only if we get caught!" Roland responded with a laugh.

Bennett ignored them and kept moving towards a clump of rocks twenty yards in front of them. The half-moon high in the sky showered them in a sparse scattering of light, enough to guide them without using the flashlights they all carried.

"Stop, you hear that?" he called back to the others.

Somewhere in the distance the whine of a turbine engine grew louder.

"There!" Bennett announced pointing towards a dark shape approaching them at speed and less than fifty feet above the ground.

"What is it?" Roland asked.

"Gunship like the ones back at Edmund's," Bennett responded keeping his eyes pressed to his night vision binoculars watching the inbound machine.

After dumping Watson's body, they had returned to Roland's house where to the delight of Bennett, he discovered he was an army fanatic and kept a small stash. But unlike Edmund, he knew how to fire the big ones. Five years in the French army had been enough to teach him the essentials of decent combat until he deserted deciding it wasn't for him. He avoided prosecution by fleeing France into eastern Europe and then eventually found his way to the United States.

Bennett rummaged through a collection of handguns, assault rifles and tactical accoutrements including the binoculars he was now holding. They took what they could carry and drove the ninety-mile trek from Las Vegas to Papoose Lake, an area of barrenness, seven miles south of Area 51. The journey took them back through Indian Springs and north along the same desolate dirt road that Bennett had been found wandering aimlessly along by Bishop two days earlier.

"Come on, under here, that gunship will have infrared," Bennett called pointing towards a small rock escarpment recessed a few feet into the cliff face.

They scrambled and pinned themselves hard against the rock wall hoping the gunship didn't detect their heat signatures under the narrow ledge. Bennett unleashed his rifle off his shoulder and readied himself. Roland mirrored his every move while Edmund pressed himself harder into the rocks.

A few seconds and the machine passed without slowing.

Up ahead they could see the terrain growing steeper and the ravine was abruptly ending. Another five minutes of walking, mostly climbing and they were back up top on the open ground at the southern end of Papoose Mountain. There the slope was more forgiving.

"Over there, that's the entrance," Roland announced pointing his rifle towards a clump of large rocks twenty feet up the side of the mountain. Bennett looked out across the dark desert valley stretching to the east, he could just make out the scattered rocky outcrops silhouetted under the dim light of the half-moon. He checked the horizon in every direction, the gunship had gone, though something else caught his attention. A small flash of white light like that of a flashlight.

Roland moved quickly leaving them behind while Bennett kept his eye on the source of the light.

"Roland wait, someone's watching us," he called.

"What? Where?"

"About three hundred yards," Bennett replied beckoning with his rifle to the east.

They stood watching the darkness, no sign of the light while Bennett scanned the area with his night vision binoculars.

"Can't see anything. Let's keep going," Bennett announced turning towards the stacked rocks.

"Who do you think they are?" Edmund asked.

"Don't know, though I reckon that gunship will be coming back real soon, so let's not waste any time."

They reached the clump of rocks and found a small narrow opening leading underground at the base.

"This used to be a mine shaft, gold mine from the 1920's. They are littered all over these parts, but this is the only one close to the mountain," Roland announced, shining his flashlight into the dark depths of the opening.

A crude wooden ladder clung to the side of the cavity disappearing into the fading beam of light.

"How far down do you think it goes?" Bennett asked.

"I don't know but mining surveys for this area had the gold vein at about two hundred feet."

"How do you know this leads to Sector Four?" Edmund asked.

215

"I don't, though it's been rumoured for a long time now there were secret passageways built during the construction back in the 1950's. The US government started building it as a nuclear bunker during the cold war, but my source says it was never completed. The same source says it was sold off to a private company. I never found out who and there is nothing in the public records about ownership."

They started the descent as each ladder rung creaked and groaned under their weight. The eighty year old timber had deteriorated well beyond its ability to hold the load and each step confirmed it.

After twenty feet, Edmund was first to fall.

45.
Tunnels

Papoose Lake
May 24, 2005

In the narrow beam of light, Bennett caught glimpse of Edmund tumbling towards him, desperately grappling the rock face to halt his fall. The ladder rungs under his boots snapped like twigs and he fell faster crashing into Bennett. Like dominoes, they dropped under the combined weight crashing into Roland, a few rungs further below. The old wooden ladder disintegrated and together they plummeted the remaining five feet onto the cold hard floor of a subterranean cavern.

Bennett clambered to his feet scanning the walls of their new surrounds with his flashlight and his handgun fixed alongside. The cavity was just on fifteen feet across and high enough to stand with room to spare. At the western end, a narrow tunnel was partly visible behind a stack of fallen rocks. The old timber framework holding the ceiling up was failing in places, made worse by the slow seepage of water trickling down the walls.

"Doesn't look very safe," Edmund declared grimacing in pain as he staggered over to Bennett's side. He had landed hard on one leg and buckled under his weight, hammering his hip against a rock protruding from the cavern floor.

Bennett turned to him looking him up and down. Edmund just nodded to acknowledge his pain, but all was okay.

Roland on the other hand had escaped injury and was already pushing past Bennett taking a few steps into the tunnel, edging around the scattered rocks.

"Roland wait, can you hear that?" Bennett whispered, ushering both men to be silent.

Somewhere deep inside the tunnel a faint whirring hum like that of a fan could be heard.

"Sounds like a ventilation system," Roland said moving further into the tunnel. The others followed.

At that moment, another sound interrupted their conversation and Bennett charged Edmund, pushing him into the tunnel. Somewhere above them the mine shaft had started collapsing inwards showering the cavern in earth and rocks, narrowly missing them. A few seconds was all it took for the entire cavern to fill.

Inside the tunnel, the three men were shaken, but it was Edmund who was panicking and clawing at the rocks, trying desperately to shift them.

"We're going to die," he screamed, pushing harder at the wall of rocks blocking the tunnel entrance.

"Charlie, calm the fuck down. We'll find a way out," Bennett yelled, grabbing him by the shoulders and showering him in light.

Roland showed no interest, instead he was exploring the tunnel with the beam of his flashlight.

"Let's see where this tunnel takes us," he called back.

He and Bennett slung their rifles across their backs and together with Edmund, they edged slowly along the dark narrow passageway towards the low humming noise.

A few minutes and their flashlights lit up something sprawled across their path. A distinctly sour odour grew more potent the further they walked and their eyes started watering from the pungent stench of rotting flesh. Up ahead a human body was visible, mostly decomposed to expose the bones. The organs had been devoured by rats and the flesh had liquified fusing into the dirtied clothing. The skull screamed a painful death with its mouth wide open and the head rolled back.

Edmund buckled over and dry reached, he had never been exposed to such a noisome sight and it shook him hard, pinching his nose and backing away.

Bennett didn't falter in his stride, pushing past Roland to inspect it more closely under his flashlight. Carefully pushing it over with the edge of his boot, he noticed something fall from a pocket.

"What is it?" Roland asked.

"Nevada driver's license in the name of Alex Spedman, 58 years old," Bennett replied picking it up and rolling it over in his hand.

Roland stood staring at the corpse for a moment, a sullen look had overcome him.

"Do you know this man?" Bennett inquired.

"Yes. He was an old friend who went missing about a year ago. A few weeks before he disappeared, I saw him in Las Vegas where he was meeting someone from the Government. He wouldn't tell me who, but they claimed to have worked at Sector Four. I tried to contact him a few times in the days after the meeting, but that was the last I saw of him. Poor Alex."

He continued staring at the corpse, "How do you think he died?"

"Painfully by the look of it. Too far decomposed to see any obvious cause of death," Bennett answered.

"What's that over there?" Edmund asked pointing towards another dark object further along the tunnel.

A second body similar in appearance to the first became visible under their flashlights except this one had no identification. The level of decomposition was the same and like the first one, they appeared to have suffered an excruciating death.

They pushed past it and kept moving slowly, edging closer to the humming sound. It was barely wide enough for them to walk single file and the timber supports every few yards had collapsed in places letting earth spill across the floor. The air was dense with the foul stench of death no matter how far they distanced themselves from the bodies.

"There is light up ahead," Bennett announced as they approached a slight bend in the tunnel.

"Looks like a hatch," he added.

A steel door mostly concealed by earth and fallen rock marked the end of the tunnel. It was slightly ajar, allowing a soft yellow light to filter through from behind it. Painted on the door were the words 'Entry Strictly Prohibited' and the world renowned ionizing radiation symbol beneath it. Under the warning appeared the words 'United States Government'.

A small rock had wedged open the door an inch and earth had spilled through jamming it in place. Bennett tried to pull it open, but it only moved a few more inches until the rocks blocked its path.

For the next couple of minutes, they tossed loose rocks aside and dug away the damp soil. Above them the old timber planks lining the ceiling were cracked and warped, creating the unnerving feeling it would collapse at any minute. Edmund was the one most nervous and hurried the others along.

"I was right about this place," Roland declared as he and Bennett yanked at the door.

They heaved with all their strength and slowly it creaked open, accompanied by a loud grinding squeal until the gap was wide enough to squeeze through.

"Hang on Roland!" Bennett ordered as he grabbed Roland's arm halting his rush to climb through.

He raised his gun and together they stepped through with him leading the way.

46.
<u>Sector Four</u>

Papoose Lake
May 24, 2005

"There's the source of the humming sound," Bennett said pointing towards the overhead ventilation ducts.

"What is this place?" Roland stuttered, confused by his surroundings.

The darkness of the tunnel had been replaced with a dim yellowish haze, enough to display a long rectangular room roughly fifty yards long by twenty wide. The ceiling was over forty feet above them. Along each side were steel clad rooms with small windows embedded like those of portholes on a ship. Each were no bigger than one foot in diameter. A solid steel door the size of a small truck was evenly positioned in the middle of each room, all with four sturdy hinges and a triple bolt locking system.

"Your guess is as good as mine, I'm not sure I want to know what's behind these doors," Bennett replied curiously covering the first of the rooms under the beam of his flashlight and handgun.

Edmund, the scientist among them, was more intrigued and stepped in close to look through the first small porthole. Through the darkness he could see a faint green light shining from the other side, though not enough to reveal the interior.

"Give me your flashlight," he called to Bennett.

The window glass was thick, possibly an inch which made shining the light through it diffract in all directions.

"What do you see?" Roland asked impatiently.

"Can't really see much, looks like a laboratory of some kind. Wait there's something...!"

The steel door shuddered from something on the inside ramming it. Edmund was thrown backwards onto his ass mostly from the sudden shock of what he thought he'd seen. Bennett grabbed the flashlight and jumped to the porthole.

"Holy fuck!" he exclaimed.

"What was it?" Roland screamed desperately.

"Don't really know, a large animal or beast," he replied still shining his light into the room and added, "Can't see it now."

"Did you see its eyes?" Edmund asked lifting himself back onto his feet and limping across to Bennett.

"Yes, larger than dinner plates and eerie black, almost glistening," he replied without taking his eyes from the interior of the room.

"That's what I saw too," Edmund added.

Bennett could feel another migraine coming on and remembered his purpose. "Come on, we need to find the second level."

They walked faster past another six rooms all the same size with the faint green light inside. At the end of the main room was a single normal sized doorway clearly marked with an exit sign. On the wall next to the door was a glass covered box like the emergency fire alarms in commercial buildings except this had one distinct difference.

Inside the box was a single blue crystalline looking object no bigger than a golf ball. On the underside of the box, a red push button protruded. Warnings in large letters lined the wall on each side.

EMERGENCY EVACUATION
Press red button for activation
Exposure in 15 seconds once activated

"What do you make of that?" Roland asked.

"Containment of whatever is in those rooms I would think," Bennett answered, mesmerised by the blue object.

"What is it Bennett?" Edmund asked witnessing the strange look on his face.

"Not sure, something about that blue object is familiar, like I know exactly what it is. My memories are still very scattered," he replied moving to the doorway and reaching to open it.

He stepped through into a dimly lit stairway.

"It looks like we're on the lowest section," he said shining his flashlight up the steps.

Above them the staircase vanished into darkness.

"This is level six," Roland said shining his flashlight on the rear of the door.

On the door, a large numeral six was stencilled in red. Under the sign, the words "Exobiology Storage - Restricted Access" were painted.

Roland stood staring at it.

"Exobiology, what's that?" he asked.

"The study of extraterrestrial life," Edmund answered slowly returning his thoughts to what he had witnessed in the room.

Bennett turned and looked at Edmund, he was having a similar reflection.

"I can't believe this is happening, it is all true. All this time, we were right, this base does exist," Roland muttered still staring at the sign.

"Come on, no time for I told you so speeches," Bennett commanded.

They commenced the climb as somewhere high up the stairwell, a group of people could be heard descending the stairs. Their boots pounded the concrete echoing down the narrow stairwell but without haste in their steps.

"Guards coming," Bennett whispered to Roland.

Roland unstrapped his Colt battle rifle from across his shoulders and took aim up the stairwell. Bennett did the same. Together they advanced leaving Edmund to catch up.

"Looks like about five passing through level two," Bennett confirmed through his night vision binoculars.

"In here," Edmund called from outside the door to level four.

Above them, the sound of the guards stomping grew closer and Bennett reversed up with Roland at his side. Together they all entered level four.

It opened onto a long narrow corridor leading to a massive hangar. Though mostly covered in darkness, a sparse scattering of lighting around the perimeter alluded to its size, a football field across.

Bennett moved quickly to the left with his gun raised. Roland did the same to the right.

"Place is deserted," Roland whispered.

Bennett checked his watch, "Three am, no wonder!"

The floor space was lined with rows of dark objects covered by green tarps, some larger than passenger airliners while others the size of small buses. To their right, the row seemed endless but to their left, four massive hangar doors measuring thirty feet across stood side by side. Each extended upwards fifty feet to the ceiling and sat atop two parallel steel roller tracks embedded into the concrete floor.

"What is this place?" Edmund muttered gazing up at the enormity of the high ceilings and across the vastness to the far side.

No one answered him.

Roland had raced twenty yards across the floor to the closest object and yanked on the tarp, it didn't budge. He explored the underside, shining his flashlight onto the silvery metallic skin of a massive craft. The light beam slithered and refracted off the surface in all directions seemingly magnified tenfold and the sudden abundance of light displayed the detail.

The craft was long, reaching eighty feet in length and cylindrical, twenty feet across resting on four vertical struts, twice his height. Overall it gave resemblance to a gargantuan cigar, though all he could see was the underside. The metal skin was like nothing he had ever seen before and under the light, glistened as though wet.

Roland was in awe, an alien space craft, he thought, until something caught his eye. A distinct marking reflected off the beam of his flashlight.

47.
Level Two

Sector Four
May 24, 2005

Roland stood confused, deflated.

"For decades, people worldwide have been reporting the unusual appearance of long cylinder-shaped UFO's in the sky. Until a few minutes ago, I was going to say this confirms the existence of alien spaceships. Then I saw this," he said as Bennett appeared at his side.

He lifted the beam of his torch and exposed a small metal plate welded to the underside. On the plate was inscribed the words, 'Ramadon Missiles'.

"As you can see, this is American made."

"Ramadon Missiles? That sounds familiar?" Bennett asked.

"Yes they are the world's largest producer of ballistic missiles and were just recently taken over by the Orionis Andromeda Corporation for half a trillion dollars. Biggest deal in history," Roland answered.

Edmund interrupted the conversation.

"And it means Eckhard Banks now supplies ninety percent of the world's high-tech arsenal, but worse than that is his nuclear capability. He builds and sells nuclear weapons and even though the United Nations condemn him for it, legally they cannot stop him."

Bennett could only vaguely remember Ramadon Missiles.

"Who is Banks?" he asked.

Roland answered him.

"Eckhard Banks is the owner of the Orionis Andromeda Corporation. The guy is worth billions and most of his wealth has been made from war. Orionis can mass produce just about every tactical air weapon in the world including intercontinental nuclear missiles. Speculation has it that he has over five hundred nuclear warheads stockpiled somewhere just in case world war three starts and one side runs out! Banks is a complete lunatic, a man obsessed with money and power. I remember reading an article about him as a child drowning his younger brother so he would be the single heir to his father's wealth. Seriously, what kind of kid thinks that? None of it could be proven and was written off as a tragic drowning accident, but the local Sheriff was adamant he'd killed him."

"Do you think these are missiles?" Edmund asked motioning with his hand towards the cylinder above them.

"No not in the traditional sense," Bennett interjected inviting a quizzical expression from the others.

"I believe this is a large dispersal device. See look there," he said pointing his flashlight towards rows of small openings on the underside.

The whole surface resembled a giant cheese grater, covered in small circular recessed sections, some open with the lid protruding downwards a few inches.

"But to disperse what?" Edmund asked.

Somewhere behind them, a door swung open and a man dressed in a white lab coat walked through. The others dropped to the floor behind the concealment of the tarp as a bank of lights started flickering on across the hangar.

Bennett leapt to his feet.

The man in the lab coat had been busy staring at his clipboard, flicking light switches on and he didn't see the dark figure launch at him from behind. Bennett sprinted the twenty yards in silence and like an Olympic long jumper, he lifted himself from the floor and dropped his boot into the man's back pushing him forward. In one smooth fluid action, he wrapped his arm around the man's neck and lowered him unconscious to the floor.

"He won't be out for long," Bennett called to Roland while at the same time, he reached down and snatched the man's access card from his coat pocket.

"There must be over a hundred of these cylinders," Roland said looking out across the expanse of the hangar floor as more lights powered to life.

"Closer to two hundred," Bennett replied turning abruptly to a sound behind them.

The man was starting to stir, first his eyes flickered and then his head moved. He opened his eyes engaging Bennett's as Roland stepped forward and with the butt of his rifle, slammed it unforgivingly into the man's head.

"There he will be out for a little longer now!" he smirked.

"We can't stay here, we need to get to level two," Bennett interjected in an authoritarian tone.

They hurried back to the door they'd entered through.

"Okay we ready?" Bennett said not waiting for the answer and opened the stairwell door.

It was clear, no sound of the guards as they edged their way up past level three and onto the landing outside the level two door. Bennett and Roland stopped, waiting for Edmund to catch up and with their guns leading the way, they pushed the door open.

It was different to the other levels. A wide brightly lit corridor greeted them in silence with another closed doorway at the far end, thirty yards away. Two dark grey doors lined either side, each clearly marked starting with 21A and 21B closest to them. A card swipe device was mounted on the wall next to each door.

"Damn," Bennett said pointing with his eyes to a security camera fixed on the ceiling.

Roland reached up and smashed it with the butt of his rifle.

"I guess they will definitely know now!" Bennett mumbled, hurrying along the corridor towards the last two doors.

"So, what's your plan when we get into this room?" Roland asked checking behind as they progressed.

"I have no idea. Hopefully it becomes clear when we are there!" Bennett laughed sarcastically.

"There it is, room 21C," Roland announced pointing to a set of double doors unlike the ones they had just passed. The two doors side by side were much larger and wider.

"Xavier!" Edmund yelled from five yards further back.

Bennett had lost his balance and had collapsed to the floor unconscious. In front of him, Roland hadn't noticed.

"Oh shit, Charlie stay with him," he called and grabbed the key card from Bennett's hand.

He lifted his rifle and slid the key card across the scanner pad. The doors swung slowly inwards and Roland readied himself behind his rifle sights, partly shielded by the opening doors.

48.
Room 21C

Level 2, Sector Four
May 24, 2005

The room was brightly lit and devoid of life, just an elaborate padded chair fitted with head and arm restraints in the centre of the room. Behind the chair, a sophisticated looking machine made up of two long slender robotic arms dangled from the ceiling. Each had a robotic claw on its end and appeared more like a sadistic torture machine from a horror movie.

They carried Bennett's limp body across to the chair and positioned him.

"We're in the right room. Look!" Roland directed Edmund's attention towards a bank of cabinets lining one wall.

Inside one of the cabinets a metal tray contained six glass cylinders roughly six inches tall by two inches in diameter. Each had a metal screw lid and inside a tiny grey object drifted, as if swimming.

Edmund stood staring for a few seconds.

"Charlie, come on. We have to work out how to use this machine," Roland yelled.

"Those things… they are what is in Bennett's head, right?" he said pointing towards the canisters.

"Yes, now come on!"

"They are alive, parasites of some kind," Edmund added still drawn to the peculiar entities that distinctly resembled tiny metallic jelly fish with bundles of lengthy transparent tentacles protruding from the underside. Each ebbed and flowed together with the motion of the creature's body as if dancing. To Edmund they were beautiful and hypnotic.

"No, they are machines… not alive at all. Here look at this," Roland said thrusting a folder of documents into his hands, breaking his fixation.

Inside was a series of A4 size pages containing handwritten notes about nanotechnology and micro-computer chips. Some contained detailed schematic drawings of the tiny machines inside the canisters with the main body housing a mass of microscopic computer circuitry around a CPU, no larger than a pin head.

"Says here these things embed themselves into the spinal cord and invade the brain starting with the temporal lobe. That would explain the loss of memory," Roland said flicking through pages of other documents while Edmund fired up the computer.

Roland continued.

"The long thin tentacles act as neurotransmitters designed to connect with the human nervous system into the brain relaying and receiving messages."

He paused.

"Well this isn't good. Says these things eventually take full control of the human host with death occurring between thirty to ninety days."

"As I said, parasites!" Edmund muttered.

"Yes, but man-made parasites," Roland acknowledged and added, "This might help."

He handed Edmund a ten-page bound document labelled, 'Extraction Procedures'.

Edmund snatched it and opened the first page.

"Surely it can't be this easy," he muttered racing over to a keyboard attached to the side of the machine.

"Sit Bennett up straight and restrain his head into the head cage," he said as he read out loud, "Make sure his head is strapped in tight, can't be any movement."

He continued reading, flicking over to the second page before his fingers danced across the keyboard and the machine vibrated to life. At first a series of long harmonious beeps sounded and then as if the chair came to life, the sides extended around him, conforming to his shape and restraining his limbs. The same occurred around his throat while behind him, the mechanical arms uncoiled. Slowly they extended towards the back of Bennett's head. Both arms moved slowly in unison to within a few inches of his head and stopped.

At the end of one arm, a thin blue beam of light pinpointed the back of Bennett's neck, moving in a circular motion before stopping. The other arm lifted, aligned itself with the blue dot and slowly, a long hollow needle protruded forward. Edmund and Roland watched as the needle tip caressed the skin. A speck of blood dribbled from around the insertion as the needle pierced the flesh.

For the next two seconds nothing happened. Then the arm shot forward, deep into his neck and Bennett's eyes sprung wide open.

His body started convulsing, twisting violently against the restraints and though his agonised howls were distracting, Roland was first to react to the door bursting open behind them.

49.
Level One

Level 2, Sector Four
May 24, 2005

Two guards dressed in dark grey battle fatigues charged the room, shooting as they advanced. The first bullet hit Edmund in the shoulder and the second sliced through his chest. Roland anticipated the attack and dropped to the floor firing as he fell, killing the leading guard. The second retaliated with a volley of shots and Roland rolled sideways to cover himself behind Edmund's body. The rounds smacked into Edmund's lifeless body and ricocheted off the floor, one shattering a glass canister.

Roland returned fire and the guard retreated to the corridor with Roland quick on his heels, firing as he ran. The guard turned, squeezed his trigger to the clunking sound of the slide slamming back and his magazine empty of bullets. The last thing he witnessed before he died was the muzzle flash of Roland's gun.

At the end of the corridor, an amber warning light was flashing while an irritating siren signalled reinforcements were soon to arrive. Back behind him, Bennett had regained consciousness though he still shook and convulsed uncontrollably, battling the clutches of the chair. His face contorted with a combination of agony and fear while a floodgate of sweat had opened, drenching his clothes. Beside him, blood pooled outwards across the white tiles from under Edmund's body.

Roland stood staring for a moment, out of respect for his dead scientist friend before he scanned the corridor and raced to Bennett. The needle had retracted and exited his neck, leaving a thin trail of blood. From inside the hollow tip of the needle protruded a miniscule metallic claw tightly grappling an object covered in blood. He leaned in for a closer look as the chair retracted its hold on Bennett.

Measuring less than a few millimetres, Roland recognised the object straight away. The main body consisted of shiny silver metal and at one end, a bundle of dark thin fibres like cotton thread, dangled lifelessly towards the floor. He peered over at the canisters of parasites, it was the same.

"What happened? Is it out?" Bennett asked, dazed and slurring his words.

"Yes, you passed out. Charlie, bless his soul, got it out."

Bennett glanced sideways at the two bodies massed in blood.

"Edmund! Is he dead?"

"Yes, a couple of guards found us, both dead now but poor old Charlie didn't make it."

Bennett pulled himself up from the chair and lost his balance, slipping to his knees. Roland grabbed him.

"How's your memory now?" he asked.

"I can remember more of my younger past but nothing recent, that's still a blank," he replied looking around the room.

"Is that what was in me?" he asked pointing towards the canisters.

Roland briefly explained the minute devices.

Bennett made no reply, he instead looked down at Edmund's body. He'd only known the man for two days, yet he felt a deep saddening wash over him.

"Can you walk? We can't stay here, more guards will be coming," Roland said.

"Yes, I think so," he replied shaking the grief from his mind.

Roland helped him to his feet and though he was a little fragile at first, he quickly reached full stride. Together they entered the corridor as the stairwell door swung open with a platoon of guards charging through.

"This way Bennett," Roland yelled yanking at him towards the closed door to their left.

Bennett fired a series of rapid shots at the guards, dropping one to the floor and forcing the others to retreat into the stairwell. Behind him, Roland swiped the access card and the door opened inwards while Bennett fired two more covering shots at the stairwell door.

They stepped through into another high ceiling hangar.

"Here help me?" Bennett called running across to a row of cabinets next to the door.

Together they heaved and pushed one across the door.

"That should hold them off for a short while," he said as he joined Roland to view their surroundings.

The hangar was distinctly smaller than the one on level four and the lighting gave them full view across the fifty-yard expanse. To their left, workbenches crowded with tools and machine parts lined the wall. To their right, four cubicles sat side by side, behind glass panels. Inside each, a bank of mainframe computers blinked red and green.

The hangar floor was mostly empty, except for three small vehicles resembling oversized golf buggies parked on the far side.

"What's that?" Roland asked pointing towards the centre of the hangar.

They walked to within a few feet of a huge square opening in the floor and peered down into the darkness of a deep elevator shaft. Evenly spaced across the opening were four massive vertical hydraulic pistons, each over ten feet in diameter and extending upwards into the ceiling. Below them the same shaft and pistons dropped away into the darkness of the lower levels.

"Maybe it's how they get their craft to the outside, a launch pad somewhere higher up," Roland commented looking up.

"It's big enough!" Bennett sneered.

"Yeah if you're transporting jumbo jets!" Roland laughed.

The cabinet holding the door shut jolted an inch as the guards pushed and heaved to move it.

"Wait here, I have an idea." Bennett sprinted across the hangar, around the edge of the elevator shaft and climbed into the closest buggy. It was larger than he first thought, nothing like a golf buggy at all. It resembled a small aircraft pushback tractor with the accompanying power as it roared to life under his boot.

The cabinet slid another inch as the guards gained traction and one pushed his gun through firing a blind shot narrowly missing Roland. But it wasn't the gun that almost killed him, it was Bennett driving the tractor head on into the cabinet at a speed that threw him sideways in shock. The force slammed the door shut crushing the guard's arm and crumpling the cabinet. Bennett yanked the hand brake on and jumped down.

"Sorry Roland, the thing got away on me!" he joked but Roland wasn't amused.

On the other side of the door, they could hear the guard's agonized screams and the others yelling commands for reinforcements.

"Come on, there's a lift on the other side," Bennett called pointing towards the other tractors.

They moved quickly across the floor and entered the lift, pressing the level one button.

"What's the plan Bennett?"

"There's something here I have to destroy, I remember that much now," he said.

"What is it?"

"Some advanced weapon that's far more destructive than our nukes."

The lift ascended slowly while he explained to Roland what he could remember about the president's visit. He kept it brief.

"That certainly explains why Banks is involved, but I am not sure what he gains if the US, Russia and China nuke each other off the face of the earth," Roland added.

Bennett made no reply, instead he raised his gun as the lift jolted to a halt and the doors slid open. Roland mirrored his move and together they stepped quickly out onto a massive steel platform like that of an aircraft carrier. In the centre, an unusual looking aircraft sat idle while beneath it, four men dressed in grey overalls busied themselves disconnecting hoses and checking their clipboards. They hadn't noticed the lift door open.

Bennett and Roland darted ten paces to behind a stack of fuel drums out of sight of the men.

At first glance, the craft resembled a B2 stealth bomber with its flat triangular wing, distinct lack of vertical tail fins and long flat fuselage. However, unlike the B2, the outer metal skin resembled a mirror, polished silver reflecting light in every direction and under the hangar lights, it glimmered. It stood ten feet above the deck on sturdy struts and passenger jet size wheels. Two massive twenty-foot-long cylindrical jet engines were mounted at the ends of both wings giving the craft a sense of enormity. It was difficult to distinguish whether it was man made or alien.

The steel platform was wide and on the far side, four launch tunnels side by side gave signs of the night sky and a myriad of stars. To their left, a door opened and two pilots walked through, both wearing the same black flight suits and metallic silver helmets. One broke from formation and engaged conversation with the workmen in overalls while the other climbed up inside the craft. A minute later, he entered the craft and the four engines commenced start up into a high pitch squeal.

"I have to get onboard that craft," Bennett shouted over the increasing deafening whine of the engines.

"Do you think the weapon is on it?" Roland called back.

"I don't know but my gut feeling is saying yes," he replied.

Roland nodded and raised his rifle above one of the drums and took aim.

"Okay get ready!" he called.

Bennett caught on quickly to what he was about to do.

The first high powered shot went unheard and a workman dropped to the floor. The next three rolled off in the same time it took for the other workmen to realise their colleague had been killed by a sniper. Above them, the pilots continued their start-up sequence as Bennett leapt to full sprint across the platform under the watchful eye of Roland's rifle.

He raced past the four workmen slumped lifeless on the floor and landed on the first tread of the ladder as it lifted into the underside of the craft. He was onboard leaving Roland behind on the platform, alone, as the lift doors opened.

50.
Bomber

Airspace over Nevada
May 24, 2005

Bennett examined the interior of the aircraft, a chamber normally housing sixteen B83 thermonuclear warheads had been vastly refitted. A ten-foot tubular shaped device hung from the ceiling pointing downwards at the bomb doors. At the upper end, thick black cables connected it to a computer fixed to the aircraft's sidewall. It resembled a massive spear with a deep red crimson tip measuring three feet in length.

The craft's cockpit had no door, revealing a brightly lit instrument panel and the pilots immersed in switches and the controls. Keeping from their sight, Bennett edged closer to inspect the spear.

"Lucifer's Funnel!" he mumbled to himself.

He had recalled the crimson red chunk of crystal nicknamed 'Lucifer's Funnel', discovered at the Roswell UFO crash site. This displayed similar qualities.

"Fuck this isn't good," he swore silently as the computer activated and the monitor illuminated. Lines of code appeared rolling down the screen until the computer beeped.

The screen had gone blank except for two lines displayed in green.

Coordinates received...
Enter confirmation code>

As more memories slipped into place, he raised his gun and charged the cockpit.

One of the pilots reached for their gun and Bennett responded pressing his handgun into the pilot's chest and firing one round. As quick as he did, he spun to aim the gun at the other pilot's head.

"Okay don't shoot!" she said, a definite panic resonating in her voice.

"What is that weapon back there?"

"It's the code thirteen pulse weapon, thought you would have known that. You are Jon Bennett aren't you?" she replied giving Bennett a quizzical look.

"How's that possible? There hasn't been enough time to decode the schematics," Bennett said. He had a vague recollection the code had been taken from him a few days earlier.

"Reversed engineered from the weapon onboard the alien craft," the pilot answered.

"What alien craft? It was destroyed at Roswell," Bennett said.

"Another one was discovered in Antarctica. It has a fully intact pulse weapon, but no one knows how to operate it," she answered glancing forward at the instruments.

"He was my friend you know," she added pointing at the dead co-pilot.

Bennett ignored her.

"If it was reversed engineered then why do you still need the thirteenth code schematics?" he asked.

"Too many unknowns in the technology, the engineers could only achieve ten per cent capability, that is why the code was still needed."

Bennett nodded. He didn't suspect the woman was lying.

"What's your target today?"

"Somewhere in Northern China close to the Russian border but I don't know exact coordinates until I check the computer in the back."

"Shenyang and Zavitinsk, were these results of the weapon?" Bennett asked.

The pilot nodded.

"Why?" Bennett demanded.

She was about to answer as an orange light flashed on the panel.

"Radio message!" the pilot confirmed as Bennett reached for a headset hanging next to him.

"Blue pulse one, I repeat. You have a stowaway. Take immediate caution, subject is extremely dangerous. Lethal force is authorised. Base out."

"Respond, tell them the subject has been eliminated and don't do anything stupid. If you know who I am, then you know I can probably fly this," Bennett said to the pilot's surprised look. She didn't know about Bennett's fighter pilot background.

"This is blue pulse one, subject has been eliminated, proceeding to target."

"Good now change course, heading one eight zero and lock in the autopilot," Bennett demanded, looking outside into the dark early morning sky and the endless constellations of stars.

They were eight hundred miles east of the Aleutian Islands and at forty-five thousand feet, cruising close to Mach four.

"Where are we going?" the pilot asked.

"You don't need to know, now get up," Bennett ordered.

From the moment Bennett had stepped into the cockpit, his eyes had been busy absorbing the instrument panel and acquainting himself with the aircraft. It was greatly different to what he knew, far more modern and the panel was littered with three times the instruments he was accustomed to.

The pilot unharnessed herself and stood.

"Remove your helmet."

She lifted the helmet to expose a woman in her early thirties, short dark hair and a thin petite face. Her eyes expressed fear as they repeatedly glanced over at her dead co-pilot.

Bennett marched the woman rearwards with his gun pressed hard into her back.

"If you are going to shoot me then at least look me in the eyes to do it," she said just before her legs went limp and she collapsed to the floor.

"No, I'm not," Bennett whispered having slammed the butt of his gun into the woman's head.

He quickly stripped the laces from her boots and bound her hands to the bulkhead behind the cockpit. There he left her slumped with her arms above her head, while he slipped into the control seat and disengaged the autopilot. It had been many years since he'd sat behind the stick of a military jet and the sheer size shocked him as he banked hard towards the east. The wingspan was over four times larger than the F4 Phantom he used to fly in the Navy, but it was noticeably faster and unexpectedly more agile.

"Blue Pulse One, Blue Pulse One, please maintain your course of two seven zero. Base out."

Bennett paying no attention to the radio message, pushed the nose down and steered the opposite direction descending through thirty-five thousand feet.

"Blue Pulse One please respond."

Radio silence followed for a moment until a new voice crackled through the headset.

"Mr Bennett, I would appreciate you returning my two-billion-dollar aircraft."

Bennett hesitated before responding, "This is unfair, you seem to know me, but I don't know you?"

More radio silence followed as Bennett pushed forward on the throttle to test his new toy with a combination of high-speed manoeuvres banking left and right, diving and pulling up near vertical. In the rear, the unconscious pilot was flung back and forth, pivoting from her bound hands.

"Mr Bennett, I hope you are enjoying your playtime in my aircraft, but this might help persuade you."

A screen to his right illuminated with an incoming video stream. In the centre, a woman battered and bruised knelt with her hands bound in front. To her left a man stood holding a black handgun to her head that hung loosely forward behind a mop of long chocolate brown hair.

Bennett watched as someone out of camera shot, grabbed her hair and yanked her head back. At that moment, a floodgate released an avalanche of memories. Not just one or two, it was everything all at once. First the codes, Jeremiah, the treachery of Dom Whittaker, *The Trust* and the recent events.

However, it was the penetrating crystal green eyes staring at him, screaming for his help that triggered his greatest memory; his love for her.

"I'm sorry Jon," Nicholette uttered.

The video feed was a tight frame showing only Nicholette and the gunman while the location offered no clues, just a small dull coloured featureless room.

"You lay one hand on her and I will kill you," Bennett said calmly using all his power to brush off the anger consuming him.

A man out of picture spoke.

"Bring my plane back and she won't be harmed. If you don't, then she dies and the baby dies along with her."

The baby, Bennett remembered, it wasn't only about Nicholette.

"Okay you win, I will return it. Just do not harm her," Bennett conceded.

He corrected course towards Papoose Lake and calculated seventeen minutes arrival time. The largest screen in front of him showed their airspeed approaching Mach five while back behind him, the pilot was awake and wrestling her restraints, trying desperately to work the boot laces loose.

"Why are there no g-forces, we're at Mach five," he called back to the pilot.

"G-force dampener reversed engineered from the alien craft."

"What else was reversed engineered from it?"

"Not much but did you wonder how you're going to land this bird! There is no runway where we are heading," she laughed.

"Enlighten me then?"

"Untie me and I'll show you!"

Bennett just laughed, "I guess we both die if I can't work it out."

He continued to study the control panel and the assortment of levers each side of him, yet nothing stood out. He'd flown Harrier Jump Jets a few times in the navy, so he understood vertical take offs and landings, but this aircraft lacked the controls to rotate the engines downwards.

He pushed the nose into a steep descent towards Nevada having crossed the Californian coastline a minute earlier at thirty thousand feet. The darkness of night had passed and the sun's warm rays were making their presence felt inside the cockpit.

"Has anyone flown the alien craft?" he asked.

"No! The engineers had no luck finding the controls or the engines for that matter. They suggested part of the ship was possibly cloaked but of course, no one knows how to uncloak it. They did manage to find the weapon imbedded in the underside."

"Have you seen it?"

"No, don't have the access authority," she answered and asked, "Have you worked it out yet?"

"What?" he hinted.

"How to land!"

"No but I'm sure you don't want to die," Bennett replied.

The barren mountainous landscape of Nevada filled his windshield as he banked over the top of Indian Springs and tracked north at eight hundred knots. In the distance at about eight miles, he could see the vast expanse of Groom Lake and Area 51 nestled into the western edge.

He slowed to six hundred knots and dropped to five hundred feet as he approached Papoose Lake tucked tightly between two rugged mountain ridges. Pulling the speed back another fifty knots, he guided the bomber over the eastern mountain, scanning the surface for signs of the launch platform concealed among the terrain. The first pass revealed nothing and he circled back.

"What's wrong Bennett? Can't you find the door?" the pilot laughed.

"What the fuck!" Bennett called.

In his hands, the flight stick ceased responding and the aircraft dropped, nose first towards Papoose Lake.

51.
<u>Capture</u>

Above Sector Four
May 24, 2005

"What the fuck is going on? Someone else has control."

"We're being flown in remotely. Just sit back and enjoy the ride Bennett," the pilot laughed.

Bennett had visions of the tractor beams used in the movie Star Wars to pull spaceships in as he watched the mountainside open and a steel platform sliding forward from within. The jet slowed to a few knots and hovering like a helicopter, it edged across the platform, lowering until the wheels skidded to a halt.

The platform was long and narrow extending out a hundred yards from deep inside the mountainside and roughly the width of a six-lane freeway.

Heavily armed guards swarmed the deck, a row of five on each side, all aiming their rifles at the cockpit. Each wore dark military battle dress without insignia. Behind them, two black Humvees with an M2 machine gun mounted on top, rolled in at speed and took up position.

Bennett sat watching but it wasn't the soldiers or the high calibre machine guns that had his attention. Further over, a group of people were walking quickly towards the jet. On their outer cordon four armed guards moved at the same pace, constantly checking the platform and the sky.

In the middle of the group, a woman dressed in black army pants and a bloodied grey singlet was resisting every step of the way, enticing the constant prodding by the guard behind her. Her hands were bound tightly at her front and her lean muscular arms flexed as she wrestled violently to break free.

Bennett smiled at her rebellious spirit, it was one of the traits he loved so much about Sponarava. To the left of the guard, two people heavily concealed under long black overcoats and darkened masks kept pace with the group. At first sight, they looked like Russian hitmen straight out of an assassin movie. But it was to hide their identities from the overhead spy satellites.

They reached the aircraft and stopped twenty feet from its nose. The guard lashed out with the butt of his rifle into the back of her legs and she collapsed to her knees. He took three paces back and aimed the muzzle at her head while the two masked persons moved closer to the aircraft.

The taller of the two placed a headset on and spoke.

"Mr Bennett, as you can see, I have control of the aircraft, there is nothing you can do," he said glancing back at their prisoner.

It was the same voice he'd heard on the radio and he couldn't help thinking he'd heard it before. A deep dominant but arrogant sounding man with a hint of perhaps a Texan accent.

"Please exit the aircraft," he added maintaining a polite tone.

Bennett sat watching, contemplating his next move while the pilot laughed.

"They will kill you Jon," Nicholette yelled as the guard silenced her with his rifle to her head.

The taller man turned and walked the few paces to the guard where he stopped and beckoned for the man's side arm, a Russian made MP-443 Grach. He lifted the Grach and aimed it squarely at Nicholette's head, a few inches from her face. She had been dazed by the guard's strike, but her eyes screamed anger and defiance.

"Bennett, you have ten seconds, or she dies!"

Pushed into a corner with no options, he stood, gave them one last look from the cockpit and opened the aircraft's hatch. He climbed down the air stairs leaving the pilot behind.

The guards rushed him, stripped his weapon and threw him against the deck binding his hands with zip ties. He was lifted to his feet and dragged across to the others where for the first time in four days, he locked eyes with his fiancée.

"Thank you for returning my aircraft," the tall man said.

"Who are you?" Bennett demanded.

"Oh, I am sorry, I didn't introduce myself. My name is Eckhard Banks and this place here, much to everyone's speculation," he replied waving the gun around him, "Is Sector Four."

"But it doesn't matter who I am, you and your beautiful mother to be, will soon be dead," he continued as he caressed Nicholette's face with the muzzle of the gun.

Bennett snapped forward attempting to break free from the guard's hold, "You hurt her, I will kill you, you hear me asshole!"

Banks laughed, "Oh Jon, you were always a fiery one, it's something I've always liked about you. The same with your girlfriend here, she is just like you, defiant to the end. It's a real shame I must end the services of Hansel and Gretel, but you failed me on your last contract, the Soldier still lives."

He and Nicholette exchanged glances, both had the same realisation, Banks had been their silent client and they'd been eliminating his enemies for him, one by one.

"Kill him!" he directed the guards and turned towards Sponarava and lifted his gun.

"Say your goodbyes."

The guard closest to Bennett stepped forward a few paces and prepared to squeeze the trigger.

52.
Shooter

Sector Four
May 24, 2005

"WAIT!"

The other masked person spoke for the first time and to Bennett's shock, was an all too familiar voice. More memories ambushed him and this time, they were far more devastating.

"Rose! ... Is that you?" he challenged as the guards hesitated, waiting on their instructions from Banks.

He nodded and gestured with his hand to lower their guns.

Weakened by disbelief, Bennett slumped to his knees.

"Why Rose? I don't understand."

Knowing Sponarava had never trusted Rose, he caught a glimpse of her 'I told you so' expression and brushed it aside. Rose's dramatic changes since St Marika's mental hospital four years earlier had raised too many flags for her, though Bennett dismissed it, arguing the eighth code nanobots flowing through her veins were the reason.

The gaps in Bennett's recent memories had filled, now vividly fresh. It was Banks who had entered his code into the sphere, but it had been Rose who activated the final symbol. Banks had ordered the memory suppressor implant, but strangely, it had been Rose who helped him escape into the desert.

A nearby guard terminated his radio call and walked briskly across to Banks, "Sir, we have three minutes of satellite blackout remaining."

Maintaining the facility's invisibility meant they could only open the launch bays when the imaging and spy satellites were not overhead.

"Judith be quick, you have one minute," Banks ordered.

"Who's Judith?" Bennett asked, bewildered.

Rose removed her mask, ignoring the scowling disapproval from Banks and answered, "I am sorry Jon, there is much you do not know about me."

She continued, "My birth name is Judith-Rose and I am not your father's biological sister, I'm his half-sister. We had the same mother, but different fathers," she said quickly.

"Then why all the fucking secrecy Rose?" Bennett growled returning to his feet with the guards struggling to restrain him.

"Like I said, there is much you do not know. Unfortunately, we are running out of time for me to tell you."

"Eke darling, we need to take them inside, I do owe Jon an explanation," she asked with a hint of authority over Banks in her voice.

Agitated at her revealing herself, Banks raised his gun at Sponarava's head.

"They must die," he commanded nodding his head at the guards.

Hailing every ounce of strength, Bennett broke from the guard's grip as Banks pulled the trigger. The other guard slammed into him and they toppled to the deck. The crack of the single gunshot struck him like a heart attack, but the ensuing heavy thud of a body near him fuelled his raging anger.

As he leapt to his feet, the guard slumped forward, half his face torn from his head. On the hangar floor, the other guard perished as blood pulsated from a one-inch hole in his neck.

"SNIPER!" someone yelled.

The guards scattered, running for cover escaping the incoming barrage of bullets from a gunman hidden amongst the nearby hills.

Further over, Banks was stumbling, holding his gun hand tightly against his body, blood drowning his clothes. He'd been shot by the sniper, blowing half his hand off at the exact moment he had squeezed the trigger.

Bennett looked up to the rewarding sight of Sponarava charging towards the closest guard, snatching his gun and tapping a round into his head. She spun and with two shots, took out the next two closest guards while the sniper continued to drop the retreating men, one by one. Amongst them, Banks and Rose fled.

Under their feet the platform retracted slowly into the mountain as the men atop the Humvees unleashed the ferocity of the M2 machine guns. Neither of them knew the enemy's position and as one slumped forward onto his gun with a bleeding hole in his head, the sounds of a high pitch turbine drowned out the yelling and gun fire.

From inside the mountain hangar, a sleek gunmetal grey monster hovered a few feet above the deck and quickly gained forward speed. Hanging off each side, three massive gun turrets oscillated in search of the target while the single pilot lifted the craft skywards. Bennett recognised the same futuristic gunship he'd seen at Edmund's house.

Dropping to his knee, Bennett fumbled with his bound hands to grab Bank's bloodied Grach off the floor and he fired twice. Twenty yards over, one guard had ceased his retreat and was firing on Sponarava's position. Bennett's first shot hit him in the shoulder spinning him sideways while the second ripped a gaping hole through his head. It was the second time that day Sponarava's life had been saved.

As the remaining guards vanished into the darkness of the mountain hangar, Sponarava and Bennett embraced before removing their restraints. Under them, the platform continued rolling.

"Not much time, we need to take that," Bennett said pointing towards the bomber.

"What about Banks and Rose?" she hesitated.

The second Humvee charged them, the gunner not relenting on the trigger. In the hills, the rattle of electric Gatling guns echoed as the gunship closed in on the sniper. Like a massive bird of prey stalking a rabbit, it swooped across the hundreds of small ridgelines scattered down the mountainside pushing the gunman into the camouflage of the low shrubs. From under a clump of salt bush, he watched the gunship bank towards him and the ferocity of the Gatling gun followed.

"Sorry Jon, you're on your own now," he mumbled as a white flash appeared on the horizon to the west over Papoose Lake.

A silver missile streaked across the ground at low altitude and slammed head on into the gunship. It erupted in a fireball spearing nose first into the ridge where the fuselage disintegrated in a tumbling red and black mushroom cloud. The sniper remained motionless as the sudden deafening roar of two fighter jets passed overhead at fifty feet. Both expressed United States markings.

Another missile skimmed the deck and incinerated the Humvee in a direct hit.

"Come on, get to the bomber," Bennett called.

Behind them another two gun-mounted Humvees rushed from inside the hangar, each firing wildly to intercept their escape.

Off the southern end of the platform, a dark intimidating shape ascended, edging a few feet above the deck. With the added ferociousness of the under-wing missile clusters, the Apache attack helicopter rose and unleashed its fury on the first Humvee.

Like a savage wild animal avenging its fallen, the second Humvee slammed down on the brakes and spun in a trail of tyre smoke. The gunner opened fire and the Apache responded unkindly with its Gatling gun shredding the Humvee as if paper.

"GET DOWN!" Bennett screamed at the sight of a silver flash in the northern sky.

53.
Tank

Sector Four
May 24, 2005

A missile hit the bomber followed by a second and a third. Overhead at a hundred feet, the two fighter jets pulled near vertical attitude with their afterburners lighting up the early morning sky, disappearing east. Back on the rolling platform the bomber was a burning carcass with nothing to salvage.

Shielding themselves from the intense heat, Bennett and Sponarava picked themselves up and dragged each other towards the hangar. Thirty feet over, the Apache hovered like it was waiting for something. Further to the west out across Papoose Lake, a squadron of four Blackhawks skimmed the dry lakebed rushing towards them. While a few hundred yards to the south, a lone heavily camouflaged figure with a Barrett M82 sniper rifle strapped to his back, clambered the escarpment below the platform.

"What now?" Nicholette asked.

"Take our chances inside, we have no option," he replied taking a quick peek around the corner into the dimly lit hangar.

"Is it bad?" she asked pointing to the thin stream of blood down his arm.

"I'll live, had worse!" he chuckled. In the shootout he'd been hit, a small sliver of flesh ripped from his shoulder.

She laughed for the first time, breaking into a huge smile and he grabbed her, pressing his lips against hers. It lasted briefly and they pushed each other away.

"What do you think he's waiting for?" she beckoned towards the Apache.

"Don't know but I think it's safe to say he isn't here for us."

Above them, the mountainside started rolling down as the Apache unleashed its armament. Eight Hellfire missiles slammed into the mountain above the hangar knocking the massive sliding hatch off its tracks and it tumbled under the immense weight down the mountainside, crashing to the lakebed. The hangar was exposed.

"I think that answered your question!" Bennett called over the rumble of rocks falling past them and the increasing thump of rotor blades as the first Blackhawk arrived overhead.

Returning a smirk, she raised her gun and entered the hangar with him close behind. On the far side, a large elevator door slid open and a heavy armoured vehicle rolled through.

"What's that?" Sponarava called.

"Looks like some kind of small tank."

As it moved closer, Bennett noticed similarities to the gunships with its reflective black metal surface and distinct lack of sharp defining edges. A stealth battle tank was a more apt description, he thought.

They watched it gain speed, crossing the hangar floor on four sets of sturdy wheels towards the Apache and the Blackhawk edging into the hangar. Mounted on the top, a long wide cannon with distinct similarities to a giant telescope overhung the front like the cannon on a modern day army tank.

Behind it, a group of armed guards spilled from the elevator and commenced shooting until the Apache's chain gun ripped through them one by one. Bennett and Sponarava ducked for the cover of a nearby tug tractor as the first Blackhawk skidded onto the deck releasing its payload, ten heavily armed United States army commandos.

"HOLY FUCK!" Sponarava screamed. Bennett remained silent, he'd seen it before.

A pulse of vibrant blue light had shot from the tank's cannon, vaporising the Blackhawk and incinerating the last two commandos as they leapt to the deck.

The next pulse obliterated the Apache before the pilot had time to flee.

In the sky above the hangar, twenty commandos fast roped down from the other Blackhawks and leapt onto the hangar floor, shooting as they dropped.

"Are you Bennett?" the lead commando called as he ran to take cover behind the same tug tractor.

"Yes, who are you?"

"Major Dirk Wilson, Bravo Unit, Special Forces Sixth out of Bragg."

"What's your mission Major?" Bennett asked.

"Special assignment under the hand of the US President directly, neutralise this facility at any cost using lethal force and retrieve some advanced pulse weapon."

Bennett nodded, "How did you know me?"

"Secret Service Agent Ryan Adams is on-board a squadron of incoming Sikorsky Super Stallions. He's five minutes out. His instructions were to find you and pass on a message."

"Message, what message?"

"We are at DEFCON TWO, the Chinese and the Russians are in the final countdown for a full nuclear attack on the United States. Exposure to the world of this facility and the pulse weapon used on Zavitinsk and Shenyang need to be made in the next hour or life on this planet as we know it, is about to change in a real bad way. The President is refusing to ready our nukes, he believes you can change it all. But we are running out of time Bennett. There is unrest in the Oval Office, the Secretary of Defense and the Joint Chiefs are at each other's throats and there's whispers of a coup to overthrow the President. If that happens then shit, it's game on, you know, a world nuclear war."

Sponarava interjected, "So what do we do?"

Wilson looked at her, he knew her past and part of him admired her while part feared her.

"We need to commandeer the bomber and the weapon used to destroy those sites in Russia and China," Wilson responded.

Bennett laughed.

"What's funny?" he asked.

"You're F15's just took it out!"

Wilson said nothing, looked down in disbelief reaching for his radio.

"Stallion One, this is Bravo Six, do you copy?"

"Bravo Six go," the pilot of the lead Sikorsky replied.

"We have a problem. The bomber and weapon were destroyed by our friends in the sky."

Another voice came across the radio.

"Bravo Six, contingency plan is authorised," Adams replied taking charge of the radio transmission.

"Contingency plan?" Bennett asked.

"We capture Banks and make him confess, uplink a video to the Russian and Chinese Presidents."

"What if he doesn't?" Sponarava added.

"Then we are screwed," Wilson replied before adding, "But Bennett, I've read your brief, if anyone can make him talk, you can."

A pulse of blue light shot across next to them and slammed into a neighbouring tug tractor. Like the helicopters, it disintegrated in a flash of intense white heat and consumed the three commanders covering behind it.

"We need to take out that tank, the Sikorsky's will have no chance if we don't," Wilson ordered over his radio.

Dodging the crossfire, five commandos broke from the firefight with the remaining guards and engaged the tank. It swung tightly towards them, lowered its cannon and fired. The deck under the commandos erupted vaporising all five. Wilson watched on in horror as the next two pulses killed more of his men.

"Cover me," Bennett yelled as he snatched a grenade hanging from Wilson's battle jacket and sprinted towards the tank.

As if sensing his intentions, it spun towards him and lowered the canon. Bennett nearly snapped his ankle as he darted left and jagged right to slide awkwardly under the pulse. The heat from the pulse's proximity scorched his skin and feeling like he had been set on fire, he kept his momentum clambering onto the rear of the tank.

To his surprise, there were no hatches or windows and it was too small to accommodate a driver. The cannon was ten feet long and three feet in diameter narrowing to a six inch muzzle opening at the front. At the rear, it extended from inside a large globular cannister made of thick glass resembling a massive light globe on its side.

It started turning towards the remaining tug tractor where the others continued to suppress the guards retaliatory fire. Next to him, a flash of blue light ignited inside the bulb, intensifying in vibrance as each second passed.

As the canon reached full charge to fire, he pulled the pin, jammed the grenade down the muzzle and leapt from the tank. Less than ten strides later, it exploded sending him hurtling and stumbling to his knees. Behind him, the tank's cannon had been torn apart and ripped from its mounting. The gunfire eased as the commandos flanked the enemy shooting them as they retreated into the elevator.

"Come on," Bennett called.

They raced to the elevator while the commandos separated and disappeared down the stairwell.

"Bravo Six do you copy?"

Wilson reached for his radio, "Bravo Si….".

He collapsed to the floor, blood squirting from a fist size hole in his neck.

"Fuck … TAKE COVER!" Bennett yelled pushing Nicholette into the elevator as more rounds smacked around them, slicing through the dead guards.

54.

<u>Treason</u>

Level 1, Sector Four
May 24, 2005

Yet as quickly as it had started, the shooting ceased with the loud bone breaking thud of a body falling fifty feet from the ceiling. One lone guard had positioned himself high above them and had taken out three of the commandos until he met his fate. At the hangar's opening, that fate walked through, a lone silhouette carrying a Barrett M82 sniper rifle and as he stepped past the fallen soldier, he fired another round into his head for added measures.

Nicholette dropped to Wilson's side, trying her best to stop the bleeding, but it was in vain. He died staring at her with the radio blaring in the background.

"Bravo Six please respond."

Bennett grabbed the radio, "This is Bennett, Bravo Six is down."

"Roger that. What is your status?" Adams asked.

"Proceeding with the contingency plan," he responded watching the sniper materialise into a familiar face.

"Whittaker! So good to see you, but how did you know we were here?" Bennett called leaving the sanctuary of the lift.

"After you and Nicholette vanished in Bolivia, I spent the past five days trying to find you. Where the fuck have you been is more the question?"

"That's a long story, how did you find us?"

He extracted a small black device from his jacket pocket. At first it looked like any ordinary cell phone but as the screen illuminated, it was clearly a tracking device with a small green flashing dot in the centre.

"I discovered this among my father's stuff, just never knew what it did. The start-up screen asked for a code signature. I had no idea, so at a guess, I typed your name in and it started tracking you. For days it had you in the Las Vegas area but nothing specific and then early this morning, it started beeping with exact coordinates. I found nothing at the coordinates except the barrenness of this mountain until half the fucking mountainside opened up and a fancy looking silver jet launched."

Bennett interjected, "Don't tell me, the device showed me onboard it."

Josh nodded.

"It tracks my code's signature, don't ask me how, but those implanted with the eighth code nanobots have a unique signal emitting from their bodies. It has something to do with the person's DNA and how the nanobots communicate at the cellular level."

"Hate to break this up boys but we need to find Banks, remember that little world war three thing!" Nicholette announced.

"World war three, what do you mean?" Whittaker quizzed, confused.

"No time to explain," Bennett grunted.

"Eckhard Banks is behind those attacks in Russia and China. We need his recorded confession to stop a full nuclear strike against us and we need it now," Nicholette explained.

"Bennett do you read?" one of the commandos called on the radio.

"Go ahead."

"What happened to Wilson?"

"Shot by a guard hiding in the roof. He's dead. Where are you, any sign of Banks?" Bennett replied.

"Level two, we just secured a large hangar with minimal resistance, no visual on Banks."

"Okay good, there are medical labs on that level. Banks is injured and needs medical attention. Secure those labs, we're on our way," Bennett ordered.

Vzzzt Vzzzt Vzzzt

"What's that noise?" Whittaker beckoned towards the dead team leader.

Bennett grabbed Wilson's body and rolled him over.

"Sat phone's buzzing!" he observed and pressed the accept button.

"Hello is this Major Wilson?" the caller asked.

"No, he's dead, who is this?" Bennett replied.

"This is the United States Secretary of Defense, George Whitman. Who am I speaking to?"

"This is Jon Bennett."

"Mr Bennett, you and Wilson's men need to stand down and vacate Sector Four immediately. Your presence is jeopardising a greater mission," he ordered.

"What greater mission Sir?" Bennett asked.

"That is not your concern Bennett, you have your orders now get out."

"Is this order authorised by the President?" he pushed.

"Who the fuck do you think you are Bennett? Do not question me! I am the United States Secretary of Defense. You have your orders, now fucking get on with it or I will have you arrested," he barked down the phone.

"With all due respect Sir, I don't take orders from you," Bennett returned with the same arrogant demeanour and hung up the call.

He pondered momentarily, hoping he hadn't just made a mistake of colossal proportions for himself and picked up the radio while the others stood watching him, beckoning for an explanation.

"Adams, do you read? We have a problem."

There was no response.

55.
Adams

Level 1, Sector Four
May 24, 2005

As the thump of rotors washed out the radio silence, Adams fast roped down from the first Super Stallion. With urgency in his stride, he sprinted across the hangar to Bennett and the others.

"Doesn't change our mission Bennett, our fate rests with that confession from Banks. The Secretary must be in cahoots with him, the President can deal with that. Thirty minutes ago, we went to DEFCON ONE and full nuclear launch readiness. The President will not launch until one of the others launch first and that could happen at any minute now. The Russian President doesn't appear to be keen to press their red button either. However, our latest intelligence indicates leadership problems at the Kremlin and a likely uprising by the military in the wake of the pressure by the Generals to strike first. If the military take control, they will launch, no question about that," Adams instructed after Bennett had quickly briefed him about the phone call from Whitman.

Sponarava interjected, "What about negotiations, surely the Presidents are talking."

"Yes, they have been in positive negotiations, but the real threat comes from the Chinese President. He won't come to the table, he believes both Russia and the United States are staging this to destroy China and his country will end up the only target. We have limited intelligence coming out of Beijing."

Adams continued, "There is no more time for talk, we are seriously running out of time. Bennett you need to get that confession."

He yanked a small body worn camera from his jacket and handed it to him.

"Just press record."

The radio blurted to life.

"Bennett, you copy. We're pinned down on level three. Banks was on level two but slipped through and now somewhere on the lower levels," the commando declared.

"Level four has aircraft, he may be attempting to fly his way out. Lock it down, we're on our way," Bennett responded.

Adams grabbed the radio, "Sergeant, this is Adams. We need Banks alive."

They descended to level three to the sounds of an intense gun battle as the lift doors crept open.

"GET DOWN!" Whittaker screamed. He was the first to see the guard raise the rocket launcher.

The blast flung them sideways as the lift cables tethered and it jerked violently downwards a few feet at the mercy of gravity. The rocket grenade had missed, impacting high through the ceiling and severing half the cables.

Swiftly regaining his balance and under the onslaught of gunfire, Bennett dragged Nicholette's dazed body to the safety of a nearby shipping container. She'd been hit the hardest by the blast wave and was smashed against the wall. Whittaker upon seeing the rocket, had pushed Adams and they missed the impact, scuttling to the safety of a forklift five yards from the lift. Fifteen feet over, the commandos covering behind timber crates and containers were down to eight men and losing the battle.

The lift had opened onto another hangar of enormous proportions and like level two, there was a massive shaft in the centre. The same four huge vertical hydraulic pistons stood evenly spaced across the void, each extending up through level two. Fifty yards on the opposite side of the shaft, the stairwell was guarded by Banks's men, a small group of six but with the advantage of position and weapons the commandos had never encountered. Resembling smaller portable versions of the tank cannon, they fired a football size pulse of blue light that on impact, disintegrated a human body into mush.

The commando sergeant radioed, "Adams how far away is Charlie Unit?"

"Sixteen minutes," he responded peering around the forklift for a visual on the commandos on the far side of the hangar.

"We don't have sixteen minutes, their weapons are too advanced," the sergeant radioed back.

"Charlie Unit?" Whittaker beckoned.

"Backup unit waiting at Greech Air force Base."

"Last minute contingency plan, you know, in case things went to shit!" Adams added responding to Whittaker's amused look.

"Well I think it's safe to say, things are going to shit!" Whittaker laughed as another barrage of gunfire ricocheted around them.

"Adams… The stairwell, we have to get to it. It's the only way down," Bennett shouted from ten yards away above the constant crackle of gunfire.

As another rocket grenade launched, the shipping container to their right erupted, and lifted, toppling back down onto its side crushing two of the four commandos covering behind it.

"We can't stay here, we're sitting ducks," Bennett called as another rocket struck the forklift, hurtling Whittaker and Adams through the air.

As they recovered, a group of three commandos weren't so lucky, a grenade had shattered a timber crate into a thousand splinters and as if shot from a mini gun, the tiny timber darts tore through the men's flesh.

All three fell, screaming in agony and crawled inch by inch towards the others, slipping in their own blood. One of their teammates broke from behind his cover and sprinted the short ten yards to their rescue. It was the last thing he did.

An energy pulse of blue light shot across the hangar and struck him in the back. At first nothing happened and the soldier kept running, but then his body exploded outwards as if he'd swallowed a stick of dynamite. Blood and flesh splattered across the floor, leaving nothing recognisable.

"Poor bastards," Whittaker murmured.

"We have to help them," Adams demanded as a deluge of blue energy pulses rained down on the commandos, killing one more.

"Who's that?" Sponarava called.

From somewhere behind them, a dark shape appeared running towards the injured men. In his hands he carried an unusual looking assault rifle and as he lifted to fire it, a long beam of blue light exploded from the barrel.

"GET DOWN," he barked and squeezed the trigger again and again, each time launching a blue pulse towards the guards.

In the time it had taken him to run the thirty yards and fire six rounds, the guards had scattered into the stairwell. He kept firing until he reached the first wounded soldier and dragged him to safety while the other commandos rushed for the others.

"Man, I thought you'd be dead," Bennett called.

Maintaining his sights on the stairwell door, Xavier Roland shouted, "What is going on Bennett?"

Each time the door crept open an inch, he let off an energy pulse and it slammed shut.

"No time to explain, the world is on the brink of a full-scale nuclear war. Our only chance to prevent it is Eckhard Banks," Bennett replied.

He gave a brief introduction to the others feeling their gratitude, he had saved their lives. Sponarava wasn't so trusting. She turned to Bennett and whispered, "Jon I feel like I know this man, something doesn't sit right with me and you know what my premonitions are like."

Bennett took the weapon from Roland partly because he trusted her warnings, but more to satisfy his curiosity.

"This gun is unbelievable, it only targets human flesh, no effect on physical structures at all," Roland explained.

"How did you get it? What happened after I left," Bennett asked examining the weapon and turning it over in his hands.

It was quite light considering its lengthy size, he thought. He took aim towards the stairwell and depressed the trigger. It vibrated slightly, buzzing lightly in his hands as a thin but short beam of blue light expelled from the muzzle. Swamped with the vision of the laser gun battle scenes in Star Wars, he watched the short pulse of light shoot across the hangar and vanish into the door with no trace of damage.

He nodded his approval and handed it to Whittaker, "I think you'll like this."

"I hid after you left until the shooting started. Found a stash of those weapons up on level one," Roland replied.

Adams interrupted, "Come on Bennett... Banks remember?"

"We need to secure that stairwell, take out the guards from behind," Bennett instructed and added, "Come up from level four."

"How?" Adams asked.

Bennett pointed towards the four hydraulic pistons, "Whittaker and I will go down those, you keep them pinned down with this." He threw the energy weapon to Roland.

"I'm coming with you," Nicholette demanded.

"No, you stay here," he answered pulling her close to kiss her and whispered, "I need someone I can trust up here."

She nodded not knowing he had just lied to her.

56.
Level Four

Loaded with weapons, Bennett and Whittaker approached the elevator shaft hesitating at the edge to peer down into the semi darkness of the levels below.

"Seems too quiet!" Bennett commented feeling uneasy about the stillness.

"Cover us," he called to the others.

As they fired three short bursts, Bennett leapt the five-foot gap to the closest piston. He grappled the shiny surface, slipping at first, but regathered pushing his body hard against the smooth metal. He shimmied down a few feet as Whittaker jumped.

Using their hands and boots as resistance pressing against the metal, they slid slowly down the pistons. As Whittaker released his grip to prepare the jump to the level four platform, his left boot slipped.

"FUCK!" His muscular weight dragged him downwards, clutching hand over hand to gain friction on the surface.

Like a sledgehammer plummeting from the sky, Whittaker's rifle swung from his back and whacked Bennett in the head, severing his grip. As an immediate reflex and simulating a backstroke swimming start, he pushed with all his might, outstretching his arms, but missed the ledge.

In one continuous motion, Whittaker used the momentum of the collision to catapult himself out and swing through the air. With his knuckles turning white, clenching the ledge, he hung for a few seconds watching Bennett disappear into the darkness.

"Bennett, can you hear me, are you okay?" he called on the radio.

At first there was silence, then the radio crackled to life.

"Fuck that hurt! I'm okay. You will have to go on without me, I think I'm on level five," Bennett responded.

"I'm sorry Jon, my screw up."

"Just get going and secure that stairwell, I will find my way back up," Bennett replied as he peered into the darkness of level five.

Thin slivers of light drifted down from the levels above and in the distance, he could just make out the dim green light of the exit sign above the stairwell door. As his eyes adjusted, he could see he was inside another hangar but much smaller and distinctly older. The walls were concrete, unlike the upper levels constructed of steel and the paint was perhaps the original by the state of the flaking. His conversations with Roland came to mind, maybe it was the original underground structure built during the cold war. Surrounding him were the massive pumps and fluid reservoirs used to push the pistons up and down.

He climbed through the machinery onto the floor and moved towards the stairwell as the radio blurted, "Bennett, you there?"

"Yeah go."

"We have the stairwell secured, heading down to level four, where are you?" Adams asked.

Whittaker had made quick work taking down the six guards on level three. One grenade and two shots were all it took and the stairwell was clear.

"Approaching the level five stairwell now," Bennett responded as a dim orange light to his right caught his attention.

He stopped and stood staring, not quite comprehending what he was witnessing or the bizarre feeling he was experiencing. It was huge, beautiful and strangely hypnotic. He kept watching for a moment.

"Bennett, where are you?" Adams called.

"Give me one minute."

"Fuck Bennett, hurry the fuck up, we don't have a minute!"

He shook off the eerie feeling and ran to the stairwell where sighting the level six door triggered an idea.

"About fucking time. Why'd you take so long?" Adams screamed.

Bennett ignored his suspicions and rushed to Nicholette. She was looking paler and he knew she was suffering, though too stubborn to let on. Time wasn't just running out for the United States, it was running out for her as well.

"Banks has to be on this level, the one below is empty, just darkness down there," he said.

"Sir all clear," a soldier declared as he opened the door a few inches.

The commandos took the lead, rushing into the hangar and spreading out among the scattering of cylinder shaped craft.

"Geez, this place is bigger than I first thought. There must a thousand of those cylinder things," Roland said as Bennett pushed past him.

As they had previously encountered, the hangar was littered with the cylinders, mostly covered under tarps, except this time, the lights were on and the true volume was on display. Directly opposite them, the four elevator pistons stood tall reaching into the upper levels. At the furthest end at about eighty yards, a row of five futuristic gunships sat idle, a formidable sight even in their inactive state.

"Stay focussed everyone," Bennett commanded as he and Adams led the way, keeping their guns at eye level.

Whittaker remained back twenty yards with his sniper rifle covering them while Sponarava and Roland stayed close to Bennett. The eight commandos held the flank and moved fast and deliberate towards the gunships.

"Can you hear that?" Adams called.

"Sounds like a hangar door opening," Roland said.

"No, it's the platform lowering, that's the pistons you can hear," Bennett replied pointing towards the shaft behind them.

As Bennett rushed back to the shaft, the whistling squeal of turbines firing up, drowned out the hissing of the pistons. One of the gunships was engaging its engines, two enormous turbines mounted on the ends of fifteen feet delta shaped sub wings.

"Not good! If that platform gets here, that gunship is out of here and I'm betting Banks is onboard it. We have to stop it," Bennett declared watching the platform, eighty feet across slowly lowering towards them.

"TANK!"

Sponarava was running and yelling as an energy pulse shot over her head and obliterated a cylinder next to them.

As the shock wave hit, Bennett was hurled over the edge of the shaft and yet again, he found himself at the hands of gravity, clinging by one hand and staring up into the eyes of Whittaker.

57.
Drone

"Give me your hand," Whittaker called.

Further along the hangar, the amplified clatter of the commando's gunfire intensified as more of Bank's guards with pulse rifles rushed from behind the gunships.

"Adams, we need that fucking backup," the commando sergeant yelled into his radio.

Adams answered, "Ten minutes. Do not let that gunship leave, but remember we need Banks alive."

"We have to stop that platform coming down," Bennett grimaced as he wrestled the edge to extend one hand to Whittaker.

Above them the platform was drawing closer, passing through level three and as Whittaker yanked a grenade from his belt, an energy pulse struck. It tore through the floor to his right, catapulting him ten feet through the air and smacking him hard against the deck. The grenade clattered to the floor and rolled to the edge.

The tank fired again and with a sizzling screech, the pulse passed within inches of his body. At first all seemed okay, until the stench of burning flesh vilified his nostrils and the agonising pain crippled him all over.

Bennett rushed to his side, ripped his own jacket off and doused out Whittaker's burning arm. The tank fired another round, this time missing and exploding somewhere further along the hangar.

"We're running out of time to stop the platform, it's almost here," Whittaker said clenching his teeth from the pain as Bennett dragged him with one arm while shooting at the tank with the other.

The tank fired another round, blasting the wall next to them. As the concrete and steel erupted, Whittaker leapt to his feet.

"Crazy fool!" Bennett muttered as he watched him sprint low towards the platform and dive for the grenade with a pulse igniting the floor behind him.

He pulled the pin, waited and tossed it high. With the timing of the explosion critical, the grenade detonated with a deafening boom a few feet under the platform. Fire and smoke tumbled outwards washing over them and as it cleared, the pistons remained. Taking noticeably longer to recharge, the tank pulled back and waited to fire.

"Whittaker, you okay?" Bennett called rushing to grab him.

"Look, it's cracking," he pointed as Bennett whisked him away towards the closest row of cylinders.

At first, small hairline cracks like spider webs appeared in one of the pistons and as they grew, the piston buckled sideways under the enormous weight of the platform. Sounding like a screaming cat, the steel twisted as the other three pistons lurched towards it and jammed the platform in place, ten feet above the floor.

"Good luck getting out now Banks!" Bennett muttered.

"Bennett, you copy. Banks is onboard the gunship, we have a confirmed sighting and it's about to lift off," the radio blurted.

"Copy that, we've blocked his way out," he replied as he heard the sizzling hiss of an energy pulse shoot across the hangar followed by a crackling boom as it exploded somewhere close.

"Banks is using the tank to blast their way out," Whittaker called as another pulse struck the remaining pistons and the platform tilted an inch.

"The tank, it's a drone. Must be a control room nearby," Bennett added.

"Up there, I spotted it earlier," Whittaker replied pointing to a large window and a landing perched high up one side of the hangar.

A near vertical staircase led up the side of the wall to a landing twenty feet above the floor. A row of windows the length of the landing exposed a large room with monitors covering one wall. In the doorway, a man dressed in the same dark military battle dress as the guards stood jerking and rolling a small black device in his hands.

"There's the drone controller. I'll take care of him, you go get Banks," Whittaker called leaving the concealment of the cylinder's tarp.

Fifty yards deeper into the hangar, the gunfire was heavy and the commandos had lost more men against the barrage of energy pulses and rocket attacks. Roland had joined the battle and charged wildly at the guards, snapping at the trigger of his pulse rifle in a frenzy and killing as many as he could until the weapon unexpectedly started beeping and the firing stopped.

He looked down, a small LED screen on the side was illuminated in red and flashing in time with the beeps.

... CRYSTAL DEPLETED ...

"Fuck!" he muttered as a guard stepped in front of him, grinned and raised his pulse rifle.

The impact was nothing short of being hit by a stampeding bull as he was flung ten feet across the floor. Rolling to his back, a dark figure brushed his face and two gunshots followed, clobbering his eardrums. He opened his eyes to the guard falling lifeless to the floor with two holes in his chest.

"Roland, you okay?"

He refocussed from the dead guard to look into the eyes of Sponarava standing over him with her hand out to help him up. She had seen him charge the guards and like running line support in a game of football, she was just behind him and knocked him out of the way.

"Thanks, I owe you," he said accepting her hand.

"You can pay me back later," she laughed momentarily as a pulse shot over their heads and they retreated for cover.

From behind the cylinders, the gunship rose up like the head of a cobra preparing to strike, its underbelly canons oscillating in search of targets. It fired and imitating lightning, a beam of blue light shot forward striking the floor.

"RUN," Sponarava screamed grabbing Roland by the arm as the floor shook like an earthquake.

The pulse vanished as if consumed by the floor but then, like an air bubble reaching the water surface, it blew outwards. As they sprinted for their lives, a two feet radius of concrete and steel erupted behind them and knocked them tumbling, concussed and bleeding.

The machine screamed past, skimming the cylinders and launched two pulse spears at the tilting platform. It started to crumble, crack in half and collapse.

They dragged each other to their feet as Adams rushed past, "Come on, we can't let that gunship escape."

Behind them, the commandos were neutralising the last few guards after commandeering their own pulse rifles.

By the time Adams and the others reached Bennett, he had emptied his magazine at the gunship. The bullets had deflected off its skin like tacks against steel while the pilot continued to blast the platform, unphased by Bennett's presence.

"We don't have long, there has to be a weak spot on that thing," Bennett called to Adams appearing at his side with the other two.

Roland grabbed Bennett's arm and pulled him around, "Ahh Jon! We got ourselves another problem."

58.
<u>Banks</u>

Twenty yards out, the tank drone was bearing down on them at speed. The first pulse went unexpectedly high passing well overhead and striking the ceiling on the other side of the elevator shaft. The next exploded a few yards from their feet and the blast wave threw them tumbling to within an inch of the shaft.

"RUN!" Sponarava yelled leaping to a sprint until she glanced over her shoulder and saw that Bennett hadn't moved.

He stood watching the tank as if attempting to stare it down.

"JON ... WHAT THE FUCK! ... RUN!"

She raced back and grabbed his arm as the canon fired again. This time, it hit its target.

"Look!" he said pointing back behind the tank.

"Is that Whittaker?" she quizzed, glancing back along the extension of his arm.

On the landing forty yards further over, Whittaker stood manipulating the tank's remote control like a kid with a video game controller for the first time while inside the room, the guard bled out onto the floor.

Bennett acknowledged him with a hand wave and turned to the burning roar of the gunship slipping through the air. The pulse had decapitated the right-side engines and it banked right, smacking nose down into the deck. The screeching of metal scraping against metal was excruciating to their ears as the wounded machine slid uncontrollably into a row of cylinders and burst into flames. Like a freeway car pileup, a chain reaction of cylinders colliding ensued, each exploding.

"Come on, we need to get Banks out," Bennett yelled sprinting into the heat of the burning wreck.

As if on cue, Banks staggered from the wreckage, one hand wrapped in a bloodied bandage. In his other hand, he held a handgun at eye height.

"That's far enough Bennett," he shouted.

Bennett slowed, lifting his hands in surrender, continuing to edge small steps closer.

"It's going to blow," he nodded towards the river of fuel flowing from under the wreckage.

Banks glanced sideways.

In one smooth continuous action, Bennett leapt forward two paces, struck the man in the throat, snatched his gun and turned it on him. Banks buckled over gasping for breath as Bennett grabbed and shoved him from the wreckage, seconds before the fuel ignited.

The fuel tank erupted and like a ten foot wave smacked them tumbling end over end before slamming them without mercy, headfirst into the deck. Like a gazelle attempting to evade a lion, Banks jumped to his feet and sprinted, until his boot clipped a piece of burning debris. He stumbled at the same moment Bennett tackled him, grabbing him by his jacket and threw him without effort onto the hangar floor, head first.

"You run like a scared goat," Bennett laughed.

"Fuck you Bennett, you have no idea what you've got yourself into. You'll be going to prison for the rest of your life when I'm finished with you."

"Then enlighten me, what have I got myself into?" Bennett returned dragging him to his feet and pushing him across the hangar, well away from the small inferno devouring the remainder of the gunship and a dozen cylinders.

The remnants of the Bravo Unit appeared behind Adams while Roland and Sponarava stood close by watching Bennett throw their prisoner into a nearby chair.

"Charlie Unit has landed. Let's get this done," Adams commanded.

Banks screamed confidence in his posture, sitting tall and showing no sign of fear. He looked over those around him like he was assessing their fate, each one of them including Bennett.

"Banks I am curious, what do you gain from starting a nuclear war?" Bennett chose as his lead question.

Banks laughed, "What are you talking about Bennett?"

"The devastation in Shenyang and Zavitinsk, that was your bomber. The Russians and the Chinese think it was a nuclear strike against them," Bennett said taking the pulse rifle from Roland.

He aimed it at Banks.

"You going to shoot me Bennett?" Banks glared in return.

Examining the space age weapon and rolling it over in his hands, "They don't know about the advanced weapons you build here, like this one. Do they?"

"Our work here is sanctioned by the United States Government and perfectly legal," Banks refuted.

Bennett glanced sideways at Adams who shrugged with an uneasy nod of his head.

"But does that involve designing and building new weapons of mass destruction and testing them on other countries. Energy pulse weapons capable of annihilating whole cities. I'm sure the United States Government didn't sanction that!"

Movement to his right broke the conversation.

"Adams, we found this one hiding down the back. For an old duck she can fight," one of the commandos announced still wiping blood from his mouth where she had struck him.

Ignoring Bennett, Rose broke from the soldiers and rushed to Banks.

"Eke I am so sorry," she said quietly in his arms.

"It's okay sweetheart, these men have been misinformed and have made a grave error coming here today. I think they are going to find this out soon," he reassured her in a raised tone.

Distracted by her presence and the overt display of affection, Bennett's purpose momentarily stumbled. In all his life, he had never seen her show affection towards anyone, she had always been cold.

"Hello again Jon," she turned to face him while Sponarava's grip tightened on her handgun, resisting the urge to shoot her.

Raising his gun, he stepped towards her, "Rose you have much to explain, I don't even know where to start. Are you in on this fool's plan to start a world war?"

Banks answered, "Judith, Jon seems to think I am behind those dreadful events recently in Russia and China. He is claiming I used some secret weapon to destroy those military installations. Tell him, he's misinformed."

Rose didn't say anything at first, instead she lowered her eyes.

"So, Rose is it true, have I been misinformed? I've seen your prototype energy weapon on the bomber, I know its potential capabilities," he asked leaning forward to within an inch of her face.

"Yes Jon you have been misinformed," she hesitantly replied.

"Bennett you're making monumental mistakes again. How's this going to look for you? The world remembers you for your fuckup in Kuwait and we all know how that went, all those innocent people killed," Banks baited.

"See now you are misinformed asshole, I wasn't even there."

"We seem to be missing someone. Where is Whittaker?" Banks asked cutting him off.

"How do you know Whittaker?"

Banks raised his bloodied hand, "He did this didn't he? I know plenty about Joshua Whittaker, but clearly there are some things you don't know about him. You and your beautiful fiancé over there really disappointed me on your last contract. Oh! Which reminds me. You need to reimburse me the one million dollar deposit."

Bennett and Sponarava shared a quick glance.

"I find it hilarious your target has been right under your noses all this time," he smirked.

"What are you talking about Banks?" Bennett demanded.

"The Soldier of the New World, it's Whittaker. Now I'm going to have to take care of the contract myself, seeing you two failed."

"Jon!" Roland yelled.

Bennett turned to the sounds of a scuffle and Banks laughing.

59.
<u>Plans</u>

Struggling to hold herself upright, Sponarava battled the onset of a seizure, swaying left and right into Roland's arms as he cradled her gently to the floor. Bennett rushed over, took her shaking body in his arms and held her against his chest.

"She's going to die Jon!" Banks laughed.

Fuelled by pure anger, Bennett leapt to his feet, raised his Beretta and fired one round.

"JON NOOOO!" Rose screamed.

"WHERE IS THE SPHERE?" he howled, breath and spittle spraying the prisoner.

Missing Banks's groin by a few millimetres, the bullet had torn through his trousers, grazed his leg and perforated the chair. As Rose rushed to push him away, he backhanded her in the head with his gun, tearing her cheek apart and showering blood across the floor.

"Tell me, where is the sphere or you die?" he yelled, unleashing a left-hand blow across Banks's face.

As he stood over him and rammed the gun muzzle down his throat, a loud emphatic voice echoed over his shoulder.

"BENNETT PUT THE GUN DOWN!"

Another outburst followed, exuding greater urgency and with the accompaniment of a short burst of automatic gunfire into the ceiling.

"DROP THE GUN NOW! You have two seconds or you die."

He half lowered his gun, raised his other hand in hesitant surrender and slowly turned towards the voice. Charlie team had arrived, except their weapons weren't aimed at Banks. Instead, he was confronted with the threatening sight of three rifle muzzles inches from his face and the soldiers glaring over their gunsights at him.

A few paces behind the soldiers, a dark skinned man in his late thirties wearing grey United States Army battle fatigues, stood scoping Bennett with his M16 rifle.

Further over, the other Charlie Unit soldiers were disarming Adams and his team while Sponarava suffered the tail end of her seizure with a few sporadic spasms, draped across the floor. Roland was more subdued laying his gun down quickly, showing a surrendering gesture with his hands and backing away.

Bennett reluctantly lowered his gun to his side and it was snatched by the soldiers. "What the fuck is going on?"

The dark skinned man lowered his rifle an inch. "My name is Lieutenant Chad Petersen, I have direct orders from the United States Secretary of Defense to place you under arrest."

Adams spoke, "Lieutenant, there appears to be some confusion here, our orders are directly from the United States President."

"Change of plans!" He nodded to his men.

One by one the remaining Bravo team were shot, a single bullet in their head.

"YOU FUCKING ASSHOLES!" Adams screamed locking eyes with the muzzle of the lieutenant's gun.

Bennett propelled himself sideways into the closest soldier, driving his full weight at him and snatched his gun with lightning speed. As the lieutenant's head filled the gun's crosshairs, his legs buckled and all went momentarily dark. The gun slipped from his hands and clattered to the floor. The other soldier had reacted with reciprocating speed, spearing his rifle butt into Bennett's head.

"WAIT," Banks hollered.

Wiping the blood from his face, he lifted himself from the chair, "No need to kill them yet."

Sponarava's seizure had passed and she climbed awkwardly to her knees. Next to her, Bennett massaged the agonising throb in the back of his head, feeling the sticky warmth of blood seeping through his fingers. They embraced eyes with a smile and a reassuring bold nod.

"Hey lieutenant you piece of shit, I am guessing the President knows nothing of this!" he called.

The lieutenant remained steadfast, preoccupied with his gun on Adams while Banks spoke, "Like I said Jon, you don't know what you've gotten yourself into!"

He reached down and ripped the camera from Bennett's jacket, "Do you really take me for a fool?"

Bennett held silent as the soldiers clawed at his clothes and body, uncovering the two knives strapped to his left leg and the Glock on the right.

"What's this?" one demanded.

Inside his jacket pocket, they extracted a small orange rectangular metal box. One side was double glazed revealing the interior.

"A souvenir! I like mementos from my travels," Bennett responded with a sarcastic smile.

Earlier when he'd fallen to level five, he'd remembered the emergency evacuation warning on level six and the lethal potency of the blue crystal inside the box.

Banks like he'd seen a ghost and with urgency in his stride, stepped in extending his hand, "Be careful soldier! That little thing will kill us all."

As if a newborn baby, Banks caressed it lightly, turning it over gently to examine the golf ball size piece of blue crystal firmly fixed inside it.

"What are all the cylinders?" Bennett interrupted him, nodding at the mass of craft lining the hangar floor.

"Earth's readjustment!" Banks replied.

Bennett rolled his eyes. "What the fuck do you mean by that Banks?"

"You of all people should have worked that out. We needed an efficient mechanism for the widest dispersal of the blue crystal. Those cylinders as you call them, are destined for low orbit and when the time comes, will re-enter the atmosphere scattering the fine crystal dust over thousands of miles."

"You're a mad man Banks, you're no different to *The Trust*, that was their plan to exterminate most of humanity."

Banks turned to the lieutenant, "Put this somewhere safe and do not break that glass, it's not a pleasant death if you do."

"*The Trust!*" he laughed, "You comparing me to those Nazi fools is an insult."

"You're no different!" Bennett snapped back.

"Bennett, now that's where you are wrong."

He and Rose shared a sly glance. "Our goals are about preserving humanity. Hitler and *The Trust* were about war and domination, exterminating their enemies first, as an inauguration to their Fourth Reich. I wasn't about to allow the Nazi occupation of our planet."

Rose spoke, "For so long *The Trust* was untouchable, the men controlling it had powerful and unbreakable ties deeply entrenched inside our governments. Then four years ago, that all changed, thanks to you Jon. When you cut the head off the snake, it opened the doorway for us."

"You killing the six commanders was all we needed to acquire their assets. Their deaths threw the organisation into chaos and it didn't take much to kick their nest wide open. After that, it fell like dominoes," Banks added.

"Jon your predictability is what we relied upon," Rose said, "I knew you wouldn't let up on destroying them once you became aware of their purpose."

Banks raised his voice. "Enough of this! Bennett all you need to know is that you served us a purpose, just a cog in the wheel. There are sacrifices that must be made for the greater good of humanity's survival. Once it starts, nothing can be done to stop it. There is no military institution on this planet that can prevent what we have developed."

"Are you listening to yourself Banks? Rose, how can you support this absurdness, billions of innocent lives will be murdered including children?"

She said nothing.

"So the strikes on Shenyang and Zavitinsk were a result of your pulse weapon?" Bennett challenged.

"Of course they were, two birds one stone was the way we saw it. Our pulse weapon prototype needed testing and why not start a nuclear war at the same time. When the world is still reeling from the attacks, a few billion more dead people won't seem unfathomable. The crystal radiation would be written off as nuclear fallout."

"Yeah but the United States is annihilated at the same time by the Russian nukes. Not leaving you much to conquer!" Bennett scoffed.

"You're a psychotic mass murderer, you will never get away with this!" Adams yelled as the lieutenant drove the butt of his rifle into his head.

Banks ignored Adams, "You might find this interesting! Do you remember Meredith?"

"Killer satellite developed by the US Government to intercept inbound ballistic missiles and then stolen by *The Trust* I recall. I also remember crashing and destroying her somewhere off the West Australian coastline four years ago," Bennett said.

"The Orionis Andromeda Corporation was contracted by the US Government to build Meredith, she was the product of my engineers. Yes, you destroyed her, but she has two sisters, both active over the United States and programmed to destroy anything the Russians throw at us. So you see Jon, the United States will remain untouched while Russia and China burn."

"The Secretary of Defense, how does he fit into this?"

"George shares our dream..."

A sudden flash of blue light cut him short.

"GET DOWN!" the lieutenant screamed.

60.
<u>Crystal</u>

An energy pulse shot past the lieutenant, striking a tight congregation of Charlie Unit to his right. Their bodies instantly shredded like minced meat while the rest of the unit dashed for cover, shooting at the tank as they fled.

The wall behind the lieutenant exploded in a myriad of concrete, steel and vibrant blue light, hurling him through the air as the small orange box slipped from his hands.

Bennett leapt, striking the closest soldier in the throat with his bladed hand and snatched his gun. In one smooth effortless action, he snapped around and squeezed the trigger. Blood and brains jettisoned across the floor and the soldier fell, dead. The second soldier retaliated holding firm his finger on the trigger.

Each round missed as Adams stampeded the soldier, crash tackling him to the floor like a footballer desperately blocking the game winning try. As the rifle clattered across the floor, they exchanged punch for punch until the shimmering steel of a long Bowie knife stopped Adams mid strike.

The soldier lunged, slicing the air as Adams jerked half a step backwards narrowly missing the path of the razor edge. The next dropped low and as he deflected it, the blade nicked his hand, leaving a track of bloodied flesh dangling.

"ADAMS," Bennett yelled.

Catching movement in his peripheral vision, Adams dropped to his knees. Bennett rushed them unleashing a tight arc of automatic gunfire missing Adams by the narrowest of margins and obliterating the soldier's chest and head.

"Jon, they're getting away." Sponarava yelled, watching Banks and Rose flee towards the rear of the hangar with the lieutenant at their side.

Commandeering a rifle from a dead soldier, she gave chase, firing while randomly stumbling, reeling from the straggling aftereffects of the seizure. Her first burst of rounds missed. Her second didn't.

One of the three bullets ripped through Rose, tearing through her torso and she crumpled into the lieutenant's arms. Banks raced ahead abandoning them and not once looking back, absorbed in his own self-preservation.

"Nik gun three o'clock," Bennett screamed.

The warning came too late.

Gunfire cut her down and she hit the deck screaming, snatching at the gaping bloodied hole in her arm.

Tyres screeched and as if lightning had struck, an energy pulse cauterized the air above them. The drone had stormed their position, skidding to a halt and firing its canon. Both soldiers were instantly torn apart, limb from limb as the flash of blue light torpedoed through them.

Further over, atop one of the cylinders, Whittaker lay belly down manipulating the drone's remote controls. To him, it was an exciting childhood memory, a recount of the endless hours conquering the digital enemy on PlayStation pumping his veins with adrenaline. Scattering the soldiers like rats escaping a fire, he kept firing the canon, waiting an impatient few seconds each time for it to recharge.

While the Charlie unit retreated from the barrage, Bennett and the others rushed towards a closed doorway in the depth of the hangar through which Banks had disappeared. On his tail, the lieutenant laboured with Rose bleeding over his shoulder.

KABOOM!

"Fuck!" Whittaker yelled at no one, tossing the remote control aside and grappled for his rifle.

61.
__The Box__

At the last second, Whittaker caught sight of the trailing exhaust plume as a rocket grenade careered into the drone. It detonated, ripped open as if a can of sardines and the soldiers responded without hesitation, rushing forward past the burning wreck.

He flattened himself against the cylinder's roof and commenced shooting, quickly shifting the crosshairs from soldier to soldier. Each time he squeezed the trigger, a soldier slumped lifeless to the floor giving Bennett and the others time to race towards the doorway. But as more soldiers emerged from behind the mass of cylinders, he lost his advantage.

One of the advancing Charlie team raised a rocket launcher to his shoulder and Whittaker's cylinder erupted, lifting and catapulting fifteen yards across the floor, end over end. Whittaker was tossed helplessly with it.

"Whittaker," Bennett screamed, breaking from the others and sprinting the twenty yards to the upturned cylinder, firing at the enemy on every stride. One found its mark and the soldier fell, showered beneath his own spray of blood.

Whittaker clambered across the floor fumbling desperately for his rifle as gunfire strafed him from fifty yards away. He was pinned down, edging nervously inch by inch towards the upturned cylinder.

Further over, Sponarava clutching her blood-soaked arm, charged the last few yards to the door.

"It's locked, we need a key card," she yelled, yanking at the handle.

Adams and Roland were on her heels, churning through the final remnants of their ammunition as a Charlie Unit soldier rose up above them atop the closest cylinder. He raised his Colt M4 assault rifle and depressed the trigger, holding it low to his hip and sweeping it from left to right.

The bombardment of rounds sent them scuttling, ducking and weaving as they fled until the last two bullets struck flesh. The firing stopped, replaced with the subtle metallic chink of the empty magazine hitting the cylinder roof.

Bennett sprinted and rolled to his back, sliding the last couple of feet out of the firing line of the advancing soldiers. He looked up and shot his last bullet.

The soldier clutched at his throat as the severed artery spewed his life down the front of his battle jacket.

"Adams is down" Sponarava called, kicking at the door without it budging in the slightest.

At her feet, Adams laid suffering in silence, two rounds had decimated his intestines and blood oozed to the floor, pooling under his body.

Bennett grabbed Whittaker and together they sprinted, dodging the incoming barrage and sliding the last few yards into the cover of the doorway's recessed section. The door was set back a few feet into the hangar wall, enough to give them some protection from the incoming gunfire.

"Bennett, I have six rounds left," Whittaker yelled.

"I'm out," Bennett conceded.

"We need a key card, can't bust it down, it's solid steel," Sponarava yelled as she pressed hard against Adams's wound, fighting to stop the bleed and forgetting her own mangled arm.

"FUCK." Bennett was infuriated.

"It's all good." Whittaker pulled a white plastic card from his pocket and tossed it to Bennett.

"I figured the dead guard didn't need it," he laughed.

An electronic click sounded as Bennett swiped the card across the scanner and the door lock released, opening an inch.

"We need to get going, I'm almost out," Roland called, firing single controlled shots desperately to keep the enemy back however, he was failing.

Bennett turned to Whittaker, "I have an idea. Can you see the small orange box at about thirty yards?"

Whittaker looked in the direction Bennett was pointing and spotted the box the lieutenant had dropped earlier.

"Yeah," Whittaker replied finding it in his rifle scope.

"Can you hit it?"

"Don't insult me Bennett!"

"Okay you will have to move quick once the box is pierced," Bennett instructed.

Nicholette gave him a doubtful concerned look and he felt her thoughts. He grabbed the rifle from Whittaker and pushed the others through the doorway.

"I'm the only one immune to the crystal radiation, it's the safest option."

Whittaker hesitated, ready to argue until Bennett shoved him through the doorway and slammed the door shut behind him.

The first group of soldiers broke from their cover and swamped the doorway in rapid gunfire.

He turned and sprinted for the closest cylinder as bullets licked at his footsteps. He landed hard on his belly spinning himself around to face the soldiers running towards him.

"Fuck I hate these things," he mumbled.

He wasn't used to the enormous length of the gun. The Barrett sniper rifle was cumbersome and heavy to manoeuvre quickly in tight spaces as the rounds started hitting around him. He pulled himself in tight behind one of the wheel struts and panned across the floor with the scope.

"There you are!" he whispered and gently squeezed the trigger.

The rounds hitting around him didn't stop and more soldiers appeared running towards him.

"Fuck!"

He had missed the box.

One of the soldiers stopped, dropped to his knee and lifted a rocket launcher to his shoulder.

Bennett readjusted his aim and fired.

The rocket released and shot high across the hangar, striking one of the three helicopters at the rear. The fireball engulfed and detonated the other helicopters next to it, casting out a blast wave that tossed Bennett like paper from under the cylinder's feet.

He was out in the open and dazed from the impact.

Twenty feet over, the closest three soldiers had dropped their guns and were clutching desperately at their throats, struggling to find their last few breaths. Each howled like a dog hit by a car as their bodies convulsed in a violent bone breaking seizure and dark red blood spewed from every orifice.

Bennett's second round had struck the box and shattered the glass.

Looking out across the hangar floor at the thirty or more soldiers screaming their last few seconds of life, he felt sickened at the sight. The scene was like he'd seen four years earlier in Namibia when *The Trust* had conducted their experiments on the villagers. It was a vision he'd chosen to wipe from his memory, but now it had been resurrected as he watched the victims fight, their bodies liquefying to a mush of skin and bone. The blue crystal radiation was pure evil and Banks planning to disperse it in the atmosphere was incomprehensible, he thought.

He grabbed as many weapons as he could carry and raced to join the others.

62.
<u>Sphere</u>

Halfway along the corridor, a body covered in blood blocked his way. Adams was buckled over holding his belly looking ghostly pale and labouring with every breath. He glanced up as Bennett approached and he grimaced from the growing pain.

Bennett dropped to his side and Adams grabbed his arm, "I am sorry Jon, we tried. Good luck to you and every poor soul on this planet now."

He convulsed in a coughing fit spewing blood.

"Where are the others?"

He pointed towards the end of the corridor, "Gone to find Banks. I told them to leave me."

"We need to contact the President," Bennett said handing him a cell phone he'd taken from a dead soldier.

"Why, can't do much now without that confession," Adams stuttered.

"You're wrong, I have the confession."

Bennett pulled a small silver device from inside his jacket and held it up to Adams. In his hand was a covert video recorder the size of a cigarette butt. He'd found it when rummaging through Roland's armoury and took it in case they needed evidence that Sector Four existed.

"You're a genius Bennett!" Adams coughed more blood and used all his strength to dial the President's private cell phone.

A moment passed.

"Jon, we have Banks cornered," Whittaker appeared running along the corridor, but pulled up quickly when he caught sight of Adams slumped across the floor.

He had died during the conversation with the President and Bennett was just terminating the call.

"The President has been briefed," he said, reaching down to close Adam's lifeless eyes.

"Nicholette says he's in the sphere chamber," Whittaker announced.

They ran fifty yards along the same narrow corridor past four closed doorways and around two corners until they reached a wider section. Roland was busy tampering with a scanner on the wall while Sponarava sat on the floor, dazed after another short seizure.

"The sphere maybe in there," she blurted out, pushing herself to her feet at the sight of Bennett.

"Yeah but we can't get in! It's a retina scanner so unless you can get us the right set of eyeballs then we aren't getting in," Roland added.

"You will never get your hands on the sphere Jon."

They all turned towards Bank's voice crackling through an intercom on the wall next to the scanner. On the ceiling above them, a small camera gave Banks a clear view of the chamber door.

"It's over Banks, you missed the other covert recorder I was wearing. The President is right now playing your confession to the world. The Secretary of Defense has been arrested for treason and will spend the rest of his life in prison. As for you? Well you've committed mass murder on a grand scale so both the Russians and the Chinese will be wanting their retribution. Something I am sure won't be good for you!" Bennett said slowly and confidently into the intercom.

A few seconds of silence followed.

Inside the chamber, Banks was for the first time in his life, no longer in control and starting to panic. The lieutenant was attempting to lever open a steel hatch, corroded shut from years of moisture seeping down through the mountain. Behind it was their only escape, a long steep tunnel leading to the outside.

Leaning against the wall next to him, Rose was slouched over and bleeding badly from a gunshot wound. Sponarava's bullet had hit her in the back, slicing through the lower edge of her heart and exploded out her chest leaving a fist size hole. Banks knelt beside her and held her close pressing against the constant stream of blood oozing from under his hands.

"Eke you have to leave me here, I'm not going to make it… save yourself," she said, reaching into her pocket and extracting a small silver disk roughly two inches in diameter.

Further over, the lieutenant continued to push and pull at the hatch, edging it open an inch.

"Banks, I will trade your life for the sphere," Bennett called through the intercom.

He waited but no reply came from inside the chamber.

"Perhaps there is an escape tunnel in there?" Sponarava suggested.

Bennett nodded, "Kehlstein had one, so yes quite possible."

The cell phone rang and he answered it.

He hung up. "We have another problem. The Russians don't believe the recording is authentic, they say it's a trick. Two Russian subs have just been detected in the Pacific north of Hawaii, surfacing to firing depth."

"Fuck not good," Whittaker responded.

"How many nukes are we talking about?" Sponarava asked.

"I don't know but it sounds full scale. Both sides have access to over six thousand nuclear weapons. One Russian sub carries sixteen long range ballistic missiles each with four nuclear warheads capable of striking anywhere across the United States. That means over sixty targets from just one sub," Bennett answered.

"And there are two subs we know of in the Pacific," Roland added.

"It's a good thing we're underground then hey!" Whittaker smirked to lighten the glum atmosphere.

Bennett yelled into the intercom, "Banks, millions of innocent Americans are about to die because of your doing. The Russians are launching a nuclear attack, will the satellites protect us?"

At first there was silence and then, a broken voice aired.

"I am sorry Jon, Eckhard wasn't completely honest with you. The satellites are programmed to protect the central regions only, the east and west will be annihilated."

"Rose how do we reprogram them?"

"You can't from here and even if you could, it's too late. The process takes three hours," she replied in broken speech, interrupted by her struggle to cope with the pain.

"Where is Banks?"

The intercom remained silent.

"There must be something we can do," Sponarava said.

"Yeah maybe you talk to the Russians, they'd love to hear from you," Bennett answered sarcastically referring to the large bounty on her head.

"I'm going to die anyway," she snapped back.

"Give me the phone," Roland demanded.

He paused and looked at Sponarava, "You saved my life earlier today and now I can repay you."

Bennett gave him a puzzled look and handed him the cell phone.

He dialled, waited and then spoke in fluent Russian. The others glanced at each other, bewildered and confused. Sponarava and Bennett had no problems understanding what he was saying however, Whittaker had no idea.

"This is Papillon, my access authority is Romeo... Charlie... Alpha... nine... two... seven... six. I need you to transfer me on a secure line to Dimitri Kryuchkova."

Both Bennett and Sponarava took two quick steps back and raised their guns at him.

63.
Dimitri Kryuchkova

Kryuchkova was the head of the Russian Federal Security Service and before that, the KGB. He was the man who had issued Sponarava's arrest warrant and had authorised the lethal force for her capture. In addition, he had placed the one million Euros bounty on her head.

Roland raised one hand in the air and shook his head. "Trust me!" he said in English.

"You better know what you're doing," Bennett replied, not lowering his gun.

A few seconds later and it became clear Roland was talking to Kryuchkova explaining where they were and about Banks's grand plan. It was obvious from the conversation they knew each other well, but then the mood changed abruptly.

"She is dead, I witnessed it about two hours ago. Shot by the American soldiers," he said staring at Sponarava.

He hung up.

"You have some explaining to do," Bennett demanded.

"Yes I do, but first you need to contact your President and tell him to stand down. Kryuchkova is still very influential in the Kremlin. If anyone can change the course of events, he can. This is the best chance we have at authenticating your recording."

Bennett grabbed the cell phone and made the call.

"Now start talking Roland or Papillon, whatever your name really is?" Sponarava commanded.

"I was engaged to his daughter until she fell victim to leukemia and died a few years ago. My real name is Jean-Marc Cardot and until a few years back, I was employed by the Russian Intelligence Directorate, that is how I came to meet Kryuchkova and his daughter. For the past few years I haven't been involved in espionage until you, Bennett appeared on my doorstep with Charlie."

"Why?" Bennett asked, though he was expecting the answer.

"One million Euros! The reward for her. I knew you would lead me to her."

"So why the change of heart?" Sponarava asked still with her gun aimed at him.

"Nicholette there is no need for the gun, you saved my life and I honour my repayment. That's why I told Dimitri you are dead so maybe you can lead a normal life without that bounty hanging over you. You remind me so much of my late fiancée and not a day goes by without the anguish of losing her. I don't wish that upon Jon."

Sponarava lowered her weapon as the phone rang.

"It worked, the Russians are standing down," Bennett announced as he hung up the phone.

He shook Roland's hand as the others joined in the excitement of the moment.

"Jon we need the sphere," Sponarava said pushing away from Bennett's embrace.

He tried the intercom again but still no response came from inside the chamber.

"Wait here, back in a minute," he called as he sprinted towards the hangar.

Less than two minutes later he returned carrying a rocket launcher. He hurled it to his shoulder, yelling at the others to move and fired. The explosive spear shot along the corridor with a deafening rush and slammed into the chamber door. Fragments of the wall and fire erupted outwards, knocking them off their feet.

Bennett charged into the fire, pushing aside the remnants of the burning door. The others were quick to follow, each with their guns ready and squinting through the smoke.

The doorway led into a smoke filled room where small spot fires burned. The rocket had shattered the door into pieces that had been sprayed across the room. Across the far side, a steel hatch hung open and a body covered in blood was sprawled next to it. Bennett raced over to it. The lieutenant was dead with a bullet hole in the back of his head.

"Jon, over here!" Whittaker called.

Under a larger section of the door, Rose was pinned covered in blood, most of which was from her gunshot and not the grazes from the explosion. In her hands she grasped an object the size of a basketball and covered in alien looking symbols.

Nicholette was first to react, pushing past the rest of them to pry the sphere from Rose's blood covered hands. A slight humming vibration emanated from inside as she held it.

"Is she dead?" Whittaker asked.

Her eyes flickered open to stare at Bennett, "I am sorry Jon, you are too late."

"Where is Banks?"

"Gone, through there!" she replied pointing towards the open hatch.

"Jon, should the sphere be doing this?" Sponarava inquired as the humming intensified in her hands and her fingers vibrated.

Bennett looked to her and then back at Rose who gave him a defeated look. He grabbed the sphere and rolled it over. On the underside, the small detonator disk had been screwed into place initiating the self-destruction sequence.

"NOOOO!" he screamed as all three hundred symbols lining the sphere's surface started flashing a vibrant blue light.

"It's for the best Jon," Rose added.

"We have to get out of here and fast, the sphere's auto detonation has been activated."

"YOU BITCH!" Sponarava yelled and slammed the full weight of her fist into Rose's face, breaking her nose and shattering her cheek bone. She recoiled for a second strike when Bennett wrestled her away.

"How long do we have?" Roland asked.

"Roughly fifteen minutes, we detonated one at Kehlstein a few years back. The symbols will stop flashing one by one counting down until there are none left," Bennett answered as the first symbol stopped blinking its blue radiance.

"What happens then?" Roland again.

"Big fucking explosion of nuclear proportions."

"Fifteen fucking minutes, how the fuck are we going to get out and far enough away in fifteen fucking minutes?" Whittaker banged his fists against the wall.

Bennett was pacing back and forth, thinking.

"I have a crazy idea that none of you will believe, I'm not sure I do myself. We need to get to level five, but first I need to dispose of the blue crystal in the hangar," Bennett quickly said making his way towards the hangar door.

He stopped and called back to Whittaker and Roland, "Bring Rose?" while Nicholette glared daggers at him.

It took him three minutes to locate the small piece of blue crystal among the putrefied bodies on the hangar floor and then somewhere to shield it. A coffee flask sitting on the worker's bench was perfect, the inner glass and metal outer covering would be enough he hoped, as protection.

He gathered the others and they ran as fast as they could to the stairs and down onto level five.

Eleven minutes until detonation.

Level five was mostly shrouded in darkness except where the elevating platform had collapsed, allowing light to filter down from the hangar above. Whittaker carried Rose's weak body flopped over his shoulders, unburdened by her light frame weighing just under a hundred pounds while Roland hung close to Bennett. Sponarava stayed back behind Whittaker. Her mind was in turmoil, she and the baby would now die without the Sphere.

They waded through the debris from the fallen platform until they reached a side hangar illuminated in a faint orange haze. Bennett stopped, staring into the hangar.

"There is my idea!" he announced to the unanimous jaw drop.

64.
<u>Escape</u>

"Are you kidding, is that what I think it is?" Roland muttered as he pushed past Bennett to step deeper into the hangar.

Above him, the lights activated by his movement, flickering to life exposing a massive black circular shaped object glistening as if wet and over eighty feet across. It resembled a giant upside down saucer propped up high above the floor by three long thin struts. Bennett couldn't help think it reminded him of the ferocious tripod machines in the classic H.G. Wells science fiction novel, 'The War of the Worlds' as he walked closer.

The height of the craft was at least two building stories at the highest point sloping down to a few feet at the outer extremities. There was no obvious entry point and the underneath was completely smooth without markings or detail of any kind.

"It's the alien craft from Antarctica," Rose stuttered.

"I cannot believe this!" Roland exuding with excitement and like a kid in a toy shop, ran through under it.

"Biggest waste of time and money that was," she added, interrupted by a blood coughing fit.

Bennett gave her a bewildered look.

"The technology is way beyond us, our best scientists didn't know where to start," she added.

"Hey, can I remind you all why we're here and that time is running out fast," Sponarava interjected holding out the timer in her hands. She had brought along the sphere to keep check of the time remaining though deep down she was holding desperate hope it would stop. Half the symbols had ceased flashing meaning seven minutes remaining.

"This was your plan Jon? Fly an alien spaceship out of here, a flying saucer that the best scientists don't even understand?" Whittaker screamed, sensing their death was inevitable.

"Bennett laughed, "Well I did say it was a crazy idea. It's just that I have this weird unexplainable feeling like I know how to fly it. It started when I first laid eyes on it."

He reached out and caressed the metal of the closest tripod leg.

"Whoa!" He pulled back quickly rubbing the sudden burning sensation tingling through his fingers.

"What just happened?" Roland added.

Above them the alien craft transformed. The outer skin turned iridescent silver and the underside materialised into a conglomerate of detail showing the entry hatch and two large bay doors. In the middle, a large red glass dome five feet across extended downwards two feet. On closer inspection, the dome surface presented as more consistent with that of a brilliant cut diamond reflecting light in every direction.

"The pulse weapon I suspect," Bennett declared in response to the curious looks on the faces around him.

The overall shape of the craft had altered as well. Though it retained a mostly circular aspect, three long cylinder shaped sections side by side protruded from the main body giving the distinct indication they were the engines.

The hatch slid open and a set of stairs extended smoothly and silently to the floor.

"Rose is that normal?" Bennett called.

"No, it's never done that before. It took the scientists over a year just to find that hatch and it wasn't how you just did it. How did you do that?"

"No idea, but I think it's responding to my thoughts if that's possible."

"Hey even if you can fly this thing, how are we going to get out of here. Have a look around, can you see an exit?" Whittaker said.

"They got it in here somehow and it wasn't by the platform. Must be somewhere leading to the outside. Go have a look and hurry," Bennett responded glancing at the sphere.

"About five minutes," Sponarava confirmed holding it out to show the last third of symbols flashing.

"You're all going to die," Rose coughed holding her chest.

Bennett vanished up the stairs into the craft where he was ambushed by the sudden overwhelming onset of disorientation. Around him the craft's interior presented larger than the outside and it unbalanced him. The lighting was subdued by a soft green glow emanating from the walls while under his feet, thin trails of white light gave direction towards what looked like the craft's cockpit.

The main cabin behind the cockpit was circular in shape, about eighteen yards across and empty. The cockpit was nothing like the fighter jets he was used to and at first sight, there appeared to be no instruments or flight controls. One hard metallic seat sat alone at the far end, clearly not intended for a human by its miniature size and the unusual contours.

To his surprise, he was drawn to it like the alien craft was communicating with him, giving him instructions.

He took a few cautious steps driven by both curiosity and something inside him dictating his moves that he couldn't fight. He tried to shake it loose, but the longer he remained in the craft, the more powerful the feeling grew, like he was possessed by someone or something else and it was taking control of his body.

The space surrounding the chair started mutating and structures raised abruptly from the floor while next to him, the chair beckoned him. It too had changed shape and as he sat, started moulding to his body shape. As if alive and made of liquid metal, the chair expanded and circulated around the extremities of his body crawling up to cover his head and face.

Outside, Roland and Whittaker had discovered level five was much larger and older than the darkness was allowing them to see. An emergency evacuation sign on the wall showed them the direction, a long escape tunnel hidden behind a set of large hangar doors. They pressed a switch next to the sign and the doors rolled back slowly, revealing the late afternoon daylight.

Bennett's mind had intertwined with the craft and he could see the cockpit at arm's reach around him. As if the entire front of the ship was made of glass, the outside was suddenly visible in one hundred and eighty degree panorama view. He could see Rose laying on the hangar floor in her expanding pool of blood and the men in the distance, running towards the craft. Behind them he could see the escape tunnel angled upwards towards the blue sky.

Somewhere close he could feel Nicholette's presence, but something was not right. It caused him to panic and the craft immediately released him.

"Jon, can you hear me?" she called as his surroundings reverted to the green glow of the craft's interior and her violently shaking him.

"It's okay Nic, I can fly this thing, but don't ask me how because I have no idea. It's like I've done it before in another life!" he explained.

"I think I know what you mean, it's kind a familiar to me too," Nicholette responded and added, "But we have about one minute until this thing goes off."

The sphere was down to the remaining thirty symbols.

Back behind them, the other men were entering the craft.

"WHOA!" Whittaker stammered as he took his last step and lost his balance. Roland eagerly pushed past him and fell to the floor disorientated.

"Someone get Rose and strap yourselves in, we're almost out of time," he called.

Back behind him, four seats had protruded from the walls responding to his thoughts.

He turned to Nicholette, "You might want to get rid of that thing!"

She laughed at her own stupidity, "Fuck!" and ran to the hatch, tossing it.

Bennett let himself go and the spacecraft consumed him, wrapping the control seat around him. Two objects the size and shape of tennis balls appeared in his hands as an extension of the seat. Each in combination with his thought processes, controlled the speed and direction of the craft by turning and rotating them.

As his mind interacted with the ship's interface, the engines engaged without a noticeable sound and the craft lifted a few feet above the floor, defying gravity. He summoned his thoughts towards the tunnel and the craft responded with a slight tilt of the control in his right hand. It was all happening as if he'd done it a hundred times before, but he struggled to comprehend how it was possible.

Resting on the hangar floor below them, the sphere counted down through the last three symbols. Bennett tilted the control in his left hand and the craft accelerated into the tunnel while his passengers remained unaware they had exited the mountain. Inertia dampeners inside the craft made it impossible for them to feel the roll and acceleration as Bennett pushed it skyward.

The last symbol ceased flashing.

65.
<u>Retribution</u>

Two miles south of the mountain, a lone vehicle sped across the rough terrain bouncing and losing traction on the loose rocks. The driver kept check of his rear view mirror and maintained the pressure on the pedal. The car, an old Jeep suddenly shuddered and a low pitched whistling like wind through a louvre made him slam down hard on the brakes.

"I don't believe it!" Banks mumbled as the alien craft passed twenty feet overhead and pulled vertical through the clouds.

He jumped from the car and stood watching the clouds for a couple of seconds silently cursing Bennett as a flash of brilliant white light lit up the entire sky. He shielded his eyes from the searing intensity as the air around him turned suffocatingly hot and he was deafened by what he thought was thunder directly overhead.

To the north, the mountain's belly was ripped open and the nuclear mushroom cloud rose from within. It had erupted in shades of crimson red, violet blue, orange and grey that clawed skyward while the blast wave raced out across the desert. Like a heavy door slamming in a gale-force wind it smashed unforgivingly into Banks tossing him across the ground.

He climbed to his feet rejoicing at the thought he'd survived, but then something unusual caught his eye. The ground around him started shaking and sliding while the base of the mountain appeared to rise.

He threw himself back into the Jeep and planted his foot on the pedal. The back wheels spun wildly on the loose rocks until the tyres grabbed traction and he gained speed. The jeep's steering jerked left and right in his hands until the front wheels buckled under the strain of the earth moving. The vehicle slipped sideways to give Banks a ringside view of his fate. He looked out the window as a fifty foot wall of molten earth tumbled towards him.

At that moment, Eckhard Banks ceased to exist as the ground rose up and fused his body into the earth.

66.
<u>Rose</u>

"I always loved you Jon, that is the truth."

The sudden onset of a woman's voice startled him. He had been mentally consumed by the alien ship and the others had become a vague presence behind him except for Rose, who now stood beside him. She was crystal clear to him and strangely, much younger and no longer suffering the effects of a gunshot.

"What? I don't understand, how are you here with me?" he asked still interconnected with the chair and the alien ship.

"I have so much to explain and I don't have much time."

"What do you mean not much time?"

"I am dying Jon, you saw my injuries."

Bennett was confused, his mind was racing with questions and all the time, he was feeling the presence of something else inside his head. How was Rose clearly visible while the others were blurred shapes, he speculated looking behind into the cabin where they were seated.

"I never fully believed the Monk when he spoke about the true purpose of the eighth code nanobots, it all seemed ridiculous but now I can see it," she continued.

"See what?"

"The robotic microorganisms not only assist the human body heal and extend our lives, but they are actually reprogramming our DNA, transforming our bodies and minds."

"What the fuck are you talking about Rose? What do you mean transforming?"

"It wasn't until I entered this craft that I realised. You and I have the eighth code in our bodies and only we can see everything inside this craft. Only you can operate it and though I cannot, I can still see what you can. The others cannot except

Nicholette has partial vision only because her strain of the eighth code was altered by *The Trust's* scientists."

Bennett drifted momentarily thinking.

"The Monk said the code is being used to implant members of an alien race on Earth, a covert invasion to put it simply. Each injection of the code is unique with a separate extraterrestrial identity but takes thirty years for the full mutation to occur. Your father was only a few years off when he was killed."

Bennett didn't fire an argument, it explained his understanding of the alien craft and the feeling he was riding shotgun with someone or something else.

"What happened to you Rose? I thought you were dedicated to the Monk. How did you get tied up with Banks?"

"Very long story Jon. We became lovers in our younger years and our relationship only grew stronger as the years passed. It was something we kept secret and at times, proved near impossible. But it wasn't just my love for the man, it was his vision for a perfect life that lured me. We both dreamt of a utopian world and he was prepared to do anything to achieve it. He convinced me when he murdered his younger brother, just so he was the sole heir to his father's wealth. Killing his parents was the icing on the cake to demonstrate his commitment."

"Geez Rose, I always thought you as insensitive but never that cold."

She continued talking though Bennett could see she was tiring and her speech starting to stagger.

"Then there was the Nazis and the Fourth Reich! Eckhard wasn't about to let *The Trust* inflict the planet with their rule."

She hesitated, "I never realised how personal it was to him."

"Why personal?"

"Eckhard's father was a founding member of the *The Trust*, originally their primary financier. This was the reason Eckhard murdered his parents, not just to get his hands on his father's billions. He wanted a seat at the table of *The Trust* and be part of their 'New World' vision."

"What happened?"

"They refused him membership and I think it was because they suspected he had killed his father. This infuriated him, tore him apart in the early days until we conceptualised our plan."

She continued. "*The Trust* tried to kill him though they never anticipated his resolve. He diverted his newfound wealth to hiring a small army of mercenaries to protect him twenty four seven while he built his empire."

"How'd you get involved with *The Trust* then?" Bennett asked.

"He had me infiltrate them to keep tabs on their progress, thinking we could utilise their already established networks. That's how I met the Monk and discovered we had a common goal, the destruction of *The Trust*. At first, I believed the Monk's prophecies of the arrival, but he never once articulated on what it all meant. That started to make me suspicious, so it didn't take much for Eckhard to convince me the Monk was a fraud. It's a shame he had to die because now I can see the truth in the things he said."

"You killed him?" Bennett quizzed.

"Yes, I had to, he and his guardians posed the greatest threat to Eckhard's plans. After *The Trust* was dismantled, he turned his attention towards Eckhard's business empire. Too much time and money had been invested for some religious oracle to tear it all down."

"So why help me escape after I was implanted with the memory suppressor? You must have known I would have died anyway."

She didn't answer his question and instead said, "There is an upside to me killing the Monk. I found the Mayan Sphere."

"Yeah and it just went nuclear so hardly the upside," Bennett scoffed.

"No Jon, that was the Sumerian Sphere. It had been taken from Saddam Hussein's treasures by a British soldier serving in Iraq."

Bennett didn't care about learning why she helped him, his attention had diverted towards saving Nicholette and their baby.

"Where is the Mayan Sphere now?"

"Australia..." she stuttered and vanished from his sight.

"ROSE!" he screamed.

67.
Lost Codes

As if sensing his heightened anxiety, the alien craft released Bennett and he slipped from the chair. He ran and fell awkwardly, stumbling to his knees suffering the craft's disorientation effects.

Rose was strapped in her seat on the opposite side of the main cabin while the others were either side, all unconscious or dead, he wasn't sure.

Suddenly Nicholette's eyes sprung open and she gasped for a breath, "What happened, where are we?"

"Rose knows the location of the last remaining sphere," he called.

She was alive though clinging to the edge, her breathing was almost non-existent and her pulse near gone.

"ROSE WAKE UP, WHERE IN AUSTRALIA IS THE SPHERE?" he yelled at her, grabbing and shaking her urgently.

Her eyes twitched and she slurred, "Behind waterfall...under rocks..."

"Do you mean the waterfall at Viktor's Sanctuary?"

She nodded briefly.

Nicholette was next to him, "Jon the First Code, we need the First Code."

With her last remaining strength, Rose reached out and grabbed his arm. Her eyes flickered open and closed, her body shuddered violently as the final few pints of blood drained to the floor.

She opened her eyes staring directly at him, pausing for a couple of seconds and whispered, "I am the First Code Jon."

Her head rolled to the side and her life extinguished.

He ripped open her blouse scattering buttons in every direction. The first code tattoo was vanishing fast with her death, but it was futile, four of the thirteen symbols had been obliterated by the bullet's exit. Panic struck, he pushed and prodded at the fleshy edges of bloody chest wound trying desperately to reconstruct the tattoo.

It was gone.

"Nooooo!" Nicholette screamed, "It's my fault, I shot her."

Bennett took her in his arms and held her tight. "I am so sorry Nic."

She burst into tears while inside his pocket, the cell phone started vibrating.

68.
Archway

West Antarctica
May 26, 2005

Two days later, shuffled along by an armada of Secret Service, Bennett stepped from the gang plank of a nuclear submarine, the USS Alabama onto a small narrow dock built deep inside the West Antarctica Ice Sheet. Originally constructed during World War II by the Nazis, the dock served as the only doorway into a massive subterranean chamber mostly formed naturally by glacier movements over thousands of years. Completely hidden from the world, the chamber concealed the planet's greatest secret.

It had been a hectic forty eight hours since escaping the detonation of Sector Four. Nuclear war had been diverted however, both the Russians and the Chinese were demanding immediate access to details of the pulse weapon. Nicholette had collapsed for the final time, slipping hopelessly into a coma and rushed to Johns Hopkins Hospital in Baltimore. There she remained on life support for both her and the unborn baby. Together with Roland and Whittaker, Bennett had dashed across the Pacific to Australia and recovered the Mayan Sphere hidden under rocks behind the waterfall at Viktor's Sanctuary, just as Rose had instructed.

Prior to that, he had received an interesting phone call from the President, pleading for his cooperation to hand over the alien craft in exchange to learn the truth of why the Thirteenth Code was so important. At first Bennett was hesitant, not trusting until an offer was presented, one he couldn't refuse.

Nicholette and the baby were going to die, that was the unanimous prognosis of the medical staff at the hospital. Her body was shutting down quickly, it was just a matter of time and in their opinion, less than two days.

When the President announced the CIA had tracked down Jeremiah's location, Bennett knew it was his only chance of saving Nicholette. Jeremiah held knowledge of all thirteen codes but more importantly, the First Code. In return he agreed to meet with the President at an undisclosed location in Antarctica while he kept the alien craft cloaked, far from the government's reach.

Fourteen hours underwater onboard the Ohio-class nuclear submarine wasn't what he had expected and to surface inside the cavern under the ice took him by surprise. Either side of him, the Secret Service agents kept watch as they ushered him from the dock into a long brightly lit corridor. At the far end, an elevator door slid open.

Two of the agents entered the lift while Bennett followed watching them select level three. Neither spoke a word as the lift slowly ascended, creaking and groaning all the way. The lift doors opened and the men nodded for Bennett to exit.

"Jon, thankyou for coming. I hope your travel was comfortable." The President stepped forward extending his hand as a formal greeting.

Bennett took his hand, nodding acceptance. "What is this place?"

The lift had opened onto a room, forty feet square resembling a miniature NASA control room. Two walls were lined floor to ceiling with monitors displaying satellite feeds from around the world. Three men dressed in white overalls busied themselves at keyboards not distracted by the presence of the President or the swarm of Secret Service agents loitering around them.

"This cavity is a hundred feet below the ice surface, formed over a million years ago we believe," the President said pointing towards the wall sized window to their right.

Bennett stepped closer to peer down into an enormous cavern eighty yards across and bordered by sheer vertical ice walls, glistening under the floodlighting. An array of twenty huge lights were spaced evenly around the extremities of the floor. Each light pointed in the same direction, to the west showcasing a massive golden archway in the ice wall.

Bennett stood staring, trying to comprehend what he was witnessing.

"It was discovered by the Germans sometime around 1944 during the war." The President said as he walked to his side at the window.

"What is it?"

"Come I'll show you," the President replied and he led Bennett back into the lift, descending to the cavern floor.

Leaving the narrow confines of the lift, they stepped onto a steel pathway wide enough to walk side by side. The floor was the natural ice and though the air seemed unusually warm, the ice showed no sign of melting. Like the steel path they walked on, there were others leading to a large platform suspended in the centre of the cavity. Raised on top of the platform, two heavy artillery cannons like those seen on the deck of a Navy destroyer were perched high facing the archway. Lower down on either side, smaller calibre miniguns lined gunner trenches carved into the ice however, there was no sign of soldiers. The entire floor space was deserted.

Bennett stopped briefly to take in the enormity of the space, rising up as far as he could see. The walls had cracked in places, some wider than his hand.

They reached the base of the archway.

A solid steel door, fifteen feet high and the same wide, stood closed under the archway. Painted across the door in red paint were the words.

ENTRY PROHIBITED

"Why the artillery? What's behind the door?"

The President ignored the question.

"We first learnt of this place shortly after the second world war, a few small references in Hitler's secret documents was all we had, but it took us ten more years before we actually found it. The Nazis had spent years excavating into the ice to reveal this archway. Carbon dating suggests it is over seven million years old."

Bennett broke abruptly from scrutinising the archway to stare at the President.

"What? It can't be!"

He returned to look more closely at the archway rising thirty feet above him. The ice had been excavated from around it, leaving it free standing.

"It's solid gold and over two hundred tonnes in weight," the President announced.

"WOW! Now that's some serious value there!" Bennett walked closer, outstretched his hand to caress the smooth shiny surface.

"Whoa, it's hot, why's it hot?"

"That we don't know, but each year it gets a few degrees warmer. Most of the ice around it wasn't excavated, it has melted with the increasing temperature."

The President hesitated a moment. "Jon, this is not the reason I asked you here."

He turned towards the control room set high up the side of the ice wall and nodded.

Air hissed as the steel door's locking system released and started opening, slowly rolling back into the ice wall. Lights flickered on, one by one down a long straight tunnel, carved from years of drilling by the Germans.

"The technology in the 50's and 60's didn't allow us to fully explore what is down here. It wasn't until the past ten years with our advancements in ground penetrating radar, did we discover its true size."

"Size?" Bennett quizzed.

"It's massive!" the President replied, handing Bennett a folder he'd been carrying since leaving the control room.

Bennett opened the folder exposing a sheath of glossy photographs.

"Are they structures? They look like skyscrapers?" he asked flicking through dozens of images generated by the radar.

"Yes, it's a small city and like the Archway, it's over seven million years old. Most is frozen in the ice shelf, but some parts of the city are inside cavities like this one."

Bennett stood shaking his head in disbelief. "Do you have any idea who built it?"

"Yes!" the President replied.

69.
<u>Enoch</u>

West Antarctica
May 26, 2005

"Jon, what's down that tunnel is the greatest secret this government and a handful of others have ever kept. Only a very small group of people know it exists and we need to keep it that way for now. Not even *The Trust* or Banks knew it was here. Keeping it hidden was a gargantuan task in itself. So what you are about to learn cannot be disclosed, do you understand that?"

Bennett laughed. "You seem to forget where I once worked. So yes, I understand though I'm a little confused why you are telling me, it's not like I have the security clearance anymore."

"Yes that is true however, this might provide you some answers. Have a look on the rear side of the Archway," the President requested.

Bennett obliged and stepped behind the archway.

He stood staring, shocked at first.

"The symbols, they are the same as those on the spheres," he responded.

"Yes that is what I thought you'd say," the President replied.

"So whoever built this archway also built the spheres," Bennett concluded.

"Yes."

He pointed to the images in Bennett's hand, "Take a closer look at the structure in the centre."

Bennett held it up, studying it intently. At the centre of the tall structures, a circular disk the size of four football fields became evident.

"What is it?"

"For the past thirty years, excavations have been underway down here. It's been slow going and costly but what we discovered is unbelievable, an alien civilisation, dead for millions of years.

Thousands frozen in the ice without the slightest physical evidence of decomposition like a human body."

"And the circular disk?" Bennett asked.

"Spacecraft!"

From somewhere behind them a small vehicle similar to an extended golf buggy arrived driven by one of the Secret Service agents. Next to him sat another agent. The President walked towards it offering his hand as an invitation for Bennett to take a seat, "It takes ten minutes to reach the excavation site."

They climbed onboard and the buggy lurched forward into the tunnel.

"What do we know about them? Like where are they from? How'd they die?" Bennett asked.

The President nodded. "Now this is where it becomes really interesting. Their anatomy is nothing like ours. What we believed at first were lifeless corpses, were in fact, living bodies in a state of dormancy. Thousands of them in stasis throughout the city. But then a few years back, something extraordinary occurred."

He paused a moment, leant in closer to Bennett and whispered, "One woke up!"

"What? Seriously?"

"They call themselves Jeremiah!" the President answered catching a glimpse of Bennett's bewildered expression and quickly added, "Jeremiah is not an individual as you believe, it's the name of their race. They originate from a planet system similar to ours over a thousand light years from here, across the expanse of our galaxy."

He paused allowing Bennett to absorb the information.

"Sixty-six million years ago, their planet was destroyed by a powerful enemy and they fled, discovering Earth not long after the Cretaceous extinction event."

Bennett interrupted him, "The what event?"

"The asteroid collision that killed off the dinosaurs. They arrived in the years after that, to a burning planet and an uninhabitable surface. Instead they chose Mars as an alternative."

"What? Mars doesn't sustain life," Bennett interrupted.

"It once did," the President abruptly replied.

Bennett gave him a surprised look.

The President continued his briefing. "The Monk had been correct in his warnings. When the pulse weapon is fired continuously at the planet's surface, it starts an unstoppable chain reaction of devastation."

"Is that what happened to Mars?"

The President nodded. "The Jeremiah's enemy annihilated their cities and in the process, crippled the planet. The result is what we see today, a desolate landscape with a thin layered atmosphere of mostly carbon dioxide."

"What about the surface images sent back by the Mars probes? There wasn't signs of previous life, certainly no evidence of alien structures! How was that covered up?"

"Could you imagine the shocked looks at NASA when the first images of the Mars surface returned showing evidence of a previous civilisation," the President chuckled.

Bennett laughed, "Yeah I bet. That's one huge event to cover up."

"We couldn't allow the real images into the public space. The world's not quite ready for the reality of aliens you'd have to agree."

Bennett nodded.

"Most of the destruction lies below the surface and was not visible, but some areas were exposed from wind erosion. Luckily the preliminary images sent back only showed a small section but it was enough to confirm Mars was once inhabited."

"So how did they end up here?" Bennett asked.

"A small group of Jeremiah escaped undetected from the burning planet and headed to Earth, crashing into the polar ice shelf. Here they rebuilt their cities concealed under the ice though more importantly, hidden from their enemy lurking in space. But then their queen died and the Jeremiah started becoming extinct. She had been their last reproducing queen."

"Reproducing queen?" Bennett quizzed.

"As I said, the Jeremiah have quite different anatomy to us and though they have physical characteristics similar to humans, their biology is very different. They are best likened to bees; they can only reproduce from a fertile queen. Only one escaped the red planet and when she died here on Earth, it meant the extinction of their race had become inevitable. However a Jeremiah's life cycle can last for over a hundred thousand years, regenerating every few thousand by undergoing a period of deep sleep similar to the hibernation cycle of a bear. These periods of dormancy can last a few thousand years."

"Is that what they are in now?"

"Yes and most are due to wake sometime in the next three years."

"Enoch was first, one of a small group of three that awaken in the ten years preceding a full awakening."

"Enoch?" Bennett asked.

"That's what it calls itself."

"Are we going to speak to Enoch now?"

'Yes, I hope so," the President answered.

"You hope so?"

"Jon we have a problem that maybe you can help with," the President said waiting no time to continue, "Only one person could communicate with the Jeremiah."

"The Monk!" Bennett interjected. For some strange unknown reason, it was all starting to make sense to him.

"Yes, don't ask me how or why he is the only one, but he was. His death is causing quite a degree of angst with Enoch and the other two Jeremiah."

"Not sure how I am going to help," Bennett refuted.

"No one has ever flown the alien craft except you. We are optimistic that also means you can communicate with them," the President answered as the buggy slowed around a bend in the tunnel and shuddered to a halt.

"Why the urgency to reopen the dialogue with them?" Bennett asked. Ever since stepping foot inside the ice chamber, he had sensed the President was holding information back.

"The Monk was the Chairman of the World Defence Coalition, a select group of trustworthy billionaires and prominent world leaders. Enoch had appointed him to this position to prepare us and hopefully prevent the end of the world."

"Mr President I am lost. World Defence Coalition, end of the world, you're going to have to give me a bit more."

"Yes of course. The Jeremiah are not the only alien race we have encountered."

Bennett knew where the conversation was heading. "Roswell?"

The President nodded. "Yes. There were three alien beings onboard that craft that crashed at Roswell. Two died on impact while the third survived for the best part of a week. It was different to the Jeremiah in both appearance and communication abilities. What we learnt from that being in 1947 was gravely disturbing, but it had little significance at the time until the Jeremiah showed up."

Bennett engrossed in the conversation didn't notice the bright ball of light slowly approaching them from further along the tunnel.

The President continued. "It was a scout, searching for the Jeremiah."

"What?"

"The alien that crashed at Roswell was here looking for the Jeremiah cities. They have been at war with them for hundreds of millions of years and have one goal, the total annihilation of the Jeremiah species. It's only a matter of time before one of their other scouts discover them here under the ice."

"It's too late, they are coming!" Bennett mumbled.

"How do you know?" the President asked.

"That just told me," he replied pointing towards the emerging white light.

At first glance, the light shimmered growing brighter revealing what appeared as a humanly figure enshrouded in a white robe and long hair flowing. Watching it move closer, Bennett couldn't escape visualising the depiction of God from biblical drawings. Then as the light started to lose its luminance, a tall spindly figure edged slowly towards them as if floating weightless across the floor.

The President turned, bowed his head and extended his hand like he was befriending a lost dog. Behind him the two agents stepped a pace forward, fingers releasing the clips on their holsters.

"This is Enoch," the President announced to the floor.

Standing erect at ten feet tall, the Jeremiah displayed some physical similarities to humans with its long slender arms and legs. The outer covering was vastly different with lizard like skin, the colour of milky grey and glistened as if wet.

Narrow shoulders laid the base for an elongated but thin head that tilted downwards to stare at them with two small bulbous black eyes. Long dark hairlike follicles dangled loosely either side down past its shoulders while two tiny slits resembling fish gills beneath its eyes allowed it to breathe.

"What now?" Bennett mumbled back at the President.

Enoch raised its arm extending three long slender talons and slowly lowered its head towards them. Bennett held his ground as it moved closer to within a few inches, its black eyes mirroring his reflection.

Unbeknownst to him the President and the agents had collapsed to the floor.

70.
Provenance

Indian Ocean
2,000 miles southwest of Perth, Australia
May 26, 2005

Bennett woke, dazed and disorientated. The President and his agents stood watching him as one reached down to help him up.

"What happened?" Bennett stuttered as his surroundings materialised into focus, he was back onboard the USS Alabama.

"You were teleported somewhere, the city possibly. The Monk always thought so but he could never confirm it. He used to say only the Jeremiah were permitted to walk free inside the city and that's why we have never been given access."

"I remember somewhere brightly lit and claustrophobic, suppressing my vision. Enoch and the other two Jeremiah were there, talking to me in English I think, well that's what it sounded like," Bennett said.

He continued, "It was the same feeling I had when I controlled the craft, like someone or something was inside my head, sharing knowledge and guiding me."

"They communicate telepathically," the President stated.

Bennett nodded recalling his experience, "It was like wearing some incredibly advanced virtual reality device."

"What did they tell you?" the President asked.

"More than I was prepared for. Our future doesn't exactly sound secure."

"How long do we have?" the President asked, clearly distressed and it was evident he had prior knowledge of where Bennett's conversation was heading. It was the first time Bennett had sensed fear in the man's voice.

"A little over three years for the first fleet of ships to arrive."

He hesitated, staring into the President eyes. "Earth will be completely destroyed and humanity wiped out."

The President mumbled, "We have suspected this for some time though it always lacked confirmation."

Bennett had a sudden flashback of what Charlie Edmund had said about the object hurtling towards Earth, the 'Death Star' in his words. Was that the fleet of ships? He wondered.

"How long was I gone?" Bennett asked.

"Six hours! But that's not unusual, the Monk was sometimes gone for days at a time."

Bennett continued. "Their enemy will stop at nothing to eradicate the Jeremiah and in just over three years, that enemy arrives and like they did on Mars, will bombard this planet. Energy pulses each equivalent to ten thousand atomic bombs will rip Earth apart."

The President studied Bennett. "Do you know why the whole planet and not just their city under the ice?"

"Provenance!" Bennett responded.

The President stared at him for a few seconds, overcome with a look of guilt, "How much did they tell you about Provenance?"

"Three hundred thousand years ago after their Queen died, they set about a plan to continue the existence of their species. Seeding the Earth with their kind was the only solution, giving evolution a helping hand. Homo Sapiens became the result of their DNA manipulation with the Neanderthal migrating out of Africa. But it partly failed."

The President broke in, "Provenance has been one hell of a secret to keep. Very few people know and to be honest, I have always struggled to accept it as truth. The Monk was relentless in his sermons about humanity evolving from extraterrestrial life. To hear it from you now confirms what he claimed however, he never mentioned anything about it failing.

"Modern man did evolve from their interference, that much is true. However, the Neanderthal DNA sequencing proved too restrictive and it never fully evolved. As a result they intervened again, five thousand years ago introducing a new genetic code strain into the human population."

"Was it successful?" the President asked.

"It was effective in about one percent. Evolution diverged, on one side were humans and the other, a hybrid species. The one percent were the hybrids. They retain all the physical characteristics of humans for now though over time, they will fully evolve into the Jeremiah species. This takes thousands of years with the final few years lying dormant in a cocoon similar to a caterpillar metamorphosing into a butterfly."

"The Monk never spoke of hybrids," the President interjected.

"The Jeremiah's accelerated evolution means now there are thousands of these hybrids dispersed across the planet, living among the population not knowing they possess the dominant genetic code of the Jeremiah species. This is why the entire planet will be destroyed."

"The Jeremiah can protect us, the Monk always talked of their plans to build an orbiting defence system using the thirteenth code pulse weapon. Did they speak of this?"

"Yes," Bennett answered.

He continued, "They are the original engineers of the pulse weapon and their enemy stole it, used it against them."

"So do you now understand why we need that alien craft you took from Banks?" the President asked.

Bennett nodded. "Yes, they need it to supplement their defence system. To be more specific, it is the red diamond they need. Lucifer's Funnel as we call it, was manufactured from crystalline material only found on their home planet. After their home world was destroyed, they were unable to build more weapons. The orbital defence system needs nine of these funnels, they are one short. Without the ninth, the combined power can only achieve eighty percent, not enough to take out an entire fleet of ships."

The President already knew about the plans to build a defence system using the pulse weapon in close proximity to Earth, just outside the orbit of the moon. He didn't know it was the Lucifer's Funnel they needed.

The President broke from the topic. "I've always wondered how the code carriers like yourself came to exist. The Monk had never said."

"First you have to understand why the Spheres. The Jeremiah needed test subjects, humans for perfecting their genetic code. They selected three civilisations, first the ancient Sumerians of Mesopotamia followed soon by the Egyptians and finally the Mayans of South America. They presented, arriving in great flying machines and were received as Gods, beings of far advanced technology and power. They came offering precious gifts, the most significant of these were the three spheres. Each were bestowed with the promise it would give the leaders great endless power to destroy their enemies. All the Jeremiah asked for in return was the sacrifice of their thirteen best warriors. It was from these warriors they machined their survival, through the perfect genetic code."

The President gave him a quizzical look.

"I am a descendant of the thirteenth warrior," Bennett announced.

He continued.

"Each descendant carries the codes upon their chest and hold the cognitive awareness of the Jeremiah, meaning they can telepathically communicate with them. In my case, I also have the ability to operate their technology like the craft."

"Why the codes? I mean why the thirteen codes?" the President asked.

"The technologies embedded in the spheres were the gift, not the sphere itself. The Jeremiah set it as an intelligence test, when the technologies could be unlocked then humanity was ready for the next stage in the evolutionary process of the brain. Deciphering and understanding those technologies were the first key step in the cognitive transition to a Jeremiah brain. Their intelligence is far beyond that of the smartest humans and mostly as result of over ten billion years of their own evolution."

The President's cell phone chirped and he stepped away to answer it.

Less than two minutes he returned.

"Jon, we have to get you back to Baltimore pronto. Nicholette has taken another turn for the worse. This time the doctors aren't hopeful."

71.
<u>Salvation</u>

Johns Hopkins Hospital
Baltimore, USA
Sixteen hours later…

Bennett staggered from Nicholette's ward, mentally jaded. The latest news from three different specialists had been devastating. His fiancé and baby had less than twenty-four hours to live. The inevitable had arrived.

"Bennett!" A far off voice from down the hallway.

He looked up to the familiar sight of Josh Whittaker rushing towards him. He looked excited, waving something in his hand.

"I have it," he called from ten yards away to the disapproving glares from two grumpy nurses seated at the ward desk.

"It's too late," Bennett muttered pushing past him heading for some fresh air to think more clearly.

"Jon wait!" Whittaker grabbed his arm and extended a small black leather bound document wallet towards him.

"What's this?"

"Open it," Whittaker demanded, struggling to conceal his excitement.

Bennett opened the wallet.

"What? This is not possible. Where did you find these?"

"My father had a hidden online storage account, gigabytes of information."

Bennett flicked through the sheets of paper, thirteen in total.

"I don't believe it," he exclaimed separating one particular sheet from the others.

He stood frozen, fingers trembling, watching the symbols reveal themselves from behind the scattered text. He was one of few who could decipher the hidden codes from what appeared as written ramblings on the page, some English and some alien.

"Is it what I think it is?" Whittaker asked tugging at Bennett's arm to arouse his attention.

Bennett slowly nodded, engulfed in the thoughts of what it meant. "Dom must have scanned each page of Viktor's codebook and faxed them to that storage account sometime just before his death in Tehran."

"Or he had them all the time!" Whittaker added.

Bennett didn't care for details, he was mesmerised by the hope he held firmly in his hand, an impression of the First Code.

"Where's the Mayan Sphere?" Whittaker asked.

"Somewhere safe. Come on, we don't have much time, help me get Nicholette out of here," Bennett ordered.

Was it too late for the First Code to reverse the damage done? Could it save their lives? He was struggling to overcome the thoughts of defeat.

72.
<u>Posterity</u>

Undisclosed location
Atlantic Ocean
Six months later.

A cool afternoon breeze lapped gently across the tiny island, palm trees swayed in rhythm while underneath, two lovers embraced in the joy of their creation. The code had worked. The sphere had activated with an incredible display of bright blue blinding light and Nicholette's life had been rescued from the brink of her last few dying hours.

"She's so beautiful Jon," she whispered.

Bennett hadn't stopped staring at the small baby sleeping peacefully in her arms while he bathed in the warm aura of happiness surrounding her and their newborn child. Two weeks earlier, Lilyana had been born a healthy seven pound baby girl showing no signs of the trauma from her mother's ill health. Nicholette had lingered for a month after the lifeless remains of the microscopic nanobots departed her body, each day determined to give all her strength to the survival of their child. Then suddenly it all changed, inexplicably awaking one day strong as if never effected by the parasites.

Bennett pulled her tight into his arms and kissed her forehead. "Yes as beautiful as her mother."

Since Antarctica, Bennett had taken the place of the Monk but not because the President needed him as their communicator. He held a grave secret that grew more threatening by the day.

"I lied to the President," he blurted. He couldn't withhold it any longer.

"What do you mean?"

"I am not sure the enemy is coming. They may already be here."

He paused in thought.

"I think the Jeremiah are the enemy!"

"Why do you think that?" she asked.

"Visions I started having a few months ago, like the entity inside me is trying to warn me."

"Why build the defence system if there is no enemy coming?" Sponarava was baffled by his sudden disbelief.

"I don't know, maybe to use on us. I am not sure their home world was destroyed by their enemy as they say."

"I don't understand, why withhold something like that from the President."

"Trust! I don't know who to trust, but I do know starting a war with the Jeremiah would be certain suicide for humanity. I need more time with them, learning their ways and finding their vulnerabilities. Our success against them I think hinges on what I can learn from my entity and whether I can maintain cognitive control during the metamorphosis."

The subtle cry of hunger broke their conversation and they both peered down into the awakening crystal green eyes of Lilyana Bennett.

Neither knew what lay dormant in her genetic code though Bennett knew one thing, he was metamorphosing quicker than expected.

73.
<u>Redemption</u>

Washington

The President approached the podium to an eagerly awaiting audience of reporters, he had an announcement he'd promised to make.

Three thousand miles away, Bennett sat in front of his television glued to every word.

A smile broke quickly accompanied by a sense of relief.

The President had officially cleared his name of all the wrong doings of the Kuwait incident and had just briefed the world on the truth.

His reinstatement to the CIA would be effective immediately.

He sat watching as the President left the podium and the coverage reverted to the studio where the commentator rehashed Bennett's past history covering his lawful achievements. They knew nothing of his real deadly past.

He eased back into his sofa and for the first time in many years, he had some peace of mind.

Paul Gilmour